KAREN ROBARDS

Scandalous

POCKET BOOKS
New York   London   Toronto   Sydney

Pocket Books
A Division of Simon & Schuster, Inc.
1230 Avenue of the Americas
New York, NY 10020

This book is a work of fiction. Names, characters, places, and incidents are products of the author's imagination or are used fictitiously. Any resemblance to actual events or locales or persons, living or dead, is entirely coincidental.

First Pocket Books printing March 2001

POCKET and colophon are registered trademarks of Simon & Schuster, Inc.

For information regarding special discounts for bulk purchases, please contact Simon & Schuster Special Sales at 1-866-506-1949 or business@simonandschuster.com.

The Simon & Schuster Speakers Bureau can bring authors to your live event. For more information or to book an event contact the Simon & Schuster Speakers Bureau at 1-866-248-3049 or visit our website at www.simonspeakers.com.

Design by Lisa Litwack. Illustration by Alan Ayers.
Hand lettering by Iskra Johnson.

Manufactured in the United States of America

10 9 8 7 6 5 4 3 2

ISBN 978-0-7434-6739-1
ISBN 978-0-7434-2452-3 (ebook)

Scandalous *is dedicated to my readers. Working on it has been a true labor of love, and I hope you enjoy it. I also can't forget the men in my life: my husband Doug, and sons Peter, Christopher, and Jack. Without their help, none of this would have been possible.*

February, 1810

The earl of Wickham, handsome, rich, and only thirty-one, smiled in anticipation as he scanned the lush green landscape for his quarry. A telltale movement in the brush, a gesture from a servant, and the earl jerked his gun to his shoulder. A shot exploded, the sound reverberating with shattering suddenness through the shimmering waves of heat that were, at the moment, baking the island paradise that was Ceylon. It did not come from the earl's gun.

The watcher gawked in disbelief as the earl was flung forward as though kicked in the seat of his breeches by a giant boot. Blood gushed geyserlike from his back as he slammed face first into the ground; almost instantly the back of his fine linen shirt was awash in crimson. His servants, held in place until then by the same shock that froze the watcher on a hill some quarter mile away, reacted at last and rushed in a frantic, screaming mass to his side.

It was too late. The watcher knew it even as he cried out in horror himself. His horse shifted beneath him, frightened by his noise. The spyglass that he held to his eye wavered and dipped, losing focus on what he watched—and found, instead, a thicket of trees just beyond the panicked, chaotic scene, and, glimpsed through leafy branches, a rough-looking thug leaping onto the back of a scruffy horse, a rifle clutched in one hand as he spurred his mount away.

The watcher realized, with the same sense of impossibility with which he had witnessed the earl's violent death, that the fleeing thug was the most probable source of the gunshot.

Marcus had just been murdered before his eyes.

Shock held grief at bay; what fueled him was rage. A dark, violent mushrooming of fury that brought an explosion of curses to his lips and vengeance to his heart. Clapping the spyglass shut, he set his heels to his horse's sides.

He had arrived too late. He could not help Marcus now. But he could, perhaps, stop his murderer from getting away.

❧ 1 ❧

" 'Tis sorry I am to be the bearer of ill tidings, Miss Gabby."

More than sorry, Jem Downes sounded positively miserable over the news that he had crossed an ocean and parts of two land masses to bring her, Lady Gabriella Banning thought. His rheumy brown eyes met her widening gray ones sadly. Behind him, the aged butler, Stivers, bowed himself out, closing the door with a muffled click. The smell of damp from Jem's clothes overrode the faint scent of sulfur from the coal fire and tallow from the candle sputtering at her elbow. Jem's hat was in his hands; his travel-stained clothes were splotched with moisture and dotted with shiny-wet raindrops from the unrelenting downpour outside. His boots and trousers were flecked with mud. In the ordinary way of things, the family's lifelong servant would never have dreamed of presenting himself to her in such a state. The fact that he had not waited for the morrow, or even to put off his soiled apparel, spoke volumes about his state of mind.

Almost unconsciously, Gabby braced to receive the blow. Her lips compressed and her spine stiffened until she was sitting regally erect behind the massive desk tucked into the corner of the estate office, to which she had retired after dinner to go over the household accounts. Until this moment, her biggest worry had been whether or not just a few more shillings could be squeezed from the estate's already pared-to-the-bone expenditures. Jem's words caused her heart to give a great lurch, and effectively drove the family's financial picture from her mind. Nevertheless, she fought to preserve a calm demeanor. The only outward sign of her sudden anxiety was her rigid posture, and the convulsive tightening of her fingers around the quill she held. Conscious of this last, Gabby carefully put the pen down near the ink pot, and placed her pale, slender hands flat upon the open ledger in front of her.

Outside, thunder crashed with enough volume to penetrate even so deep within the fortresslike walls of Hawthorne Hall. The fire in the hearth flared suddenly, no doubt because windblown raindrops had found their way down the chimney. To Gabby the sudden thunderclap and the subsequent surge of light and heat seemed almost portentous. With difficulty she repressed a shudder. What now? she thought, staring hard at Jem. Oh, dear Lord in heaven, what now?

"You have seen my brother?" A lifetime of living with the meanest sort of bully had taught her the value of maintaining an outward imperturbability, no matter what disaster was about to befall. Her tone was as cool as hock.

"Miss Gabby, the earl is dead." Clearly aware of the terrible import of his news, Jem twisted the soft felt hat in his hands until it was almost unrecognizable. Fiftyish, with short grizzled hair and sharp features, he had the slight, wiry frame of the jockey he once was. At the moment his posture, hunched under the weight of what he had to tell her, made him seem even smaller than usual.

Gabby drew in a short, sharp breath. She felt as though

she had sustained a physical blow. Rejection of her plea, even a reprimand for daring to make it, if Marcus was in personality anything like their father, she had been prepared for—but not this. Her half brother, Marcus Banning, who, upon their father's death some eighteen months before had become the seventh Earl of Wickham, was a mere six years her senior. Two months previously, when it had become obvious that the new Earl was in no hurry to come to England to claim his inheritance, she had sent Jem with a letter for her brother to the tiny island of Ceylon, where Marcus had lived most of his life on a tea plantation owned by his mother's family. In it she had explained their circumstances as concisely as she could, and asked Marcus for permission—and funding—to take their sister Claire to London for her long overdue come-out.

She had sent Jem off with little hope. Still, something had to be done. Claire was already nearly nineteen. Gabby could not bear to think of her sister marrying Squire Cuthbert, the stolid, middle-aged, long-widowed owner of the neighboring property, who was her most persistent suitor, or Oswald Preston, the local curate, by default. Both, in their different ways, were top over tail in love with Claire, and, having been unwelcome at Hawthorne Hall during their father the sixth Earl's lifetime, were now frequent visitors. Claire was kind to them because kindness was an integral part of her nature, but the thought of her wedding either the portly squire or the sanctimonious Oswald was enough to make Gabby ill.

"My brother is *dead?*" Gabby repeated slowly. A knot formed in her stomach as the ramifications began to ricochet through her head. "Jem, are you certain?"

A foolish question. Ordinarily she would never have asked it. Jem was not likely to make a mistake about something so enormous as the death of the new earl, after all.

Jem looked, if possible, even more miserable. "Yes, Miss

Gabby. Certain sure. I was there when His Lordship met his end. He was out with a party hunting a tiger, and the beast charged from cover when none expected it. Someone fired in a panic, and the shot struck him. He was gone just like that. Nothing to be done."

"Dear God." Gabby closed her eyes, feeling suddenly light-headed. In the months since her father's death, she had both hoped for and dreaded the coming of Marcus, the half brother she had met just once in her life. Everything would be changed with the advent of the new earl: her position, and that of her younger sisters, was bound to alter. For the better, she had hoped, although, as fate had taught her to, she had feared it might be for the worse.

But what could be worse than seeing Claire, and Beth after her, suffer the same fate she had herself? To be alternately bullied and ignored by a father with an abiding contempt for females and not even the smallest scrap of natural affection for his offspring; to be kept so short of money—and this when their father was a very rich man—that the amount of food on the family table was ofttimes insufficient; to be left to wither away on the vine with scant prospects for a husband or children or any life beyond the vast isolated acreage of Hawthorne Hall?

Suddenly Gabby knew what could be worse: to lose their home entirely, and the funds that had allowed them to live adequately if not well in it. To be forced to leave Hawthorne Hall, to make their own living as—and this was if they were fortunate—governesses or companions. Beth was too young to take up any post, Gabby realized as she tried calmly to consider it, and Claire—would anyone hire Claire? Claire, whose beauty was so arresting that she turned heads when she did no more than walk down the streets of York, which was the nearest town of any size?

No respectable woman would be likely to offer employment to Claire, Gabby realized with a deep sense of forboding. At the ripe old age of twenty-five, with her nothing-out-of-the-ordinary looks and the limp that had resulted from an accident she had suffered at age twelve, she herself was the only one of the three who was in the smallest degree employable. Would she be allowed to keep her sisters with her in any position she was fortunate enough to obtain?

Not likely. Almost assuredly not. Especially not once a prospective employer set eyes on Claire.

What were they to do? The question curled, cold and snakelike, around Gabby's heart, bringing near panic with it. Suddenly Squire Cuthbert and Mr. Preston began to seem almost like lifelines in a raging sea. Certainly, if faced with the choice, Claire would consider marrying either better than being cast upon the world with little more than the clothes on her back.

But wait, Gabby told herself firmly, trying to quell her rising fear, it was early days yet. There had to be other alternatives. It was just that none had as yet occurred to her.

"Did he leave—a family? A son?" A last faint hope fluttered in her breast as Gabby opened her eyes to look at Jem again.

"His Lordship was unwed, Miss Gabby, and childless, I think. Doubtless he would have chosen a proper English bride when he came home to take his place as earl."

"Yes." Gabby took a deep, steadying breath. Whatever was to become of her and her sisters, there were immediate steps that had to be taken, people who needed to be notified of the earl of Wickham's death. She had so recently performed the same functions after the demise of her father that she felt quite like an old hand. Mr. Challow, her father's chief barrister, would need to be informed, for one, and Cousin Thomas . . .

Gabby went cold at the thought.

With Marcus's death, the earldom and all that went with it passed to the nearest male heir, the Honorable Thomas Banning, son of her father's late cousin. Her father had loathed Thomas, and Thomas, together with his horrible stiff-necked wife Lady Maud and their two simpering daughters, had returned the earl's animosity with interest. She had seen him and his family perhaps half a dozen times in her life, most recently at her father's funeral. He had been barely civil to her and her sisters, and his wife and daughters had not been even that.

She, Claire, and Beth were now at Thomas's mercy, Gabby realized with a sick sensation in the pit of her stomach. Her father, in his terrible misogyny, had made no provisions in his will for his three daughters, as she had learned to her dismay only at the time of his death. They had no income, no funds of their own. They had been left totally dependent on the generosity—or lack of it—of the new earl.

Not for the first time, Gabby wondered if her father, upon dying, had found himself in hell.

Terrible as it was for a daughter to entertain such a thought, she could not help but feel that, if so, it was a reward well earned by the misery he had caused, and continued to cause, those whom he should have most cherished in life.

Perhaps Thomas would allow them to continue to live at Hawthorne Hall, Gabby speculated without much hope. It might please his wife to have *Matthew's miscellany,* as she disparagingly called Gabby and her sisters because each was the offspring of a different, subsequent countess of Wickham, as dependent poor relations.

But then Gabby thought again of Claire, and knew even

that faint hope was misplaced. Maud would not want Claire within a mile of her own whey-faced daughters.

"Miss Gabby, His Lordship writ you a letter."

At Jem's words, Gabby's attention focused on him again.

"A letter?" Her voice, she was surprised to discover, revealed no hint of her distress.

"The night before he—before he was took. He was on the trail after that tiger I told you about when I caught up with him, away off in the wilds with just those heathen native servants of his. He called me into his tent and gave me this to give to you." Jem fumbled in the leather pouch that hung at his side, and extracted a slightly crumpled and stained letter, which he passed to her.

Gabby took it, broke the seal, and spread it out. It was a single sheet containing just a few lines scrawled in a firm black hand. Another sealed sheet, wrapped inside the first, was revealed as she unfolded the missive. This she set aside.

My dear Gabby, the letter began,

My own knowledge and the tales I have heard of our father lead me to believe that you have, if anything, understated the case in which you have been left. I beg your forgiveness for not attending to the matter earlier. Indeed, I freely confess that I have been remiss in not seeing to the welfare of my sisters, and hereby give you permission to take our sister Claire to London for the Season. You do the thing up in high style, and draw on my funds as needed and at your discretion. A letter to that effect is enclosed, which I suggest you present to Messrs. Challow, Mather and Yadon, attorneys at law, with my compliments. As it happens, my circumstances are such that I find myself viewing a trip to England with favor, and may join you in London myself before many weeks have passed. I look

forward to furthering our acquaintance, and to reac-
quainting myself with Claire and baby Beth, at that time.
Yours most sincerely, Wickham.

Unexpectedly, Gabby felt a lump form in her throat as she stared down at the bold script. Her brother sounded both likable and as if he were disposed to have a care for them, and this sheet of paper, along with his scarce-remembered visit to Hawthorne Hall when she had been no more than eleven, was all she was ever to know of him.

It seemed hard. But then, she had learned, such was life.

The other sealed letter was indeed addressed to Messrs. Challow, Mather, and Yadon, she saw as she picked it up, then glanced again at Jem.

"Gabby, Gabby, is that *Jem* you're talking to?" The library door flew open without warning. Lady Elizabeth Banning, an exuberant red-haired fifteen-year-old still faintly round with puppy fat, burst into the room. Like Gabby, she was dressed in the unrelieved black of mourning for their father although the obligatory period of time for such had passed, for the simple reason that they were the newest gowns any of the sisters possessed. The dispersal of funds for the purchase of mourning garments had been reluctantly allowed by Mr. Challow after the death of their father, although by rights, he said, he should not be approving any expenditures at all without the sanction of the new earl, whose funds they now were. Even continuing the minimal allowance that had in the past permitted Gabby to run the house had been the subject of some debate within the law firm, he told her, with the consensus being that, without notice from the new earl, the best course of action was to let things go on as they had been until they received instructions to the contrary.

"Oh, Jem, it *is* you! What did our brother *say?*" Beth's

spaniel-brown eyes had fixed on Jem at once, sparing Gabby the need to answer her original inquiry. She bore down on the pair of them, firing questions as she came. "Did you find him? Did you give him Gabby's letter? What did he say? Can we go? Can we go?"

"I'm sorry, Gabby, I tried to stop her, but you know how she is," Lady Claire Banning said with a sigh as she followed her younger sister into the room. Not even her sober black gown could detract from Claire's dazzling combination of silky raven curls that spilled in charming profusion over slender shoulders, huge, thick-lashed golden-brown eyes, porcelain-pale skin, and perfect features. In addition, her figure was round where it should be round, slim where it needed to be slim, and altogether delectable. "She just could not contain herself one moment longer."

If Claire could just have her season, Gabby thought, looking at her sister almost achingly, she would be overrun with eligible gentlemen wanting to marry her. The sad thing was that here, right under her own hand, was the very instrument that would have given Claire the future she needed, that she was entitled to by right of birth, that she deserved.

Marcus had granted permission for Claire to have her season. He had practically given Gabby *carte blanche* to fund it, too.

But Marcus was dead. The letters he had sent were now no more than worthless scraps of paper. As soon as Cousin Thomas was apprised that he had become the earl of Wickham, they would be very fortunate indeed not to be cast out of Hawthorne Hall forthwith.

A growing despair knotted Gabby's stomach. What she had to tell her sisters was too, too cruel. If only, she thought, throat aching, Marcus had survived just a scant three more months, just until Claire had had her season. . . .

"For goodness' sake, Jem, can't you talk? Did you or did you not find our brother?" Beth demanded, bouncing like an excited puppy around the man who had taught her and her sisters to ride and hunt and fish and enjoy almost every imaginable outdoor pursuit. Over the years the sisters had come to regard him as coconspirator and friend rather than servant, and were on terms of disgraceful intimacy with one who was in actuality no more than a groom.

Jem looked even unhappier than before. "That I did, Miss Beth, but. . . ."

He glanced helplessly at Gabby, who looked down at the letter in her hand and took a deep breath, willing herself to sound composed as she broke the dreadful news.

At that moment Beth spied the letter, and with a quick movement and a gleeful cry snatched it from her sister's hand.

"Beth, wait. . . ." Gabby groaned, grabbing for the letter, but speech was more of an effort than she had imagined and her protest was too strangled to deter her sister, who danced out of reach with a tantalizing grin. To learn how close all their hopes had been to being realized could only make the truth harder to bear. . . .

"Oh, Beth, try for a little decorum, do," Claire put in crossly, throwing herself down in a chair near the fire and trying to pretend that she, too, was not vitally interested in the contents of the sheet that Beth now eagerly perused. "I declare, I've never in my life seen such a hoyden as you're turning into."

"At least I don't break my neck craning it to look into every mirror I pass." Beth retorted, glancing up for a moment to glare at her sister. Then as she returned her attention to the letter her face broke into a beatific smile and she looked at Claire again. "Oh, Claire, you're to have your season! Our brother says we're to go."

Claire's eyes widened, and soft color rushed into her cheeks as she sat up straight in the chair. "Beth, truly?" Her gaze flew to her older sister. "Gabby?"

She sounded almost afraid to believe that so wondrous a fate could be hers.

As indeed, Gabby thought, looking at Claire with a sudden sharp sensation that she could only conclude was heartbreak, she was right to be. What she would not give to be able to provide this one thing for Claire. . . .

At that moment the fire popped as loudly as a sharp clapping of hands and flared again, higher and hotter than before, momentarily drawing everyone's startled attention to it. The color of the flames tinted the pale skin of Gabby's hands an eerie shade of red, she saw, glancing down at the letter to the barristers that still rested beneath them. She had no doubt that her face was turned the same, suddenly most appropriate, hellish hue.

Because the most dreadfully sinful notion had just occurred to her. . . .

"Read it for yourself." Beth thrust the letter at Claire, then perched on the arm of her sister's chair, watching the older girl's face with an air of jubilant expectancy. When Claire reached the end, she gave a little squeal of excitement. The two younger girls put their heads, one bright red and one raven black, together and began reciting the words aloud with increasing glee.

As her sisters read, and the fire died back down, Gabby made a decision. She was, she discovered with some surprise, a true Banning after all. Gaming ran strong in their blood, and now it was her turn to wager all on a daring throw of the dice. She stood, a too-thin woman of no more than medium height clad in head-to-toe black bombazine, her untamable chestnut hair dragged into a reasonably neat chignon at her nape, her pale, squarish face with its small, straight nose and decided mouth and chin brought to sudden vivid life by the fierce resolve that glowed from her usually calm gray eyes, and walked with the deliberate care she had learned to take to conceal her limp around the desk until she reached Jem's side.

"Have you told anyone else of this? Talked to anyone on the ship, perhaps, or since you landed in England?" Gabby asked for his ears alone as they watched her sisters poring over the letter once again. Jem looked wretched as, finishing the missive for what must have been the dozenth time, both girls looked at each other and began to chatter excitedly. Gabby's whisper turned urgent. "What I am asking you is, who else knows of my brother's death?"

Servant and mistress were of much the same height, and their eyes were nearly on a level. Jem glanced at her, his brow deeply furrowed.

"No one in England, Miss Gabby, save you and me. I wouldn't be talking to strangers about family business, on the ship or anywheres else, now would I? A few know in Ceylon, I reckon, but mostly natives and such."

"Then I am going to ask you to do me a very big service." Gabby spoke rapidly, before her nerve could fail her. "I am going to ask you to pretend that you left my brother's side immediately after you received these letters, and never witnessed his death at all. I am going to ask you to pretend that, as far as you know, the earl is still alive and in Ceylon and will be home in his own good time."

Jem's eyes widened. As he met her determined gaze, his lips pursed in a soundless whistle.

"Miss Gabby, I can do that, and for you I will willingly, as you knows, but the truth of it is bound to come out sooner or later. Such like that always does, and then where will we be?" Jem's low voice was both alarmed and cautionary.

"In no worse case than we are right now, and perhaps a great deal better off," Gabby said firmly. "All we need is just a little time, and a little luck."

"Gabby, aren't you excited? We're going to *London*," Beth exclaimed rapturously, springing up from the arm of the chair and dancing forward to envelop her oldest sister in a suffocating hug. "Claire will have her season, and we'll get to see the sights. Oh, Gabby, I've never been beyond Yorkshire in my life."

"None of us have," Claire chimed in. Her eyes were glowing with anticipation and her step was light as she joined them, although, conscious of her status as a mature young lady, she refrained from jumping up and down with the heedless abandon shown by Beth.

"London will be a treat for all of us." Gabby, returning Beth's hug, managed a credible smile. A sideways glance showed her that Jem was looking at her with as much alarm as if she'd suddenly grown horns and a tail.

"Does this mean we can have some new gowns?" Claire sounded almost wistful. Claire loved pretty clothes, and had upon many occasions spent hours poring over the fashionable sketches in such publications as the Ladies' Magazine that, banned from the house by their father, still had chanced to come her way. Without being overly vain, Claire was very aware of her own beauty, and such matters as the latest hairstyles, or the design of a gown, were important to her. She had longed for a season in the worst way, but given their circumstances had known that her chances of ever having one were remote. To her credit, she had been very good about the prospect that it was never to be. But now—now she could have one after all. Despite the risks,

Gabby was suddenly fiercely glad to be able to provide Claire with such a chance.

"Certainly we may," Gabby said, refusing to look at Jem again as she well and truly threw caution to the wind. "An entire new wardrobe, in fact, for each of us."

The fire in the hearth popped loudly and flared again just then, causing Gabby to jump. As her sisters exclaimed more over their unprecedented good fortune, Gabby could not forbear casting the hearth a sideways, slightly nervous glance.

Why could she not escape the feeling that, no matter how pure her motives, some sort of hellish bargain had just been made?

2

little more than two weeks later, the earl of
Wickham's ancient coach lumbered clumsily
over rain-pitted roads, bound for London. Stivers and Mrs.
Bucknell, the housekeeper, along with a footman and a
maid, had been sent on ahead a few days before to open the
family townhouse on Grosvenor Square, which had been
closed for more than a decade, and engage such additional
staff as was deemed necessary to run it. Still muttering dire
warnings whenever Gabby came within earshot, Jem rode
on the box beside John-Coachman, his hat brim pulled low
over his eyes to shield against the drizzle. Inside, Claire and
Beth chattered excitedly, watched over by Twindle, the now
elderly governess who had joined the family with the advent
of Claire's mother and stayed on in the face of that lady's
demise. Sitting beside Claire on the worn plush seat that, despite all their efforts to freshen it, still smelled faintly musty,
Gabby smiled when necessary and looked out the window
at the boggy moor they were leaving behind. The soaked
heath, gray sky, and unceasing rain were as familiar to her as
the confines of Hawthorne Hall, she realized, and as surprisingly dear. She had known no other home, and it cost her a

pang to realize that, however this game played out, her future, and that of her sisters, in all likelihood lay elsewhere.

Having made up her mind to seize the day while she
could, she had suffered sleepless nights and many qualms
of conscience ever since. The wrongness of what she was
doing unsettled her; but to allow her sisters to suffer for
want of a little resolution was, in her estimation, more
wrong still. She quieted her conscience by reminding herself that, even if something did not happen to bring the
whole scheme tumbling down around her ears, she did not
mean to keep up the pretense forever; as soon as Claire was
safely married she meant to "receive word" of Marcus's
death, and then the sham would come to an end. How
wrong could what was actually no more than buying a little
time to get themselves creditably established be?

"Is your leg paining you, Gabby?" Claire asked, turning
her attention to her older sister as Beth was now engaged in
a spirited discussion with Twindle over the sights that it
might be proper for a very young lady to visit while in
London. Astley's Ampitheatre and the beasts at the Royal
Exchange were, in Twindle's judgment, just passably acceptable. Covent Garden—". . . and how you came to be
knowing of that place, Miss Beth, I can't begin to think . . ."
was definitely not. Having grown accustomed over the
years to Gabby's infirmity—indeed, she and Beth never
even thought of it as such; Gabby's damaged leg was as
much an accepted part of her as her straight-as-a-horse's-
tail hair—Claire didn't sound overly concerned.

"Was I frowning, to make you think so?" Gabby asked
lightly, summoning a smile. "My leg is fine. I was just running over a list of all I have to do when we reach London."

"Do you think Aunt Salcombe will consent to sponsor
Claire, Gabby?" Beth broke off her conversation with

Twindle to ask with a worried frown. Although too young herself to partake of the pleasures of balls and routs and evenings spent at such fabled bastions of the *haute ton* as Almack's, she had entered into the preparations for Claire's come-out with gusto.

"I can't say for certain, of course, but I am hopeful that she will. After all, she did invite me to make my come-out under her aegis when I turned eighteen, saying that, as she had no children of her own, she would adore to present her niece to the *ton*. And you are as much her niece as I am, and a far better prospect to make a splash." This last Gabby, with a twinkle, directed to Claire. What she forebore to add was that, when the invitation had arrived all those years ago, she had been over the moon at the prospect of a London season, until her father had laughed and said that obviously his sister Augusta did not realize that her eldest niece was now a cripple and would disgrace her in any ballroom which was unfortunate enough to suffer her presence. Gabby had not been privileged to see what the earl had replied to his sister, but the invitation had been turned down and never repeated. Crushed at first, Gabby had come to realize, in retrospect, that it was probably for the best. She could not have left Claire and Beth, then eleven and eight, with no one but Twindle and Jem to buffer them from their father's excesses even for the few months of a single season, and to have abandoned them forever via marriage, which was, after all, the ultimate goal of all that frivolity, would have been impossible. And her father would never have let her take her sisters to live with her, either to London or her new husband's home. What Matthew Banning possessed, he possessed completely, whether he valued it or not.

"Lady Salcombe is a very high stickler, Miss Gabby." A shade of anxiety darkened Twindle's narrow face as she spoke. From the circumstance of having lived in London for years before coming to Hawthorne Hall, Twindle was at least vaguely familiar with a number of the great lords and ladies who made up the fashionable scene.

"Well, if she is not inclined to help us then we must make shift without her," Gabby said with assumed cheerfulness. Though green to the ways of London, she was not so green that she did not realize that the assistance of her father's sister was of paramount importance in making Claire's introduction to the *ton* the success it should be. Being herself firmly on the shelf, Gabby was, she felt, perfectly qualified to act as her sister's chaperone. As the daughter of an earl, even such an eccentric and reclusive one as Lord Wickham had been, she and her sisters must command a certain place in Society. But she knew no more of London and town ways than she had read of in books, heard about from Twindle, and observed from watching her father's usually less than top-drawer guests over the years. And she had almost no acquaintances there. As she had told Claire, if Lady Salcombe refused to help them they would manage—somehow. But not nearly so well, or so easily, as if that lady agreed to stand their friend.

Always at the back of her mind lurked the knowledge that they must make the most of this time she had snatched from the jaws of fate: there could be no more than this single season for Claire.

"Do we not have any other relations in town who could assist us if Aunt Salcombe refuses?" Beth asked curiously.

"Besides Cousin Thomas and Lady Maud, you mean?" Gabby smiled as Beth made a face. "There are various assorted relations, I believe, but I prefer to start with Lady Salcombe. She is, or used to be, quite a pillar of society, you know."

Gabby sought to turn the conversation then by wondering aloud if the village she could see from the window was West Hurch, or not. Just as she thought it best to keep the knowledge of Marcus's death and the truly desperate nature of this trip from her sisters and everyone else save Jem, so, too, did she think it best not to make Claire and Beth overly conscious of the unconventional nature of their family structure. Although it was true that she at least did have fashionable relatives other than their father's kin, it was doubtful that any of them could, or would, be of much help in facilitating Claire's come-out. They had never visited Hawthorne Hall, or evinced any interest in herself or her sisters that she knew of. The problem was that each of the earl's offspring had had a different mother, and those mothers had varied widely on the social scale. Marcus's mother, Elise de Melancon, had journeyed to London from Ceylon for her season amid hopes that she would make a great match. She had been both an acknowledged beauty of unexceptional birth and a considerable heiress. Her union with the earl of Wickham had satisfied all parties, although after a scant two years with her new husband the beautiful young countess had been so little enamoured of married life that she had taken her baby son and fled back to Ceylon. Upon that lady's death a few years later, the earl had once again visited London to find a bride. This time his unknowing victim had been Gabby's mother, Lady Sophia Hendred, as well born as himself but neither particularly beautiful nor particularly rich; she had died in childbed some three years after Gabby's advent. Claire's mother, Maria Dysart, a beauty of no more than respectable birth and no fortune at all, had caught the earl's eye on a jaunt to Bath and had been considered to have married above her when she wed the recent widower. She had lasted just long enough to produce Claire before succumbing to what was described as a wasting disease. Beth's mother had been an obscure clergyman's daughter. Fortunately for the legions of unmarried ladies still out there, by the time the former Miss Bolton had fallen down the stairs at Hawthorne Hall, breaking her neck, the earl had suffered the riding accident that had confined him to a wheel chair for the rest of his life. No other countess had graced Hawthorne Hall with her presence, and it had been left to Gabby to act as mistress of the house, and surrogate mother to her younger sisters, a role that had suited her very well.

"Just think, Claire, by this time next year you'll probably be a married lady," Beth said with wonder, bouncing a little on the seat. With all the lurching the carriage was doing, such movement seemed redundant, but Beth had been unable to sit still ever since learning that they were going to London.

"I have been thinking of that," Claire confessed, sounding faintly troubled. Her eyes met Gabby's. "To tell the truth, I—I'm not sure I wish to be married, after all. I don't want to leave you two behind—and—and I am much afraid that the gentleman will turn out to be—well, like Papa."

This piece of frankness left the other three occupants of the carriage without anything to say for a moment. Gabby was the first to recover her power of speech.

"You need not marry anyone if you don't wish to," she said stoutly, and meant it, too, despite everything, though the possibility that all her desperate scheming might be for naught sent a sudden chill down her spine. This was an outcome she had not considered; she could only hope that Claire, with her soft heart to make her susceptible and her breathtaking looks to provide her with opportunity, would tumble headlong into love upon being exposed to a world full of eligible, and, it was to be hoped, handsome and charming men. If not—well, they would cross that bridge when they came to it. "And as for worrying about your prospective groom being like Papa—well, I don't think very many gentlemen are—are mean with money, or reclusive, or—or so unloving to their wives and children as he was, so you need not concern yourself overmuch about that."

"No indeed," said Twindle feelingly. "His Lordship was quite unique in that regard, believe me."

"And perhaps Gabby and I and Twindle will come to stay with you, after you're married," Beth added with a grin. "So you need not worry about losing us, either."

Gabby, taking care to keep her expression under control as her youngest sister, in all innocence, hit the nail squarely on the head, again directed the conversation into safer channels.

They passed that night in Newark, continuing on the next day. Their first glimpse of London was had at sundown. The carriage topped a rise, and suddenly there was the city spread out before them like a banquet. Crowding the windows, they marveled over the spires and rooftops, the seemingly never-ending cluster of buildings, the meandering silver ribbon of the Thames, all glittering jewel-like under the rays of the setting sun. However, by the time the carriage entered London proper, clattering across the bridge into streets crowded with vehicles of every description, it was, due to a series of maddening delays, full dark, and Gabby thanked providence for the light of a rising moon. Progress was necessarily slowed, and soon even the novel sights of the metropolis ceased to make them forget their fatigue. Plastered to the windows once again, they at first viewed with wonder the bustling tide of humanity through which they wound their way. Illuminated by newfangled gas street lamps which lent a yellow glow to the smoky haze that lay like a blanket over everything, the sights of London were as fascinating to their country-bred eyes as visions of another world. Then they realized that those citizens on foot seemed, for the most part, to be both ragged and dirty, while those on horseback or that could be glimpsed aboard passing conveyances appeared standoffish and in many cases positively surly. Odiferous smells began to permeate even the walls of the carriage, making them wrinkle their noses and glance at each other in consternation. The cause was soon identified as narrow ditches, thick with floating refuse, that ran alongside the roadways. Shabby half-timbered buildings crowded so closely together on both sides of the road that they seemed after a while to create a single, wall-like facade. This was bisected at irregular intervals by narrow dark alleys into which dangerous-looking characters disappeared like rats down a hole. Observing one particularly evil-looking fellow, Claire echoed the sentiments of all by expressing thanks aloud that the shabby appearance of their carriage and the faded condition of the crest on the door made an assault by robbers unlikely. As they at last entered the posher environment of Mayfair, identified in a thankful tone by Twindle, the traffic thinned and the streets grew markedly less populated. By the time the carriage swayed to a halt on the cobblestone street outside Wickham House, the moon was climbing the sky and there were few people about. The occupants of the carriage were hungry, exhausted, irritable, and, in Claire's case, extremely travel sick. It was with relief that Gabby, who was closest to the door, sucked in a breath of fresh, relatively sweet-smelling air as Jem opened it and let down the steps, then held up a hand to help her alight.

"Thank heavens. Much longer, and we all would have been ill," she said. Bestowing a quick smile on her frowning servant as she gained the dark, windy street, Gabby gathered the billowing folds of her cloak closer about her person in response to the unexpected, although not entirely unwelcome, chill of the April night. At least, she thought in the spirit of trying to find a positive thought to dwell on, the rain had ceased, though puddles stood on the street, gleaming black in the moonlight.

" 'Tis not too late to draw back from this mad scheme o' yours, Miss Gabby," Jem said in a worried undertone. As Gabby glanced at him their gazes held for a pregnant instant. The worst thing about servants who had known one from the cradle, and, indeed, had practically helped to raise one, was that they felt quite free to speak their minds whenever they chose, Gabby reflected with some annoyance, however unwelcome their observations might be.

"Yes, indeed it is too late. I have quite made up my mind, Jem, so you may as well stop pestering me about the matter." Her tart reply was as low voiced as Jem's warning.

"Mark my words, missy, no good will come of it," he muttered direly, then was forced into silence as Beth appeared in the door of the carriage. Beyond casting him a sharp look, Gabby ignored him after that, looking about her instead as she waited for her sisters and Twindle to be handed down. Gaslights burned on each corner of the square. Their flickering glow, coupled with the bright moonlight, made visibility quite good. A wheeled cart rattled along farther down the street, she saw, pushed by a pie man calling out "Meat pasties! Meat pasties for sale!" as though he had not much hope of being attended to. Another carriage, newer and far more fashionable than their own, swept by, its wheels rattling over the street, its flickering lights and open curtains permitting Gabby just a glimpse of an elegant lady and gentleman inside. In the grassy area at the center of the square, a pair of ragged-looking urchins conversed with another, lantern-bearing man whom Gabby guessed—hoped—was the watch.

"Really, Claire, you are far too old to go casting up your

accounts in carriages." Beth, having reached the street, directed this complaint up at the open carriage door.

Gabby had to smile a little at Beth's outraged tone, but otherwise she paid scant attention to her sister's grumbling. Instead she turned her gaze to Wickham House, and was pleased with what she saw. From outward appearances at least, Stivers and Mrs. Bucknell had done an outstanding job. For all that it had been closed for years, the house appeared in no different case from its neighbors around the square. Indeed, it might almost have been held to have been one of the handsomest among them. Certainly it looked as well kept.

"Next time *you* may sit across from her." Beth scowled and brushed disgustedly at her black skirts as she moved to stand at Gabby's elbow. Claire, who had just appeared in the doorway looking as pale and woebegone as a daffodil after a storm, called down apologetically, "I'm truly sorry, Beth."

"Now, Miss Beth, Miss Claire can't help being sick, and you know it, so just give over, do. And as for you—using cant terms is never becoming in a young lady, and so I've told you time out of mind," Twindle said in a scolding tone, appearing in the aperture as Claire, clutching Jem's hand, began to climb down.

"Being sick all over one's sister is even less becoming in a young lady than using cant terms, if you want my opinion," Beth retorted. As Twindle and Jem fussed over a still-apologizing Claire, Gabby, long innured to such petty squabbles between her sisters, turned her attention back to the house.

Its facade was impressive, she noted with some pride: made of brick with elegant stone steps and iron railings, Wickham House stood four stories high. The amount of work Stivers and Mrs. Bucknell had done in just a few days to make the dwelling ready must have been staggering: all appeared pristine, from the gleaming brass knocker on the door to the immaculately swept steps to the sparkling glass in the four rows of windows. But what was most surprising was that the lamps on either side of the door burned bright with welcome, and every room in the house seemed to be lit up. Although the curtains were drawn, light glowed behind them, making the grand house appear almost as though a party was being held inside.

"Stivers timed our arrival to a nicety, don't you think?" Beth said with admiration, breaking into Gabby's thoughts. Behind them, John-Coachman was already beginning to unload the baggage from the roof by the simple method of untying the bundle and then tossing individual pieces to the ground. Having turned Claire over to Twindle, Jem stood below, catching the newly liberated pieces and assembling them into a pile.

"Have a care with that one. It contains Miss Claire's vanity case," Twindle shrilled from some paces behind them, alarm obvious in her voice.

John-Coachman's reply was an unintelligible mutter, followed by a thud and a moan from Twindle.

"Stivers appears to have done a remarkable job," Gabby agreed, making a mental note to instruct the butler to be more sparing with candles in future. Under the circumstances, she did not mean to spend more than she must. Such profligacy was unlike Stivers, she thought with faint puzzlement as, treading warily, she began to ascend the steps. Steps were ever difficult for her, and only by maintaining a slow, careful pace could she be relatively confident of not stumbling. Beth was just behind her, and Claire, supported by Twindle's arm, brought up the rear.

The door opened before Gabby reached it. A strange footman peered out at them: one of Stiver's new hires, no doubt. Behind him, the hall seemed as well-lit as the assembly rooms at York, where, in the months before their father's death, Claire had, under Gabby's chaperonage, twice attended dances.

"Hello," Gabby said, summoning a smile for the footman as she gained the top of the steps. "As you have no doubt guessed, I am Lady Gabriella Banning, and these are my sisters, Lady Claire and Lady Elizabeth. And this is Miss Twindlesham."

"Yes, my lady, we were expecting you all the afternoon," the man said, stepping back with a bow and opening the door wide. "Shall I send someone down to carry in your bags, my lady?"

"Yes, thank you," Gabby said, walking past him into the hall. What immediately struck her was how warmly alive the house felt. Despite having had no members of the family in residence for a decade past, it seemed almost to hum with vitality. The marble floor gleamed; the chandelier sparkled; the tall pier glass to her right reflected walls papered in a soft cream and green pattern that looked surprisingly unfaded, and the mirror's ornate frame, as well as the frames of various paintings adorning the walls, were so bright a gold that they might well have been recently gilded. The deep reds and blues of the oriental carpet underfoot were as vivid as if it had been laid down the day before. The banister of the wide staircase that rose steeply on the right was silky with polish. Not the faintest musty scent or odor of mildew could be detected, sniff though she might. Spring flowers in a Meissen bowl added their scent to the smell of beeswax and—dinner? Surely not. Surely Stivers could not have timed their arrival as precisely as that.

As she drew off her gloves, Gabby realized with a deepening frown that there was even a slight buzz of conversation in the background. It seemed to emanate from beyond the closed pocket doors that led to the salon on the left; the dining room, she supposed.

"Miss Gabby, Miss Beth, Miss Claire, welcome!" A smile warmed Stivers's usually cadaverlike face as he hurried toward them from the back of the house. "Miss Gabby, forgive me. I have been on the watch all afternoon, and would have been on hand to open the door to you myself, but I was called to the kitchen to settle a slight dispute. That chef of His Lordship's—well, you know how Frenchies can be—has no notion of how to go on in a proper English kitchen. But I handled the difficulty, I fancy, quite well! I only hope that his foreign concoctions suit your palate, Miss Claire." This last was added on a fatherly note.

"Stivers, you have been very busy. I commend you," Gabby said as Claire murmured something inaudible in reply to this reference to her notoriously delicate stomach. The feeling that something was amiss was growing ever stronger within Gabby's breast. She frowned at Stivers. "But what do you mean, that chef of His Lordship's? Have you purloined someone's cook?"

The question was meant to be half in jest, but the joyous grin that transformed Stivers's face in response alarmed her to the core. In all the years he had served them—and that was all the years of her life and more—Gabby had never known Stivers to look *joyous*.

"No, Miss Gabby. It's *His Lordship's* chef, that he has brought with him from foreign parts. His Lordship, your brother, the earl of Wickham. He is here, Miss Gabby."

For a moment Gabby could do no more than stare at the butler in stupefaction.

"Wickham? Here? Whatever are you talking about, Stivers?" Gabby demanded when she regained command of her tongue. Just then the doors to the presumed dining room were thrown open. What seemed like a positive crowd of dazzlingly dressed people spilled into the hall, laughing and chatting as they came.

"We shall be late for the farce," complained one woman, a ripe blonde in a shockingly low-cut yellow gown who laughed up into the face of the man to whose arm she clung. He was tall, well built, black haired, clad in immaculate evening attire, and at the center of the approaching throng.

"My lord," Stivers said with a deprecating cough.

The black-haired man's gaze swung around inquiringly. Perceiving the newcomers, he, along with the entire party, came to a halt. Gabby was suddenly conscious of being the cynosure of all eyes. Aware of the poor appearance that she and her sisters must present in their travel-stained, out-dated mourning gowns, and of the slight scent of sickness that, she feared, clung to them all, she was conscious of an inward shrinking. Then it occurred to her that she was being made to feel uncomfortable by strangers who were most incomprehensibly making themselves at home in *her* house. She stood a little straighter, squaring her shoulders, raising her chin, and regarded the interlopers with eye-brows lifted in faint hauteur.

For an instant, no longer, she and the black-haired man locked eyes. His, she saw, were a dark blue, deep set beneath thick black brows. He looked to be in his early to mid-thirties, and his skin was very tan, as though he had spent much time exposed to a hot, unEnglish sun. His features were chiseled, his face hard and handsome. His broad-shouldered, narrow-hipped form was well suited to the frilled shirt, long-tailed black coat, silver waistcoat, black knee breeches, and silk stockings which he wore.

"Ah, so you have arrived at last," he said genially, just as if he knew them well and had been expecting them, and disengaged himself from the lady at his side. "Ladies and gentlemen, you must give me a moment to greet my sisters."

Gabby felt her jaw go slack as he strolled toward her.

"Gabriella, I presume," he said with a slight smile as she goggled up at him, and, possessing himself of her suddenly nerveless hand, carried it to his mouth. "Welcome to Wickham House. I trust your journey did not prove too tiring?"

❧ 3 ❧

She was unremarkable in every way save for the hauteur with which she regarded him, he thought. The hauteur nettled him: the daughter of an earl she might be, but she was also well past the first blush of youth, shapeless as a stick, dowdy in unbecoming, head-to-toe black, faintly disheveled, and, unlike the high flyer on his arm, possessed of looks that would never merit so much as a second glance from a connoisseur of women such as himself. He set himself to banishing the hauteur from her manner, and, he congratulated himself, succeeded admirably with his very first words. In fact, by the time he raised her hand to his lips, she looked as shocked as if he'd struck her. Her parted lips quivered, but no sound came out. Her eyes widened on his face until they were the size of coins. The delicately-boned hand he brushed against his mouth was suddenly cold as ice—or a corpse's. And, speaking of corpses, what small amount of color there had been in her face drained away in seconds, leaving it deathly pale.

Her response was extreme even though the unexpected presence of her brother in London must come as a considerable surprise. He was barely able to stop himself from frowning as the thought occurred to him: was her response *too* extreme? Did she, in fact, *know*?

Not unless she was possessed of the second sight, he assured himself. How could she, after all? The trail which had brought him here was known to no one save himself and a few—very few—trusted confederates. He had chased Marcus's killer all the way to Colombo, then lost him. Instinct had taken him to the port's crowded dock area. There he had picked up the scent again, and followed it clear to London, where he had found his quarry at last, rotting in a rented room in a flophouse so disgusting that the scent of a corpse could pass unnoticed for three days. Someone had clearly gotten to the gunman first. That someone was, he guessed, his quarry, his *true* quarry. The man who had ordered Marcus's death. The message with which Marcus had summoned him to Ceylon had read, in part, *Come at once— believe it or not, I've found what you seek.* He hadn't believed it, not really, but had gone nonetheless. But still, he'd been too late—Marcus had been killed before his eyes, ironically lending credence to his message. Now all he could do was try to flush out the man who had ordered Marcus's death. The best way to do that, he'd decided, was to assume Marcus's identity in hopes that the killer, befuddled into believing that his first stooge had failed him, would try again. So far, though, the scheme hadn't worked. Having flaunted himself throughout London without success, he was coming to the reluctant conclusion that the man he sought was intelligent enough to lay low.

Now here was Marcus's sister, looking at him like he had just crawled out from under a rock. But she could not know he was not Marcus. Not unless she'd had a spy in Ceylon.

Still, he looked at her carefully, sizing her up with a keen intelligence veiled by lowered lids. She was dressed in deep mourning suitable for the death of a close relative, and her astonishment at seeing him seemed disproportionate to the circumstances. But if she were truly in mourning for any recent death, she would not now be in London planning to launch her sister into the *ton,* which, courtesy of the voluble Mrs. Bucknell and the less loquacious but corroborating Stivers, he knew was the reason for the ladies' very inopportune intrusion into his plans. A closer glance was sufficient to disclose that the garments she wore were not only not in the current style, but well worn. Her bereavement, then, was most likely a long-standing one.

What, then, was he to make of her reaction to his presence? Was she, perhaps, of that stamp of female who was overset by the least departure from the ordinary?

Looking at that square jaw, he wouldn't have thought so.

"M—Marcus?" she said. Her voice was low and hesitant, and surprisingly husky.

"Am I really such a surprise, dear sister?" he asked lightly, releasing her hand and smiling down into her widened eyes. Still a shade wary, he looked closely into their depths. The gray irises were as cool and clear as the never-ending English rain. Their very clarity reassured him: this woman—this proper English *lady*—was the keeper of no secrets. In him, she saw no more than the obvious: her older brother, head of her family, a man she did not know who, now that he came to think about it, held her future in his hands, arrived out of the blue to possibly interfere in her and her sisters' lives. Looked at that way, her astonishment could be reinterpreted as at least partly consternation, and became more understandable. Clearly, whoever the mourning was for, it was not for Marcus Banning, seventh earl of Wickham. In other words, not for him.

Relaxing slightly, he looked beyond her to where the

other three females in the party stood regarding him with no more than the normal amount of surprise and interest. The gaunt old woman sizing him up with a narrowed, weighing gaze he immediately recognized as some kind of an upper servant, naturally protective of the young ladies in her charge. The beautiful girl—indeed, she was ravishing enough to make his eyes widen before he got his expression under control—who leaned on the old woman's arm had to be the second sister, Claire. And the plump, smiling youngster with the carroty hair was Elizabeth.

Of course.

"Marcus, is it really you?" The youngest one, Elizabeth, came forward then, hands extended to greet him, a bounce in her step, delight in her voice. Before she had quite reached him she was stopped in her tracks by a quick sideways grab by Gabriella, who seemed to have recovered her wits if not, entirely, her composure. Halted but uncowed by her sister's restraining hand on her arm, the younger girl grinned up at him cheekily.

"It is indeed," he answered, taking her hands and smiling back at her. Gabriella had let her hand fall away from her sister's elbow with obvious reluctance, and he barely resisted casting her another assessing look. Instead, he kept his gaze focused on the youngest one. "And you, I fancy, must be Elizabeth."

"Yes, but, remember, I am called Beth."

"Beth, then." He was still smiling as he released her hands and his gaze flicked beyond her to the remaining sister. Though he did not look her way again, he was increasingly conscious of Gabriella's growing frown and that she watched him as a bird might a snake. "And you are Claire."

The beautiful one smiled shyly at him. God, she was

lovely. It was going to take some doing to keep the idea that she was his sister firmly fixed at the forefront of his mind.

"Yes."

While his answering smile still retained its avuncular quality, he shifted his attention to the servant. Gabriella's unwavering regard continued unabated, making him increasingly uncomfortable. Whatever ailed the woman, his best course of action was to appear unaware of any unusual behavior on her part, he decided. Following his gaze, Gabriella turned slightly and made the introduction, her voice as husky as before but less hesitant now: "This is Miss Twindlesham, who has taken care of us all for lo these many years."

He bowed. "Miss Twindlesham. Welcome to Wickham House."

"Thank you, my lord." Miss Twindlesham's expression relaxed, and as she smiled primly at him he got the feeling that he had passed some sort of a test. Claire continued to smile at him, too, and young Beth positively beamed at him. The only one of his newfound relations who did not look delighted to make his acquaintance was, in fact, Gabriella. Instead, she was watching him with a wary frown.

He smiled at her with, he hoped, a good approximation of brotherly fondness.

"Will you not introduce us to your sisters, Marcus?" Belinda appeared beside him, twining her arm in his. The wife of Lord Ware, an elderly, infirm peer who lived year round at his seat in Devonshire, she traveled annually to London where, despite having a taste for gaming and an open appreciation of men, she was nevertheless everywhere received. He had met her at a card party not long after he had arrived in town, and she had been his mistress since that date. But her proprietary air was beginning to grate on him, and, while she was held to be a beauty, her rather mature looks could not hold a candle to those of, say, his newly met middle sister.

As he made the introductions, he allowed no trace of what he was thinking to show on his face.

"Lady Ware, allow me to present Lady Gabriella, Lady Elizabeth, and Lady Claire Banning, and Miss Twindlesham."

Gabriella, he saw, with what must be an innate ability to judge quality, held out a mere two fingers to Belinda. She murmured something appropriate while looking as if she did not count herself completely honored by the introduction. The two younger ladies smiled and held out their hands, and Miss Twindlesham sketched a curtsy. He concluded the introductions with a careless wave of his hand toward the other members of his party. "Also, Lady Alicia Monteigne, Mrs. Armitage, Lord Denby, and the Honorable Mr. Pool."

The exchange of polite greetings was interrupted by Stivers, who, after a quick conference with the footman, approached to hover at his shoulder.

"Yes, Stivers?"

"My lord, the carriages have been brought 'round."

He nodded in acknowledgment. "Thank you." Then, to the assembled group, which, he thought with some amusement, resembled nothing so much as a flock of curious peacocks crowding around a quartet of beset crows, he said in a louder voice: "It seems that, if we are not to miss the evening's entertainment entirely, we must go. Gabriella, Claire, Beth, we will talk more on the morrow. In the meantime, Stivers will take excellent care of you, I know."

The theatre party grew boisterous again as good-byes were said, and assorted hats, greatcoats, sticks, and cloaks were handed around. Then the door was opened, and they headed out into the night, which, even though it was now April, had grown teeth-chatteringly cold. His last over-the-

shoulder glimpse of his new sisters showed him that
Gabriella, who still stood in the center of the hall with the
others clustered around her, had turned all the way around
to watch them go. Their gazes met for only the briefest of
moments before the closing door blocked her from his
view. But even as he swung inside the waiting chaise and
settled himself next to the warm, sweet-smelling armful
that was Belinda, he could not get her expression out of his
mind. It took him a few minutes to recall where he had
seen such a look before, but when he did the memory was
unsettling: it had been during the peninsular campaign, on
the face of a young soldier he had seen get hit in the midsection by a shell. In the seconds before the boy collapsed
and died, the look in his eyes had not been pain, or terror,
as one might have expected, but utter disbelief.

That was what had been in Gabriella's eyes as she
watched him disappear into the night: utter disbelief.

❧ 4 ❧

"I must say," Beth said with enthusiasm, turning to her sisters as the door closed behind the exiting party, "our brother is *something like!* Did you ever see anyone more handsome, or more complete to a shade?"

"In any event, what a surprise to find him here. Although he *did* say in his letter that we might expect him to join us in London in a few weeks. He seemed quite nice, actually. Certainly he has an air." Claire's voice turned reflective as she glanced at Gabby. "Do you think we might be able to get one or two new gowns made up immediately? I could see that Lady Ware and the others thought us the veriest provincials. And Lady Ware's gown! Did you ever behold anything so ravishing? Do you not think that something similar would look well on me?"

"Not unless you were planning to set yourself up as Haymarket ware," Gabby snorted, recovering her wits to some degree now that her supposedly deceased brother was out of sight.

"That dress was certainly not meant for young ladies in their first season," Twindle agreed. "And as for you, Miss Beth, what have I told you about using cant terms? You will give people a very pretty opinion of you if they hear you talking so."

"Miss Gabby, Miss Claire, Miss Beth, Stivers only just now sent to tell me you had arrived." Small and round as a dumpling, Mrs. Bucknell came bustling into the hall, her florid, rather plain face wreathed in smiles despite the scandalized tone of her voice. "Was there ever such a surprise as His Lordship being here? And for all that I thought he might send me and Stivers straight back home again, as he had already set up here as a bachelor establishment, no sooner did Stivers tell him that you meant to come to town for Miss Claire's season than he bade us stay and take the place in hand, which we did, you may be sure," she tut-tutted. "You look fagged to death, the lot of you, and you especially, Miss Claire. You'll be wanting to go straight upstairs, as any but a nodcock such as Stivers would know, and have a can of hot water sent up to you, and refresh yourselves. Then would you be wanting supper served in the morning room, Miss Gabby, seeing as how the dining room is still at sixes and sevens from His Lordship's dinner party? Or a nice tray in your rooms?"

Gabby gathered her resources enough to greet the housekeeper warmly, and answer her questions.

"Miss Claire, for one, would be wishful of retiring to bed," Twindle said firmly, shepherding Claire toward the stairs. Mrs. Bucknell, clucking at the severe trials travel imposed on those with a delicate constitution, undertook to show them to their chambers herself. Twindle glanced back over her shoulder at her younger charge. "Miss Beth, I leave it to your own and Miss Gabby's discretion as to whether or not you retire for the night as well, but just let me remind you that London is not going anywhere. It will still exist on the morrow."

Beth looked imploringly at Gabby. "If I went to bed

now, I could not possibly sleep so much as a wink. Claire, I cannot believe you would be so poor spirited as to retire to bed on our first night in town."

"I would not do so, but I have the headache, and my stomach is behaving in the most disgraceful way," Claire said apologetically as she began to climb the stairs.

"Of course you must go up, Claire. Beth, do you go upstairs too, and at least wash your face and hands. I'm coming as well, as soon as I've had a word with Stivers. In about three quarters of an hour, if you like, you and I will take a light repast—Mrs. Bucknell, something cold will do—in the morning room. After that, I for one am going to bed. If you hope to see anything of London tomorrow, I suggest you do, too. Otherwise, you'll be as cross as a bear."

Beth made a face, but obediently started to follow Claire and Twindle up the stairs. When they had climbed enough to be out of earshot, Gabby turned to the butler.

"Stivers, was he indeed here when you arrived?" she asked in a low voice.

Stivers frowned at her. "His Lordship, do you mean, Miss Gabby?"

"Yes. His—His Lordship. Was he already in residence here at Wickham House when you arrived?" Despite her best effort to remain nonchalant, her voice had an urgent undertone.

"Why, yes, Miss Gabby. I apprehend from something his man—Barnet, that is—said that His Lordship arrived in the country some two weeks ago, and came straight away to London, meaning to travel down to Hawthorne Hall at some later time."

Her expression must have revealed something of her feelings, because he added anxiously, "Is aught amiss, Miss Gabby?"

Gabby's mind was racing. All her scheming and worrying, her arguments with Jem, her sleepless nights, had been, apparently, for naught. Marcus was alive and well and, indeed, here at Wickham House. And seemingly perfectly pleased to see them, too.

It was unbelievable. How could Jem have made such a mistake? Perhaps her brother had been merely wounded, and had recovered. But Marcus didn't look as if he had been recently ill—or, indeed, ever ill for so much as a day in his life, for that matter.

Something did not make sense.

"No, nothing is amiss, Stivers," she lied, and from somewhere summoned up a rather weak smile. "I was just rather surprised to encounter my brother here, is all."

"Indeed, Miss Gabby, it was a surprise to Mrs. Bucknell and myself too, but it is surely a happy day for us all when the earl returns to take up his rightful place, is it not?"

"Yes, indeed it is," Gabby replied with a forced smile, and began to walk toward the stairs. With one hand on the banister she paused, glancing back at Stivers.

"Jem went around to the stables with the coach, did he not? Would you have a message sent to him that I need to speak with him right away? Put him somewhere where we may be private, and tell him that I will join him presently."

"Yes, Miss Gabby."

Stivers was too familiar with his young ladies' long-standing bond with the groom to express any surprise. As he turned away with a bow, Gabby, her thoughts in a whirl, headed up the stairs. She tried to recall everything she could remember about her brother from the one time she had met him, when her father had for some unknown reason summoned his heir to Hawthorne Hall. Marcus had been a spindly youth of seventeen, not over-tall, with black hair and pale skin and—what color eyes?

Of course, they must have been blue. A deep indigo shade. Hadn't she just seen them again, scarcely more than a quarter of an hour since? Eyes did not change.

But the rest of him had changed greatly from her memory of him. Had the youth she just vaguely remembered really grown up into that tall, muscular, splendidly handsome man?

Obviously he had, as impossible as it seemed.

He had been quiet, and rather shy. She remembered that. And bookish—she remembered that, too. And homesick. The few conversations she had had with him had centered on his grandfather, whom he loved, and his longing to be back with him at their home. Gabby remembered envying him for having a loving grandfather and a happy home to go back to, even if it was on some heathenish island, as her father called it.

And then someone had come for him, and he had left Hawthorne Hall, just like that. If she had questioned where he had gone, and why, she did not remember the answers. Probably she had not asked. Her father had not been the kind of man of whom one asked idle questions.

Or, indeed, any questions at all.

"Miss Gabby, I've put you in the countess's apartments, if you've no objections. And this is Mary, who will be waiting on you. Mary, this is Lady Gabriella. See you take good care of her."

Jolted from her thoughts by Mrs. Bucknell's words, Gabby looked up to see the housekeeper holding open a door for her. The young maid standing beside her, eyes nervously downcast, bobbed a curtsy at her new mistress. She was a slender, freckle-faced, sandy-haired girl, obviously unsure of what to expect. Gabby summoned a smile for her, and, trailed by housekeeper and maid, passed into the chambers allotted her.

The countess's apartments consisted of two rooms. The first was a large bedchamber, elegantly appointed in soft, slightly faded shades of rose and cream. The walls were hung with cream-colored damask. The hangings and coverlet on the large four-poster were of rose silk with a deep, knotted fringe. The curtains drawn over the two long windows at the front of the apartment were of the same material. A fire—a luxury that had been permitted in the bedrooms at Hawthorne Hall only since her father's death—burned cozily in the hearth. The second chamber, which Mrs. Bucknell described as her dressing room, was outfitted with a variety of mirrors, a dressing table littered with an interesting assortment of bottles and boxes, and several tall wardrobes. Her as yet unopened trunk already waited before one of them. At the far end of the room, a cream-painted six-panel door with a crystal knob was set into the wall. It was closed.

Mrs. Bucknell must have seen her gaze resting rather thoughtfully upon that door, because she said, "That leads to His Lordship's apartment. As this chamber was the largest of those suitable for a lady, and required very little in the way of refurbishing, I took it upon myself to put you in here, Miss Gabby, thinking that you wouldn't mind being next door to your brother. I hope I did right?"

Although Gabby wasn't entirely certain that she was telling the truth, she reassured Mrs. Bucknell that she had done just as she ought, managed to rid herself of the woman when the promised can of hot water arrived, and with Mary's help quickly washed her face and hands and tidied her hair before leaving her room again. It was her intention to get downstairs before Beth, so that she might have a few minutes of private conversation with Jem to see where, exactly, the mistake had been made.

Stivers was on the lookout for her. He materialized from the nether regions of the house just as she reached the first floor.

"I have put him in the library, Miss Gabby. If you will follow me," he replied to her inquiry.

Gabby nodded her thanks, and did as she was bid. Ushered into a tall, paneled room lined with books, she waited until Stivers had withdrawn and the door was firmly shut before advancing on Jem, who stood before the fire, his hands clasped behind his back, a worried frown on his face.

"You have heard that my brother is in residence?" she said in a low voice, her arms crossing over her chest, her hands rubbing her upper arms nervously. Her gaze met his. "Tell me, if you can, how that is possible?"

Jem shook his head. He looked as disturbed as Gabby felt.

"It *ain't* possible, Miss Gabby. For certain sure it ain't possible. His Lordship your brother was shot dead on that island o' his. I saw it happen with me own two eyes."

Gabby drew a deep, slightly shaky breath. "Perhaps he was wounded, but did not die."

"Miss Gabby, he was *dead*. Begging your pardon, but His Lordship had a hole blowed clean through his heart. I knows dead when I sees it, Miss Gabby. I ain't such a green one as to be mistaken about that."

Gabby stared at him. "Jem, you *must* be mistaken. If you are not, then—then this man who says he is my brother is—is either a ghost, or an imposter."

Jem looked grim. "I don't hold with believin' in ghosts, Miss Gabby."

"Nor do I." Despite the warmth of the room, Gabby shivered as she considered the other possibility. "But an imposter—that is so unlikely as to be ludicrous, you know. Besides, he knew our names, mine and Claire's and Beth's." She frowned slightly as she remembered that he had called Beth Elizabeth before her sister had corrected him. He had played with baby Beth all those years ago when he had come to Hawthorne Hall, and called her by the diminutive then. In his letter, he had referred to their youngest sister as Beth. And, too, he had called her Gabriella, when he had known her as Gabby all those years ago. . . .

But by itself, calling his sisters by their full given names meant nothing. Many years had passed, after all, and he was a grown man now, with probably only the vaguest memory of them all.

Just as her memory of him was vague.

"What do he look like, this lordship?" Jem asked slowly.

Of course, Gabby realized, feeling relieved. Jem had lately seen her brother; he could identify him without a doubt.

"He is tall, and well set up, with black hair and blue eyes. Very handsome."

Jem looked doubtful. "Well, I don't know about the handsome part. That's a thing for the ladies to decide, I'm thinking. But as for the rest—aye, it fits close enough, I reckon."

"Then he must be Marcus." Gabby felt a stirring of profound relief. With her brother wonderfully, amazingly alive, and in London, and from all indications perfectly willing to provide Claire with a come-out, her troubles were at an end. She would not have to carry through with her scheme after all. The missive that she had already sent to Mr. Challow, with Marcus's letter enclosed, was no longer a lie. She was *not* attempting to deceive anyone; Claire need be in no particular hurry to marry. . . .

"Miss Gabby, whoever the gentleman be, who he can*not*

be is His Lordship. Not unless his corpse has risen and is walking about above ground."

Jem's grim words punctured her growing bubble of happiness. Deflated, she met his gaze. Why had she even allowed herself to hope that this would be easy? In her experience, nothing in life ever was.

"You must see him, then," she said. "That is the only way to be sure."

"Aye. That's just what I was thinking meself."

"He has gone out. It will likely be late before he returns."

"With your permission, Miss Gabby, I'll wait in here 'til I hears him come in. Then I'll nip out into the hall and get a good look at him, with him being none the wiser."

"I'll wait with you."

Jem shook his head. "There's no need for that, Miss Gabby. You go on up to bed, and I'll tells you the truth of it in the morning."

Gabby shook her head. "I couldn't shut my eyes until I know."

Just then they heard the sound of voices in the hall as Beth, having come downstairs, inquired as to whether or not her sister had put in an appearance yet.

Gabby sighed. "I must needs join my sister for a while. I'll have Stivers bring you something to eat in here. After Beth has retired for the night, I'll be back."

"No doubt I'd be wasting my breath to argue," Jem said, frowning at her.

"Yes," Gabby agreed tranquilly. "You would."

With that she left the room to join Beth. They partook of a cold supper, and then explored the house. Beth went into transports over everything from the elegant drawing room to the cunning garden to the mews at the back of the house. Gabby, though less vocal, was equally impressed. By the time her sister had at last gone to bed, and Gabby had pretended to retire too so as to rid herself of Mary and Stivers and the rest of the hovering staff, it was past midnight. Accustomed to dressing herself—the sisters had of necessity shared one maid, who had been left behind at Hawthorne Hall—she shed the nightdress into which Mary had tenderly fastened her and without difficulty donned a fresh gown, which at least had the virtue of being clean although it was nearly identical to the one she had earlier discarded. Then she brushed her hair, rewound it into its customary knot at her nape and crept back downstairs to join Jem in the library.

Although not surprised, he was not best pleased to see her, and they spent the first quarter of an hour in a spirited though low-voiced discussion about the advisability of her presence. Defeated, Jem at last gave up. Then they set themselves to wait, one on either side of the fire, and wait was exactly what they did. An hour passed, and then another, and another. The clock on the mantel had just chimed four o'clock, and Gabby was having all she could do not to fall asleep in her high-backed leather chair, when the unmistakable sounds of someone entering the house jolted her fully awake again.

On the opposite side of the fire, Jem, too, sat upright. They exchanged speaking glances as the distant click of a closing door and the muffled tread of heavy footsteps reached their ears. Then, almost at the same moment, they stood. Gabby was in the lead as they tiptoed toward the library door.

ᴥ 5 ᴥ

The tall, dark figure that was—or, possibly, was not—the earl of Wickham walked across the shadowy entry hall to pick up a candle that had been left burning for him on the table. His caped greatcoat swirled about his legs, and added even more width to already broad shoulders. Another figure, his dark bulk slightly taller and far broader even than the earl's, emerged suddenly from the salon to the right, a hand carefully cupped around the flame of a candle that he, too, carried. Wickham checked, as if surprised. Then the figure joined him, and the two began to converse in low tones that Gabby, strain though she might, could not quite overhear.

"That be Barnet, His Lordship's man. I runned across him in the kitchen earlier," Jem muttered in Gabby's ear as they crept along in the dense shadow cast by the stairs. Pressed close against the cool plaster wall, Gabby was conscious of her rapidly increasing pulse rate. Something about the sight of the two very large men talking together so quietly in the dead of the night struck her as sinister. For the first time, she was truly ready to believe that the man who called himself her brother might indeed be an imposter, bent on who knew what nefarious scheme.

"Well, is he Wickham?" she hissed at Jem. The slow prickle of apprehension that crept down her spine when she considered that he might not be was unpleasant. What she craved was for Jem to recognize his mistake, 'fess up, and tell her that he had made an error of monumental proportions and that Marcus really was alive and was, at that very moment in fact, talking to a veritable giant in the entry hall, thus allowing her nerves to settle and them both to retire to a well-earned rest.

"I keep tellin' ye, Miss Gabby, it *can't* be His Lordship." Jem shook his head at her. "Though I ain't had a proper look yet, I know what I know: His Lordship's dead."

They were still edging forward, protected from view by the sheltering staircase and the darkness at their end of the hall. The only illumination came from the pair of flickering candles. The uncertain light transformed the men's bodies into solid dark shapes, and played over their faces in an ever-changing symphony of light and shadow. Recognition of any individual feature was going to be difficult at best, Gabby realized, and felt like kicking herself for not divining earlier the impossibility of what they were attempting. Identification of this sort was best left to the bright daytime hours, not the vagaries of night and candlelight.

Right now she could be warm and safe in her bed. . . .

The fall happened so fast that she could do nothing to prevent it. One second she was easing along the wall, a hand pressed flat against it for guidance and her gaze fastened on their target, and the next she had caught her toe on something—a corner of the rug, perhaps, or the leg of the narrow console table she had just passed? She stumbled forward, and in the process came down hard on her weak leg. It collapsed beneath her so that she was catapulted willy-nilly into a headlong dive.

"Who goes there?" The barked question was uttered just as she landed with a *smack* face down on the cold marble floor. Luckily, since she ended up measuring her length, her hands broke the worst of the fall. Jem let out a hoarse exclamation and, abandoning what was now a futile attempt at concealment, flew to her side. He crouched over her, his gnarled horseman's hands gentle as they closed on her shoulders, his voice urgent as he besought her to tell him if she was hurt.

Gabby ignored him. Eyes wide with horror, fingers curling nervously against the cold, unyielding surface on which she lay, she turned her head toward the men who, just as she had feared, were even now staring at them.

From her new vantage point, looking up at them from approximately their ankle level, the pair looked terrifyingly huge—and menacing.

Both candles had been lifted high. With Jem beside her, she was caught in a long finger of candlelight. Gabby blinked as she struggled to see past the twin flames to the faces of the men who were holding them. She could discern nothing beyond the glitter of their eyes; then, as her gaze traveled downward, she gasped aloud as she realized that a silver-mouthed pistol was now pointed directly at her, grasped in her supposed brother's very capable-looking hand.

"Why, 'tis Gabriella," he said with obvious surprise, employing a far different tone than the harsh bark with which he had demanded to know their identities. Without further ado, the pistol disappeared again into the pocket of his great-coat. Then Wickham, if indeed it was he, set his candle down on the table and moved unhurriedly toward them. His man followed, candle still held high to better illuminate the scene.

Gabby swallowed convulsively, and ignored stabs and

throbs of pain from various parts of her anatomy to struggle into a sitting position. That was as much dignity as she could achieve for the moment, she admitted to herself, quickly twitching her skirts into position to conceal her lower limbs. Standing was, just at present, beyond her. Taking a quick mental inventory of the damage she had suffered, she realized that her hair had been knocked partly loose from its pins, and long chestnut strands straggled witch-straight around her face. Her palms stung from their unexpected contact with the floor. Her knees tingled and throbbed. Her left hipbone and weak left leg ached abominably.

She could only trust that she had not done herself real harm.

Then she glanced up, to find Wickham—for so she could not help but think of him, whatever the merits of the case—and his man looming above her. Suddenly her physical condition became the farthest thing from her mind. Wickham was looking her and Jem over with a frown, his eyes narrowed in a speculative fashion that Gabby misliked. His man openly scowled at them over Wickham's shoulder. He had the hulking build and squashed-looking features of a pugilist, and on that face, a scowl was as frightening as an openly voiced threat.

"What, pray tell, are you doing, creeping about the house in the middle of the night?" The very quietness of Wickham's voice made it, perversely, scarier than a shout would have been. Meeting his gaze, Gabby felt her mouth go dry.

What *was* she doing creeping about the house in the middle of the night, indeed?

Before Gabby could come up with a halfway plausible lie, Wickham's eyes narrowed on her face.

"Spying on me, sister?" he asked in a falsely affable tone that made the hair on the back of Gabby's neck rise. His gaze stayed fixed on her, eyebrows lifted in what was almost a parody of polite inquiry.

She took a deep and, she hoped, unnoticed, breath.

"Not at all," she said coldly, prepared to dodge a direct and probably unbelievable lie by informing him that her actions were certainly no concern of *his*. Before she could finish, however, Jem shot to his feet and placed himself squarely between her and the others, looking for all the world like a small, aged, but admirably valiant lapdog attempting to guard its master from a particularly fierce pair of marauding wolves.

Gabby's rueful conclusion was that the lapdog was more likely to meet with success.

"She be no more your sister than I be, you blackguard! *You are not my lord Wickham,* and I for one knows it. My lord Wickham is dead!" Jem's voice was shrill with indignation.

Gabby's jaw dropped at that inopportune utterance. She watched, frozen, as the pistol reappeared, so quickly that it might almost have been done by sleight of hand, this time to point with unmistakable menace at Jem.

"No! No!" she gasped, horribly afraid that she was about to witness murder done. To reveal so much, under these circumstances, was quite possibly a fatal error. Dear fool, she thought with an inner groan, what were you *thinking?* Clutching at Jem's arm—he automatically clasped her elbow to assist her to rise without ever removing his gaze from the pistol—she surged painfully upright. Gaining her feet, ignoring the ache in her leg and hip, she placed a hand on Jem's shoulder for balance, and summoned a—she hoped—teasing smile for the man with the gun. "Jem was funning, of course. Really, Marcus, have you *no* sense of humor?"

There was the smallest of pauses. Beside her, Jem made a restive movement but remained prudently silent, no doubt realizing too late that to issue his challenge in the dead of the night when they were alone with the imposter and his henchman might not have been entirely wise. The pistol continued to point unwaveringly at him. It occurred to Gabby then that if what Jem alleged was true, they just might be in the gravest of danger. *Mortal* danger.

Too late now. She very much feared that the damage was done. The words could not be unsaid, and she could only hope that she had managed to smooth them over. If not, there was no one around to come charging to the rescue: her sisters and Twindle were deep asleep some two stories above, and the servants were at the very top of the house. They were at his mercy, defenseless.

"That hound won't hunt, my dear." Wickham's silky-sounding drawl made her go cold with fear. "So you might as well abandon the attempt. Permit me to say that you're a very poor liar. You've been looking at me like I was a ghost since you first set eyes on me." He gave a short, unamused laugh as his gaze held hers. "The question is, now what's to be done?"

His eyes glinted black in the candlelight. Gabby felt her heart give a great lurch as the pistol was leveled at Jem with, she feared, deadly intent. Jem's arm shot out, pushing her more fully behind him, and her fingers dug into the groom's shoulder as she watched a long, bronzed thumb ease back the hammer. . . .

The sound of the gun being cocked seemed as loud as an explosion in the breathless silence.

Then Gabby, even while staring down the mouth of the gun, bethought herself of something, and felt the tension that had stretched her nerves tight as bow strings ease.

"All right, whoever you are, that's quite enough," she said tartly, trying again if her injured leg would bear any weight; it seemed that now it would, and, trusting her own two feet to support her once more, she cautiously removed her hand from Jem's shoulder and slipped around to stand beside him. There was a severe expression on her face as her gaze met the imposter's. "You might as well quit waving that pistol about. It is quite useless to try to frighten us with it any longer, you know. I am perfectly well aware that Jem and I stand in no danger from it."

Beside her, Gabby felt Jem quiver. He rolled an anxious eye in her direction, which she ignored. The false Wickham looked at her rather meditatively.

"Indeed?" His fingers moved, seeming to caress the shiny metal beneath them with real affection. The weapon was, she noted, fully cocked, and still aimed at Jem. Still, she knew she was not, could not be, mistaken. "How so?"

"A shot would rouse the household," she pointed out calmly. "Which you must know as well as I do. Too, a pair of bloody corpses in the entryway would present their own problems: the bodies would have to be disposed of, for instance, and every trace of blood scrubbed away, all before anyone came upon the scene. Then you would have Jem's and my disappearance to account for. Hue and cry would be raised for us, and you would inevitably come under the kind of close scrutiny that, under the circumstances, I am quite sure you would rather avoid."

He met her gaze for the briefest of moments.

"You're a mighty cool customer, madam, I'll give you that," he said with a slight, wry twist of his lips. Despite a protesting murmur from his henchman, who stood just behind him glowering at them over his broad shoulder, he carefully eased the hammer down into a safe position and repocketed the pistol. "So which is it, do you think, Gabriella? Have I refrained from shooting the two of you because I fear bringing the household down around my ears, or because the task of disposing of two—how did you put it, bloody corpses?—is beyond me?"

"I have no idea." Gabby's voice was unruffled. "Nor do I particularly care."

"You rascals, by this time tomorrow the Runners will be after you," Jem said with relish, having apparently decided, now that the pistol was out of sight and the imposter was responding so lightly to Gabby's challenge, that the enemy was well on the way to being routed. "If 'twere me, I'd be taking to me heels as soon as ever I could. I dunno but what impersonating a belted earl ain't a hangin' offense."

This, Gabby could not help but feel, was unnecessary provocation. The false Wickham's gaze flicked to Jem, running over him from the top of his salt-and-pepper head to his sturdy boots, giving the impression that it missed nothing in between.

"You know, you are growing most tiresome, the pair of you. I really cannot have you spouting your nonsense all over London." His tone was thoughtful. Crossing his arms over his chest, he regarded them out of narrowed eyes.

"Let me take care of the bloody nuisances for ye, Cap'n," growled the hitherto silent giant at his back. "*I* won't 'ave no problem riddin' us o' a pair o' plaguey corpses."

"Then I see I need no longer hold back." The imposter looked at Gabby with a sardonic smile. Jem immediately thrust her behind him again, almost oversetting her in the process, and reached inside his coat, withdrawing from an inner pocket a pistol that Gabby had not even known he carried. Horrified, she watched as he brandished the pistol at their adversaries, facing them with the gloating expression of one who held all the aces even though he had to tilt his head back to look up into the faces of the taller men.

"You'll keep a proper distance from Miss Gabby, ye

scoundrels," Jem said through his teeth. "Miss Gabby, do you go back along to the book room and lock yourself in. I'll deal with . . ."

The imposter's fist shot out so fast that Gabby barely saw it move, and connected with Jem's chin with a wicked-sounding crack. Jem's grizzled head snapped back, and without a word he crumpled to the floor, landing with a sickening thud. The pistol skittered harmlessly across the floor. Grinning, Barnet moved to scoop it up.

For a moment Gabby could only stare in horror at her fallen champion, who sprawled senseless almost at her feet. Then her accusing gaze shifted to her ersatz brother, who looked maddeningly calm as he rubbed his knuckles with the thumb of the opposite hand. Behind him, his henchman chortled approval as he pocketed the pistol. At the sound, her spine stiffened and she felt her temper begin to heat.

"You have now run your length," she said icily to her false brother. She crouched rather clumsily beside Jem, ascertained with a touch that he still breathed, and glared up at the man looming over them. "Whoever you are, whatever game you are playing at, this farce is now at an end. If you do not turn yourself about, instantly, and leave my house, taking that—that sniggering ape with you, I shall scream the place down."

"Unwise to utter threats you can't carry out, Gabriella." There was a taunting note to his voice.

"Oh, can't I just?" Gabby retorted, and opened her mouth to scream.

In that instant he was upon her, swooping down like a bird of prey, one hand clamping hard over her mouth, his arm encircling her waist, all before she could get out so much as a squeak. Fighting with all her might, Gabby was still easily bested. In a matter of seconds she found herself hoisted clear off the floor in an awkward her-back-to-his-front hold that imprisoned her arms even while he continued to press his hand over her mouth.

"That's the ticket, Cap'n." Barnet hovered close, nodding approval, as Gabby fought for what might well be her life. "Now we'll see 'ow much screamin' she'll do."

"Let me go," Gabby cried, but nothing emerged but an unintelligible croak. The imposter's palm completely covered her mouth. His long fingers dug painfully into the soft flesh of her cheeks. She could not scream; she could scarcely breathe. She could, however, kick, and this she proceeded to do with abandon despite the pain it caused her, smashing her heels—it was a pity she wore only soft slippers, she reflected furiously—into his shins with a viciousness she had not realized she was capable of. Squirming madly, she bit at his hand. Her teeth sank deep into the fleshy part of his palm. As the salty taste of his skin filled her mouth she felt a fierce spurt of satisfaction.

"Damn it to bloody hell," he yelped, jerking his hand away. Mouth free, Gabby sucked down a great gulp of air and screamed for all she was worth. Just as quick as that, he shoved a wad of what felt like balled-up leather deep into her open mouth, stifling the cry almost at birth.

Caught by surprise, she gagged and choked as she tried to spit the oily-tasting thing out again. It was suffocating her. . . .

"Serves you right, my girl," he said grimly, his eyes staring inimically into hers as he shifted his grip to lift her high against his chest. Struggling with all her might, gasping for breath as she tried to expel the gag with her tongue, sweating with anger and fear, she writhed frantically in his arms as he held her clamped against the hard wall of his chest. But her struggles weakened as her need for air increased. Her heels, flailing futilely against empty space, gradually stilled; her squirming lessened and then ceased altogether.

His arms were unbreakable bands imprisoning both her arms and her legs; it was, she realized with growing despair, impossible to win free.

For the time being it was all she could do just to breathe.

"Take him away and keep watch on him until I tell you otherwise," he said to Barnet, indicating Jem, who still lay unconscious on the floor, with a jerk of his head. "At the moment, I feel a pressing need for some private . . . conversation . . . with my dear little sister."

❧ 6 ❧

*D*isdaining to let her head touch his shoulder, Gabby kept her neck stiffly erect and held her head high as she was borne along the cavelike hallway with as much ease as though she weighed no more than a feather—which in fact, she reflected grimly, she scarcely did. He was so much larger and stronger than she as to render any kind of physical contest between them laughable. Whatever he chose to do to her, there was little she could do to stop him. The very helplessness of her position infuriated her, for which she was thankful. It was better, far better, to be angry than afraid. Fear rendered one weak. . . .

Although it was too dark to read his expression clearly, she could see his eyes, and she glared into them, hoping to silently convey all the unflattering sentiments the foul-tasting gag prevented her from giving voice to.

Whatever he planned, she warned herself, her only chance of avoiding it lay in keeping a cool head.

"I collect you launched your little ambush from the library." A thin thread of light showing beneath the closed library door obviously prompted his comment.

He did not even sound out of breath, she reflected furiously, while thanks to his gag she fought for every lungful of air, and, whether from that, or exertion, or—she hated to think it—fear, her heart thumped painfully in her chest.

Stopping at the door, he managed, by dint of a little deft juggling, to turn the knob without loosening his hold on her. When the door swung open he carried her into the library and pushed it shut again with his foot.

"You were lying in wait for me, weren't you, you and your servant? Unwise, under the circumstances, don't you think?"

As she couldn't answer, and he obviously knew it, the question, uttered as he carried her across the library, took on a purely rhetorical quality. The fire had burned low in the hearth, Gabby saw, but it still gave off a faint orange glow that illuminated the area immediately around it. He deposited her in the same high-backed leather chair in which she had been sitting before. Imprisoning her wrists in one large hand, he crouched in front of her, looking at her speculatively. His wide shoulders blocked her view of much of the room. His hard-planed, swarthy-skinned face was too close for comfort. His dark blue eyes bored into hers; his mouth was set in a thin, hard line. With the best will in the world she could not deny that he was a heart-stoppingly handsome man. The acknowledgment did nothing whatsoever to make her loathe him less. Spine ramrod straight, chin up, she eyed him with open hostility.

He continued reprovingly, "What you should have done was kept your suspicions to yourself until you could lay them before Mr. Challow or another of his ilk. Confronting me in private with none but an elderly, undersized groom to protect you was nothing short of bird-witted."

As Gabby was thinking much the same thing, his words served merely to heap coals on the fire of her seething anger. Of course, it was of some small comfort to reflect that she had not intended to confront him at all; the confrontation had come about as a result of her fall, which had been entirely accidental. Still, had she taken the night to consider before attempting to determine the truth surrounding the appearance in London of her supposed brother, the outcome of the subsequent unmasking would have been very different.

"Now," continued her tormentor in a goading tone that made her long to spit in his eye, "purely as a result of your own foolishness, you find yourself at *point non plus.*"

He smiled at her. The smile was slow, self-satisfied, with a definite mocking quality. To keep herself from kicking him—and it was a near run thing; his shins were right in front of her feet—she reminded herself that, with her soft slippers, what that would primarily achieve would be hurt to her own toes. It would certainly not win her release.

In an effort to avoid succumbing to temptation, she forced herself to concentrate for a moment or so on the purely physical. The heat from the fire felt uncomfortably warm now; probably because she was already overheated from her battle with him. The high neck and long sleeves of her kerseymere gown did not improve matters, and the tickling of her nose by a wayward strand of her hair added a final element of discomfort. She shook her head in a vain attempt to shift the errant lock; it fell right back to where it had been before.

Of course. Such was always her fate.

She wrinkled up her nose in silent protest, and glared at him. His gaze, she noted with some dismay, was fixed on her forcibly parted lips. Her breathing faltered as it occurred to her that, perhaps, murder was not all she had to fear. . . .

"If you try to scream, I'll put it back," he warned. Then, to her considerable relief, he fished the gag from her mouth. She coughed and shuddered as it was withdrawn, then drew a deep, lung-filling breath.

The gag, she saw as she worked her dry jaw and lips, trying to restore them to a semblance of normal feeling, consisted of one of his leather driving gloves, now wet from her mouth. He glanced at it with obvious distaste before tossing it onto a nearby table. His attention then returned to her. He was so close that she could see the faint vertical crease between his thick black eyebrows, the lines at the corners of his eyes, the individual whiskers that made up the shadow darkening his cheeks and jaw. The firelight added dancing orange lights to his cropped black hair, and was reflected in the indigo of his eyes.

"Do you now intend to strangle me at your leisure?" The question was pure bravado, uttered despite her swollen-feeling tongue.

He laughed, but it wasn't a pleasant sound.

"Don't tempt me, my dear. You are mighty inconvenient, you know. Now, I am going to ask you some questions, and you are going to answer me. Truthfully, mind."

He gave her wrists an admonitory shake. Gabby's eyes narrowed at him. She could smell the odor of strong spirits that clung to him, as well as the fainter underlying scent of tobacco. It occurred to her, upon identifying the first smell and getting a closer look at the restless glitter in his eyes, that her captor might be just a trifle well to live. Not inebriated, precisely, but definitely feeling the effects of too-liberal imbibing. She knew the look of a man in his cups from bitter experience, and recognized it before her now.

Her lip curled with contempt.

"Although it may be hard to believe given your own obvious proclivities, some of us do make a habit of telling the truth," she said. Her lips and tongue now worked almost normally.

He smiled sardonically at her.

"I hope you are not meaning to imply that *you* tell the truth."

She bristled. "Of course I—what do you mean?"

"It is obvious to anyone of the meanest intelligence that you are running a rig here."

Gabby's eyes widened in astonishment. "*I* am running a rig? That's rich. Especially coming from someone who is *pretending* to be my poor dead brother."

"Ah." His smile broadened. "But that presents us with an interesting question: if you knew that Wickham was dead, then what, pray, were you doing journeying to London, sending your servants to open Wickham House, and planning to launch your sister into the *ton,* when you should more properly be in Yorkshire in deep mourning? I confess, that piques my interest."

She shot him a fulminating look. Scoundrel or not, he was abominably quick, she had to qive him that.

"I hardly knew my brother. It is not to be wondered at that I do not feel the need to go into mourning for him—" she sounded defensive, realized it, and lifted her chin haughtily "—and in any case I see no need to justify my actions to you."

"Now, there's where you're wrong. You see, to all intents and purposes *I* am now Wickham. And you—and your servant, of course—are, I apprehend, the only ones who know otherwise. A very ticklish position for you to be in, *sister.*"

Gabby said nothing for a moment as she considered her situation. He was still crouched in front of her, a hand encircling each of her wrists now. Though he held her loosely, his fingers curled around her wrists like the lightest of shackles, she knew that there was no possibility of breaking free. Given her relative lack of strength, his hands might as well have been iron shackles in truth. His body blocked any possible means of escaping from the chair, much less the room, still less him.

Her gaze met his; he was no longer smiling. His eyes were narrowed and intent, gleaming black in the flickering firelight. His mouth was a hard, straight line.

He looked totally ruthless, she thought, and capable of anything, up to and including her murder. The full extent of her own vulnerability assailed her, rendering her, for a single, hideous instant, most horribly afraid. An inward shiver shook her; goose bumps prickled to life on her flesh. The only other time she could remember feeling so helpless was . . .

No. She wouldn't remember. She *would not*. She was no longer the same person she had been on that day.

When she had vowed never, never in her life, to allow herself to be afraid of any man again.

Sitting up a little straighter, disregarding the strong hands imprisoning her wrists and the big body blocking hers and the mortal danger she might very well be in, she looked him dead in the eye.

"If you leave this house, right now, and give up your pretense, you have my word that I will not set the Runners on you, nor tell anyone else of your deception."

For a moment their eyes deadlocked. Then he made a derisive sound that was as much a snort as a laugh, and abruptly stood up. As quickly as that her hands were free. Before she could do more than register the fact—much good would it do her anyway, she thought bitterly, as any blow she could deliver would have about as much impact on him as a mosquito bite—he was bending over her, his hands wrapping around her throat. He did not squeeze, but let her feel the strength in his hands while slowly, easily tipping her chin up with his thumbs.

His hands were large, long fingered, and warm. Wrapped around her neck like a wide, tensile collar, they intimidated without a word. Gabby's eyes widened. Her heart began to pound. She could feel the color leaching from her face. Clutching the arms of the chair to keep from grabbing his wrists—that, she thought, was just what he expected her to do, and therefore she would not do it—she took a deep, steadying breath. If he meant to strangle her, she had not the physical strength to prevent him. Her only hope lay in her wits.

"Let us have one thing very clear between us: you are—*totally*—at my mercy." His smile was detestable.

He bent over her, his hands almost caressing on her throat, his gaze holding hers. As she stared back into his eyes, trying to present a fearless mien while she searched desperately for a way out, *any* way out, she could feel the skirt of his voluminous greatcoat puddling on her legs. Something hard brushed her knee.

His pistol, she realized with a fierce rush of excitement. If she could only get her hands on his pistol he would sing a very different tune. . . .

"A man who would threaten a woman—" she said with calm precision, sliding her hand stealthily inside his greatcoat pocket as she spoke. The pocket was warm, silk lined, and capacious. To her searching fingers, the pistol felt hard and smooth and, when she hefted it, heavy, and as welcome as a blessing. "—is beneath contempt."

"Nevertheless . . ." he began, only to break off as, with the pistol still inside his pocket but now held securely in her hand, she eased the hammer back. The sound of the pistol being cocked was sharp and apparently, to his ears at least, unmistakable. The look of surprised comprehension on his face was almost comical. Gabby permitted herself a savage smile as she pulled the pistol free of his pocket and shoved it hard against his ribs.

Their eyes met. For an instant, no longer, neither of them moved, or spoke.

"You will now unhand me." Gabby's voice was very cold, and very positive.

He glanced down then, as if to assure himself that the object threatening him was indeed a pistol. Then, eyes glittering, mouth tight, he slowly and with obvious reluctance lifted his hands away from her throat.

"That's very good. Now step back. Slowly. And keep your hands where I can see them."

He did as she ordered, straightening and taking first one, then a second, then a third step backward. His movements were cautious. His gaze, after that first glance at the pistol, never left hers. Still bothered by the errant strand of hair, Gabby risked removing one hand from the pistol to shove it behind her ear.

"I should perhaps warn you that that particular pistol is possessed of a hair trigger." The statement was casually conversational in tone.

Gabby smiled grimly. "Then you had best make certain that I have no cause to flex my finger, hadn't you? A little farther back, if you please. Just there."

She scooted forward until she sat on the edge of the slippery leather chair, planting her feet firmly on the carpet, the pistol gripped in both hands and pointed unwaveringly at his midsection. He stood watching her from perhaps three feet away, his hands, palms out, lifted to shoulder height in front of him, his mouth hard. The front of his greatcoat hung open, revealing his immaculate linen, his black breeches and the muted silver of his waistcoat. His jaw was set; his eyes glinted unpleasantly. In fact, he looked

very much like a man bested by a woman, and one, moreover, who greatly disliked the fact. Gabby couldn't help herself: she smiled.

"Now, what's to be done with a villain such as yourself?"
she pondered aloud, thoroughly enjoying the sensation of
having turned the tables on him. "Should I shoot you out
of hand, or merely hand you over to the authorities as soon
as may be?"

"You must do as you please, of course, but while you
consider your options you might also consider this: if you
reveal to the world that I am not Wickham, I shall be forced
to thrust a spoke in your wheel by confessing that
Wickham has, in fact, met his end."

Gabby's eyes narrowed at this—a more telling threat
than he knew—and her voice grew waspish. "You can reveal nothing if you are dead, sirrah."

"Very true, but I cannot think that you really wish to figure as a murderess. They hang, you know."

"To shoot a man who has held a gun on and threatened
to strangle one certainly cannot be considered murder," she
protested indignantly.

He shrugged. "Do you mind if I lower my arms? My hands
are beginning to tingle. . . ." He did so without waiting for her
reply, shaking his hands as though to restore circulation to
them, then crossed his arms over his chest and regarded her
quizzically. "Murder is a question for the courts to decide, of
course, but by the time the decision is made, whether or not
you are eventually found innocent will scarcely matter: only
think of the scandal. I am sure you cannot wish to bring so
much notoriety down upon your family."

Gabby's lips compressed. To admit that he had a point,
even to herself, was a struggle. But what he said was, she
feared, horribly, hideously true. If she wished to find a top-

of-the-trees husband for Claire, they could afford no hint of scandal.

She smiled grimly. "Your warning has a great deal of merit, I must admit. If I shoot you, I shall take care to conceal the fact."

His brows lifted. "Thus placing yourself in the dilemma you earlier pointed out to me: disposing of the—er— bloody corpse. You won't be able to shift me yourself, you know. I outweigh you by, at a rough guess, a good six stone." His gaze flicked beyond her, and his expression brightened. "Excellent timing, Barnet. You must . . ."

Whatever else he said was lost as Gabby instinctively cast a glance over her shoulder. Barnet was nowhere in sight; the door to the library remained closed. Even as she registered those facts—it took no more than a split second—and realized that she had been played for a fool, a flurry of sound and movement snapped her attention forward again. It was too late: having leaped toward her in that moment of her inattentiveness, he grabbed her wrist in a brutal grip that hurt, turning the pistol to the side even as he attempted to wrest it from her grasp. . . .

Whether she truly meant to pull the trigger she was never afterward sure. In any case, the pistol went off with a kick like a mule's and a terrible explosion of sound.

He gave a sharp cry and staggered back, a hand clapped to his side. Their gazes, hers horrified, his shocked, met and held for an instant in which time seemed to stop.

"By God, you've shot me," he said.

She was staring at him as if she expected him to keel over dead at any moment. Her horrified expression brought a wry smile to his lips even as he clapped his hand hard over the place where the bullet had gone in. However much she might wish it, he knew from the location of the wound that he would not die. There were no vital organs that he was aware of located just above the hipbone.

He was, however, bleeding. Profusely. He could feel the warm welling of blood against his palm. Strangely enough, it did not hurt. Not yet, at any rate, although he was sure that, when the first shock had worn off, it would.

His "sister" had surprised him. That rarely happened anymore. He had survived for so long in this dangerous game because he was, at heart, a cautious man. But who would have guessed that a scrawny old maid of an English lady would have the gumption to challenge him, much less turn his own pistol on him and pull the trigger?

Not he.

The amusing thing about it was that, after leaving the theatre and seeing Belinda home, he had declined an offer to stay and keep her company for the dangerous but necessary exercise of trolling the city's likeliest gaming hells in hopes of presenting such a tempting target that his quarry would be lured into the open. That was the kind of work where he could expect to be shot, and he had, most correctly, been on his guard the whole damned night. How ironic was it that, no sooner had he entered a house where he could reasonably expect to be safe, than he had encountered a creature who had proved to be more dangerous than any of the thugs who skulked through London's meanest streets?

A creature who was even now regarding him with wide gray eyes and parted lips, her slender body—which, incidentally, he had discovered in the course of carrying her about, possessed its fair share of feminine charms—seemingly poised, most ridiculously, to rush to his rescue?

A creature who was beginning, despite all the reasons why it shouldn't be happening, to interest him exceedingly?

"You shot me," he said again on a faintly disbelieving note, holding her gaze. Then the shock began to wear off, and the wound began to throb. It was all he could do not to sway at the sudden stab of pain.

❧ 8 ❧

"'Tis your own fault. You should never have tried to take the pistol. Oh, dear God in heaven, you're bleeding." This last came as he lifted his hand from his side to glance down at it and Gabby saw that his palm was bright red with blood. She still sat on the edge of the big leather chair, one hand now clapped to her cheek, her eyes wide with horror. The pistol, having dropped from her nerveless fingers scant seconds after it had discharged, lay on the carpet at her feet. The acrid scent of gunpowder hung heavy in the air.

"Worried that you might yet have to dispose of my bloody corpse?" That this was accompanied by a flickering ghost of a smile in no way mitigated Gabby's distress. She watched, stunned, as he pulled his shirttail out of his breeches and lifted the hem. A goodly portion of bronzed, muscular flesh roughened by dark hair came into view. Pushing his breeches a few inches down from the waist, he exposed a jagged, bleeding gash in his left side just above his hipbone. He glanced at it, then allowed his shirt to drop back into place and pressed his hand over the wound.

"How bad is it?" She felt sick to her stomach.

" 'Tis not serious: a flesh wound, no more."

Flesh wound or not, he was obviously feeling the effects of the injury. The hand that was not pressed to the wound found and curled around the back of a highly polished rosewood desk chair just behind him. Grimacing, he took a step back and leaned heavily on the chair. His face, she noted with a corresponding increase in her sense of horror, had, in just those few moments, grown pale.

"A surgeon must be sent for." Marshaling her wits, Gabby stood and moved with scarce concern for her aching leg to his side. The extremity of the moment prompted her to ignore the transgressions that had brought her to shoot him in the first place. He was white to his lips now, and his eyes were narrowed with what she took for pain. Placing a gentle hand on his upper arm, she looked down at where his hand was pressed to the wound. His greatcoat was thrust back, along with the tails of his coat, and his fingers lay partly against his waistcoat and partly against his shirt. Blood seeped through them, trickling down over his knuckles like teardrops tinted red. She winced.

"We must find something to staunch the blood. . . ."

He made a derisive sound. "Don't tell me that, having done your utmost to kill me, you now propose to act the nurse? If you want to do something useful, help me off with my coat. The infernal thing is damnably in the way."

He was almost panting now. Obediently Gabby reached up to grasp the collar of his heavy greatcoat as he shrugged the arm on his hurt side out of it. Moving behind him to ease the other arm free, she heard the muffled thud of footsteps rushing down the hall, and glanced instinctively toward the door. He apparently heard the same thing. Clenching his teeth, sweat popping out on his forehead, he looked at her.

"You were right about the sound of a shot bringing the

household down upon us, it seems. Which is it to be, Gabriella? Do we keep each other's secrets—or not?"

The door to the library burst open just at that moment. Jem, a piece of rope tied to one wrist and dangling in front of him, charged inside, followed by the enormous bull of a man that was Barnet clutching the pistol that Jem had carried earlier. Jem was obviously uncowed by the threat posed by the pistol, and this appeared to confound Barnet. In addition, both were disheveled, red-faced, and looked thoroughly alarmed, and Barnet sported a swelling, half-shut eye.

"Miss Gabby! Miss Gabby! Thank the Lord you're alive. If the bastard's done ye any harm. . . ." Jem skidded to a halt, his voice trailing off and his eyes widening on the pair of them—the imposter, pale and sweating, leaning heavily on the chair back with one hand pressed to his bleeding wound; Gabby, obviously unhurt, standing by his side, clutching his heavy greatcoat in both hands—as the true state of affairs burst upon him.

"Never say the little wench managed to shoot ye, Cap'n," gasped Barnet, who, like Jem, had come to a stunned halt while drinking in the scene. He pointed the pistol at Gabby, who shrank instinctively toward the imposter.

"Put it away, Barnet," Wickham said, his voice testy.

"Hoo, it's unloaded anyway," Jem crowed with triumph as he hastened toward Gabby.

"Why, you . . . "Casting a darkling glance at Jem, Barnet swallowed the rest, pocketed the pistol and rushed to the wounded man's side, sparing a single censorous flick of his eyes for Gabby on the way. "Blimey, miss, you shouldn't've done it, and that's all I 'ave to say."

"If Miss Gabby shot him, ye can be certain sure the bounder deserved it," Jem said, firing up in his principal's defense. As he spoke, he freed himself of the rope and cast it aside. "Aye, and it'd be a good day's work for her if the blackguard was kilt."

"Jem, hush," Gabby protested, fearing that a resumption of hostilities between him and Barnet was about to occur before her eyes.

Barnet, however, had no more than a single venomous glance to spare for Jem. As he crouched to lift the stained linen and look more closely at the wound, his attention was all for his master. "Cap'n, Cap'n, 'ow bad are ye clipped? Cor, ye must be more jug-bit than I thought to let a slip of a thing like miss 'ere blow a 'ole through you."

"Miss Gabby be *Lady Gabriella* to the likes o' you," Jem spat, one hand closing around Gabby's wrist as he tried to pull her away.

"Jem, let go. You must see I cannot leave. . . ." Gabby cast the servant a distracted glance.

"On the contrary, I wish you would leave," the imposter said. His voice was labored, and he was suffering Barnet's attempt to use the bunched tail of his shirt to staunch the blood with a patience that was its own testament to the suffering he was enduring. "Barnet can do everything that's necessary for me, believe me. We have only to come to an agreement—come, ma'am, are we enemies or allies?—and you may take yourself off with my goodwill."

"Mighty pretty behavior it would be in me to just leave you like this," Gabby said indignantly.

His expression was unreadable. "If it comes to that, shooting me was not exactly pretty behavior either, so if I were you I wouldn't trouble my head overmuch about the niceties now."

Gabby gasped. "You were threatening to strangle me!"

"You must have known that I would not have done so, however."

He winced, Barnet having apparently pressed on a particularly tender spot. For a moment Gabby almost felt like congratulating Barnet.

"You would not have done so . . . !" she broke off, shaking her head as the sight of him, pale and bleeding and leaning heavily on the chair, brought her back to a sense of proper priorities. "For the moment, that is neither here nor there. A surgeon must be sent for."

The imposter shook his head. "I told you, Barnet can do for me. Come, give me your decision."

"Cap'n, miss is right. We'd best get a surgeon to you."

"I don't want a damned sawbones—and have a care, Barnet, or all your 'captains' will undo us," the imposter said through his teeth. A scarlet stain had already soaked through the wadded handful of once immaculate linen, and begun a slow but seemingly inexorable spread across the silver-gray waistcoat. It was obvious that without the support of the chair, the wounded man would not have been able to stand.

" 'Tis not a *surgeon* we need to send for, but the Runners," Jem said, glancing at Barnet with grim glee. "You huge brainless oaf, I warned you there'd be a heavy reckoning to be paid for this night's work."

Barnet surged to his feet, fists clenching, the blood-stained tail of his master's shirt left forgotten to unfurl like a scarlet banner.

"Listen, ye banty leprechaun, I've still enough starch of me own to do for you and the lidy 'ere, and I'd advise ye not to forget it."

"That'll do, Barnet," the imposter said sharply, and with a glance at him Barnet subsided, grumbling, to tend the wound again.

"Now you're for it, ye scoundrels," Jem said with satisfaction as the muffled thunder of many pairs of feet stampeding down the stairs filled the library. Confused-sounding voices exchanged exclamations, which were as yet too distant to be completely understood. "Ye'll find yourselves in the Old Bailey afore the day is out, see if you don't."

"Why, if that's so you can be sure I'll wring your scrawny little neck first, jest to rob you of the joy of witnessin' it," Barnet growled.

"In here! In the library. Come quickly," Gabby called, raising her voice so that it could be heard out in the hall. A babble of anxious cries answered her, and what sounded like a positive herd of people pounded in their direction.

"Don't fash yerself, Cap'n, I'll not be lettin' 'em take ye without a fight." Eyes wide with alarm, Barnet once again surged to his feet.

"No, hold, Barnet," the imposter said, restraining his henchman with a hand on his arm. The imposter looked at Gabby. "The time is at hand, it seems. Are we keeping each other's secrets, Gabriella, or not?"

Pursing her lips, Gabby met his gaze. His eyes were dark and narrowed. His brow was beaded with sweat and furrowed with pain. His waistcoat was marred by a spreading stain, and his dangling shirttail was scarlet with blood, which dripped from the hem to form a small but growing puddle at his feet. Beside him, Barnet, restrained by the hand on his arm, stood snarling at the open door like an animal at bay.

"Certainly not." She shook her head, appalled at the very idea. To even consider keeping her silence about his false identity was unthinkable. It would not only be wrong, it could be dangerous. He could turn on her at any time. Or, if she had perchance rendered him physically unable to do so, he could instruct Barnet to dispose of her and Jem as the only others who knew of the switch. Going along with the pretense that this threatening stranger was her brother Marcus,

Earl of Wickham, made the poor scheme she herself had hatched for her own and her sisters' deliverance seem positively innocent in comparison. This was fraud on a grand scale, a dangerous scale, and she would have no part of it.

The imposter's mouth twisted wryly at her response, and he looked as though he meant to say something more. Just then Stivers skidded into view outside the open library door, clad in breeches and braces that had been pulled on over his nightshirt, bare feet thrust anyhow into unlaced shoes. Spying them, he bounded forward only to check on the threshold, his expression aghast as he surveyed the lot of them. Behind Stivers, Claire, Beth, Twindle, Mrs. Bucknell, and a variety of servants, all in their nightclothes with various covering garments thrown over the top, appeared, jostling and bumping into each other as they stumbled to a halt, vying to see past the butler into the room.

"Come on, Cap'n, I'll be gettin' ye out o' 'ere," Barnet muttered.

Attempting to draw his resisting master's arm over his shoulder, looming above him like an angry, protective giant, Barnet now seemed bent on flight. The imposter, repelling Barnet with an impatient gesture, looked steadily at Gabby.

" 'Tis a pity you and your sisters will be obliged to miss the season," he said with an air of gentle regret, his voice quiet enough so that it could not be heard beyond the four of them. "The accepted mourning period for a brother is a year, I believe, is it not? And afterward, no doubt you will find your circumstances much changed."

Gabby stared at him. She had only to tell what she knew, and he would be exposed for the charlatan he was. In his injured state, even with Barnet's help, he had little hope of escape. Any punishment he might suffer would be well deserved. . . .

But she and her sisters, who certainly deserved nothing of the kind, would suffer, too. Once word of Marcus's death was out, Cousin Thomas would assume his rightful position as the new earl, and she and Claire and Beth would be sentenced to a life spent, at best, as poor relations.

With all the surety of an incontrovertible truth, it hit her that permitting this man, whoever and whatever he was, to act the earl would surely be better for herself and her sisters than allowing Cousin Thomas to assume the title.

Unless, of course, he murdered her and Jem before her plan for securing the future could come to fruition.

All hung on what she did next. Her gaze met the imposter's, and held. It was time to choose the path of honor and truth, the path of personal safety. . . .

Which was also the path of poverty and loss, for Claire and Beth as well as herself.

"You are undoubtedly a scoundrel," Gabby said through her teeth, meeting his gaze. It occurred to her that if she had made a hellish bargain when she chose to keep Marcus's death a secret, then here before her must be the devil himself, come to drive the bargain home. Then, finding that what she had thought was a choice was really not one at all, she raised her voice so that she could be heard by everyone.

"You had best allow us to send for a surgeon, *Wickham*," Gabby said clearly, still holding his gaze. The imposter greeted her change of heart with the merest flicker of a smile and a slight inclination of his head. Beside him, Barnet stared at her suspiciously. At her own side, Jem gasped and then seemed to swell with indignation.

"Miss Gabby . . . what . . . Miss Gabby . . . !"

Transferring her gaze from the imposter—no, Wickham now, she reminded herself—to her servant, she caught Jem's eye even as he began to sputter denials, and shook her head.

"Keep silent," she whispered fiercely for his ears alone. Face working as he took in what had just occurred, Jem nevertheless obeyed, looking for the briefest of moments as if he were being forced to swallow a particularly nasty-tasting dose of medicine. Then his mouth closed with an audible snap. His gaze flew to Barnet and he looked at the bigger man with the kind of loathing he generally reserved for would-be horse thieves.

Then there was no more chance for private discourse of any kind.

"Begging your pardon for intruding, my lord, but I was awakened from sleep by what sounded like a *gunshot* in the house." Despite being practically thrust into the room by the combined efforts of those behind him, who spilled in after, Stivers managed to retain his dignity as well as his feet.

"Gabby, what's happened?" Claire, breaking through the logjam of people to hurry across the room to Gabby's side, spoke at almost the same moment as Stivers. Claire managed to look fetching even while sporting a lace-trimmed cap tied under her chin to keep her curls silky smooth through the night, and demure although only a rather shabby lavender shawl had been thrown over her billowing nightdress. Behind her, Beth, wrapped up in a blue damask coverlet with her hair in long braids, stopped short just inside the door to stare at Wickham.

"Marcus is *bleeding*," she said.

A chorus of gasps ensued as the eyes of all the newcomers focused on Wickham. For a moment the gathering stood frozen. Then they all rushed forward almost as one, exclaiming and chattering among themselves as they crowded around. Gabby found herself jostled, and glanced around to discover that she was hemmed in on all sides.

"Oh, Marcus," Claire gasped, clutching at Gabby's arm

as she took a closer look at the injured man, whose blood now spilled freely onto the carpet as his shirttail, which was wet through, could absorb no more.

"My lord!" Twindle wrung her hands in horror as she took in the full measure of the disaster. "Oh, dear, my lord, you look pale as can be. Here, here, use this to press against the wound." Tearing off the nightcap which she wore tied over her braided and wound gray locks, she passed it to Barnet. Barnet accepted it with a look of revulsion, but nevertheless folded the snowy linen into a pad and knelt again to press it to the wound.

"O' course 'e looks pale. Look, there's a bloody great 'ole blown in 'im," scornfully averred one of the newly hired footmen, who then blushed under Twindle's withering glance.

"The watch must be summoned at once. Only tell us who did this, my lord," cried Mrs. Bucknell, who was glancing wildly around as if expecting to find a burglar hiding in the shadows.

"I fear it is quite my own fault: I was clumsy with my pistol," Wickham said to them all, in a voice that was surprisingly strong. "I am ashamed to admit that I put it in my coat pocket, thinking it unloaded, and when I went to take it out again it went off."

"Stivers, as you can see, His Lordship is wounded. I was just sending Jem to fetch you." Gabby took charge with the ease of long practice. Clearly, if constructive action was to be taken, she would have to organize it. "A surgeon must be sent for right away. I am sure you will know where one is to be found."

"Yes, Miss Gabby." Clearly shaken by the sight of his bleeding master but with the air of one rising nobly to the occasion, Stivers acknowledged the directive with a brief bow. With an imperious gesture at the still-blushing footman he retired into the hall, said footman following at his heels.

"I told you, I need no surgeon. Barnet can do all that is required." Wickham, practically draped over the chair now, gave Gabby a commanding look.

"Don't be an idiot," Gabby responded crisply, passing Wickham's coat on to a servant. Wickham's mouth compressed at this blatant disregard of what he plainly considered to be an order, but he made no reply. Perhaps, Gabby thought, judging from the now ashen hue of his face, he was growing too weak to argue. "Barnet"— the surly-looking giant crouched at Wickham's side returned her gaze warily— "can certainly assist, but a surgeon must and shall look at that wound."

Wickham remained silent. Barnet hesitated for the tiniest moment, then put in gruffly: "I'd say you're in the right of it, miss."

"Lady Gabriella, to you," Jem growled. Gabby gave Jem a very hard look, warning him without words to mind his tongue.

The little crowd of servants and family members instinctively looked to Gabby for further instructions. A glance at Wickham showed that he was sweating profusely and slumping ever lower over the back of the chair, while the drops of blood at his feet grew so numerous that they were beginning to run together to form a puddle.

"Barnet, I think it would be best if you helped His Lordship to his chambers to await the surgeon. Francis—" Gabby spoke to the footman who had accompanied them from Hawthorne Hall "—you may assist Barnet. Mrs. Bucknell, if you would please fetch lint, clean towels, and hot water upstairs, I'll see what can be done to staunch the blood until the surgeon arrives."

Long accustomed to running a household, Gabby spoke with authority. All addressed sprang into action.

"Miss Claire, Miss Beth, I think it best that we return to our chambers. We can do nothing but get in the way here." Twindle looked from one to the other of the younger girls.

"I shall never sleep a . . ." Beth's voice trailed off under Twindle's stern look.

"Gabby, how came *you* to be present? And Jem . . ." Claire, still standing at Gabby's side, asked with a frown even as Twindle tried to draw her away.

Before Gabby could reply, there was a collective gasp from the servants.

" 'e's fainted," Barnet proclaimed hoarsely. Looking around, Gabby saw to her dismay that Wickham had indeed lost consciousness. His face was gray, his eyes were closed, and he sagged bonelessly against Barnet, who had caught him with both arms around his waist. Even as Gabby watched, Barnet made some adjustments to his grip, then lifted Wickham like a babe.

Fear in his face, Barnet looked from his master, whose big body now hung limply his arms, to Gabby.

"Miss, I . . . 'e . . ." he gasped.

"Carry His Lordship abovestairs," she directed calmly. Barnet nodded, looking relieved at having someone to tell him what to do, and headed toward the door with Wickham's deadweight in his arms. Gabby turned to follow, glancing over her shoulder to add, "Mrs. Bucknell, fetch those supplies I requested *now,* please. Jem, I might need you as well. The rest of you will do the most good by going back to bed."

❦ 9 ❧

By the time the surgeon arrived, dawn was at hand. The first faint fingers of light were beginning to probe around the edges of the tightly drawn curtains in the earl's bedroom, and down in the street the clatter of wheels and the bell of the muffin man could be heard. The servants, so lately sent back to their beds, were once again stirring. Wickham, now stripped to the waist, his breeches loosened and eased down on one side to expose the full measure of the wound, his boots off, lay on his back in the middle of the vast, crimson-curtained four-poster that was the centerpiece of the chamber, his black head propped on a pair of soft down pillows. The coverings had been pulled to the foot of the bed, and, despite the faintly ashen cast to his face, his skin looked very bronze in contrast to the white sheets.

Considering how large the elaborate carved rosewood bed was, the degree to which he managed to fill it was surprising, Gabby thought. His shoulders spanned almost half the width of the mattress, and his stocking feet reached nearly to its end.

Even injured and undressed, he looked formidable. Gabby shivered inwardly as she remembered how helpless she had felt when he had wrapped those big hands around her neck.

It occurred to her again that this was a dangerous game she played. But at the moment, unless she was willing to jeopardize all she held dear, she didn't see any other way out.

For the immediate future, at least, she did not think her connivance put her life at risk. Her modesty, now, was a different matter. In truth, she found the situation into which she had been thrust more than a little unsettling. She had helped to nurse her father through his final illness, and occasionally had been called upon to assist at times of accident or illness among the tenants at Hawthorne, and so was not a complete stranger to the male form. But as a maiden lady somewhat stricken in years, she had never expected to find herself in such close proximity to a nearly nude, blatantly virile stranger.

Trying her best to take no notice of the broad bare shoulders, the wide chest with its thick wedge of black hair, the muscular abdomen, or—blush!—his navel, which was almost fully exposed, Gabby still, with the best will in the world, could not completely focus on the task at hand. In the course of tending to him, it was impossible to keep her fingers from learning the faintly coarse texture of the hairs on his chest, or stop herself from noticing the heat and satiny smoothness of his skin, or the hardness of the muscles beneath, or the faint musky scent of him. Still, she was determined to take his nakedness in stride. At the moment, he was her patient, no more, no less.

Thus, though she perched rather warily on the very edge of the bed, her manner was calm and efficient as she did her utmost to stop the loss of blood, which was, in her judgment, the biggest threat to his well-being. Both hands, one on top of the other, maintained a continuous pressure on the thick pad of lint and towels she had lain over the still bleeding wound, and she was careful to let her eyes stray no farther than her own hands and the pad beneath them—at least, no more often than she could help. It was the second such pad she had employed in the past hour. The first pad had been soaked clean through.

So much blood. The question that troubled her now was, how much more could he stand to lose?

"If you're trying to torture me, ma'am, you're succeeding very well." Wickham, who had regained consciousness some few minutes after being lain in his bed, watched her out of narrowed eyes. His voice was weak, but a sardonic note was evident nonetheless. Brow furrowed, he moved restively in a vain attempt to escape her ministrations. "Your *treatment* hurts more than the getting of the wound."

"Lie still," Gabby said sharply. "You only do yourself harm by moving about."

"Considering that you put the hole in me in the first place, I am sure you will forgive me if I tell you that I find your expression of concern less than convincing."

"Obviously you have not considered: if you die, having set yourself up as Wickham, then I am left in no better case than I was with my true brother dead."

"Ah." He smiled a little, although the effort obviously cost him. "Then I perceive I may safely trust my well-being to your hands."

"I am sorry to say that you may."

"Ow!"

The exclamation came as she shifted her position to apply pressure directly over the place where blood was beginning once again to break through. Beneath her palm, she could feel the telltale warm dampness. . . .

"Just bind the damned thing up and be done with it, why

don't you?" He shifted again as she bore down relentlessly on the pad. "Pressing on it like that hurts like the devil."

"I would say that you are well served, then." Her voice was cool and untroubled as she continued to apply pressure.

He grimaced, and sucked in air audibly through his teeth. "Oh, would you? No doubt you would greatly enjoy subjecting me to thumb screws, or perhaps the rack, as well?" His gaze rolled around to his henchman, who had about him a helpless air as he hovered beside the bed. "Get me something to drink, Barnet. I'm dry as a desert."

"Yes, Cap—uh, milord."

As Barnet moved away to do as he was bid, a soft rap sounded on the chamber door. Jem, an expression of grim disapproval on his face that had only grown more pronounced since Gabby's claiming of the imposter as her brother, went to answer it. There was a low-voiced exchange of conversation, and then Jem opened the door wide.

"The surgeon's arrived," he said sourly. As the portly, white-haired surgeon entered with a bustle of importance, Gabby caught a glimpse of Stivers and Mrs. Bucknell, their faces worried, among a congregation of servants who seemed to have gathered in the hall outside the earl's bedroom. Under the circumstances—who knew what her false brother might blurt out in a state of semi-consciousness, or under the influence of pain?—she had thought it best that only she, Jem, and Barnet should attend the injured man.

"Water? *Water?*" Wickham, spluttering, protested in an outraged tone even as Gabby kept her head turned to observe the entrance of the surgeon. "I want wine, or spirits. Take that away, and bring me something decent to drink."

Barnet, who had tenderly lifted his master's head from its nest to assist him in sipping from the glass he had brought, barely managed to keep said glass from being dashed to the floor by snatching it from Wickham's hold in the nick of time. As a result he allowed the wounded man's head to drop with a little less care than he had shown in lifting it.

"Damn it to hell, Barnet. Are you trying to kill me, too?"

"Sorry, Ca—er, milord."

The surgeon reached the bedside then, rubbing his hands together, bowing at Gabby. "I am Dr. Ormsby, my lady. Now, let me see, what have we here? A bullet wound, I was told? Yes. Excuse me, dear lady, if I could just have a look. . . ."

Gabby relinquished her place without a murmur, and stood up.

"Get off. I have no wish to be mauled by such as you." Wickham glared at the surgeon, who was in the act of lifting the blood-stained pad to peer beneath it. Surprised, Ormsby dropped it and stepped back, looking very much affronted.

"My lord . . ."

"Don't be such a baby," Gabby intervened, speaking crisply to Wickham. "Of course the surgeon must look at that wound. If you are afraid of being hurt, I am not surprised at it, but it is something that you just must set yourself to endure."

Wickham transferred his glower to her. "I am *not* afraid of being hurt."

"Oh, I thought that must be it," Gabby said.

He looked at her as if he wanted to throw something at her.

"Very well," he said through his teeth, to the surgeon. "Examine me, then. But have a care what you are about."

Gabby was careful not to smile as Ormsby, now wearing a slightly wary expression, once again lifted the pad away from the wound. He pursed his lips, and probed, and tested the patient's hipbone and abdomen with his hands. By the time he looked up again, Wickham was several shades paler than before, and sweating profusely. Though not a sound had escaped his lips, Gabby was very sure the examination had hurt.

Under the circumstances—the man had threatened her life, and Jem's, after all, among many other notable transgressions—she was not entirely sorry.

"The bullet is still lodged in the wound," Ormsby pronounced, straightening up at last and addressing his words to Gabby. "An operation for its removal will have to be performed."

The look on Wickham's face was pure horror.

"I'll not have any bloody sawbones cutting on me."

"Blue Ruin, milord." Barnet reappeared at the bedside at that timely moment, proffering a silver flask. Wickham, tight-lipped, looked at his henchman and nodded. The flask was put into his hand, his head was lifted, and he drank.

" 'Twill be easier if he's drunk," Ormsby said approvingly, already removing his coat.

"I told you, I'll not have. . . ." Wickham's voice was a growl. He was once again lying back against the pillows, his eyes mere glittering slits, his jaw clenched.

Gabby's lips compressed. It was an effort to remind herself that his recovery was as important as if he were her true brother.

"If the bullet is in there, then it must be removed for healing to occur," she said shortly.

"If the bullet stays where it is, there can be little doubt that the wound will putrefy," the surgeon agreed, handing his coat to Jem and rolling up his sleeves. "Is there hot water? Excellent."

Gabby had indicated the pitcher and basin with a nod.

"There is really no choice," she said to Wickham. He met her gaze for a long moment, during which she was silently given to understand that he considered his current situation to be entirely her fault. Then he looked at Ormsby, and nodded curtly.

"Very well. But be damned careful what you're about."

The surgeon inclined his head. "As I am always, my lord."

Barnet proffered the flask again as Ormsby, with a great many self-important flourishes, began to lay out his instruments on a small table he directed Jem to carry to the bedside. This time Wickham drank deep. Then he looked at Gabby again.

"Time for you to leave," he said.

Gabby, who could discover in herself not the smallest desire to witness the upcoming surgery despite a burning wish to be somehow revenged on his faux lordship, nodded. But Ormsby glanced around just then, shaking his head at her.

"I will need someone to assist me, my lady. Of course, if you care to send in one of the maids . . ."

"Barnet can do all the assisting that is required," Wickham growled, having just downed another long swallow from the flask.

The surgeon made expressive eyes at Gabby.

"Damn it, man, don't make faces behind my back. If you've some ob—objection to Barnet, tell me f—flat out." The slight stumble to Wickham's voice was, Gabby realized, an indication of the contents of the flask at work.

Ormsby looked pained. "It may become necessary, my lord, to employ your man—big, strapping fellow that he is—to hold you, uh, steady. I should not like to slip with the knife."

The thought obviously appalled Wickham.

"If you should so slip, my good man, I assure you that the consequences will be extremely unpleasant." Wickham all but bared his teeth at Ormsby, who took an instinctive step back from the bed, before being distracted by Barnet once again wordlessly proffering the flask.

"Very good notion, that," Ormsby said in a low-voiced aside to Gabby as Wickham once again drank deep. "Very, um, forceful man, your husband."

"He is not my husband."

Ormsby gave her a rather surprised look. Obviously, in his opinion no lady would be caught dead in the bedchamber of a man—especially a half-naked one—who was not her husband.

"He is my brother." Gabby's voice had a snap to it as she was forced to utter the lie. Although, she told herself, she might as well get used to it. For the forseeable future, to all intents and purposes the shameless blackguard in the bed *was* her brother.

"S—sweet sister, I would still ask you to quit the room." Wickham had obviously overheard her mendacious claim of kinship and found it amusing. Just as obviously, whatever was in the flask was doing its work: his cheeks were faintly flushed now, and his limbs sprawled heavily against the mattress. "Your servant—Jem—may render what as—assistance is required. I have no—no desire for you to witness the upcoming b—butchery."

"Hardly that, my lord," Ormsby replied, affronted. "Indeed, I'll have you know . . ." *My lord* shot him a glittering look. Ormsby swallowed. "But that is neither here nor there." He lowered his voice and glanced at Gabby again. "My lady, given that your brother is a large man, obviously quite strong, I fear that—in the thick of things, you know—more than one servant might be required to, er, hold him down."

Gabby glanced at Wickham, who was regarding the pair of them suspiciously but was too occupied with draining the flask at Barnet's prompting to interrupt. A servant could of course be summoned to take her place, Gabby thought—but under the circumstances, would that be wise?

If all should be revealed, she would lose as surely as Wickham.

"Go now," Wickham said, lowering the flask from his lips and scowling at her.

" 'Tis best that I stay," Gabby replied firmly, meeting his gaze with quelling intent. Wickham apparently either deciphered her message, or no longer felt inclined to argue. In any case, he made no further protest.

Having finished his preparations, the surgeon glanced at Barnet and nodded. Looking grim, Barnet put the flask aside and then sat down heavily on the edge of the bed.

"Bite on this, milord," he said, twisting a linen handkerchief between his fingers until it formed a tight coil. Despite his deepening inebriation, Wickham appeared to comprehend the significance of that. He grimaced, then opened his mouth so that Barnet could insert the handkerchief between his teeth. Barnet then wrapped his big arms around his master's arms and chest.

What followed was unpleasant in the extreme. Ormsby probed for the bullet; Wickham writhed and made guttural sounds of pain through the handkerchief clenched between his teeth. Blood flowed like claret at a wedding. As Ormsby had predicted, Barnet alone was not enough to hold the patient still. Jem, looking disgruntled, was called upon to sit on Wickham's ankles, and press his hands down tightly over his knees.

By the time the bullet was extracted, Gabby was sweating almost as profusely as Wickham.

"Hah! Got it." Ormsby held up the bloodied, mishapen lead ball with an air of triumph, then deposited it in the basin Gabby held for him. Wickham, groaning, having arched his back clear off the bed at the crucial moment despite the combined efforts of Barnet and Jem to hold him down, shuddered as the bullet left his flesh. Then he collapsed limply upon the mattress as blood welled like water into the hole Ormsby had left and overflowed. Clucking importantly, Ormsby began to try to staunch the blood. Panting, his head resting back against Barnet's shoulder, Wickham spat the twisted linen rope from his mouth.

"I think I'm going to be sick," he said in a guttural tone. As Jem scooted off his ankles and Barnet held his head over the side of the bed, he was, indeed, violently ill. Gabby barely managed to get the basin in place in time.

≈ 10 ≈

By the time Gabby emerged from the earl's chamber, she was lightheaded with weariness. Having cauterized the wound, dusted it with basilicum powder and bound it up, and left behind a goodly number of potions to be administered at various times under various contingencies, Ormsby had left, promising to return on the morrow. Wickham, exhausted from all that had been done to him and still very much under the influence of Blue Ruin, had already drifted off. Barnet had expressed his intention of remaining at his master's side for the duration. Jem followed Gabby out into the corridor, which was, thankfully, deserted, the gathering of servants who had been there earlier having presumably escorted Ormsby out en masse, so eager were they for news.

"If you have anything to say, and I can see that you do, you may just save it for later. I am too tired to hear you out," Gabby said grumpily to Jem, reading his intention in his eyes. A purpling bruise showed very distinctly amongst the salt-and-pepper bristles on his jaw. Gabby was reminded of the blow that Wickham had struck him. Fiery for all his small size, Jem wasn't likely to forget or forgive that any time soon.

"This be a nice sort of bobbery for a lady to be gettin'

herself mixed up in, Miss Gabby, and you knows it." Jem, too, spoke in a lowered voice, but his words were no less vehement for all that. "Them in there is as fine a pair of hang gallows as I've ever cast me peepers on. Shooting the villain was the best notion you've had. He . . ."

"Think what you like, but you'll keep your tongue between your teeth," Gabby interrupted ruthlessly. "Whoever he is, he cannot be worse for us than Cousin Thomas."

"A right idiot Mr. Thomas may be, but at least wi' him we wouldn't have to fear being murdered in our beds," Jem retorted. "Them rascally thieves deserves to be transported if not outright hanged. Only let me be sendin' to Bow Street . . ."

He broke off abruptly as Mary came along the corridor bearing a can of hot water. Spying Gabby, she dropped a quick curtsy.

"Good morning, Mary."

"G' mornin', mum. Mrs. Bucknell thought you might be wishful of having this in your room about now, mum," Mary said.

"I shall be very glad of it indeed, thank you, Mary. You may take it inside. I shall be with you directly."

As Mary did as she was told, Gabby once again looked at Jem.

"If we reveal that the man in there is not Wickham, he will reveal that Wickham is dead," Gabby said flatly. "With Wickham dead, Cousin Thomas succeeds to the title. You know what Cousin Thomas is: with him as earl, we—all of us, my sisters and I, you, the rest of the staff—would soon be in the direst of straits. This way is not good, but it is better than the other, believe me."

Jem frowned, then shook his head doubtfully. "If you be bound and determined to do this, Miss Gabby, then you knows I'll stand buff," Jem said. "But to my way of thinkin' it be a bad mistake. Them thievin' rogues . . ."

A chambermaid appeared at the top of the stairs, walking toward them with her back bent under the weight of the coal bucket she grasped with both hands. Jem broke off what he was saying. Seizing the opportunity thus afforded her, Gabby moved toward the door to her chambers.

"I am going to bed," she said to Jem as the girl passed with a quick bob. "And I suggest you do, too."

"I doubt I'll ever close me eyes peaceful-like again with this house full of rogues and rascals like it is," Jem said bitterly. "And with me bunkin' down in the mews like I am, who's to keep a watch on 'em for you, eh, tell me that?"

"Fortunately, there's no need for anyone to keep a watch on them at the moment. They are bound by the heels. The one is wounded, and the other must wait on him. Which means that they will hardly have the leisure to trouble themselves about us." On this optimistic note, Gabby put her hand on the doorknob.

"Aye, that's true enough, unless they decide that riddin' the world of those who can testify to their crimes be more urgent than carin' for their wounded, in which case we'll be regularly dished. You keep your eye out, as I will do, and don't you go a-trustin' of 'em an inch, Miss Gabby, you hear?"

With that grim warning ringing in her ears, Gabby made it inside her apartment at last, and gave herself up to Mary's care. Shortly thereafter, she surrendered to utter exhaustion and lay down upon her bed. Within minutes she was fast asleep.

∽ ∽

"You'll wake her. Come away at once."

"But it is past midday." The dismayed whisper belonged to Beth.

"She is clearly very tired then." Claire's cooler tones were equally low-pitched.

"Gabby *never* sleeps this long."

"Her rest is usually not disturbed by a gunshot in the middle of the night."

"Pooh. Gabby is not such a milk-and-water creature as to sleep the day away for such a cause as that. You and I were disturbed by it too, and we're up. I am persuaded that she would not wish to miss our first day in town."

"You just want to get out and see the sights," Claire retorted. Gabby's lids lifted just enough to allow her to perceive her sisters hovering near her bedside. Claire was holding onto Beth's arm, trying to drag her away. Beth, scowling at Claire, resisted. Of course, neither of them had any notion that she'd been awake the entire night. Claire continued, "Don't waste your time trying to tip *me* a rise."

"And to think Twindle is always scolding *me* for using cant terms." Beth shook her head. "You just never use them when she's about."

"Come away, do." With what Gabby considered true nobility, Claire ignored the temptation to launch an answering salvo. "Let Gabby sleep. We can go shopping tomorrow."

"Shopping?" Beth practically hooted. "If that's your notion of a day well spent, I think it's pretty flat. I . . ."

"All right, I'm awake," Gabby intervened with a groan, opening her eyes fully and easing onto her back. The curtains were still tightly drawn, leaving the bedroom gloomy with shadows. Still, it was obvious from the glow around the edges of the windows and the noises that she could now hear quite clearly from the street that the day was well advanced. For a moment she felt a fluttery little thrill that went a long way toward erasing her exhaustion: they were actually in London. . . .

"Now see what you've done," Claire said on a scolding note to Beth as they both turned to look at Gabby. "Would it have hurt you to let her sleep?"

"Indeed, I have far too much to do to sleep the day away. What o'clock is it, anyway?" Gabby said, rubbing her tired eyes with both hands.

"It's gone *eleven*." Beth's tone was scandalized, as if sleeping so long was the most depraved thing she had ever heard of. Indeed, their father, an insomniac for years, had never allowed any member of his household to sleep much past dawn. Even though he had been gone for well over a year, ingrained habits were, they had discovered, hard to break.

"So late," Gabby mocked, and gestured at Beth to open the curtains. As Beth obeyed and bright daylight flooded the room she blinked off the last remnants of drowsiness and hoisted herself up against the headboard. Her troublesome hair, never very secure in its pins, tumbled down around her shoulders as she did so, and she became keenly aware of various newly acquired aches and pains. The dull throbbing in her hip and leg was the worst. As she winced at it she remembered all too clearly the fall that had caused the ache. Coupled to that memory was another, even more unpleasant one: in the next room was a man pretending to be her brother; a man, moreover, who had bullied and threatened her and whom she had most deservedly shot. A man who was a dangerous criminal, and whose dark secret she knew . . .

At the thought Gabby shivered. She supposed she should consider herself lucky that she had been awakened by her sisters, rather than his henchman come to murder her in her bed.

But such thoughts were best saved for another time. There was no doing anything about the man in the next room just at present. And the speediest way to be rid of him was obviously to carry on with her original plan to get Claire creditably established. Then the situation would be very different, and the scoundrel would be well advised to look to himself.

"See how tired she looks. You need to learn to think of others besides yourself sometimes, Beth."

Beth swelled with indignation.

"Beth is right, Claire. I should *not* like to miss our first day in town," Gabby said hastily, before the argument could begin.

"See?" Beth said with lofty dignity to Claire.

Claire, appearing to forget for the moment her status as a young lady, stuck out her tongue by way of reply.

"Pull the bell, would one of you? I must get up. We've a call to pay on our Aunt Salcombe, for one thing, if not today then as soon as possible, and no doubt we'll soon be receiving calls ourselves . . ."

Gabby's gaze ran over the pair of them. Both were clad in more of the outmoded mourning, which was all she had to wear herself. That deplorable state of affairs she meant to remedy without delay. The sooner Claire was properly dressed, seen, courted and wed, the easier she would breathe. No matter how she tried to rationalize the situation in her mind, there was no getting around the feeling that she was sitting atop a powder keg that could explode in her face at any moment. "Claire, you need clothes. Indeed, we all do. A pretty dash we should cut in what we own now."

Claire, who was in the process of crossing the room to pull the bell cord, nodded in emphatic agreement.

Beth groaned. "Never say we're going shopping."

Gabby threw back the covers and swung her legs over

the side of the bed, determinedly ignoring the pain in her hip and knee as her feet hit the carpet. "That's exactly what we're going to do."

By the time Gabby was dressed, she had quieted Beth's protests about the day's itinerary by promising that she should view all the sights of London just as soon as she and her sisters were fit to be seen. Which, in their present apparel, even Beth, who was peering out the window ogling fashionable passersby in what Claire termed the most vulgar way, was brought to own they were not. Then, in response to Claire's inquiry, Gabby was obliged to give an almost entirely mendacious account of how she and Jem had come to be first on the scene of Wickham's wounding. As the three of them left her apartment and headed downstairs, they had a most unfortunate encounter with Barnet, who was emerging from the earl's chamber, a frown on his face and a tray containing an untouched bowl of broth and a glass of ale in his hands.

"How is Wickham faring?" Beth asked him, when Gabby would have passed by with a curt nod.

"Not so good." Barnet looked anxious. " 'E's weak as a kitten, and as you can see, 'e won't eat."

"I won't eat that bloody dishwater, you mean." Wickham's voice, thin but belligerent, could be heard through the open door.

Barnet looked helplessly at Gabby. "You 'eard Dr. Ormsby yourself, miss: 'e said 'e's to 'ave naught but liquids until 'e checks 'im again."

"Perhaps if we . . ." Claire began, reaching to take the tray from Barnet's hands.

"Gabriella! Is that you? Come in here," Wickham ordered peremptorily.

Gabby frowned. Her inclination was to ignore the mannerless rogue, but such uncharacteristic callousness on her part would no doubt provoke a great deal of curiosity in her sisters. The wounded man was supposed to be their brother, after all.

"Gabriella!"

"Give that to me," Gabriella said shortly, taking the tray from Claire. It was surprisingly heavy, she registered as her gaze met her sister's. "Wickham's sickroom is no place for you and Beth. Go ahead downstairs and tell Stivers to serve luncheon, and I will join you in just a few minutes."

"But Gabby . . ." Beth cast an interested look through the door, which was held open by Barnet's bulk. But the arrangement of the earl's apartments was such that only a pair of gold brocade armchairs set before the fireplace could be seen.

"Go on," she said firmly, turning to enter the room.

"Miss, you can take that back in there if you choose, but I've been told to have the kitchen put up some good slices o' beef and maybe a puddin'. The c—I mean, 'is Lordship'll 'ave my 'ead if I don't obey orders."

"He won't have mine, however," Gabby said, with more certainty than she felt. Giving her a look of respect, Barnet held the door for her. She walked into the room, and Barnet closed the door behind her. Faintly she could hear his and Claire's and Beth's footsteps fading away down the hall.

She was alone with a man she had every reason to fear. The thought made her hesitate. She paused, glancing toward the bed, conscious of feeling rather like Daniel as he stepped into the lion's den.

❧ 11 ❧

She looked slim and delicate and as nervous as a subaltern in a room full of generals. Her eyes were wide as they fixed on his face. Her skin was pale. Good, he thought with a spurt of satisfaction. He hoped he made her nervous. He wanted to make her nervous. Nervous enough, at least, so that she would think twice before revealing the truth about him to anyone else.

Being tied to a bed while he recovered from the wound she had inflicted on him was, in his opinion, a recipe for disaster. To begin with, he had no way to prevent her from going back on their bargain. He could only trust that her own self-interest would keep her tongue between her teeth.

But that trust was, at best, a fragile thing. The fine line he'd been walking since he'd stepped into Marcus's shoes had, now that she and her servant knew of the deception, just been pared down to the most insubstantial of silk threads. Before, he'd only had to worry about running into someone who knew either Marcus or himself. As Marcus had lived all his life in Ceylon and had never set foot in England except for one brief visit many years before, and he himself had spent his earliest years in Ceylon before moving to India, the possibility was real but, he'd considered, sufficiently remote to make the deception workable. Still, he felt like he'd been walking on eggshells since his assumption of Marcus's identity.

The events of the previous night had turned those eggshells into liquid, and he was very much afraid that he was sinking fast.

"Come here," he said to her in much the same tone that he would have employed with one of the men under his command.

Her spine stiffened, her chin came up, and her eyebrows lifted haughtily. Despite the unbecoming black dress that looked like it had been made for a woman twice her age and size, she was suddenly every inch the great lady, and he, from the expression on her face, was so much dust beneath her feet.

If he hadn't felt so infernally weak and uncomfortable, he would have smiled.

"*Please* come here, my dear Gabriella," he amended, before she could turn on her heel and leave the room, as her expression indicated she might well do. "There is something I wish to say to you."

"What is it?" Her tone was ungracious, but she came. He suspected, however, that her obedience had more to do with the weight of the tray she held than any act of submission to his will.

"I would remind you of our bargain."

She seemed to stiffen again, and her steps faltered briefly. Her voice was cold as she answered, "You may be sure that I need no reminder. I won't go back on my word."

"You must tell no one, remember."

"What, do you think I'll go chattering of this to all and sundry? I won't." She didn't sound particularly happy about it. "To have it known that I have agreed to such a thing will not increase my credit with anyone, believe me."

"If it's any comfort to you, it certainly increases your credit with me."

"It's not." She set the tray down harder than was necessary on the bedside table, so that the spoon rattled and the broth sloshed. As he noticed that the tray was the same one he had just rejected, he scowled.

"I told Barnet to take that back to the kitchen and get me something fit to eat." His tone was abrupt again, more abrupt than he had meant for it to be.

"Barnet was merely following Mr. Ormsby's orders when he brought this up."

She frowned at him. The curtains were pulled back from the long windows that looked out over the courtyard at the rear of the house, and bright sunlight touched her face. Her eyes really were the clear gray of rain water, he noted in passing, and her profile was as delicate as a cameo's. She was possessed, as he had first learned last night when he'd held her in his arms, of a far greater share of feminine charm than was apparent at first glance. The disparity between the image she presented to the world and the woman he caught quick glimpses of intrigued him.

"That pap will kill me more surely than the wound you gave me," he said sourly, taking a surprising degree of pleasure in watching the play of sunlight over her face. As he had intended, she looked guilty. Good. He wanted her to regret blowing a hole through him. Guilt was something he could use to his advantage.

"You must eat it or nothing until Mr. Ormsby says otherwise, nonetheless," she said in a severe tone. He was, he realized suddenly, quite possibly not nearly as intimidating a sight as he might wish. Lying flat on his back in bed with his head propped on a pair of pillows, unshaven, undoubtedly pale, clad in nothing more than a nightshirt with the bedclothes (newly smoothed by Barnet) tucked around his waist, he wasn't exactly in a position to enforce any commands he might give utterance to. Certainly Gabriella no longer seemed to regard him with fear. She was looking at him, rather, as if she were a governess and he the troublesome small boy in her charge. "*Can* you eat this by yourself?"

"I'm not a child," he said, narrowing his eyes at her. "Of course I can eat it by myself. If I choose to do so, which I do not."

"Show me, then." It was in the nature of a challenge. She picked up the tray and set it on his lap, then stood regarding him with her arms akimbo and a marshal light in her eyes. "Go on, pick up the spoon."

He eyed her. "I do not choose . . ."

"You can't, can you? How it must gall someone who is so accustomed to bullying the powerless to be too weak to lift a spoon!"

Mouth compressing, he rose to the bait hook, line, and sinker, and knew that he was doing so even as he did it. What made it worse was that, as he dipped the spoon into the broth and started to lift it toward his mouth, the muscles in his arms seemed to turn to jelly and his hand began to shake. Broth sloshed onto the tray.

"Let me help you." Sounding resigned, she took the spoon from his hand and returned it to the broth as his traitorous arm subsided to rest limply atop the mattress. Then, sitting down on the side of the bed, she dipped the spoon into the broth again and lifted it toward his mouth.

He didn't know whether to feel amused, affronted, or grateful at being treated like a puling infant. As he stared at her, his expression, he guessed, was a combination of all three.

"Open your mouth," she said in the tone of one as accustomed to command as he was. Surprising himself with his own meekness, he obeyed, and she tipped the warm broth down his throat with brisk efficiency. The salty liquid tasted surprisingly good, and he realized that he was hungry. He swallowed more eagerly than he was willing to let her realize as she continued to spoon broth into his mouth.

"Tell me something: how is it that you knew my brother was dead?"

The soft question caught him by surprise, and he almost choked. Coughing, he managed to swallow, and gave her a cagey look.

"I might ask the same of you," he said when he could speak.

"I will answer quite freely, to you at least: I had sent Jem to Marcus with a message. He was there when—it happened."

"Was he, indeed?" It was surprising, then, that her servant had not come to his notice. But he had gone chasing after the killer in a paroxysm of grief and fury, while Jem, it was to be presumed, had stayed at the scene. Marcus's message had said *I've found what you seek.* What he sought he sought so urgently that it overrode even his need to return to Marcus's side. Marcus was dead; there was no mending that. All he could do was search for the killer: one who, if Marcus had been correct, and his murder made it almost certain that he had been, counted murder as the least of his crimes. Following the trail of Marcus's murder was the only lead he had; he could not allow it to grow cold.

Still, he very much feared that it, too, might come to naught as had so many leads in the past months. This roleplaying was a chancy thing at best. If the killer made no move to remedy what hopefully would be seen as a mistake, he might search as diligently as he pleased without success. It was like looking for a single straw in a field full of hay.

"Well?" Gabriella was looking at him impatiently, even as she spooned the last of the golden liquid into his mouth. He swallowed, realizing that he felt much better now that there was food—even of such a tepid and unpalatable sort—in his system. Her question was unanswerable, of course. He would never, could never, reveal anything of the quest that had brought him to this place.

"You have the most . . . kissable . . . mouth," he said pensively instead, leaning back against the pillows and letting his lids droop until his eyes were half shut. To tease her seemed a poor reward for her care of him, but it had the desired effect: her eyes widened and her lips parted as she stared at him with shocked surprise. He continued with a growing smile: "For dessert, I could fancy just a taste. What do you say?"

She surged to her feet. Her movement caused the dishes to rattle, and for a moment he feared that he might find himself awash in ale. Quickly he grabbed the glass to steady it, glad to find his strength recovered enough to permit him to do so, and looked up to find her eyes flashing like silver fish in a pond as she glared down at him.

"You are a nasty, vulgar, *libertine*," she said through her teeth. "I should have known better than to feel sorry for you. I wish I'd let you starve."

With that, she turned on her heel and stalked with a great deal of dignity out the door. He smiled faintly as he admired the gentle sway of her backside beneath the too-big skirt. Really, she was not nearly so shapeless as he had at first supposed.

❧ 12 ❧

$\mathcal{G}$abby was still seething as she joined her sisters downstairs. To think that she had felt sorry for him, sat on his bed and fed him soup, began to feel a degree of comfort in his presence. She should have known better. She did know better. But he had charm enough to lure turtles from their shells, and she had fallen victim to it.

It would not happen again.

"What did Marcus want?" Beth asked as Gabby joined them at table. Taken by surprise, Gabby could only blink at her sister for a moment. Then she forced herself to push the scene she had just left to the back of her mind, and dredge up a suitable pleasant expression to go with a suitable pleasant reply.

"He wished only to inquire about our well-being. I assured him that we are fine."

Beth looked as though she would ask something else and Claire seemed on the verge of chiming in, so to give their thoughts a new direction Gabby hastily inquired of Twindle, who had joined them in the dining room, where in her opinion the most fashionable shops were to be found. This diversion worked; Claire and Twindle chatted animatedly, Beth chimed in from time to time, and Stivers's input was eventually sought. He in turn canvased the household while the ladies partook of a quick, light luncheon. Finally what was felt to be a definitive answer was returned, and the sisters, plus Twindle, sallied forth on their first daylight foray through London's streets.

To their country-bred eyes, the sights that greeted them on every front were nothing short of dazzling. On the one hand were edifices, monuments, and museums, and buildings the height and ornate facades of which caused them to marvel. On the other hand were the inviting expanses of green that were described, in a guide which Beth the enterprising pulled from her reticule, as Hyde Park and Green Park. Everywhere people thronged, in carriages, on horseback, on foot, and vehicles clogged the streets. By the time Bond Street, which both the household and the Pocket Guide assured them was the most select boulevard for the acquisition of elegant goods in town, was reached, even Gabby felt as though, if she did not take care, her jaw might hang open as Beth's had done before Claire had adjured her, in the name of saving them all from looking like the veriest bumpkins, to please shut her mouth.

At first, conscious of their own sartorial shortcomings, they were a shade hesitant about entering the establishments of the most fashionable dressmakers. Those elegant boutiques were rife with beautifully gowned ladies of the *beau monde* on the prowl for the latest styles, and Gabby felt as out of place among them as a Puritan miss mistakenly wandered into King George's court. But the silks and satins and muslins and gauzes on display were of such mouthwatering colors and textures, and the styles of the gowns themselves were so enticing, that they could not help but be drawn in, and soon found that they were enjoying themselves immensely, even Beth. By the time they had entered the rarified precincts of Madame Renard's, who was understood to be the most exclusive mantua maker in town, they were quite caught up in discussing the finer points of the current fashions and barely noticed their surroundings. After a chance remark let fall by Claire revealed to one of Madame's pinchnosed assistants that this trio of dowdy, black-clad provincials were in fact the sisters of the earl of Wickham, newly come to town for the season, Madame herself came out to wait on them, practically rubbing her hands in greedy glee.

After that, the afternoon disintegrated into such a whirl of fabrics and patterns that even Gabby was in danger of losing her head. Madame quite understood when Gabby told her that Lady Claire was the primary focus of the undertaking. A tiny, birdlike woman with an immense pile of improbably black hair and shrewd black eyes, Madame at once perceived in Claire a beauty whose successful adornment could only enhance her own reputation. The other sisters provided less scope for her talent, she admitted to her assistant in a private moment, but the older one, for all that she was a bit long in years to be still unwed, at least possessed a certain air that was, in its own way, nearly as rare and valuable as beauty. Quality, was what it was, Madame said, settling at last on a word to define what she meant. Lady Gabriella possessed *quality*. As for the younger sister, who was, lamentably, plump as a pudding, it was to be hoped that time would work its magic on her figure. In any event, Madame could only feel that she had done her noble clients a service by pointing out that Lady Gabriella, in her role as elder sister and prospective chaperone, would doubtless need a great many new outfits, too. Lady Elizabeth was not to be left out either; although she was too young to grace any *ton* parties, it would be perfectly permissable for her to be present on at-home days, and to visit among the younger set, whose acquaintance she would undoubtedly soon make. Thus her wardrobe, though simple as befitted a schoolroom miss, needed to be quite extensive, too.

By the time the orgy of shopping was completed, the ladies, on Madame's recommendation, retired to Guenther's for ices. Exhausted but happy, each was conscious of the supremely feminine pleasure of being clad in new and fashionable gowns, Madame having been moved by the size of the order given her and the illustrious nature of her clients to part with garments that had already been made up for other ladies, but not yet delivered. The discarded mourning gowns, which madame had offered to consign to the fire, had instead been earmarked for charity. More gowns were promised for the following day, with complete wardrobes to follow within the week.

"And if we do not see a marked increase in custom once the lovely one has taken her place among the *ton,* then I have no business calling myself a *modiste,*" Madame told her assistant with satisfaction as the ladies left her premises. And her assistant agreed that it surely would be so.

Not more than three quarters of an hour later, the Banning sisters finished their ices and agreed to suspend the rest of their shopping, for such necessary but minor items as ribbons and fans, for another day.

"Well," said Beth in a fair-minded fashion as they stepped up into the carriage to be driven home again, "I must say that wasn't so bad. Shopping in London is a whole different experience than shopping in York."

"Yes, for we had money to spend, which we have never had before, and the fashions are so breathtaking," Claire replied, settling into her seat. She looked rather anxiously at Gabby, who sat across from her. "Do you suppose

Marcus will cut up stiff when he receives the reckoning? I am afraid that we have been sadly extravagant. I had no notion that we would need so many gowns, had you?"

"And gloves, and bonnets, and shawls, to say nothing of those cunning half boots with the little buttons on the side," Beth chimed in. Her enthusiasm for shopping had increased markedly as she had been shown how well she could look in new clothes.

"Certainly there was no need to bespeak new gowns for *me*, Miss Gabby," Twindle said. Like Claire, Twindle looked slightly worried about the small fortune that had been spent. "As I told you, I already possess a sufficient number of gowns for my purposes, and His Lordship—quite properly—may not wish to pay for me to swan about looking grand as a duchess."

"Stuff!" Beth snorted indignantly. "Everything you chose was either gray or puce, and of such staid design . . . I should like to see any duchess who would get herself up like that."

"The colors and materials I chose are entirely suitable for my age and station, Miss Beth, and the finished gowns will be far finer than any I have heretofore possessed."

"Sad to say, that's true for all of us, Twindle," Claire said with a rueful twinkle.

"Because Papa was such a nip-farthing." Beth exclaimed. Chewing her lower lip, she glanced at Gabby. "You don't suppose our brother takes after him in that way, do you? How lowering it would be if he ordered us to send it all back."

"Our brother Wickham," Gabby said firmly, refusing to allow so much as a single image of the odious creature to enter her mind, "will be delighted to see us looking our best."

She had not the slightest idea what the rogue's feelings would in fact be if he should, by some remote chance, see what was sure to be a staggering bill, and she didn't care. Although it was not, properly speaking, their money, it was far more their money than his, at least. Of course, if one were being strictly honest, every last farthing now rightfully belonged to Cousin Thomas. But Gabby was determined not to think about that. There was no point in letting the rights and wrongs of the situation trouble her. She had made her choice, and meant to stick to it. Claire was going to come out in style just as she deserved, and that was all there was to it. Under the circumstances *Wickham* was certainly not going to be allowed to control her purse strings. He might count himself lucky that he was not even now cooling his heels in gaol. In any case, it was highly unlikely that he would even see the bills. She had directed that they be sent straight to Mr. Challow for payment.

Smiling determinedly, she said, "That fawn-colored walking dress you are wearing becomes you to admiration, Claire."

"Yes, did you not see those two gentlemen ogling her on the street? I must say, Claire, despite all your faults you are possessed of a positively *staggering* degree of beauty." Beth spoke as one stating an immutable law of the universe, rather than with any hint of envy.

"Faults? I?" Claire stuck her nose up in the air, looked down it at Beth, then laughed. "You are very pretty yourself, Beth, and that particular shade of green in your dress makes your hair look the color of copper."

"No, does it really?" Beth beamed in delight at the compliment, and smoothed a hand over the folds of her new olive-figured muslin with obvious pleasure. "Do you think it might be actually growing darker? Being cursed with carrot-colored hair is the most maddening thing in the world."

"Be thankful you don't have freckles to go with it,"

Claire advised. Beth found herself so much in agreement with this that the two of them conversed in perfect amity for the remainder of the ride home.

They returned home to find Cousin Thomas waiting for them in the drawing room. Tall, thin, and balding, with a perpetually worried look on his rather long face, Cousin Thomas rose abruptly from the gilt-armed sofa as they entered. Although their last meeting had been less than warm, Gabby greeted him with a smile and a handshake. Claire and Beth, taking their cue from her, followed suit.

After exchanging the usual pleasantries, Cousin Thomas got right to the point.

"I've heard—things will get around, you know—that Wickham's arrived from Ceylon to take his place as head of the family, and that he's somehow managed to get himself shot. What truth is there in that, if you please?"

Lying should, Gabby thought with despair, be almost second nature to her now, but it was not. She felt more than one pang of conscience as she agreed that Wickham was, indeed, abovestairs at that very moment, and, was moreover, slightly wounded from an accidentally self-inflicted gunshot. If it had not been for Claire and Beth's innocent corroboration, Cousin Thomas might well have been able to divine from her scrambled account of events that she was telling less than the truth, Gabby thought worriedly, and vowed to do better in future. After all, she was in too deep—by far too deep—to climb out now.

When Cousin Thomas left, with assurances that he would send Lady Maud and his daughters to call on them as soon as they returned to town from a visit to the older girl's new in-laws, Gabby roused herself to one last effort and wrote a note to Lady Salcombe announcing that she and her sisters were in town and begging permission to call without delay. Then, worn out from the events of the past two days, desperate to escape from Beth and Claire's chatter, Gabby retired to bed shortly after the evening meal. Despite her exhaustion, however, once laid down upon her bed she found herself quite unable to sleep. Her leg and hip ached like a sore tooth, the jarring they had suffered when she fell in the hall aggravated, no doubt, by all the walking she had done that day. To add to her inability to rest, faint sounds from the adjoining chamber reminded her of the unsavory characters separated from her by no more substantial a barrier than a locked door. Having learned from Stivers that Dr. Ormsby had been by, and that my lord was still far from being in prime twig, she judged herself fairly safe from attack, from *my lord* at least. But still, Jem's dire warnings rang in her ears. Thanks to her faithful servant, every time she closed her eyes she was afflicted with hideous visions of Barnet's hulking form creeping into her bedchamber to put a pillow over her face. In the end, she was obliged to get up, locate a small glass jar on her dressing table, empty it of its contents, and balance it upon the knob of the door that opened from the earl's chamber into hers. As a final precaution, she took the fireplace poker back into bed with her. Finally, with such reasonable safeguards in place, she managed to fall asleep.

Only to be roused, in what she judged must be the dead of the night, by the sudden smashing of the jar upon the floor. Jackknifing upright, blinking in the direction of that telltale sound, she was horrified to perceive, backlit against her dressing room door, a huge male figure striding toward her bed.

Gasping, eyes big as plates, she groped frantically among the tumbled bedclothes for the poker.

❧ 13 ❧

If it was a race, Gabby was determined to win it. Heart pounding, fists clenched around the poker, Gabby kicked free of the bedclothes, scrambled to the opposite side of the bed, and rolled to her feet before the man—whom she now recognized as Barnet—could get his hands on her. Hefting the poker in both hands now—the thing was surprisingly heavy—and raising it high overhead, she faced the intruder with pulse racing and teeth bared.

"Stay back. Stay back or I'll scream." Her voice shook. In fact, she wasn't entirely certain that she *could* scream. Her mouth was suddenly so dry with fear that it was difficult even to force out words.

"Miss! Miss, it's the Cap'n." If Barnet heard her threat, it didn't deter him. Huge and menacing-looking, he didn't so much as check his headlong rush, but came right around the bed toward her, backing her into a corner, spurring her to brandish the poker threateningly even as the hair stood straight up on the back of her neck.

"Get out of here. I'll hit you. . . ."

But it was too late. He was already on top of her and she couldn't hit him, couldn't cleave his skull in two, couldn't separate his head from his shoulders with a swing of the poker as she desperately wished to do, for the simple reason that he grabbed the iron bar almost casually and held on with one hamlike fist.

Gabby gaped up at him.

" 'E's in a bad way, miss, you gotta 'elp me."

Her back was pressed against the cool plaster wall. Her head was tilted as she stared fearfully up at the giant towering above her, who controlled the only defense she had with one-handed ease. Clinging desperately to the poker's handle, she cast a frantic glance sideways in search of something, anything, she could use as a weapon instead.

"Miss, please. 'E's out of 'is 'ead, and I don't want to be callin' no one else to 'elp me 'cause of what 'e might say." Barnet was antsy, unable to stand still, shifting from foot to foot and casting fearful glances over his shoulder toward the Earl's room even as he spoke. The tension in Gabby's muscles eased abruptly as she realized that, despite his precipitous entrance, Barnet was not threatening her. He was, instead, entreating her. "I need you to come along o' me *now,* miss. I dursn't leave 'im longer."

"You need my help?" Gabby asked cautiously. Except for the faint light cast by the banked-down fire, her bedroom was dark. It was impossible to see anything of Barnet except the bare outline of his bulk. He stood so close to her that she was getting a crick in her neck from looking up. His hand retained its almost incidental grip on the poker, and, realizing the futility of continuing to hold on, Gabby finally let go.

A faint groan and a series of muffled sounds from the earl's apartments answered before Barnet could.

"Eh, 'e's thrashin' 'himself into the grave," Barnet said in a despairing tone. Tossing the poker onto the bed, he turned and padded back toward the earl's chamber. He had, Gabby realized, discarded his boots, and she found herself thinking fleetingly of the possibly unfelicitous consequences of mixing broken glass with stocking feet. Before he disappeared into the dressing room he glanced back over his shoulder at her. "Come *on*, miss."

Retrieving the poker—not that it had been any help so far, but one never knew—Gabby grabbed her wrapper from the foot of the bed and cautiously followed him, careful to step over the pieces of glass scattered across the dressing room floor. A key left sticking out of Wickham's side of the door linking their apartments told Gabby just how easy entering her room had been.

She'd been right to booby-trap that door.

The sight that greeted Gabby as she paused for a moment on the threshold caused her eyes to widen. The bedchamber was lit by a branch of candles on the table near the bed and the fire blazed brightly in the hearth. The room was warm, far warmer than her own, and the slightly pungent smell of medicine hung in the air. Now far removed from the insolent beast who had insulted her earlier, Wickham lay flat on his back in the center of the bed, spread-eagled, writhing, his hands and feet tied to the posts with strips of cloth. He was clad only in a linen nightshirt that had rucked up above his knees.

Gabby noticed, while trying hard not to, that his legs were long and muscular and roughened by dark hair.

You have the most kissable mouth. His words came back to her, unbidden. Detestable man, she should despise him for daring to say such a thing to her. And she did. *She did.* Only, she couldn't seem to get his words out of her mind.

"Marcus! Damn it, Marcus. Oh, God, too late . . ." Wickham was obviously delirious, twisting and struggling, held fast by the strips of cloth that bound him to the bed-posts.

"Who is he?" The question emerged of its own accord as she stared aghast at the struggling figure. He had known her brother, that much was clear. Known her brother, and known of his death. Her gaze switched back to Barnet. "Who *are* you?" Her voice was fierce.

" 'Tis all over now, Cap'n. Don't go fashin' yourself, 'ear?" Barnet ignored her as he leaned over the bed, gripping his master's shoulders with both hands in a vain attempt to quiet him.

"You have him tied down." Gabby realized that she was not going to get an answer to her question at the moment, and let it go. Had she really expected Barnet to enlighten her? No.

" 'Twas all I knew to do. 'E don't know where 'e is. 'E kept tryin' to get up." Barnet met her gaze, his voice ragged. He was in breeches and shirtsleeves, his face sagging and puffy with exhaustion, with the dark arc of a bruise underlining one weary-looking eye. "That bloody—beggin' your pardon, miss—the surgeon saw the fever was on 'im when 'e last came, but could do no better than bleed 'im and leave behind a physic for me to give 'im. The medicine don't seem to be doin' no good, and. . . ." Barnet kept talking, but his subsequent words were drowned out by Wickham's shout.

"Ah, Marcus. I should have . . . No, no. I came as quickly as I could. . . ." Wickham was struggling in earnest now, straining at his bonds, his torso coming off the mattress in a violent arc.

" 'ere, Cap'n, no." Barnet cast himself across his master's struggling form, forcing him down, all the while talking to him as one would a fractious horse or child. " 'Tis all right, 'old on now."

Barnet glanced up as Gabby, having put down the poker, pulled on her wrapper and tied it as she came, reached the bedside. Wickham looked haggard, she saw at a glance. He was more gray than pale, with a thick stubble shadowing his cheeks and chin; his black hair stood all on end; the stubby crescents of his lashes flickered as they lay against his cheeks, and his lips moved soundlessly.

Had it been only that morning that she had fed him broth?

"He has deteriorated alarmingly," she said in a hushed tone.

"Aye, I'm sore afeared you've done for 'im, miss," Barnet groaned as Wickham's agitation continued unabated.

Gabby was conscious of a niggling stab of remorse. *Had* she really needed to shoot the man? Then she remembered his threats, and the feel of his hands around her neck, and gave herself a mental shake: yes, she had.

"I'm very sorry for the state he's in, of course, but as you well know he brought it on himself," Gabby's voice was firmer now. Castigating herself did no good at all, and clearly someone needed to take charge.

Barnet cast her a reproachful look. " 'E's burning up, miss. The sawbones said to expect some fever, but this is more than that, I think."

Gabby nodded.

"Shh, it's all right," she said to the man in the bed. Then, gingerly pushing stray locks of his fever-matted black hair aside, Gabby placed her hand palm down upon Wickham's brow. His skin was dry and hot as a stove. The coolness of her touch seemed to penetrate the fog he was lost in, because his movements ceased and his eyes blinked open. For an instant, no longer, Gabby found herself staring into the indigo depths of his eyes.

"Consuela," he croaked, as if his throat hurt. "My lovely impure, I would if I could, my dear, but not now. I—I find myself a trifle in—indisposed."

Gabby snatched her hand away as if he had snapped at it. His eyelids drooped again. He gave a deep sigh as his head turned to the side, and seemed to sleep.

" 'E don't know what 'e's sayin', miss," Barnet said excusingly, although the tips of his ears had turned a trifle red. He sat up with some caution. "Out of 'is 'ead, 'e is."

"His fever must be brought down." Gabby chose to ignore both Wickham's utterances and Barnet's shamefaced apology. "The surgeon must be sent for."

Barnet shook his head. "Miss, we dursn't. The things 'e says—it's too risky, miss. 'Tis not just 'is own secrets, which be bad enough, but—but other things as well, that 'e be going on about."

Crossing her arms over her chest, Gabby looked him in the eye as he came to his feet beside the bed. "What other things? Who is he, Barnet? I have a right to know."

Barnet met her gaze and seemed to hesitate.

Gabby persisted. "You call him Captain, which to my mind makes him a military man, and it is obvious that he knew my brother. And now you talk of secrets. I would feel much easier in my mind if you would tell me the truth of the matter. Otherwise I find I tend to imagine the worst— that the pair of you are escapees from Newgate, or Bedlam, perhaps."

A slight smile cracked the granite of Barnet's worried face. " 'Tis not so bad as that, miss, I give you my word. But 'tis for the Cap'n, not me, to tell you the rest, an' 'e chooses."

"God, it's hot. Damned sun. So hot. . . ." Wickham began to thrash and mutter again. "Water. Please, water. . . ."

"You shall have water," Gabby promised, softening in

spite of herself as she touched his burning hot cheek in an attempt to penetrate his delirium. She glanced at Barnet. "The surgeon must and shall be sent for."

Barnet met her gaze, appeared as if he would argue more, then bowed his head in acquiescence. After helping the servant get several spoonfuls of water into Wickham's greedy mouth, Gabby retired to her own room. There she pulled the bell rope and sent a sleepy-eyed Mary to summon a footman to roust Ormsby from his lodging. As an afterthought, she sent another footman to fetch Jem from his bed in the mews, on the not inconsiderable chance that more brute force than could be provided by Barnet alone might be required to handle Wickham. She then proceeded to dress, although dawn was just then sending feelers of light over the horizon. For the purposes of the sickroom, she told a yawning Mary, the remaining mourning gowns she had brought with her from Yorkshire would be just the thing.

Jem arrived before Ormsby. Barnet admitted him to the earl's chamber. As Jem stepped inside the two servants glared at each other with mutual hostility, and for a ludicrous instant circled each other like stiff-legged dogs. Finally, in response to a sharp call to order by Gabby, both moved to stand by the bed, one on either side. In a low voice, Gabby explained the situation to Jem, who cast darkling looks at the scowling Barnet all the while. Before Jem could do more than get started on a low-voiced but heartfelt expostulation to her to think what she was about, Ormsby arrived.

"The wound has gone putrid," Ormsby announced after a brief examination. "I will not try to hide from you, ma'am, that your brother's situation is grave. Still, I do not totally despair of his life—" this was said hastily, in apparent response to the expression on Gabby's face and the muffled sound from Barnet "—*if* my instructions are followed to the letter. The wound must be soaked every two hours in hot poultices made with this powder I shall leave with you; he must have his medicine without fail; he must be given plenty to drink; and he must be kept warm and still."

"I will see to it," Gabby replied, for the instructions had been addressed to her.

It was not to be supposed that Ormsby would not bleed Wickham. This he did, to, as he said, release the ill humors in the blood that were doubtless causing the fever. Then the first powder was poured down Wickham's throat under Ormsby's supervision; likewise was the bandage changed, and the wound soaked. As this of necessity involved revealing a great deal more of the patient's flesh than Gabby was comfortable viewing, she retreated to a corner of the room, where she busied herself preparing a flacon of watered wine.

". . . so much blood. God, Marcus. Marcus." The soaking of the wound appeared to cause great discomfort, and Wickham half awoke, crying out in seeming anguish and fighting to free himself from the ties that bound his limbs. Jem and Barnet both stood by to assist the surgeon. As Wickham began to flail and call out, Barnet appeared more and more apprehensive. Gabby's own alarm at the revelatory nature of Wickham's ramblings increased with every passing moment. When he said, plain as anything, *Damn, the little witch shot me,* she was sure, from the heat she could feel creeping into her cheeks, that her face was turning guilty scarlet. And when he began to moan once again about blood and Marcus, her alarm was assuaged only by her reflection that the surgeon, not having the least acquaintance, as she supposed, with the family, could have no notion of the import of what he was hearing.

But in this she proved to be mistaken.

"I beg your pardon, Lady Gabriella," Ormsby said, when

he had gathered together his belongings and was preparing to leave. "But is not . . . That is, I was under the impression that Marcus was His Lordship's given name."

Gabby felt her blood run cold at this unlooked-for perspicacity, but managed to keep her countenance under control.

"It is indeed," she said coolly, as though she wondered, but was too polite to ask, how he felt that such a circumstance was any concern of his.

"But then—when he keeps calling out to a Marcus, who I gather has been severely hurt or killed. . . ." The surgeon's brow knit, and he broke off under the force of Gabby's look. "Not that it matters, not at all. It just struck me as . . . But never mind."

"As it happens, my brother had a good friend, also named Marcus, who, uh, unfortunately suffered a fatal accident not many months previous. My brother witnessed it." If she had not been wishful of allaying any slight suspicion the surgeon might be harboring, she would not have said so much. Certainly, if it had been her brother Marcus who actually lay in that bed, she would not have felt it incumbent upon her to have replied to Ormsby's curiosity at all.

"That explains it, then," Ormsby said, sounding relieved. Gabby bestowed a rather tight smile on him as she personally escorted him to the bedroom door.

"That was a near-run thing," Barnet said when Ormsby was gone. Wickham, no doubt exhausted from the painful mauling he had endured, was perversely silent now that there was no one outside of their immediate circle to hear him, and in fact appeared to be asleep. Barnet continued, with a reproachful glance at Gabby: "Did I not warn you that the Cap'n's mouth would be the undoing of us? I don' min' tellin' ya, I was in a sweat the 'ole time."

"There be no *us* in this, you oaf," Jem said furiously

from the opposite side of the bed. "This be you two criminals alone, and my poor mistress only gulled into lendin' you her aid."

"You'll keep a civil tongue in your head, you dwarf, or . . ." Barnet's fists clenched.

"Enough!" Gabby said, glaring at each of the combatants in turn. "There will be no more of this fighting between the two of you. Like it or not, we must pull together if we are not all to come a cropper over this. Barnet, when is the last time you slept?"

His face softening only slightly from the dark scowl he had turned on Jem, Barnet knit his brows in thought. "I dozed a bit in the chair, not long afore I came to wake you, miss."

"Then you will oblige me by taking yourself off to your bed. Return in eight hours, if you please."

"But, miss . . . but, miss . . ." Barnet cast a harried glance at Wickham, who appeared to be sleeping peacefully.

"Jem or I will stay with him until you return. It seems clear to me that the three of us will have to bear the burden of the nursing. You are right, he is too given to saying unfortunate things when he is out of his head to trust him to the care of any who do not know the—the particular circumstances."

Jem stiffened indignantly, shooting her a look that said as plainly as if he'd spoken it aloud that, in his opinion, she'd lost her mind.

Barnet stiffened at the same time, and, staring very hard at Jem, said, "If it's all the same to you, miss, I'll not be leavin'. Though I thank you for your kindness in considering my comfort."

"It is not all the same to me," Gabby snapped. "You will do as you are told, if you please. And, though it pains me to say it, it is not your comfort that is at the forefront of my mind. It is your master's survival."

Barnet looked alarmed. "But miss . . ."

"You are of no use to him if you are dropping with fatigue. Come, you may safely leave him to Jem's and my tender mercies."

"Yes, miss," Barnet said miserably.

"Go then."

Barnet cast a pained look at his master even as he began to move toward the door. Before he reached it, he swung around, his gaze fixing threateningly on Jem. "If anythin' should befall 'im while I'm gone . . .'"

"Go." Gabby interrupted, her eyes shooting sparks at the malingerer. Barnet shut his mouth, swallowed once, and went.

"That's the way to tell him, Miss Gabby," Jem said exultantly when they were alone.

"If you do not wish to see me fall into strong hysterics, please leave off doing battle with Barnet. Do you not see that we are stuck with him, and *him*," Gabby nodded at Wickham's still form, "just as they are stuck with us?"

❧ 14 ❧

Wickham's condition stayed much the same throughout the next two days. The wound was surrounded by a red, swollen circle of flesh that was ominously hot and firm to the touch; the dark hole where the bullet had been dug out oozed putrefaction and bled afresh with each treatment. Wickham remained out of his head with fever. Which was probably just as well, Gabby reflected as she pressed a steaming poultice to his injured side for what seemed like the hundredth time in the last three hours. At least he was oblivious to most of what was being done to him—and her modesty was, to some degree, spared. If he had been awake and watching her while she did this—well, she just could not have done it, that was all.

Keeping him decently covered while at the same time treating his wound was a neat trick, and one she had not yet completely mastered. Although he wore a nightshirt, a fresh one—Barnet had changed the earlier sweat-stained one just before she had taken over from him—it was rucked up well past his waist for the treatment. She had draped—and redraped—his private parts with a blanket, but his restless movements continually dislodged the concealing cloth. The flesh that was thereby revealed intrigued her most shamefully, but she refused to give in to her baser urgings and satisfy her curiosity by actually looking at it.

What details she caught with the occasional stray glance were quite embarrassing enough.

As she sat on the side of the bed applying the poultice, she determinedly focused her gaze on the area around the wound and above, which in itself provided plenty to occupy her eyes—and her senses. To her dismay, she had already discovered that the muscular contours of his torso affected her strangely. Sometimes she would be looking at him, idly, her mind, as she supposed, quite elsewhere, when the sheer masculine beauty of the well-toned body beneath her hands would insinuate itself into her subconscious, causing her pulse to speed up and her breathing to quicken before she realized what was happening. In such cases she would immediately avert her gaze and force her thoughts to take a more proper direction. But the lowering truth was that she found the scheming blackguard physically appealing, and however much she tried to hide from it, deep inside she knew it was so.

To make matters worse, she could not help but touch him in the course of caring for him. With the best will in the world for it not to happen, she nevertheless found herself enjoying in a way that had nothing to do with nursing the sick the sensation of her hands against his flesh. His stomach, she discovered almost guiltily, was firm and resilient, with smooth swarthy skin that was as appealing to the touch as the finest kid leather. It was bisected by a trail of fine black hair that widened considerably lower down, where she was bound not to look. That stomach hair, as she learned quite by accident, was considerably silkier than, say, the hair on his chest. His navel was a secret, inward-curving oval, into which she had more than once been forced to dip a cloth-wrapped finger to wipe out liquid pooled from her poultice. His hips were narrow, with little flesh over the hard bones.

Following the line of dark hair upward—it was necessary to dry him after mounding the dripping poultice on the wound, after all—she found that his chest widened in a vee shape as it rose toward his shoulders, and that it was also heavy with muscle beneath smooth flesh. The line of dark hair widened, too, at the height where his ribs began, and coarsened, and began to curl. Although his nightshirt obscured the upper half of his chest as well as his arms and shoulders, enough was revealed so that she knew that it was covered by a thick wedge of curling—and crisp to the touch—black hair.

Suddenly, as her mind followed where her hands and gaze roamed, Gabby felt an almost irresistible desire to curl her fingers in that thicket of hair.

Shame on you, she scolded herself, snatching her hands, towel and all, into her lap for safekeeping. Worry and exhaustion must be causing her subconscious to run amok; otherwise it would not continually present her with improper images that caught her all unaware.

You have the most kissable mouth.

Wickham muttered something then, turning his head toward her, eyelids fluttering, and for one horrified moment Gabby thought that she had spoken the words aloud and he had awakened in time to hear them. But no, she realized with relief as his lashes dropped to rest once more against his cheeks, that was only her own guilty conscience at work. He remained unaware.

"You are a complete scoundrel, you know," she told him crossly. "And I do not feel in the least bit guilty about shooting you."

She did, of course, and knew she would feel guiltier

yet—quite the murderess, in fact—if he should die. If the poison from the wound should spread throughout his system, or his fever could not be brought down . . .

Well, she just would not think about that.

From somewhere below, a clock chimed the hour. It was one a.m. The rest of the family, even the servants, were asleep. Keeping them all out of Wickham's bedroom for any except the most mundane of housekeeping chores had been quite a trick. Oh, excluding the girls had been easy enough: Gabby had merely said that there were sights involved in nursing Wickham that were not suitable for their tender eyes. Explaining why the servants were not allowed to share in the nursing was tougher: Gabby had finally been forced to claim that she trusted no one, save herself and Jem and Wickham's own servant Barnet, to care for Wickham as they ought.

And had endured many a hurt look as a result.

Afraid to keep Wickham bound to the bedposts continually—he could not rest easily tied so, and circulation in the limbs was a concern—Gabby had had Barnet untie him late on the previous day. It seemed to answer admirably: he slept, and Gabby credited his relative lack of agitation to the increased comfort that went with no longer feeling himself subject to constraints.

"Hot," Wickham said quite clearly, stirring anew. For a moment Gabby looked at him with bated breath. Again she wondered if he would waken; he had seemed on the verge several times since she had taken over from Barnet. But he settled down again, and seemed to sleep. For a few moments the only sounds were the soft rasp of his breathing, and the crackle and pop of the fire.

The room *was* very warm, Gabby realized, glancing around, as it had been shut for some time now with a fire blazing in the hearth. Indeed, she quite felt the heat herself.

Her high-necked, long-sleeved mourning gown seemed stifling suddenly, and she discovered tiny beads of moisture dotting her hairline as she thrust a wayward lock back into the cumbersome knot at her nape. Grimacing, she fanned her face with the towel in her lap. Besides being over warm, the room was also redolent of not altogether pleasant scents, including the sharp mustardy smell of the reeking poultice, and, beneath it, the duller but equally pervasive odor of a feverish male body. The only illumination besides the fire came from the branch of candles on the bedside table, which added the scent of hot tallow to the rest.

The trio of candles had burnt well down, Gabby saw at a glance, and liquid pools of tallow gleamed at the base of crooked black wicks. Leaning over, she blew the candles out, one by one. The extra illumination was unneeded, and even if they added only a small degree to the baking heat and nose-wrinkling smell it was still an extra mite that she could do without. She had treated his wound so often now that she was quite sure that she could do it, if necessary, in the pitch dark.

". . . briella," Wickham said suddenly, drawing her eyes back to him with reflexive swiftness. Had he actually said her name, or was he just muttering more nonsense in his sleep?

"Are you awake then?" she asked with some asperity.

No answer. Not that she had really expected any. His eyes remained closed, and his breathing was deep and regular. Perhaps he *was* getting better, she thought, checking the temperature of the poultice with a careful prod. His face was not as flushed as it had been, and he seemed less restless tonight.

Another hour, she thought with a sigh, testing the poultice again, and she would be relieved by Jem. Aghast at her continuing determination to, as he put it, *aid the bloomin' criminal,* Jem nevertheless performed his duty with grim efficiency. Of course, when he arrived to take over he would spend every minute until she left the room scowling and grumbling, and peppering her with warnings each more daunting than the one before it. Still, she would be glad when he came; she was tired to the bone, and—and grumpy in a way she did not like to try to analyze. The man who lay half naked and helpless beneath her hands was a stranger, a criminal, and one moreover who had insulted her and threatened her and actually done violence to her person. But he was also disturbingly handsome, charming in the way she guessed all successful rogues must be, and all too blatantly masculine. It really should not have come as such a surprise to her that she should find him attractive, but she *was* surprised, and she could not like it. It was—disconcerting, to say the least.

His head moved restlessly on his pillow, his tousled black hair in stark contrast to the white linen it rubbed against. He started mumbling, saying something long and involved under his breath, his voice so low that she could understand not so much as a single syllable. Her gaze moved to his mouth in an instinctive attempt to make out the words. Even parched with fever, it was a beautiful mouth, she noticed, a little thin, perhaps, but with lips that were well-shaped and firm, as she knew from forcing a wide variety of liquids between them over the past two days.

You have the most kissable mouth.

So, she thought, did he. How would it feel if she were to press her mouth to those beautifully shaped lips?

He stirred again, lashes fluttering, as the thought formed in her mind with as little volition as storm clouds swirling into a tornado. As she realized what she was thinking, then met his suddenly open eyes on top of it, Gabby jumped as if she'd been shot. For a startled moment she stared into indigo depths. But on closer inspection it was clear that his eyes still bore the glazed look that meant he was not really aware, and his lids closed again almost immediately as if to clench the matter.

She let out a sigh of relief. Horrified to discover that her mind was capable of entertaining such a thought as pressing her mouth to his, she dropped her gaze to her task, nudged the wet mass with an impatient finger, judged the treatment complete, and scooped the poultice that she now considered quite cool enough from the wound. Thankful to be finished, she deposited it in the basin that she had set for just that purpose on the table by the bed. In a moment she could go sit safely by the fire, and wait there, perhaps perusing the book she had brought with her, until Jem arrived to take over.

At least, if she were reading *Marmion,* she would not catch herself glancing Wickham's way.

In a hurry to get away from him now, she sprinkled the wound with the basilicum powder Ormsby had left and began to bind it up, wrapping strips of linen all the way around his midsection and tying them in place. Working her arm beneath his body required considerable effort, but if the bandage was not secured in that way, she had discovered, he inevitably managed to dislodge it.

In response, perhaps, to her arm burrowing beneath his back, he moved, more sharply than before. His legs shifted—the blanket was dislodged again, of course; *not* that she looked down to make certain—and he said *please* quite clearly. As Gabby had no idea what he meant by that, and was in a hurry to get away from him besides, she ignored the mumbled entreaty, and worked on securing the bandage without letting her eyes drift either above or below the immediate vicinity of the wound.

"Please," he said again, the word husky but perfectly distinct. Gabby couldn't help it. She glanced up. His eyelids were fluttering, but his eyes did not open. His mouth—

those beautifully shaped lips—curved in what looked like the merest suggestion of a smile.

He wanted water, she guessed with some impatience. There was a half-full glass on the table; she had given him several spoonfuls each hour. When she was done with the bandage, she would tilt a few more spoonfuls between his lips before retiring to fire and book.

"Confounded nuisance," she muttered under her breath, flicking him a severe glance that he, of course, didn't see. Her hands brushed across the too-warm skin of his abdomen as she pulled the last linen strip into place and tied the ends with a flourish.

On some level he must have been aware of her touch, because his hand moved then, finding hers, closing around it. Like the rest of him, his hand was blazing hot, large, and strong. Gabby cast another quick glance up at his face. Was he perhaps trying to communicate? Possibly. It was hard to be certain. In any case, his eyes were still closed.

A little wary, Gabby nevertheless allowed her hand to be squeezed, lifted—*and deposited atop that most private of male parts.*

Gabby gasped, snatched her hand away, and shot off the bed like the cap from a well-shaken bottle of ginger beer. Her hand seemed to burn—the thing had actually stirred and grown beneath it!—and she could not help herself: she stared down in horror at the male appendage between his legs. It was huge now, jutting away from his body at a near ninety degree angle—and she had actually touched it.

She shuddered, wiping her hand convulsively against her skirt. Oh, God, she could still feel the sensation of it moving beneath her palm.

His eyes remained closed. His expression was serene. His hand, which she had flung away with no regard whatsoever for his debilitated state, rested limply on the mattress at his side, fingers curled slightly inward.

Of course, he was unaware of what he had done, she reminded herself. He was lost somewhere in a feverish dream.

Thank goodness. Her breathing slowed. Her pulse steadied. Keeping that thought firmly in mind, Gabby screwed up her courage to the sticking point. Averting her eyes, she gingerly reached for the blanket to cover him. . . .

As quick as that, he caught her wrist and yanked her down on the bed beside him. Feet flying out from under her, she landed on her still sore hip with a gasp. Before she could make so much as a move to escape, she found herself on her back with him rolled atop her, his big body crushing her down into the mattress.

⚜ 15 ⚜

She felt warm and good lying beneath him, and she smelled of—vanilla. Burying his face in the curve between her neck and shoulder, he inhaled deeply.

Gabriella. He knew who she was. Had known, in some dimly aware corner of his mind, for some time.

The scent of her was intoxicating. So was the feel of her, slender and delicately made and, at the moment, buckram stiff with tension.

He moved against her, rocking his pelvis into hers, nuzzling her neck, expecting every second to feel her fighting to be free, to hear her ordering him to let her go.

Until that happened, he meant to enjoy the moment. He slid his mouth along to the pulse point beneath her ear and rested there a moment, feeling the agitated pitter-patter with a quickening of his own heartbeat.

Whatever she was thinking—and he hated even to try to guess—her body was responding to his with an instinctive softening that made his senses heat. Her breath came faster. He could feel her breasts pushing into his chest as she drew in air.

He pulled her earlobe into his mouth, and made a meal of the tender flesh.

Her hands clutched his shoulders. Her nails dug into his skin. She quivered, moving beneath him, and gave a tiny moan. Her response set him on fire.

He wanted to make love to her with an intensity that was almost painful. He wanted her naked and moaning in his arms, kissing him with feverish passion and locking her legs around his waist.

He wanted to put himself inside her.

He couldn't have what he wanted, of course. Even as woolly-headed as he felt, he knew that.

At least, he couldn't have *all* he wanted. He was not, in the final analysis, that big a cad. But he could have something.

He slid his hand over her breast.

"Oh," she said, on a note of surprise. And from the way she said it, he knew that she liked the feel of his hand on her breast almost as much as he did.

Wasn't there some saying about the road to hell being paved with good intentions?

❧ 16 ❧

*H*is ear was right beside her mouth as his hot, bristly face nuzzled into the sensitive curve between her shoulder and neck. It seemed to her, lying pinned beneath him as he pressed his mouth against an exquisitely vulnerable spot just below her ear, that he weighed about as much as a fully grown horse.

She couldn't help it. The moist heat of his mouth just there was causing her to breathe faster. It felt . . . It felt . . .

Wonderful.

What he was doing touched a chord deep within her that she hadn't even known was there. In her entire twenty-five years of life, no man had ever caressed her in such a way. She never had been so much as kissed by a man, and she had never missed it. Indeed, she had thought that she, personally, and possibly most ladies of her class, were immune to the kinds of animalistic emotions that she knew, from witnessing them firsthand, were the unenviable lot of the male gender. When she was younger, and marriage had still seemed like an almost certain part of her future, she had speculated occasionally on the details of marital relations, the broad outlines of which were known to her. She was a country-bred miss, after all. The duties of the marriage bed she had expected to find vaguely uncomfortable, at best. She had considered them the price a gently-bred female had to pay to obtain a husband, and, in the fullness of time, children.

It had never occurred to her that she might find the physical attentions of a man . . . pleasant.

No, not pleasant, she corrected herself with incurable honesty as her nails curled into the hard muscles of his shoulders: divine. That was the only word that did the tremors racing over her skin justice. Beguiled by her own pleasure-ambushed senses into immobility, she gave herself a moment, just a moment, in which to experience something that was never likely to come her way again.

His unshaven jaw scratched over the tender surface of her neck as he brushed hot, firm lips against her skin. His mouth found her ear, pulling the lobe into the scalding wet cave, sucking on it, nibbling at it. Her lips parted; she fought for breath. The sensation was very strange, and at the same time intoxicating. Little quivers raced along her nerve endings from where his mouth performed its magic clear down to her toes. Even his weight pinning her to the bed was not as crushing as she would have supposed, given the difference in their sizes. Or at least, if it was crushing, it was crushing in a good way—a rousing way. Actually—and she didn't know why she was surprised to realize this—her body seemed designed to accommodate his. With some inborn sense of its own, it seemed ready to yield, to conform, to mold its softer female shape to his hard male form as necessary.

Gabby realized with a renewed sense of shock that he was pushing his—his—engorged shaft against the most secret, feminine part of her.

Thank goodness, she thought as she experienced the

sensation with parted lips and widening eyes, that she was fully dressed. Otherwise—otherwise . . .

The intricately pleated crimson canopy at which she stared blurred as the pressure of his pelvis rocking rhythmically into hers provoked the most amazing reactions inside her. Deep in her most feminine parts, everything seemed to be coiling tight. There was a warm, delicious—*tingle.* Her loins began to clench and throb in a rhythm that answered his.

She was growing hot. Really, really hot. Hotter even than he felt, and he felt like he was burning up.

Out of nowhere, a tiny sound emerged from her throat. With dismay, she realized that it could be characterized only as a—as a moan.

Shocked, Gabby blinked, clamped her lips together to prevent any more wayward sounds from emerging, and realized that her once-in-a-lifetime sensory experience was quickly getting out of hand.

Time to call a halt, she told herself firmly. At once. Through sheer force of will rather than any real desire to escape, she turned her head sharply, pulling her earlobe free.

Air suddenly cooling the wet lobe felt almost reproachful. Meanwhile, his hot mouth slid down the side of her neck.

She drew in a quick, shaky breath. Her eyelids fluttered, and she realized that they were, of their own volition, wanting to close. Determinedly she kept her eyes open. Her hands tensed against his shoulders, crumpling the soft linen that covered their firm, tensile width. It was time to fight free of this unexpected whirlpool of delight before she could be drawn in any further.

He shifted his weight slightly to one side; his uninjured side, she realized, wondering if it was an instinctive move in response to pain. At any rate, now that he was not lying completely on top of her, it should be slightly easier to win free.

If that was what she wanted.

It was a wayward thought, shocking in its implication, and Gabby dismissed it instantly. *Of course* she wanted to be free. Anyway, whether she did or not, she was freeing herself.

So there.

She took a deep, steadying breath. If she could just maneuver him a little more onto his uninjured side . . .

A hard warmth settled on her breast, distracting her. It was his hand, she discovered, glancing down. The sight of his long-fingered, swarthy-skinned hand splayed against the bodice of her staid black kerseymere gown made her breath catch. Never in her life had she seen anything more wanton.

Just looking at it made her mouth go dry.

"Oh," she said.

He fondled her breast, squeezed it, kneaded it like someone might a roll of dough, then pressed his thumb down over her nipple.

She liked it. Dear God, how she liked it! Her breast seemed to tighten and swell beneath his hand. Her nipple hardened to quivering attention as he rubbed it, then rolled the erect nub between his thumb and forefinger. Her feminine parts seemed to quake, and grow—liquid.

To her horror she realized that something inside her body must be melting. She was growing unmistakably damp between her thighs.

The knowledge both excited and appalled her.

Her breast fit neatly into his palm, she discovered with some fascination as he flattened his hand over it. He began to trace circles around her breast, his fingers almost teasing. Concentric circles, which grew smaller and smaller, with her nipple as the obvious ultimate target. By the time he got there, caressing the erect nub, tweaking it quite firmly through the layers of cloth, her whole body was quivering.

It felt delicious. So delicious that her toes curled in their sensible wool stockings. So delicious that she was breathing hard, almost panting really, and gritting her teeth to keep from making another of those embarrassing sounds. The melting was now accompanied by a warm, deep ache.

He moved, shifting his weight again, pressing his knee between hers. Her skirts, she discovered, were twisted somewhere around her thighs. His legs tangled with hers. She could feel the hard boniness of his bare knee, and the heat of his muscular thigh, through her stockings.

His hard-muscled thigh settled between hers as if it belonged there. She felt a sudden, disturbing flutter of panic. This was wrong, she thought. This she knew about. The male part of him went in between her legs and . . . and . . .

Oh, dear Lord, what was he doing now?

His hand left her breast to move slowly and sensuously down her body, caressing everything in its path before tugging at her skirt.

Her skirt was halfway up her thighs and being compelled higher inch by inexorable inch before Gabby recovered enough presence of mind to struggle in earnest.

"I like it when you wiggle like that," he said in her ear, the words quite distinct. Shocked to hear sensible speech emerging from one she had thought quite unaware, she went completely still.

To her horror, he lifted his head, and she found herself staring into gleaming indigo eyes.

"You're awake," she said, her voice shrill with indignation.

"Did you ever doubt it?" He smiled at her, a slow, sensous smile that made her heart lurch. Then, before she could react, before she could punch him or demand to be released or do any of the thousand and one things that crowded into her mind, he bent his head and pressed his mouth to her breast.

She could feel the heat and moisture of his mouth clear through the layers of her dress and chemise. She could feel it burning through to her already aroused nipple, dampening it, setting it aflame. Heat shot through her. Her body quivered and quaked. Another of those humiliating little moans escaped her lips. Her back arched instinctively; her hand slid around to the back of his head, pressing his mouth closer to her breast.

Horror at her own response shocked Gabby back to her senses. Galvanized, knowing that she couldn't, wouldn't, could not possibly allow this to go any further, she began to struggle wildly, shoving at his shoulders in an attempt to free herself. When that didn't work she leaned forward, quick as a pit viper, and bit his shoulder, hard.

❧ 17 ❧

"Ow!" He yelped, rolling onto his back, his hand clapping over the injured spot. A dull thud and a muffled, feminine-sounding *oomph* brought his gaze swinging around. She had apparently slid off the side of the bed to land on all fours on the floor. His gaze narrowed on the very top of an untidy auburn head that popped like a cork in water into view. "You could have just said something like, let me up."

To his surprise, he sounded oddly hoarse.

"And you would have listened?" Gabriella appeared to find nothing amiss with his voice. Gray eyes glared at him over the edge of the mattress. Fine dark eyebrows twitched together over her nose.

Ridiculously, despite various aches and pains and the inexplicable weakness that made his head swim, he discovered that he was enjoying himself.

"Of course I would have listened. What do you take me for?"

Her expression was so speaking that she didn't have to say a word. Her whole face was in view now, and the answer to his question, in a nutshell, was clearly nothing very flattering.

"Miss Gabby?" The door to his room opened without

warning. Glancing around, he discovered Jem entering without so much as a by-your-leave. He frowned. Thank God the man hadn't come in five minutes earlier. Gabriella would have been humiliated past redemption, and he found he didn't like the thought of that.

The servant closed the door and approached the bed, peering past him at Gabriella. She, meanwhile, scrambled to her feet, running a quick, self-conscious hand over her hair, which was tumbling free of its pins in a most fetching way.

"Are you all right?" Jem was frowning at her.

"I'm fine. I just—lost my balance."

She was leaning rather heavily against the bedpost at the foot of his bed, and sounded as if she were short of breath. Come to think of it, he was slightly short of breath himself, and as his gaze ran over her matters didn't improve. Discovering hidden treasure—and he considered the body hidden under that God-awful crow's dress hidden treasure—was more exciting than he could have dreamed.

"I don't recall hearing a knock, or bidding you to come in." There was a faint peremptory note to his voice as he addressed Jem. At the same moment, a quick downward glance assured him that, tangled in the bedclothes as he was, he was decent.

"Awake, are you?" Jem cast him a scathing look.

"He is indeed," Gabriella replied before he could answer for himself, her voice as collected as if she had spent the last five minutes embroidering before the fire, rather than tumbling around in his bed. Her gaze just brushed his before meeting the servant's. Her eyes were rainwater cool. What a pity, he thought dryly, that she couldn't as easily control the giveaway pinkening of her cheeks.

She was no longer looking at him, but the old man was. Lying flat on his back as the servant curled his lip at him didn't suit him; he dug his elbows into the mattress, meaning to heave himself back against the headboard and into a sitting position.

As he raised himself into a semi-sitting position, a gut-wrenching stab of pain skewered him like a white-hot poker. What the devil . . .? Clenching his teeth to hold back a groan, he stopped what he was doing on the instant, falling back against the mattress, gasping for breath. As the pain twisted knifelike through his body, he tensed against it, closing his eyes, feeling sweat break out across his forehead. When he relaxed enough to open them again, what seemed like many long moments later, it was to find both Gabriella and her henchman ranged together beside the bed looking down at him. Jem, arms crossed over his chest, frowned at him with open dislike; Gabriella regarded him warily.

"You shouldn't try to move. You could start the wound bleeding again." Her concern, if that was indeed what he detected in her voice, seemed reluctant.

"You shot me." Flat on his back again, afraid to move in case the pain should attack him once more, he stared up at her as memory came flooding back.

"You deserved it," she said. Jem nodded his head in vigorous agreement.

"God, I feel like I've been run over by a mail coach." It was a groan. In light of the unsympathetic nature of his audience, the complaint would have been better left unuttered, he realized as soon as he said it. But he hurt too much, and was too disoriented, to be as stoic as he normally was.

"You've been very ill."

The unmistakable chill in her voice earned her a frowning, sideways glance from Jem. Seeing it, and no doubt realizing that her attitude was giving rise to questions where none had existed, she managed, strictly for the servant's benefit he knew, to banish the frown from her face.

"For how long?"

Deep breaths helped, he discovered. The pain was receding.

"This is the third day."

No doubt about it. Her tone told the tale. Milady was feeling hostile, whether from the way her body had responded to his, or from his knowledge of the way her body had responded to his, he couldn't be sure. But if he had to bet, it would be on the latter.

"So you've been nursing me." A wealth of hidden meaning underlay the words, and he managed a suggestive smile although it was becoming something of an effort simply to maintain the conversation. His tongue felt thick and swollen, and the rustiness of his voice was beginning to worry him. So, too, was the dizziness that assailed him every time he lifted his head from the mattress. The pain in his side, while no longer the burning stab of agony that had made him fear he was going to pass out, was still very much present. The only other time he could remember feeling this out of curl was when his horse had been shot out from under him in the peninsula. It had landed on his leg, breaking it in three places, and made such a mess that the surgeon had in the end wanted to take the limb off. Only his own adamant refusal to permit such a thing, and Barnet's subsequent watchdoglike devotion when he'd gone unconscious, had prevented the surgeon from sawing off the leg and having done. Remembering, he looked at the pair standing over him rather suspiciously.

"What have you done with Barnet? He wouldn't leave me, I'll be bound."

Taking care not to move more of himself than was needful, he raised a hand to the wound. When he pressed, it hurt.

"I sent him to bed. He was worn out. And you should leave that alone." Gabriella was scowling at him: a reward, no doubt, for his earlier smile.

"So you persuaded him to trust you, did you? I compliment you. Under the circumstances, that's quite a feat."

Abandoning his tactile exploration of the bandage that wound round his midsection, he lay still for a moment, gathering his resolve for another try at sitting up. His gaze moved over her. There was the faintest damp spot over her breast, he discovered with interest, a tiny circle of darker black on black that would be practically invisible to anyone who didn't know what he was looking for. But he knew, and enjoyed watching her eyes widen and her arms fold quickly over her chest as she noted where his gaze lingered and realized, too, why.

"Needs must, as the saying goes." Her eyes narrowed, and her voice was wintry.

Jem nodded agreement. It was amusing to realize that of the two, the servant's was now the friendlier expression. Of course, that was like saying, of an asp and a cobra, that one was the friendlier deadly snake.

"We've been takin' care of you in shifts. Fair worn us ragged, you have, especially Miss Gabby here. For meself, I say you ain't worth it."

"Why you? Why not the servants?" Ignoring Jem, he directed his question to Gabriella.

"Because you were out of your head with fever, and chatty with it. Under the circumstances, I thought it best that the servants at least not be made privy to all your secrets."

It was her turn to smile at him. Very malicious that smile was, too. The obvious implication was that *she* now knew all his secrets.

He smiled back at her, and damn the effort involved.

"Very wise of you. If indeed they, or anyone," he gave her a meaningful look, "learned *all* my secrets, I'd probably have to kill them."

That wiped the smile from her face, just as he had intended. Both she and Jem regarded him with stony glares.

"Shame on you, you scoundrel, to go a-threatenin' of one who has saved your life. If Miss Gabby hadn't . . ."

"That's enough, Jem. One cannot expect someone of his stamp to be grateful for care rendered."

The disdainfulness of this reminded him of how haughty she could be. And remembering how haughty she could be made him remember other things about her, too—such as how very *un*haughty she'd been when he'd had his hand, and his mouth, on her breast.

If they'd been alone, that's just what he would have said.

His gaze met hers. Something in his expression must have given her some inkling of what he was thinking, because her cheeks deepened to the color of summer roses.

"Is there water?" he asked abruptly. Embarrassing her in front of her servant was not his intention, and she was too transparent to keep much hidden if he continued to tease her. Besides, he was truly thirsty. His tongue felt like a slab of leather, and his throat was as parched and scratchy as if he'd been swallowing sand.

"Yes, of course." Her annoyance at him was not proof against her nursing instincts, he was glad to discover. She moved toward the bedside table, glancing over her shoulder at her servant at the same time.

"Get a pillow under his head, please. 'Twill make drinking easier."

His eyes met Jem's, and for an instant he and the servant stared at each other measuringly. The old man would just as soon have left him lying as he was; that much was plain in his eyes. For his own part, he didn't much like accepting help at the best of times, and especially not from someone who looked at him as he might a pheasant whose neck he longed to wring. But being flat on his back made him feel vulnerable, and feeling vulnerable was not something he was used to, or enjoyed. And drinking when one was lying flat on one's back carried its own difficulties.

By way of compromise, when Jem, with an incomprehensible but obviously less than complimentary mutter, reached for a pillow, he lifted his head. When a second pillow was pressed into duty beneath the first and the servant straightened, the two of them regarded each other with dislike.

"You might throw some more coal on the fire. It's dying down." With this direction to Jem, Gabriella took the servant's place beside the bed. Sitting down on the edge of it, rather uncomfortably he thought, she took a spoon, dipped it into a glass she held, and carefully conveyed the brimming utensil toward his mouth.

"You're very good at this," he murmured provocatively, remembering how she had once fed him broth and quite unable to resist teasing her. Gabriella's lips compressed—as he had noted before, they were really quite luscious when she didn't have them folded into an angry line—but she continued with her self-appointed task.

His fingers closed around her wrist when he had had his fill of water, trapping her hand in midair as it still clutched the now empty spoon. Her skin was silky to the touch; her bones felt as delicate as if they were made of spun glass.

She stiffened. Her wrist was suddenly rigid beneath his hand. Her eyes were wary as they met his.

"Thank you for your care of me," he said quietly, so that the servant would not hear. The air between them was suddenly charged with electricity. There was confusion, and perhaps even a touch of panic, in her eyes as she registered it. Beneath his fingers, he could feel her pulse begin to race.

Completely of its own volition, his gaze fell to her lips. They were slightly parted as she breathed through them. He distinctly remembered what he had said to her once before: you have the most kissable mouth.

If it had been true then, it was doubly true now.

Even as he focused on her lips, they met in a snug line. Glancing up to meet her gaze, he realized that she was remembering, too. She stood up abruptly, pulling her wrist free of his hold.

"You're welcome," she said, her voice cool, and turned away from him without another word. Putting the glass and spoon down on the bedside table, she spoke to Jem.

"I am going to bed," she said. "Good night."

Then, without so much as another glance or word for him, she turned and disappeared through the door that joined their chambers. He watched with a darkening frown as she closed it carefully behind her.

A moment later, a decided click told him that she had locked it tight.

Left alone with Jem, he eyed the man with disfavor and said, "You may summon Barnet."

❧ 18 ❧

$\mathcal{B}$y that evening, Wickham was measurably better, reportedly sleeping a large part of the time but aware and talking when he was awake. Plainly a corner had been turned. This information, which everyone else seemed to feel was the best of good tidings, Gabby had from Barnet, as she absolutely refused to go next or nigh her pestilent "brother" ever again in her life. He was clearly a conscienceless libertine, and she was just as clearly far too susceptible to his wiles. The only thing to be done was to keep out of his way. Now that there was no longer any question of the patient's life being in danger, she excused herself from her nursing duties without compunction. With Wickham conscious, she judged it safe enough to detail a cadre of servants to assist in his care. His Lordship, according to Barnet, who persisted in giving her regular updates on his progress whether she wished to hear them or not, no longer talked out of turn, so there was little fear of any secrets being inadvertently revealed.

Even while Wickham had been lying stricken abovestairs, visitors, whom one might have supposed would stay away out of respect for the supposedly distressed nature of the household, had called in droves as word of the earl's mishap apparently spread with the speed of a wildfire throughout fashionable London. A missive had arrived from Lady Salcombe, bidding her nieces to present themselves at her house at a certain hour three days hence. Cards had been left by the dozen; with Wickham out of the woods and Gabby now ready to receive them in person, callers flocked to their door. Lord Denby, claiming a close friendship with the stricken earl, was one of the first to be admitted, on the afternoon of the day when Gabby had abandoned her nursing duties. After inquiring politely about his friend's well-being, he spent an agreeable quarter hour flirting madly with Claire.

In this pursuit he was soon joined by the Honorable Mr. Pool, Lord Henry Ravenby, and Sir Barty Crane. These visitors were unexpected, but Gabby, mindful that Claire's marriage was the ultimate object of all her machinations, and would, moreover, free her from any obligation to the rogue abovestairs, received them with all the hospitality Wickham House could muster.

Somewhat less welcome was Lady Ware, who floated into the already crowded drawing room just as the aforementioned gentlemen were taking their leave, bestowed air kisses upon Gabby and Claire as if they were bosom friends, and joined the small cluster of gathered ladies in exclaiming over the earl's accident before settling down to chat of fashionable *on-dits* about town. Although she stayed no longer than the correct quarter of an hour, when she stood up to go Gabby was conscious of a disproportionate feeling of relief. Claire's whispered admiration of the lady's gown—a simple sky-blue silk obviously designed to showcase a bosom that even Gabby had to admit was magnificent—irritated her, but not nearly as much as the note Lady Ware pressed into her hand as she took her leave.

"Something to cheer up poor dear Wickham," Lady Ware said with a naughty smile.

Gabby, accepting the sealed missive because she could think of no civil way to decline it, just managed to summon a smile in return as she battled the urge to crush the *billet doux* in her fist.

It was even more irritating that, even after she passed the note on to Stivers with instructions that it be conveyed to its rightful recipient, Gabby could not seem to rid her hands of the cloying perfume with which it had been scented. Even repeated scrubbings of her fingers, and, ultimately, a complete change of raiment, did not clear the scent from her nostrils.

Which was not, perhaps, quite properly Wickham's fault, but it was certainly something for which Gabby blamed him.

The identities of some of those who came over the next two days were most flattering: Lady Jersey, who was apparently a long-time friend of their aunt's and was accompanied by the Countess Lieven, left her card. That these ladies were patronesses of Almack's, that most august of supper clubs, and as such to be carefully cultivated, was revealed by Twindle with great excitement.

"Only the most select are admitted there, you know," Twindle told Gabby and Claire as they looked over the collection of cards with some awe. "The vulgar call it the Marriage Mart. Nothing could be more fatal to a girl's chances than to be denied admission. If the patronesses should frown on you . . . But there is no chance of that, of course. *No one* could find the least fault with *you,* Miss Claire, or with Miss Gabby or Miss Beth either, for that matter. Nothing shabby genteel *here.*"

"That's as may be, Twindle, but it is quite likely that if our aunt frowns on us Lady Jersey and her like will not be so gracious," Gabby said. She was tired as a result of passing another indifferent night. A slight headache plagued her as well, but none of that mattered when weighed against the need to secure their aunt's support.

Accordingly, four o'clock on the appointed day found Gabby and Claire ascending the steps of Lady Salcombe's house in Berkeley Square. Beth, not yet being out, had been spared this expedition, for which she was thankful. However, when apprised of the program Twindle had in mind for her entertainment instead—visiting some stuffy museum to view Greek marbles that, she said gloomily, could be counted on to put one to the blush, and were, besides, *broken*—she was openly unenthused and muttered something about only Johnny Raws being ripe for such an expedition. This brought down on her head another lecture from Twindle on the evils that were certain to befall young ladies who used vulgar cant instead of the King's English, so Beth was looking very glum indeed as she and Twindle took their leave.

Having just finished recounting this tale for Claire's benefit, Gabby was smiling as the sisters were ushered into their aunt's presence, the footman who had answered the door having determined that she was at home.

Claire was smiling, too, as they walked into the drawing room, as she usually could be counted on to do over Beth's skirmishes with Twindle. Gabby had hoped the story would have just such an effect on her sister, so that Claire would not seem quite stricken with fright when she first appeared before their aunt. It worked, although even with the smile Claire was pale with nerves. Still, Gabby thought proudly, a lovelier picture than Claire presented could scarcely have been imagined. In a simple dress of primrose muslin, caught up under the bosom by gold ribbons and set off by the most charming little chip-straw bonnet, she was a picture to gladden anyone's heart.

Except, perhaps, that of the imposing lady who, setting aside her embroidery, rose to her feet upon their entrance to her drawing room and commenced to look them both over with a highly critical eye.

"Well," she said in a gruff baritone so remarkably like their late father's that even Gabby gave a little start. "I suppose I must count myself honored that you chose to let me know that you had come to town."

✆ 19 ✆

One look at Claire's widened eyes brought Gabby's chin up. However this visit turned out, she refused to allow herself and her sister to be bullied. They'd had enough of that from their father to last several lifetimes.

"Good afternoon, Aunt," Gabby said coolly, holding out her hand. Dressed in deep orange sarsenet with a white lace bonnet perched upon her head, she was conscious of looking very well herself, although not, of course, anything to rival Claire.

Augusta Salcombe's smallish blue eyes narrowed on her nieces. Even in her youth she could never have been a beauty, and now, at what Gabby estimated must be something more than sixty, she was the kind of woman for whom the phrase *battle-ax* had been coined. Nearly six feet tall and mannish in build, she had an angular, large-nosed face topped by a coronet of silver braids. As if to emphasize their color, she was dressed in the palest gray lustring in a style several seasons old.

"Well, I'm glad to see that at least *you're* no milk-and-water miss. You've the sense to dress your age, too, which many females who are at their last prayers do not." She shook

Gabby's hand as she uttered this backhanded compliment, then turned her gimlet gaze upon Claire. Poor Claire almost visibly quaked, and instinctively dropped a small curtsy. Lady Salcombe harrumphed. "You have the look of your mother, girl. A beauty, she was, but a complete pea goose. Which goes without saying, I suppose. She wed Wickham, didn't she?" She gave a short barking laugh. "It's to be hoped that you're not as silly as she was." Her gaze moved back to Gabby. "You, too, have a look of your mother, but if Sophia ever had a spine *I* never saw any evidence of it. I've a notion you do, however. Well, sit down, sit down, the pair of you."

They sat, and refreshments were brought in. When they were sipping tea from tiny porcelain cups, Lady Salcombe looked at Gabby.

"I've heard Wickham shot himself, or some such tomfool thing. What's the truth of it?"

Gabby told her the version that had been given out for popular consumption, and Lady Salcombe clucked disapprovingly.

"What a mutton-headed thing to have done. It's to be hoped he's got more in his cockloft than that, in the general way of things. He's the head of our house now, after all, and if he's such a gudgeon as that makes him sound he's likely to be an embarrassment to us all. Well. He's a handsome scamp, from all I've heard, but that doesn't take away from the fact that he *is* a scamp: He's been in town for more than a fortnight, and hasn't had the common courtesy to pay a call upon his aunt. What have you to say to that, eh?" Her gaze fixed accusingly on Gabby.

"Why, that I should hate to be held responsible for my brother's sins, ma'am," Gabby responded tranquilly, taking a sip of her tea. Lady Salcombe laughed.

"I like you, Gabriella, and I'm surprised at that. Your father—well, that's neither here nor there now that he's gone, but you must know that we never did get on. Well, I didn't even go to his funeral. You should have read the letter he wrote me when I offered to bring you out. Such stuff. Well." Lady Salcombe shook her head, then frowned. Her gaze ran over Gabby from head to toe. "He said you were crippled?"

"Gabby is not," Claire spoke up with a touch of indignation. Knowing how intimidated she was—Claire had never been the least hand at standing up to bullies—Gabby smiled faintly at her sister, then directed her gaze back to their aunt.

"I have a limp, ma'am."

"I didn't notice it."

"It is only noticeable when she is tired, or—or sick, or must walk long distances. She is certainly not crippled." Claire's cheeks had pinkened becomingly in her sister's defense.

Lady Salcombe looked hard at Claire. "So you do have a tongue. I was beginning to wonder. Isn't there another one of you? I thought Matthew had three daughters."

"Beth is with her governess today. She is fifteen."

"Hmph. I should like to see her."

"We would be happy to have you visit us in Grosvenor Square," Gabby said smoothly.

"I may just do that. Salcombe's dead these ten years, you know, and I've no children. Besides the two of you, and your sister and brother, my closest relatives are Thomas and his girls. *Not* relations with whom I care to spend a great deal of time, as you may imagine if you are acquainted with them. I have it in mind to get to know the four of you better."

"We would be honored, ma'am." Gabby smiled at her aunt.

Lady Salcombe set her cup down, and gave Gabby a shrewd look. "Well, I don't believe in beating about the bush and never have, so you may as well tell me plainly: Have you come to town hoping to make a splash?"

Gabby put down her own cup. "Yes, ma'am, we have."

Lady Salcombe looked a visibly uncomfortable Claire over from head to toe, then glanced back at Gabby. "Well, she'll puff off easy enough, and may look as high as she chooses, too, unless I very much miss my guess. 'Twill be harder to find a husband for you, but I don't despair of it by any means. A widower with children, perhaps. You *do* like children?"

Claire's eyes widened, and she made a choked sound that Gabby at least recognized for a hastily stifled laugh. When Lady Salcombe glanced at her with a gathering frown, however, Claire turned the sound, with great presence of mind, into a cough.

"Yes, ma'am," Gabby responded, successfully diverting Lady Salcombe from Claire's small lapse. "I do like children, but in any case I don't seek a husband for myself. We are here in London to establish Claire."

"Hmmph. All females seek husbands, my dear. It is the way of our sex. But that is neither here nor there. I presume you've come to me to ask my help in launching you and your sister into the *ton*?"

Gabby had meant to broach the subject tactfully. But Lady Salcombe, who was far from anything she had expected, seemed to have no use for tact. The only possible defense, Gabby thought, was to be as direct as she was herself.

"Yes, ma'am."

Lady Salcombe actually smiled. The effect was rather like watching the sun rise over a particularly bleak landscape, bestowing on it a warmth it was never meant to possess. Out of the corner of her eye Gabby caught Claire openly staring at their aunt with a kind of bemused wonder. Claire must have felt Gabby's look, because she recovered herself almost instantly and glanced away.

"You've a great deal of sense," Lady Salcombe said approvingly to Gabby, who, unlike Claire, managed to preserve a serene expression. "I like that in a girl. I detest today's mealymouthed misses, let me tell you." This was accompanied by a darkling glance at Claire. "Well, I'll do it. I'll sponsor you both into the *ton*, *on* the condition that you let yourselves be guided by me. Sally Jersey shall provide you with vouchers for Almack's—she said she was going to call on you, by the by; I'm glad you had the sense to come see me before she did so, for now you may tell her that you're under my aegis—and Wickham shall give you a come-out ball. 'Twill require a great deal of work on my part—see to it that you're properly grateful, young misses—but I feel I owe it to the name. Plus I expect to be wonderfully diverted by it all." A sly twinkle crept into her eyes. "Maud is bringing out her youngest this year: Desdemona, or some such idiotic name, don't you know. Won't she be green when she sees this one?" She nodded at Claire, and suddenly looked almost cheerful. Claire blushed at the obvious implication.

Gabby smiled at Lady Salcombe. "Thank you, ma'am. We accept your offer most gratefully, do we not, Claire? You are too kind. But as to Wickham's giving us a ball . . ."

"I told you you were to be guided by me." Lady Salcombe sent Gabby a martial look. "If I say there is to be a ball, then there will be one. Everything bang-up, or I won't do it at all. I shall talk to Wickham myself."

An irresistible picture of Lady Salcombe browbeating her supposed nephew into providing a ball for his unwanted "sisters" made Gabby smile. She was still smiling as she got to her feet, the allotted time for a call being well past, and all she had hoped to accomplish being done.

"He won't be able to resist you, ma'am. No one could, I'm sure."

Claire rose in Gabby's wake, and Lady Salcombe did, too. "I should make you aware at the outset that flattery is abhorrent to me," Lady Salcombe said, fixing Gabby with a stern look. "Although it is true that I *am* held to be most persuasive, I believe. Well. We may as well get started without delay. The season has already begun. I will call for you this evening in my carriage and we will attend the opera together. You may bring the young one, too, if you like. *That* will let everyone know that you are in town, and under my protection. By tomorrow, your knocker should be beating a hole in your door. What else, what else? A more fashionable hairstyle, Gabriella, if you please. I shall send someone around. You, Claire, should strive to cultivate the art of polite conversation. An inability to string more than two words together at a time may be considered a sad fault, believe me. I know either of you will not mind me giving you a hint. And you may call me Aunt Augusta, the pair of you."

"We are honored, ma'am," Gabby said truthfully, swallowing any other of the possible responses that occurred to her, and dutifully pecked the weathered cheek presented to her. Claire followed suit without comment, and was thus sped on her way by a testy admonition to find her tongue before she went out again in company. Thus the sisters went away from Berkeley Square, their aunt's promise to call for them at nine o'clock that same evening ringing in their ears.

"What a dreadful woman," Claire gasped when they were safely bestowed in the carriage. "I declare, just the thought of having her take us about makes me feel ready to sink."

"You need pay her no mind," Gabby said absently. "Indeed, I count it very fortunate that she has agreed to help us. With her to sponsor us, you will be the toast of London, Claire."

"But Gabby, she terrifies me. She reminds me so of Papa I can scarcely think when she is near."

Gabby, roused from her reverie by this revelation, turned a softened gaze upon her sister and admitted that the resemblance was both uncanny and unfortunate. To make matters worse, she thought, Claire had always been too gentle natured to bear up well under harsh treatment, and Lady Salcombe—Aunt Augusta—was nothing if not abrasive.

"I shan't let her bully you, I promise. Remember, she has no authority over us. She is not our guardian, after all."

"No, Wickham is that, isn't he?" Claire sounded comforted by the reflection. Gabby, who had never thought of the situation in just that light, was instantly appalled. It was too horribly true: in the eyes of the world, the snake in earl's clothing lying at that moment sick in the bedchamber next to hers was their guardian, and had the authority to order their lives as he pleased.

The carriage reached Grosvenor Square just then. Once inside, Gabby and Claire went to their respective chambers to put off their outer garments. Still feeling out of sorts as a result of Claire's epiphany, Gabby was pulling off her gloves and thinking unpleasant thoughts as she walked along the corridor to her apartment.

A muffled shriek from Wickham's room arrested her progress just a few feet before she reached her own door. A muffled *feminine* shriek. Gabby froze, listening. There was no other sound. The hush of a well-ordered household descended as soon as the shriek died away.

But there was no denying what she had heard.

Was the man so depraved that he had taken to attacking the chambermaids? Or was he so deadened to all sense of propriety as to—as to *entertain* one such as Lady Ware in his bedroom? Was he even now indulging—or attempting to indulge—in the kind of vice he had tried to force on her?

In broad daylight? In *Wickham House*?

Gabby couldn't help it. She had to know. If it *was* a chambermaid, poor hapless creature, a rescue had to be launched. If it was Lady Ware or another of her ilk—well, such immorality had no place in a nobleman's household, and so she meant to inform him as soon as she decently could. But the man in the earl's chamber was no nobleman, she reminded herself, and no gentleman, either, as she knew to her cost.

He was, however, to all intents and purposes the earl.

Before she could determine what, if anything, was best to be done with that circumstance in mind, another sound from beyond the door made her eyes widen. Another scream, perhaps, *muffled* this time?

Was it possible that he really *was* ravishing one of the maids?

Feeling quite guilty, and even more foolish, she crept right up to the earl's bedroom door. Looking swiftly up and down the corridor to make certain that she was unobserved, she leaned forward and pressed her ear to the smooth wooden panel.

There were definitely two people in the bedroom: a male and a female. She could hear the murmur of their voices quite distinctly, although she could not make out what was being said. The male was, of course, Wickham. The question was, who was the female, and what was he doing with her?

Her imagination boggled at the possibilities.

Gabby heard Wickham say something that ended with a laugh, then listened very hard for the female's reply. If it sounded normal, as though the creature, whoever she was, was not in any distress, her best course of action would be to simply creep away and pretend that this embarrassing interlude had never occurred.

After all, no matter how much his licentiousness might offend her, she could hardly order a lightskirt out of what was, in the eyes of everyone save herself and Jem, the bounder's own house.

Realizing that, Gabby practically gnashed her teeth.

Wickham's companion spoke. Gabby listened to the giggling voice, and felt the hair stand straight up on the back of her neck.

She knew that voice as well as she knew her own.

The female in the bedroom with Wickham was *Beth*.

❧ 20 ❧

The door, fortunately, was not locked. Gabby turned the knob and took three quick steps inside the earl's apartment as the identity of the owner of that voice exploded on her consciousness. Beth—if he had done aught to Beth . . .

Heart pounding, eyes enormous, one hand still clinging to the knob, she then stopped in her tracks, goggling at the pair on the bed.

Beth sat on the near edge of the enormous mattress, back to the door, her red hair, which she wore caught up by a white ribbon at the crown, tumbling in schoolgirl ringlets around her shoulders. Her dainty, yellow-sprigged muslin had been hiked up by her careless posture—she sat leaning forward, with one leg curled beneath her—to reveal a plump, white-stockinged leg almost to the knee. If she was in distress, she gave no sign of it. Instead, she appeared to be engaged in examining, with every indication of intense concentration, a number of playing cards which were spread out before her on the coverlet.

"Beth!" It was a strangled-sounding gasp.

At this, Beth, who was clearly preoccupied, spared her a quick, over-the-shoulder glance.

"Hello, Gabby," she said, with an airy wave and a marked lack of concern. Her attention returned immediately to the cards. "Did you see our aunt?"

Gabby drew a deep, shaken breath. Her heart began to slow to its normal rhythm. Her knees felt weak. Beyond Gabby, Wickham met her gaze, quizzing her wickedly with his eyes. Gabby felt her skin begin to heat as she remembered the circumstances under which they had last met. The wicked beast had used her unforgivably—and she had permitted it. No, if truth were to be told she had revelled in it.

Determined not to let him guess how deeply mortifying she found it just to be in his presence again, she lifted her brows and coolly met his gaze.

"*Did* you see our aunt?" he asked with every indication of polite interest. Gabby, however, was not fooled. She knew when she was being teased.

"Certainly I did," she said sweetly, glad to discover that she was in full command of her voice. "And very formidable she is indeed. She calls on you tomorrow, by the by, and means to take you to task for not yet having had the courtesy to visit her."

"Unfortunately, I am confined to my bed and cannot, as yet, receive visitors," he replied with aplomb. "Our aunt will have to save her scold for another occasion."

"You received me," Beth pointed out in an abstracted tone as she continued to study the cards. "And Gabby, too, for that matter."

"Ah, but you are my sisters, which denotes a different degree of kinship entirely. And I did not exactly receive either of you, though you are very welcome, of course. You both just—er—arrived."

Gabby shot him a withering look. His eyes twinkled at

her, and for an instant, just an instant, the sheer unexpected charm of the man caught her off guard. Gabby almost forgot what a rogue he was as she teetered on the verge of succumbing to the amusement in his gaze. He was such a handsome scoundrel. . . .

The thought acted like a dash of cold water over her rattled senses, and she recovered enough to frown balefully at him. He was sitting up in bed, propped on pillows, with a fistful of cards fanned out in one hand. At least, Gabby was relieved to see, he was decently clad, in an elegant maroon dressing gown which was tied carelessly over his nightshirt. The bedspread covered the lower half of his body to the waist. He looked surprisingly healthy for one who had so lately been on the brink of death; for this he could no doubt thank the natural swarthiness of his skin. His black hair, grown too long over the course of his indisposition, waved back from his forehead in casual disorder, and several days' worth of black stubble added a piratical edge to his grin.

"Did you want me for something, Gabby?" Beth asked without looking around.

"Beth, my child, I am afraid you flatter yourself. Doubtless *Gabby* barged into my chamber so precipitously because she was looking for *me*." His eyes teased as they met hers. Gabby realized that he knew perfectly well the suspicion that had brought her bursting into his room. "Behold me at your service, sister."

She glared at him before transferring her attention to Beth.

"Beth, dear, *what* are you doing?" This question, uttered by Gabby, was prompted by a shift in her sister's posture. With sublime disregard for both the proprieties and the amount of leg she was revealing, Beth now lay sideways across the bed, her head propped on one hand, while she appeared to count the cards lined up before her.

"Marcus is teaching me to play piquet," she said, clearly missing the point of Gabby's question. "It is the most vexing thing. I have already lost my ring, my locket, and nearly all the pin money I had left over from shopping the other day. He is not enough of a gentleman to let me win, and so far has very meanly taken every trick."

Following Beth's comically despairing gesture, Gabby's gaze went to the little pile of her belongings nestled in a hollow in the bedspread.

"I told you when we began that you could expect no mercy from me." Wickham smiled faintly as his gaze flicked over Beth.

"Yes, but I could not believe you meant it. I am your little sister, after all."

"Very true. You should have reminded me earlier. I might then have pointed out to you that you have a seven hiding under that queen, thus giving you a tierce and the trick."

Beth looked, saw, and squealed indignantly as she pounced on the card in question. "A cheat! You should have said. Oh, give me back my locket! It was not lost in fair play."

Wickham grinned at her as she snatched her locket from the pile and reclasped it about her neck. Watching, Gabby was struck by how very *engaging* he looked as he bantered with Beth. If she had not known the truth, she would never have taken him for the unprincipled charlatan he was.

She would, in fact, have taken him for the earl of Wickham, Beth's indulgent older brother.

"I thought Twindle was taking you to see the Elgin Marbles this afternoon," Gabby said to her sister with a shortness brought on by her disapproval of the situation in which she found her instead.

"Oh, she did, but was there ever anything more famous? The museum was closed. And then we went for a walk in the park, and she turned her ankle, so we had to come home. She went to her chamber to soak it as soon as we arrived. There was nothing to do, so I thought I would look in on Marcus to see how he did. He was very glad to see me, too. He was quite bored, weren't you?" She glanced up at Wickham for confirmation. "And he has been telling me all about life in Ceylon."

"Have you indeed?" Gabby asked, discovering that she quite enjoyed the idea of Beth putting Wickham on the spot.

"Certainly I have," he said with aplomb. When Beth's attention returned to the cards once more, he looked over her head at Gabby. "I know I am new to the family, but I *had* expected that my sisters would at least inquire about my welfare once in a while."

The reproach in his voice—*mock* reproach, Gabby knew—was quite wasted on her. Beth, however, glanced at him sympathetically.

"It is just that we are not in the *way* of having a brother," she explained. "I expect we'll soon get the knack of it, however."

"Just as I will soon, er, *get the knack* of having sisters," he responded gravely. Beth nodded as though agreeing to her end of a pact.

Gabby, on the other hand, watched Wickham toy with Beth's affections and was—impotently—infuriated.

"Beth, get up at once. To be lounging like that on Wickham's bed is not at all the thing, let me tell you." Her annoyance with Wickham made her voice sharper than she had intended.

Involved with rearranging her cards, Beth cast her a distracted glance. "Oh, Gabby, don't be so stuffy. I declare, you're worse than Twindle about preaching propriety. Remember, if you please, that Marcus is our brother."

Gabby looked at her sister, opened her mouth, and shut it again with a snap. What could she say to that? The truth would ruin them all.

Wickham was watching her. As Beth returned her attention to the cards, he said softly, "There is really no harm in it, you know."

Meeting his gaze, Gabby found herself, much against her will, somewhat reassured.

Beth let out a sudden squeal of delight, and looked up. "Marcus, I have four of a kind."

Wickham's gaze flicked down to his own cards. "Not good. Much as I hate to concede victory to a novice, it appears you take the trick again."

Beth whooped with joy. Smiling faintly, Wickham put down his hand, then fished a coin from a pile near his elbow and handed it over.

Gabby looked at the pair of them consideringly. Her sister was now sitting fully upon the bed, both legs curled beneath her, her body close enough to Wickham's to brush against his bedspread-covered legs every time either of them moved. For an unrelated pair, to be caught in such a posture would be positively ruinous. Even for a brother and sister—which, she reminded herself, these two emphatically were not—the propriety of the situation was problematic. But clearly, despite her own warning, Beth had no intimation that anything was in any way amiss; and for all that Gabby considered Wickham a reprobate of almost frightening proportions, she was now ready to acquit him of having nefarious designs on Beth. Still, she could not in good conscience allow Beth to make herself at home on his bed.

"Beth, it is time to be getting ready for dinner, you

know. And you might want to take extra pains with your dress. We'll be going to the opera afterward." This was said with the air of one rattling a pie plate of corn before the nose of a balky horse.

"The opera! Really?" Beth, never having attended before, was not an opera fan; she was, however, always glad for any excuse to sample the seemingly limitless delights of the metropolis. She glanced around at Gabby with delight. "How famous."

Wickham, on the other hand, frowned slightly at Gabby. "You will hardly go to the opera without an escort, or a chaperone. And I understand that Miss Twindlesham is very nearly unable to walk."

Gabby gave him a glinting smile that was not one whit removed, in spirit, from sticking out her tongue. To hear a scoundrel such as he preaching propriety was *almost* amusing. "Should it be necessary, I am old enough to chaperone my sisters, I assure you."

"Are you indeed? And how old is that, pray?"

"Why, she is five and twenty. Do you not know our ages, Marcus?" Beth looked up from her cards, sounding scandalized.

"My memory is most lamentable upon occasion," Wickham apologized, recovering gracefully.

"Gabby is five and twenty, Claire will be nineteen in June, and I am turned fifteen."

"I will strive to bear that in mind." His gaze returned to Gabby. "Nevertheless, five and twenty or no, it will not serve. The three of you cannot go alone. It is no place for unaccompanied young ladies."

His tone implied a familiarity with the opera that Gabby could not suppose came from a love of music. As her father and his guests had brought a great many female companions to Hawthorne Hall over the years without being particularly reticent about their purpose or origins, Gabby was well aware that the opera was a chief place for gentlemen—or what passed for gentlemen—to pick up mistresses.

Her lip curled at him. "It is fortunate, then, that our aunt goes with us, is it not? We may thus be sure of being spared the attentions of those who are less than gentlemanly." She smiled at him. "If you'll excuse me, I must go check on Twindle. Beth, Wickham is growing weary, I am sure, and would appreciate some time to rest. He is recovering from a serious injury, remember."

"I know, I know."

Waved blithely away by her sister, Gabby bestowed no more than another hard look on Wickham before leaving them to their game. The situation was growing unexpectedly complicated, she reflected with a frown. When she had made the decision to go along with this farce, she had not foreseen that her sisters, not knowing the truth, might actually treat the blackguard as though he were their true brother. Nor had she foreseen that Wickham might attempt to play that role. She foresaw all sorts of complications ahead, but could think of nothing to do about them.

Except, of course, worry, which went without saying.

She dropped by her own room, where she found Mary waiting for her. Changing her dress and generally tidying herself was quick work. Glancing at herself in the mirror afterward, she made a face. Her aunt thought she needed a new hairstyle, did she? Well, she probably did.

Some half an hour later, having left Twindle amply supplied with sympathy and cold compresses, she returned to her own corridor to find the door to Wickham's room ajar, just as she had left it. As it was nearly time for dinner now, she felt Beth truly deserved the scold she was about to deliver. Gabby tightened her lips, glanced into the room—and discovered Claire, pirouetting gaily in her rose silk gown for Wickham's approval.

The first thing Gabby noticed, upon once again rushing into his chamber in defense of a sister, was that the expression in Wickham's eyes when he looked at Claire was very different from the one he wore when he looked at Beth. Watching him watch her beautiful sister, Gabby felt every protective hackle she possessed go on full alert.

❦ 21 ❦

$\mathcal{T}$he wolf might have been content to wear sheep's clothing when he was with Beth, but now that Claire was within his orbit he was once again revealed for the beast he truly was, Gabby thought furiously.

"Claire, dear, what are you doing in here?" With the best will in the world Gabby could not keep the sharpness from her voice.

Wickham greeted her with a slow, devilish grin.

"Oh, Gabby, Beth has had the best notion. Instead of leaving Wickham to eat alone, we will dine with him, here in his room. She will be back as soon as she has changed her dress."

Gabby was taken aback. This was unexpected. And definitely not a good idea. The last thing she wanted was for her sisters, either of them, to spend more time with the conniving scoundrel than was absolutely necessary. And the danger to Claire might well be acute. From all available evidence, their false brother was not only an unrepentant criminal but a lecherous rake as well.

Determinedly Gabby shook her head. "No," she said in the brisk tone she used when she was exercising her authority as mistress of the house. "I'm afraid that won't be possible. We will eat in the dining room as usual. Wickham will no doubt survive without our company." Seeing Claire's eyes widen in surprise, Gabby cast about in her mind for some sort of excuse to soften what, to her sister, must sound like an uncharacteristically autocratic decree. "He is, after all, not fully recovered, and I'm sure none of us wish to overtax his strength. Besides, it will make far too much work for the servants."

She added this last as if it were a clencher.

Wickham smiled at her. "But I've already given permission," he said, too gently. "And instructed Stivers to set up a table here in my room. You need not worry your head about me, you know. Enjoying my sisters' company during a delightful meal *en famille* will no doubt prove therapeutic, rather than the reverse."

Gabby stared at him. He held her gaze with as much calm assurance as if he were indeed the earl. In that moment Gabby realized the enormity of what she had done. By recognizing this imposter as Wickham, she had granted him full authority over this house and everything in it. Over Hawthorne Hall. Over all of the earl of Wickham's holdings. Over her sisters, whose legal guardian he now was.

Over herself.

Gabby felt like screaming. She felt like tearing out her hair with both hands. She was well and truly caught in a trap of her own making. What, oh what, had she done?

The knave could order things just as he chose, and there was not a thing, not one blessed thing, she could do to prevent him.

Except tell the truth, and in doing so damn herself as well as him.

In the event, except for two brief exchanges, it was, despite Gabby's expectations to the contrary, a pleasant meal.

The first exception came when Claire asked Wickham if his wound still pained him very much.

He had, with Barnet's aid, moved from the bed to one of the big wing chairs which had been pulled up to a small square table two footmen had carried in. Covered with a linen cloth, and set with china and crystal and silver that sparkled in the candlelight, it made a very charming venue for a meal. Claire, in exceptional looks as she always was when she found herself in company where she felt at ease, had roses in her cheeks to match the color of her gown as she blossomed under his easy charm. She sat at Wickham's right hand, laughing often and appearing to hang on his every word; Beth, giggling and chatting and very young indeed in white muslin, sat on his left. Her eyes glowed with what appeared to be a severe case of hero worship every time she looked at him, which was, basically, all the time. Gabby, in soft gray-blue crepe, sat opposite her nemesis, feeling distinctly out of sorts as she watched his bewitching of her sisters with a jaundiced eye. To his credit, he was equally attentive to both, and if there was an extra degree of appreciation in his gaze when he looked at Claire, Gabby thought that it would pass unnoticed by any observer less keenly alert to trouble than herself. Of the sisters, she was the only one who merited a marked difference in treatment from him. He addressed few remarks to her during the meal, and, when he happened to glance her way, his gaze held what she finally decided was a coolly assessing quality, rather than the laughing warmth he lavished on Claire and Beth. For her part, this suited her very well. It was, she thought, an acknowledgment on his part of their adversarial status. He might, with vile falsehood as a facilitator, win over the younger girls, but he would never make a conquest of her, and it was as well that he knew better than to try.

During the course of the meal, she was, therefore, an

oasis of silence in a storm of gaiety. She spoke when spoken to, smiled at her sisters when they glanced her way, ate her meal, and listened with growing irritation as the lying wretch responded with imperturbable good humor as the younger girls peppered him with questions about his life in Ceylon. She refused to notice how handsome he looked when he laughed, or how well the maroon dressing gown became his dark coloring, or how broad his shoulders were as they seemed to fill nearly all the space from one wing of his chair to the other. But something in her silent gaze must have penetrated his genial facade, and finally nettled him, because his glances at her became more frequent as the meal wound down, and less friendly. When Claire asked about his wound he leaned back in his chair, twirled his wine glass between his fingers, and responded in a way clearly intended, to Gabby's ears at least, to pay her back for not fawning over him as her sisters did.

"To tell the truth," he said with a gleaming smile for Claire and nary a glance for Gabby. "I find I'm more troubled by a bite on my shoulder. From some creature that had the temerity to crawl in bed with me, no doubt."

Gabby stiffened as the meaning of that home thrust burst upon her. It was all she could do not to react in any other way. Her eyes met his for a pregnant instant as the events that had led up to that bite replayed themselves in her mind. You cad! You bounder! You churl! she raged at him inwardly, as their gazes held. Then, to her horror, and despite exercising every bit of willpower she possessed to prevent it from happening, she felt hot color begin to creep over her face as the memory became too vivid to be borne. To cover her confusion, she picked up her glass and took a sip. The wine was sweet, fruity, and utterly tasteless in her mouth.

His eyes gleamed at her. A faint, satisfied smile curved

his lips. Gabby, seething, blushing, and helpless to do anything about either, realized to her fury that she was being
purposefully baited.

"A bedbug, do you mean?" Beth asked in all innocence.
She glanced at Gabby, who prayed that the red glow of the
fire was sufficient to mask her heightened color from unsuspecting eyes. "Never say that we have them here."

"A bedbug. Yes." Wickham still smiled only faintly, but
his eyes laughed at Gabby as they met her furious, morti-
fied gaze. To add insult to injury, he ruefully rubbed the
place on his shoulder where she had bitten him. "That is
certainly what it must have been. A particularly vicious
one, too. Rapacious creatures, bedbugs."

"Mrs. Bucknell must be instructed to air the sheets,"
Claire said with horror, also glancing at Gabby.

Gabby kept a firm rein on her temper. To openly lose it
would be to reveal far too much. "Wickham is mistaken, I
am sure. Mrs. Bucknell would certainly be most upset to
have her housekeeping called into question. I think we can
safely discount the possibility of bedbugs in any establishment she presides over." Her gaze met Wickham's. "Possibly
you are confusing a bite for something else. Another one of
your self-inflicted wounds, perhaps."

"Perhaps," he conceded, grinning wickedly at her. It was
not his intention, Gabby realized with mixed fury and relief, to reveal her disgrace to her sisters. Instead he wanted
to keep the knowledge of the shameful things he had
done—and the even more shameful way she had responded—between the two of them. So he could continue
to torment her in private, Gabby reflected grimly, like a
small boy prodding a bug with a pin.

Under her direction, the conversation was directed into
more innocuous channels. Claire was perfectly willing to

talk of fashions, the flattering number of invitations that had already been received, and the interesting intelligence that Cousin Thomas's daughter Desdemona was also to make her come-out this year. Beth, for her part, had found the park where she had taken her abortive walk with Twindle to be delightful, and recommended that her sisters explore it without delay.

"The fashionable hour to be seen there is between five and six," Wickham said. Gabby, who had indulged in a malicious hope that he would be heartily bored by the sisters' talk of matters that were popularly supposed to be of interest only to females, got the first inkling that she was about to suffer retribution when he glanced at her with a smirk and then, quite deliberately, switched his gaze to Claire. "When I am able to do so, which I devoutly hope will be in the next few days, I'll take you driving in the park. I took delivery of a new curricle on the day of my accident, and have not yet had a chance to try it out."

"That would be delightful," Claire said with a sparkling smile, while Gabby did her best to conceal her dismay; then Claire glanced at her younger sister. "Beth may come with us, and show us the lookout point she and Twindle were trying to climb up to when Twindle twisted her ankle."

"Well, actually *I* was climbing up to it," Beth said apologetically. "Twindle was trying to prevent me. She said I should fall."

"And so fell instead, thus proving indeed that good deeds are invariably punished," murmured Wickham, his expression bland in the face of Claire's transparent assumption that Beth was as welcome a participant in his proposed expedition as she was herself. Gabby sent him a gloating glance in which the word *checkmate* was fairly shouted, and, pushing back her chair, got to her feet.

"Our cozy family dinner has been most delightful, but you must excuse us now, Wickham," Gabby said with assumed affability, and glanced at her sisters. "Lady Salcombe—Aunt Augusta—is to call for us at nine, remember. I will meet you both downstairs in three quarters of an hour."

As Beth got tangled up in a heartfelt apology to Wickham for proposing to leave him to his own devices for the rest of the evening, Gabby crossed the room. She was nearly at the door when Wickham called after her.

"Gabriella."

She turned, looking at him with raised brows.

"Have you hurt your leg? I notice you are limping."

The question hit Gabby with all the force of a blow. Just why it should bother her so much that he should notice and comment on the hesitation in her carefully calibrated gait, she didn't know, nor even want to try to analyze. But it did bother her; she couldn't help it, although she knew that caring because she was not perfect was as useless as wishing she could fly. Try though she might to move normally, there was always going to be a halt to her step, and that was just a fact of her life.

Still, with Wickham's questioning gaze upon her, she could not help hearing her father's voice echoing from the misty past: *Poor pathetic creature, what good are you to anyone now? 'Twould have been better for us all had I just had you drowned at birth.*

Even after all this time, after her father had been dead and in the ground for the past eighteen months, those words still had the power to hurt. As did Wickham's gaze on her, probing the cause of her less than graceful gait, recognizing and making a point of her defect.

But just as she had refused to slink away from her father's scorn, so she now refused to allow Wickham to see how his question had caused her to shrivel up inside.

Her chin came up a notch, and she looked him in the eye. "I have been limping most of my life. I broke my leg when I was twelve, and it never healed properly."

"Did you not know that Gabby was *lame*, Marcus?" Beth asked, amazed. Knowing that Beth accepted her limp as a part of her, and intended the statement to be no more hurtful than an assertion that Gabby had gray eyes, Gabby nevertheless winced inwardly at having her affliction so crudely named. Beth, in addition to all her many wonderful traits, had ever been one to call a spade a spade. Which had both its good points and its bad.

"Gabby is not lame," Claire said fiercely, glaring at her younger sister. "She has a weak leg. If you are lame, you need a cane to get around, or a Bath chair, or—or someone to be forever assisting you." Her gaze shifted to Wickham. "Gabby may limp sometimes, but she is perfectly mobile, I assure you."

Gabby glanced at her next sister and smiled, her eyes full of warm affection. In that instant, instead of the ravishingly beautiful young woman Claire was now, she saw the tangle-haired moppet her sister had been at five years old. Claire had been the first one to reach her after the accident, the one to crouch beside her and hold her hand while one of the housemaids ran for help. Gabby had always known, although she never really liked to think about it, that her accident had had a profound effect on Claire.

"Don't be such a mutton head, Claire. I wasn't insulting Gabby. She's my sister as much as yours."

"You're a great looby if you think it doesn't hurt her to be called lame." Claire got to her feet abruptly, her chair making a scraping sound as it slid over the floor.

Beth stood, too. "Well, *you* . . ."

"That's enough." Wickham interrupted the rapidly escalating conflict with as much authority as if he did it all the time. His gaze met Gabby's. She could detect no pity for her there, and its absence made her breathe a little—just a little—easier.

He continued: "The world is full of coincidences, it seems. I, too, have a damaged leg. It was broken in three places when a horse fell on it. It took forever to heal, and still pains me when it rains."

"In general, mine only pains me when it has been subject to abuse. If I were to fall down so that I injured it, for instance, or if something heavy were to land upon it, it would hurt for some days afterward." The polite smile with which she said this was accompanied by a darkling look that laid the blame for her current pronounced limp squarely at his door.

He smiled at her. The silent message was, *your point.*

Gabby's attention shifted to her sisters. "My dears, if we don't hasten, we shall be late, and it would never do to keep our aunt waiting."

With that reminder, Claire and Beth forgot all about Gabby's leg, which was to them very old news indeed, and, with pretty *good-nights* to Wickham, hurried from the room. Gabby stayed just long enough to pull the bell rope to summon the footmen to come and clear away the table. Then she, too, headed for her room.

"Gabriella."

She was walking through the door when his voice stopped her. Glancing back, she saw that he was standing on his own, holding onto the back of the chair in which he had been sitting for support. Instinctively she started to caution him to sit down again, and to warn him against overtaxing his strength. But he was none of her concern, she reminded herself, and instead of doing either of those things she merely lifted her brows at him questioningly.

"Perhaps one of these days you and I can show each other our scars." Uttered in a soft voice, it sounded like no more than the merest pleasantry. It took a few seconds for the underlying lasciviousness of the suggestion to penetrate. When it did, she felt her spine stiffen and her eyes widen with outrage.

He grinned at her, a deliberately mocking grin that acted like a spark to the fuse of her temper.

"You are a disgusting lecher," she hissed. "Stay away from me, and stay away from my sisters."

With that she turned her back and walked with careful dignity out of his view. It was only later, as she was taking her seat in her aunt's box at the opera while Claire and Beth exclaimed over the many fascinating sights to be found in the pit below, that she realized that his infuriating coarseness had likely been done on purpose and had served one very useful function: it had stopped her from feeling like the *poor, pathetic creature* her father had named her, and given her back her dignity.

☙ 22 ❧

*H*is careful plans had been blown to hell, he reflected wryly while, as part of a concerted effort to regain his strength, he walked with slow steps around the perimeter of his bedchamber. Knowing that time was of the essence, finding himself laid by the heels was driving him mad. And Gabriella was the cause of the whole damned fiasco. From the moment he had first laid eyes on her, in her ugly black dress with her nose stuck up in the air, he had known she was trouble. What he hadn't known was just how much trouble she was going to be.

She'd threatened his cover, defied him, shot him, excited him, and now she'd made him feel guilty besides.

If he'd known her limp was a permanent affliction, he would never have called attention to it as he had, he thought, faintly aggrieved that he *hadn't* known. But when he'd seen the hesitation in her gait as she'd crossed his bedchamber, his instant fear was that he was somehow responsible for the injury. Had he hurt her as he'd snatched her up in the hall that first night, perhaps, or later, when she'd fallen off his bed? The thought had troubled him enormously. Whatever else happened, he didn't want to cause hurt to

Gabriella. But he *had* hurt her, by calling attention to the limp that was, most of the time, not noticeable. He'd seen the stricken look in her eyes, and so he'd set out to banish it with the most objectionable comment he could call to mind. He'd succeeded, too. He'd made her angry instead.

Which was, he supposed, an improvement.

"Uh, Cap'n, what would you be wantin' me do with this?" Barnet, who was in the process of changing the bed linens, held up one of Belinda's musk-drenched missives. A footman had brought it up to him when it had arrived earlier, and, as he'd been in bed at the time, he'd given it a quick perusal there. When Beth had bounced in on him without warning, he had tucked it beneath the covers and promptly forgotten all about it.

"Put it in the drawer with the others," he said with a shrug. Belinda had really been a most faithful correspondent, he reflected. Indeed, he was quite sure that he had only Gabriella's daunting presence in the house to thank for Belinda's failure to visit him personally during his convalescence. The type of naughtiness involved in calling on an ailing gentleman in his bedchamber—and entertaining him most royally there—was the breath of life to Belinda. Only the presence of a lady of the house possessed of a quelling mien, the demeanor of a duchess, and the eyes of a hawk—to wit, his oldest "sister"—would be enough to keep Belinda away.

"The bed's ready, Cap'n." Barnet gave a last twitch to the covers and straightened, looking at him expectantly.

He grimaced. "I'm sick to death of lying abed. If I lie there much longer I'll be weak as a newborn kitten. The stiff-rumped little witch almost did for me, Barnet."

Now in the process of removing empty glasses from the bedside table, Barnet gave him a disapproving look. "You oughn't to go talkin' about Miss Gabby that way, Cap'n.

'Twasn't 'er fault that you scared 'er enough to make 'er shoot you."

He stopped walking and stared at his henchman. "What magic has she wrought on you?"

"I'm sorry, Cap'n, but I calls 'em like I sees 'em. Miss Gabby's a real fine lady, and I won't be listenin' to you or anybody else be less than respectful about 'er." His tone severe, Barnet piled the glasses on a tray.

"Well, here's a high flight." More entertained than affronted, he resumed his careful walk around the perimeter of the room. "She's a royal pain in the arse, is what she is, Barnet."

Barnet turned and walked toward the door, loaded tray in hand, casting him a censorious look as he passed. "The trouble with you, Cap'n, is you're so used to 'aving females turn top over tail every time you give 'em a slip on the shoulder that you don't look kindly on them as don't."

"I don't look kindly on them as shoots me," he retorted as Barnet set the tray outside the door, then turned back into the room. When Barnet came toward him with the obvious intention of helping him back to bed, he waved him off with a testy hand. "I can put myself to bed when I'm ready. Go away, and come back in the morning."

Barnet halted and frowned. "But, Cap'n . . ."

"Go away, you traitor." A wry smile curved his lips as Barnet looked affronted at being so named. "Nay, 'twas but a jest. We've been through too much together for me to doubt your loyalty now. You may champion *Miss Gabby* with my goodwill."

Barnet argued for several minutes more, but was eventually persuaded to take himself off to bed. Left alone, Wickham looked at the bed with loathing, walked around the room a few more times, then settled down before the fire with a book he discovered on the mantelpiece: *Marmion*. It looked like the veriest nonsense, but a trip downstairs to the library for reading material more to his taste was beyond him just at present, he feared. How such a novel had come to be in his room he couldn't imagine: it was not, in the general way of things, the kind of book he would read. He preferred histories, especially those having to do with the military, or perhaps a biography . . .

The book belonged to Gabriella. Thumbing through, he discovered her name, inked in a careful, neat penmanship that made him think of her, on the frontispiece. Of course, he thought, he should have guessed. It was the kind of book that would appeal to a woman. At least, to many women. Somehow, he wouldn't have suspected Gabriella of possessing romantic notions, but if her taste in books was any indication she did.

He was glancing through it with greater interest, reading select passages with high amusement for the flowery language and orgies of sentiment that she apparently enjoyed, when he heard the unmistakable sounds of her entering her chamber. The opera must be over, then. He listened idly to the murmur of her voice talking to her maid. Her voice was soft and musical—until she was angered. Then it could become as sharp and cold as a dagger. The thought made him smile. More often than not, her voice was daggerlike when it addressed him.

Of course, much of the fault for that was his, he had to admit. He had discovered in himself a truly reprehensible predilection for teasing her.

She rose to the bait so delightfully.

The voices in her room had died away. She must, he thought, be alone, and was probably now snug in bed. It occurred to him then that she might be missing her book.

A slow smile stretched across his face. The idea of delivering it personally took possession of his mind. Though he fought against it, knowing that to involve himself with his "sister" any more than he had to was pure folly, it proved, in the end, irresistible.

Getting carefully to his feet, the book in one hand, he moved toward the door connecting their apartments. He was just a few paces away when a sharp rap on the wooden panel, followed by the unmistakable sound of the key turning in the lock, stopped him in his tracks.

He watched with a mixture of interest and enjoyment as the knob turned and the door swung open. Gabriella stood in the aperture, clad in, from what he could tell, a high-necked, long-sleeved white nightdress, a pink-sprigged wrapper, and a bright blue quilt with one end flung over her shoulder. The quilt almost covered her nightclothes, and completely concealed her shape, which he supposed was the object. Her hair she wore pulled back as she always wore it, in the clumsy knot that did nothing for her features; a frown darkened her brow. As she spotted him, her eyes first widened in surprise and then narrowed in distrust.

He waited for what she would say to him with a degree of anticipation he hadn't felt for anything in a very long time.

∞ ∞

She had not expected him to be so close. Momentarily taken aback, Gabby blinked up at him, then mentally prepared for battle. The resolve that had hardened in her during the course of the opera was not to be dissolved merely because he was standing three feet in front of her rather than lying safely abed half a room away, she told herself. In whatever posture she found him, she meant to have this out with him, now.

"Good evening, Gabriella."

Tousle haired and unshaven, still clad in his maroon dressing gown and maddeningly handsome despite his deshabille, he was far taller than she even in the flat-soled Turkish slippers he wore. The sensation of being physically at a disadvantage was unsettling; she had grown used to him ill, and flat on his back. He greeted her with a slight, gentlemanly bow, one hand pressed flat against his chest, that was belied by his dancing eyes. Gabby scowled at him. He looked unaccountably amused, and she mistrusted his amusement, for it could only be at her expense. Letting him get in the first word was probably a mistake, she thought crossly, but there was no doing anything about it now. He had already, in the course of their unfortunate association, had things far too much his own way. She meant to lay the law down tonight, with no possibility of mistake.

"If this charade is to proceed any further, we must have certain things made clear between us," she said without roundaboutation, her gaze steely with determination as it met his.

"Must we indeed?" It was no more than a polite murmur, but again Gabby got the impression that he was laughing at her. She regarded him suspiciously. "How so?"

"First and foremost, let me make this perfectly clear: I *will* denounce you for the imposter you are if you don't keep well away from my sisters, particularly Claire." It was a bald statement that permitted no debate.

"Ah, Claire." The faintest of reminiscent smiles touched his lips. "A rare beauty, she. A diamond of the first water, in fact."

Gabby's scowl darkened. "Do not mistake: I mean what I say."

"What, that you will announce to the world that I am

not your brother? Won't that be a trifle awkward for you, since you have already accepted me in that guise?"

"I care nothing for any awkwardness, if Claire's well-being is at stake." Gabby's tone was fierce.

"Do you not indeed?" His gaze swept her. A smile once again curled the edges of his mouth. "If you wish to discuss this, can we not sit down? Thanks to your hastiness with a pistol, I find that I tire more easily than I like."

Gabby hesitated, then nodded. "Very well."

"You left your book in my room, by the by." He held the book out to her, then crossed the room and settled himself into one of the pair of chairs before the fire.

"*Marmion?*" Gabby took the book, then followed in his wake. Her movements were somewhat restricted by the trailing quilt that she had thought, for modesty's sake, to drape around her person. She could not feel comfortable with the idea of him seeing her in her night attire, especially after . . . But she wasn't going to remember that. Remembering flooded her with shame, and her shame gave him an advantage. She would not allow herself to be so weak. Sitting down opposite him, she settled the book on her knee. "Thank you. I wondered where I had left it. Now, do we have an understanding? If you wish to continue in your chicanery without hindrance from me, you must leave Claire and Beth too, for that matter, well alone."

"You cannot have considered," he said in a thoughtful tone, his head resting back against the plush upholstery and his eyes meeting hers with a gleam in them that she misliked, "how difficult you might find it to actually *prove* that I am not, in fact, the earl of Wickham, now that I am well established in the eyes of the world as such. Also, I feel I would be remiss if I did not point out to you that, should you succeed in proving such a thing, you might well be considered my accomplice, having now conspired with me to defraud the rightful earl for nigh on a week."

Gabby swelled with indignation. "I did no such thing. Conspire with you, indeed!"

"Didn't you?" He smiled at her gently. "Not that I blame you, you understand. From what I have gleaned from Claire and Beth—well, mostly Beth, who is most charmingly confiding—as well as from tidbits Barnet has picked up from the servants, I gather that you found yourself in a very difficult position upon your father's death. All was left to your brother, in fact. No provision whatsoever was made for you or your sisters. To put it bluntly, without your brother's goodwill, you are penniless; and the man who stands to inherit on your brother's death is a distant cousin who is not over fond of any of you. Am I right so far?"

"And if you are, what of it?" Gabby sat stiffly erect in her chair now, eyeing him with open dislike.

"Why, then, the mystery of why you went along with my little masquerade is explained, and the fact is that you, my dear, need me even more than I need you." The very charming smile he bestowed on her was, Gabby thought, enough to make her long to throw her book at his gleaming white teeth.

"I wouldn't be so sure of that."

"I *am* sure of it, so don't think to threaten me with exposure again. It won't wash. If it makes you feel any better, console yourself with the knowledge that I feel quite brotherly toward Claire and Beth." There was a sudden, amused glint in his eyes. "Well, at any rate, toward Beth."

Gabby rose to her feet abruptly. The quilt slid, and she had to clench her fist around a handful of cloth to keep it in place. *Marmion* she clutched, forgotten, in her other hand. Her eyes glittered with anger as they met his.

"Who *are* you? You *do* have a name of your own, do you

not? I demand to know it. As well as what your purpose is in pretending to be my brother. Besides leading a luxurious life to which you aren't entitled, of course."

For a moment they stared at each other without speaking. When he replied at last, his tone was almost casual.

"I see no compelling reason for you to know anything about me."

This languid speech made Gabby's eyes blaze.

"You, sir, are a cad."

"Oh, I admit to it quite freely."

His mild tone as much as his words caused Gabby to quiver with temper.

"You *will* leave Claire alone."

He laughed, and shook his head at her as if marvelling. "So fierce, Gabriella. You can't frighten me away from your pretty sister, you know, but you might—just might—be able to bribe me away from her."

Gabby's eyes narrowed at him. "Bribe you?" she asked mistrustfully.

He nodded. His eyes laughed up at her, but his voice, when he spoke, was solemn enough.

"My price for keeping my hands off your sister is—a kiss."

"*What?*"
"You heard me."

"No." Gabby was outraged. Her face, she judged, must by now, from the volatile mix of anger and embarrassment she was experiencing, be as red as Beth's hair.

He shrugged as if her refusal was a matter of indifference to him. "Just as well, I suppose. I've been quite looking forward to furthering my acquaintance with Claire. My position as her "brother" provides me with a great deal of opportunity to do so, you know. She—delightful innocent—thinks nothing of being alone with me in my bedchamber, or . . ."

"You—you *lecher,*" Gabby almost choked on the epithet.

"Now, now. Name calling is very childish, after all."

"You won't get next or nigh her. I'll warn her . . ."

"Of her brother? I doubt you'll convince her. Claire strikes me as one who believes the best of everyone—unlike her older sister."

"I'll tell her the truth about you, of course."

"And still hope to keep it a secret? Come, Gabriella. You know better than that. She'll let it slip, and then we'll all be in the basket."

"Give me your word you'll stay away from her, then."

"I will—for the price of a kiss. On the lips, mind. None of your old-cattish pecks on the cheek."

Still clutching the quilt around her shoulders, Gabby glared impotently down at him as the argument came full circle. His eyes looked almost black in the flickering firelight, and he was clearly enjoying himself enormously.

"Would kissing me really be such a hardship? Think of the risks you've taken already for your sisters. I would consider this quite a small thing in comparison."

"No."

"It's entirely your choice, of course."

Gabby was left with nothing to say. *You have the most kissable mouth.* Unbidden and unwanted, the words scrolled through her mind. She glanced away from him, chewing her lower lip. A kiss. One kiss, to safeguard Claire. A peck on his mouth, and it was done. As he'd pointed out, it was not so great a thing, after all. What bothered her most about it, she realized with some chagrin, was that she had been wanting to kiss him, wondering how his lips would feel against hers, imagining the deed, since he had first said that about her mouth.

All she had to do was strike another bargain with the devil, and she would know.

The temptation was almost irresistible. Gabby felt like Eve must have when eyeing the apple, tantalized but afraid.

She swallowed, and met his gaze. "One kiss, and you give me your solemn word that you will stay away from Claire?"

"I give you my solemn word that I will treat Claire as chastely as if she were my sister in truth," he temporized. "I really cannot promise to stay away from her entirely, since for the forseeable future we will all be living under this same roof."

Gabby thought that over. It seemed an acceptable compromise, providing . . . "How do I know I can trust you to keep your promise? Criminals aren't, in general, noted for their honesty."

He smiled at her, a slow, intimate kind of smile that did unexpected things to her pulse rate. "As my partner in crime, you'll just have to trust me."

"I am not your . . ." Her voice trailed off. Under the circumstances, to say nothing of his mocking gaze, there seemed little point in protesting. However inadvertent her coupling of her deception to his had been, she supposed that she was now, to all intents and purposes, just what he had described her as: his partner in crime.

It was a mortifying reflection.

"Well?" He lifted his brows at her. "Have you made your decision? I don't propose to sit here and bandy words with you all night. There are many more enjoyable ways I could be passing the time—such as in planning my assault on your lovely sister's virtue."

Gabby stiffened. "You are the lowest form of life in nature."

He chuckled. "That may well be, but the question is, will you kiss me? To save your sister?"

Gabby glared at him, realized that trying to stare him down or bring him to any sense of shame about his own lack of gentlemanliness was useless, pursed her lips—and bent down and kissed him.

Smack on the mouth. Quick as that, and it was done. Really, for all her soul searching, nothing could have been easier—or more disappointing.

The warm, dry surface of his lips barely registered

with her senses. No cataclysm of emotion assailed her. Her heart and pulse and breathing remained undisturbed. In the end, all her fantasizing came down to this: as in so much else in life, kissing a man was much ado about not much.

Pleased with herself for having had the courage to face the devil she knew head on, relieved to have gotten it over with, and as a result feeling almost smug, she looked down at him with a small smile.

"There," she said. "The deal is struck."

He laughed, and, reaching up, closed a hand around her wrist before she realized what he intended. The wrist belonged to the hand that was clutching the quilt closed, and in her surprise her fingers relaxed. The edges parted and the quilt slipped, dropping soundlessly to the floor.

Without it, despite the dual protection of her wrapper and night rail, she felt naked. She could not erase from her mind the thought that he knew just what lay beneath her garments. Trying to tug her arm free, she clamped her other arm over her breasts.

Registering the gesture, his eyes gleamed wickedly at her.

She tried to tug her wrist free. "What are you doing? Let me go."

"Oh, no," he said, shaking his head. "Not yet. Not until you pay up. That little peck was no more a kiss than a crumb is a meal."

"You gave your word." She glared at him, standing perfectly still now as she preferred not to risk her dignity by fighting for the return of her wrist when she knew as well as she knew her own name that she had no chance to prevail. "I might have known you wouldn't keep it."

"So did you give your word," he reminded her. "And the rule is pay or play, my girl."

Then, without warning, he gave a sharp jerk on her wrist that brought her tumbling down into his arms. They closed around her like the jaws of a trap, and to her horror she found herself sitting on his lap.

"Let me up." Her book had tumbled with her, and was wedged between her thigh and his stomach. Panicking, she grabbed at it as the only weapon that was within reach, meaning to whack him in the ribs with it if necessary to secure her release.

"Ah-ah," he said reproachfully as he fielded the intended blow with an elbow. "Would you undo all your good work and injure me anew? What a bloodthirsty creature you are, to be sure."

As he spoke, he wrested the book from her hand with ridiculous ease. The small thump as it hit the floor only underscored her determination to win free. Deprived of her weapon, she elbowed him hard in the chest, earning from him a pained grunt, and lunged for freedom. Then his arms wrapped around her, securing her arms to her sides and her person on his lap. She found herself a helpless, furious prisoner. Determined to preserve what little dignity she had left, she disdained to struggle further. Instead, she sat stiffly within the confining circle of his arms, quivering with temper.

"When I was shooting you, I would I'd had a truer aim!"

"Ah, well, it's a sad fact of life that we all have to live with our mistakes."

"Bastard." The shocking word, which she had never uttered before in her life, exactly expressed her sentiments.

"Sticks and stones, Gabriella," he said mildly.

To meet his gaze, she had to tip her head back. Tipping her head back brought it in contact with his upper arm. That his upper arm made a solid support for her head, and was hard with muscle besides, she could not help but notice.

The fact that she noticed merely heaped coals on the fire of her anger.

"I knew you could not be trusted." Bitterness iced her voice.

"On the contrary, you're the one who didn't live up to her end of the bargain." He smiled at her then, almost tenderly. Despite her fury, that smile made her breath catch.

He was really the most damnably—and under the circumstances that was precisely the word she wanted—handsome man.

"I kissed you. You know I did." With her head resting on his arm, his face was so close that she could see every individual whisker that darkened his jaw. She could see the tiny crinkles at the corners of his eyes as he smiled down at her. She could see the texture of his skin, the shape of his ears, the twinkle of amusement that lurked in the depths of his blue eyes.

The twinkle was what did it, she thought: it told her that she was being teased. It also eliminated any last trace of the sudden, instinctive fear of a predatory man that being pulled into his arms had roused. But that didn't mean that she wasn't still angry at him, because she was. She was irate at being tumbled willy-nilly into his lap, outraged at finding herself imprisoned in his arms, and uncomfortable at sitting nestled on his thighs. Also, she didn't much like being tricked.

"That was the kind of kiss you'd give your maiden aunt on her deathbed. It doesn't count."

"It's the kind of kiss I'd give *any*body. And it does, too, count."

The amusement in his eyes grew more pronounced.

"What do you know about kissing, anyway? I'd be willing to bet anything I possess that you've never kissed a man before."

Looking up into those teasing eyes was having the most amazing effect on her, she discovered. Almost she felt her anger starting to slip away. Realizing this, she rallied enough to snap: "I'd say that's a pretty safe bet, considering that you don't seem to actually possess anything. Everything here belongs to the earl of Wickham, and you are not he."

He ignored that home thrust in favor of sticking with the original topic.

"Tell the truth now, Gabriella. You've never kissed a man before, have you?"

Gabby bristled, lifting her head from his pillowing arm as she replied. "What makes you think that?"

"The kiss you gave me is not the kind of kiss a woman gives a man. And that's the kind of kiss I meant." His voice was firm.

"I don't recall there being any particular specifications attached to the bargain," Gabby said, with her nose figuratively in the air. She was leaning against his chest now, and his arms were wrapped—rather more loosely than before—around her waist, trapping her arms as well. She could probably have pulled her arms free if she tried, but she couldn't discover in herself much inclination to do so. Instead she was almost—comfortable in the shocking position, she realized, and, just as bad, enjoying bandying words with him. "You agreed that if I kissed you once on the lips—which I did—you would treat Claire as if she were your sister in truth. *I* kept my end of the bargain. Now it is up to you to keep yours."

"Gabriella."

He was smiling at her with that tender look in his eyes

again, and the warmth of his gaze made her feel deliciously languid. "Hmm?"

"If you want me to keep my end of the bargain, you're going to have to kiss me the way I want to be kissed. Otherwise, the deal's off."

Their gazes locked. Her heart was beating far faster than was its norm, she realized, and her breathing had quickened, too. Her muscles were starting to feel weak, and her insides were as trembly as if they had turned to jelly. She was conscious of feeling very relaxed, and at the same time more than a little confused.

This man was dangerous; he was engaged in a criminal enterprise; he had threatened her life; he had handled her in a way that should fill any gently-bred female with enough shame to last a lifetime.

And yet—all she had to do was breathe, and the scent of him made her dizzy. All she had to do was lean her head back against his arm, and the hardness of the muscle there made her own muscles dissolve. All she had to do was nestle against his chest, and the warm resilience of it sapped her strength.

Sitting on a man's lap was undoubtedly sinful. It was something that a demirep might do, perhaps. Certainly no lady of quality would indulge in such a practice—would she? In any case, never in her wildest flights of erotic imagination had she pictured herself doing such a thing. Yet— she liked it. More than liked it, in fact. She would not be averse to remaining exactly where she was for hours on end.

What would it be like to kiss him as he wanted her to? What would it be like to find out for herself "the way a woman kisses a man?"

If, with twenty-five years in her dish, she had never kissed a man like that, then it was likely she never would.

She was firmly on the shelf, she knew. Romance had passed her by. No knight was ever going to come riding in on his white horse to sweep her off her feet.

If she wanted to learn what kissing a man was all about, here was her best chance.

Perhaps her only chance.

And she discovered, with some vestigial dismay, that she very much wanted to take it.

"Very well," she said, the forced crispness of her tone belying her inner quaking. "What is it exactly that you want me to do?"

❧ 24 ❧

"First put your arms around my neck."

Gabby stared into his dark, amused eyes. Then she swallowed, and, lifting her arms, slid them rather gingerly around his neck. The silk brocade of his dressing gown felt very smooth beneath her fingers. Beneath it, the broad strength of his shoulders and back felt almost jarringly masculine in contrast. His hair, crisp and cool, just brushed her fingers. She curled them into his nape in unconscious response.

"That's good." If his voice was a little huskier than it had been, she barely noticed.

"Now what?" The reason she barely noticed was because she, in turn, was finding it hard to breathe.

"Lean forward, put your lips against mine, and open your mouth."

Gabby's brows knit. "Why?"

"Why what?"

"Why open my mouth?"

"So I can put my tongue in it."

"*What?*" Gabby recoiled. He had to catch her arms to keep them in place.

"No backsliding now," he warned.

"You—put your tongue in my mouth?" It was an appalled whisper.

"Mm-hmm. And you put your tongue in mine."

"Oh, dear Lord." Gabby stared at him, desperate for a gleam that would tell her that he was teasing. He was, she decided after a searching glance, dead serious. "I don't think I can."

"Certainly you can. Come on, Gabriella, I haven't got all night. You agreed to the deal. Now do what I told you, and kiss me."

Gabby looked up at him, at the hard-planed, handsome face just inches above her own, at the indigo eyes that had somehow, during the course of their interchange, darkened almost to black, at the not quite smiling, beautifully shaped mouth.

Her heart pounded. Her palms grew damp. He was going to put his tongue in. . . . It was so shocking that she couldn't even finish the thought. What would the reality be like?

Gathering every last bit of her resolve, she clutched the front of his dressing gown and leaned forward. Her breasts brushed his chest, and the sensitive tips tingled and grew hard. His hands dropped away from her arms, moving down to rest lightly on either side of her waist, neither imprisoning nor compelling her as he seemed to wait. Gabby understood. For the bargain to be met, this was for her to do.

She pressed her breasts more firmly against his chest, then lifted her mouth to his.

This touch of their lips was, like their last, quick and tentative. Gabby couldn't help it. She brushed her mouth across his, briefly registered the dry heat of his lips and the abrasion of his unshaven jaw against her skin, then pulled back.

His eyes were impossible to read as their gazes met.

"Still not good enough. Try again. And this time, close your eyes, Gabriella, and open your mouth."

The words were a throaty murmur. She could feel their warmth against her mouth. Just a little closer, just a hair, and she would be able to feel his lips moving against hers.

At the thought, a scalding heat suffused her veins.

"Oh, I—can't." But she didn't draw away. Instead, her fingers clenched even tighter on the fabric of his dressing gown. Her body felt curiously boneless. Her breasts swelled against his chest. The place between her legs began to tighten and ache.

He had fondled and kissed her breast, run his hand over her lower body, pulled up her skirt. . . . The memory made her feel like she was going to faint. Her body seemed to burn. Desperately, shamefully, she realized that she wanted him to do it all again.

The kind of kiss he wanted led to that.

"Yes, you can. Put your lips against mine, and then slide your tongue in my mouth."

Gabby took a deep, shaken breath. There was no help for it, she realized—and she realized, too, that she didn't even want to turn back. Still hanging onto his dressing gown for dear life, she lifted her face, and pressed her lips to his. Then, remembering his instructions, she closed her eyes, and tentatively put out her tongue.

It encountered the barrier of his closed lips. As soon as she touched them, they parted, and she screwed up her courage and slid her tongue inside his mouth.

It was wet and scalding hot and tasted, faintly, of fine brandy and cigars. His tongue touched hers, stroked it, then pushed inside her mouth, claiming it with a boldness that stopped her breath. His lips molded themselves to hers, and her head began to spin. Goose bumps prickled to life all over the surface of her skin. Her stomach clenched.

Never had she imagined that a man would kiss like this. It was shocking, overwhelming, enthralling. His hand came up to cup the back of her head, and he shifted position so that her head rested against his hard shoulder. Of their own volition, her hands slid up the front of his chest until they locked behind the strong column of his neck. She felt helpless in the face of his strength, and realized that she liked the feeling very much indeed.

His lips moved against hers, compelling a response. His tongue explored the hidden crevices of her mouth. Lying across his lap, her arms locked around his neck, Gabby savored the sensations like a gourmet might savor the flavors and presentations of a rare feast. Shyly she stroked his tongue with hers, and was rewarded by a sharp indrawing of his breath.

It was good to know that she was not the only one affected by their kiss.

Then she felt his hand cover her breast.

It was her turn to catch her breath. Although two layers of cloth—her nightgown and wrapper—separated her flesh from his touch, she could feel the heat and strength of his hand with an acuity that shocked her. Her nipple swelled into his palm as if begging for attention, as if her body, remembering his touch, longed for more. Her loins clenched, then began to throb in an aching, thrilling, too well-remembered rhythm.

He ran his thumb over her nipple, pressed against it, and her body burst into flames.

Her senses were overwhelmed. She could no longer think, but only feel. She clung to his neck, returning his kiss with growing abandon, suffering his hand to caress her breast—no, loving it as his hand caressed her breast. She was trembling, she realized groggily, and her body was arching hungrily against his chest and the place between her thighs was once again beginning to melt. . . .

She could feel the male part of him beneath her thighs, she realized, and realized too that it was hard and heavy with wanting. Unable to help herself, she squirmed against it, and felt it boldly pressing up against her bottom.

That was what she wanted inside her. . . . At the knowledge, a tiny moan escaped her, only to be swallowed up by his lips.

His mouth left hers to trail tiny, nibbling kisses along the line of her jaw. Gabby's eyes fluttered open then, as she realized with the small part of her brain still capable of rational functioning that the bargain had been well and fully met. But she no longer cared about the bargain, she found, and it seemed to be the furthest thing from his mind, too, as he pressed more kisses down the side of her neck. His mouth was hot and wet against her skin, and his hand on her breast was warm and hard. . . .

The bargain was forgotten entirely as he tugged the front of her nightclothes down to expose a breast. Her eyes stayed open long enough to watch with a kind of shocked anticipation as he bared the curving white flesh with its taut pink crest. No man had ever viewed her nakedness before—but she suddenly, fiercely, wanted him to look at her, wanted him to touch her. He lifted his head then, gazing down at her breast, and gently cupped a hand beneath it almost as if he would test its weight.

Gabby's lips parted. His hand was big and dark against her tender flesh. It felt warm, and faintly rough, and . . .

His head dipped. Her eyes widened in shock as she realized that he was going to kiss her bare breast. She felt the gentle touch of his lips as he nuzzled her, and the abrasion of his unshaven jaw against her skin, seconds before he sucked on her nipple, drawing it into the scalding hot interior of his mouth.

Gabby's senses exploded. It was the most erotic thing she had ever seen, or felt. Unable to help herself, she gave a little choked cry as his tongue found her nipple, and her nails dug deep into his shoulders as she watched him suckle at her breast like a babe. What he was doing was indecent, she knew, and lewd beyond description, and yet it sent her body up in flames.

She had never dreamed that a man would do such a thing to her, or even want to. It felt wonderful, exquisite—obscene.

She didn't even know his name.

The thought came to her from somewhere, from, she imagined, that still functioning part of her brain that was now concerned with her self-preservation, and it shocked her back to reality.

He was an experienced seducer, making lascivious use of her body. In permitting it, she was no better than a wanton, as roundheeled a female as had ever warmed her father's bed.

"No!" she said, the protest sounding weak to her own ears. She began to struggle, pushing his head away from her breast, fighting to get free. She did not credit herself that she achieved her own liberation. As she tried to cover her breast with her hand, attempting to wedge it between his mouth and her flesh, he lifted his head and looked at her. His eyes glittered and his cheeks were flushed in a way that made her fear for the outcome.

"No!" she said again, with more urgency. Their gazes held. His jaw clenched, his eyes narrowed—and he let her go.

Gabby immediately stumbled to her feet, pulling her nightclothes back into place with shaky hands.

He remained seated, hands curled loosely over the ends of the chair arms, head resting against the back of the chair, looking up at her with an expression that she found impossible to decipher. Meeting his gaze, she was all too terribly conscious of the enormity of what she had done. She had let this man, this stranger, hold her on his lap and kiss her and bare and caress and kiss her breast. She could not even defend herself by claiming, this time, that he had compelled her—he had not. She would not even have consented to a kiss if she hadn't, somewhere deep inside, *wanted* to kiss him. Not even for Claire.

Her clothing was askew, and her hair, having escaped its pins unnoticed sometime in the last few heated minutes, fell in tumbled profusion over her shoulders. How must she look to him? Gabby wondered, agonized. She flushed painfully as she realized that she must now appear in his eyes as a woman of easy morals, a light-skirt, a bawd.

Which, in some measure, with him, she supposed she was.

But she would not think of that, not now. The final humiliation would be to permit him to see the true depths of her shame.

Accordingly, she took a deep breath, and lifted her chin a notch.

"I think you will agree that the bargain has been met," she said, proud of the coolness of her tone.

Then, turning her back on him, she walked with great dignity through the adjoining door, closed and locked it behind her, then all but fled back to the cold solitude of her bed.

❧ 25 ❧

As Lady Salcombe had predicted, on the following day they were beseiged with callers, some of whom had seen them at the opera and some of whom had merely heard that they were there. Several assorted relations were among them, including one of Gabby's Hendred cousins and several assorted Dysart connections of Claire's. Among the last of the relatives to arrive was Cousin Thomas's wife Lady Maud Banning, with her two daughters, Desdemona and Thisby. Thisby had been successfully puffed off the year before, and was the Honorable Mrs. Charles Fawley now. As Stivers announced the newcomers, Gabby, who along with Claire was in the drawing room chatting with earlier-arriving guests, stood to greet them.

"Lady Maud Banning, the Honorable Mrs. Fawley, and Miss Banning."

Despite the chilliness that had long existed between the families, Gabby accepted air kisses from Lady Maud and her daughters with a smile, and offered to make them known to the other guests, who, it turned out, they already knew. After a few moments of general conversation, the earlier company took their departure, and those who remained sorted themselves out into two groups: Gabby and Lady Maud, in chairs before the long windows that looked out on the square, and Claire, Desdemona, and Thisby grouped on the sofa near the hearth.

Glancing over at the trio of girls, Gabby could not prevent a purely ignoble spurt of pride. Lady Maud was herself a wispy blonde who had once been accounted something of a beauty. Her daughters were both blondes as well, one of wheaten hue and the other flax, and gifted too with their mother's slim figure. Unfortunately, though, in the girls' countenances Cousin Thomas's characteristics came to the fore: their blue eyes were rather bulbous, and their chins receded to a regrettable degree. Desdemona, who was flaxen, had a round face and, in addition, displayed a most deplorable tendency to freckle, while Thisby's face was so long that she very nearly resembled a horse. In any company, Claire was unequaled. But with her blonde cousins on either side of her, her dark beauty shone like a beacon on a stormy night.

"Well, I must say I never thought to see you looking so well," Lady Maud said in her discontented way, her gaze traveling critically over Gabby's simple but fashionable gown of azure blue crepe. As the hairdresser engaged by Aunt Augusta had arrived earlier that day, Gabby also felt reasonably confident that her heretofore unmanageable locks—which had been trimmed and styled so that a few cunning tendrils escaped from the topknot that he had deemed most suitable for her face shape—provided her cousin's wife with no fatal flaw on which to batten.

"Thank you," Gabby replied composedly, although the tone in which Lady Maud spoke them made the words seem even less like a compliment than they did on their face. As she sought for a safe topic of conversation with one who had never made any secret of her dislike for the late earl's daughters, her gaze strayed again to the girls on the sofa. "I understand from Cousin Thomas that you have been away visiting Thisby's new parents-in-law?"

"Oh, yes, the dearest people! Charles—her husband— has eight thousand pounds a year, you know, so it was a very suitable match despite the absence of a title. I fancy I may look a little higher for dear Mona, though."

The complacent glance she cast toward her younger daughter darkened as it rested, as Gabby saw, on Claire.

"Thisby is to be felicitated, certainly," Gabby said. "And I am sure I shall shortly be offering you felicitations on Desdemona's behalf, as well."

"Yes, indeed. Your sister is quite lovely, isn't she? If it were not for her dark looks—so unfashionable at the moment, unfortunately—and the fact that her parentage on her distaff side is perhaps not quite top drawer, I am sure she would quite take the *ton* by storm."

"I am still in hopes that she might," Gabby replied lightly, having no trouble recognizing jealousy when it stared her in the face, and most nobly, in her opinon, for-bearing to reply to veiled insults in kind. "By the by, Desdemona is certainly in looks today."

That last remark was not, she reflected, entirely insin-cere. Mona did look better than she had the last time Gabby had set eyes on her. Perhaps, she thought with just the tiniest, most regrettable spark of inner malice, Lady Maud had been applying bleaching lotion to her daughter's freckles as Twindle had, in the spirit of defending her charges, once recommended that she should.

Lady Maud looked complacent.

"Well, you know, I think she is, too." Her gaze traveled to the trio of girls again. "I like to see *my* girls in pale colors and modest designs, especially when they are newly out."

Though said with Lady Maud's trademark die-away smile, this was clearly another stab at Claire, whose slim, high-waisted dress of lemon muslin was as bright and airy as sunshine next to her cousins' softer pastels. Its tiny puffed sleeves and scooped neckline did indeed reveal a considerable amount of Claire's creamy skin. But certainly no more than was proper—and no more than either Desdemona or Thisby was showing, to rather less salubrious effect.

Gabby made some determinedly agreeable remark, and she and Lady Maud conversed for a few minutes on neutral topics. Then Lady Maud, with a conspiratorial smile, lowered her voice.

"I should congratulate you on the most fortunate change in your circumstances since we last met, I suppose. What a wonderful thing it is that Wickham should have allowed you to come to London, and bring out Claire. I gather he has not quite recovered from his mishap? We were shocked—*shocked*—to hear that he'd accidentally shot himself. As someone very nearly concerned—Thomas is Wickham's heir, after all—I would advise him not to be so clumsy." She laughed gently at what she plainly considered to be a witticism. "He is recovering, I presume?"

"Yes, indeed." Gabby refused to allow her thoughts to dwell on how very far along the road to recovery Wickham was. In fact, she refused to allow her thoughts to dwell on Wickham at all. "He is much better, thank you."

"You must be most thankful that the dear boy did not take after Cousin Matthew—and I would not say this to anyone but you, my dear, I assure you—in his nip-farthing ways. Indeed, quite the contrary, if what I hear is true! I understand that Wickham is to give a ball for Claire, with Augusta Salcombe to act as his hostess?"

"That's correct," Gabby answered with a smile, perceiving behind the faintly incredulous note in Lady Maud's voice the envy of one who was widely known to be quite as big a nip-farthing—as she had put it—as the late earl. In that speech Gabby also divined the real purpose behind the unlooked-for visit, which was to be sure that Lady Maud and her daughters were invited to the ball. "And a very grand one it is to be, too, if Aunt Augusta has her way, as she certainly will. You may be sure of receiving cards for it, by the by."

"Of course I never doubted that cards would be sent to us. Are we not family?" Lady Maud asked with a sniff. "Very peculiar it would look if we were not invited to our own cousin's ball, indeed." She gave a trilling little laugh, then glanced over at the girls again, and raised her voice. "Well, we have other calls to make. Thisby, Mona, kiss your cousins and let us go!"

When they were gone, Claire rolled her eyes at Gabby.

"*Kiss your cousins,* indeed," she said, mimicking Lady Maud's sugary syllables in a way that made Gabby laugh. "They treated us like lepers when we were living at Hawthorne Hall, if you recall. Do you imagine she thinks we've forgotten?"

Still smiling, Gabby shook her head. "She seemed most eager to be friends, did she not? Well, it will do none of us any good to be seen to be at outs with them. As unpleasant as they have been in the past, they are our cousins, after all. It costs nothing to smile, and be polite."

"I shall have to bite my tongue every time they come near," Claire said with a grimace, then took herself off upstairs to join the gaggle of very young ladies who were at that moment enjoying a lively coze with Beth in the old nursery.

If truth were told, Gabby mused with a smile, Claire probably would have been far happier playing games and chatting with the younger guests than joining the adults in the drawing room, though she would never have admitted to such a thing. Despite her eighteen years, Claire was still very young, after all.

Gabby still had to look over her wardrobe for a dress suitable to wear to that night's entertainment: a musical evening to be held at the home of one of Aunt Augusta's friends, to which she and Claire had been bidden that morning by a hand-delivered note. Changing her clothes up to half a dozen times a day was something she was still not accustomed to, and just thinking about it, and the night to be spent in conversation with what was sure to be mostly her aunt's elderly friends, made her feel tired already.

Of course, it didn't help that she'd gotten practically no sleep at all the previous night. Every time she'd closed her lids, Wickham's face had appeared in her mind's eye. And no matter how she had tried to repose herself, her body had remained throbbingly awake, aching for more. *You have the most kissable mouth.* Oh, God, so did he.

Such a thing could never be permitted to occur again, she told herself sternly. And to make sure it did not, she meant, in future, to keep out of Wickham's way.

She remained downstairs for several minutes after Claire left, checking over the cards that had arrived over the past few days.

Thus she was still in the drawing room, standing beside the fireplace with no possibility of concealment, when the next visitor arrived on Stivers's heels.

"The Duke of Trent to see you, Miss Gabby," Stivers said in a sepulchre tone.

At the sound of that name, which she had thought—hoped! never to hear again, Gabby felt her stomach drop. She looked up in a panic, meaning to bid Stivers to deny her presence, only to find Trent himself walking toward her in Stivers's wake.

The room spun, and for a ghastly moment, as she stared at the gaunt, grayish-hued face that had haunted her nightmares for years, she actually feared she might faint.

❧ 26 ❧

"*G*abby," Trent said, inclining his head as he strolled toward her. "Or, you having grown so grand, must I needs call you Lady Gabriella now?"

At a gesture from Trent, Stivers bowed himself out before Gabby could think to bid him to remain. Of course, Stivers would never have left her had he known. . . . But all he knew was that Trent had been a friend of her father's, one of many of whom Stivers had violently disapproved. Left alone in the drawing room with one whom she had hated and feared above all others for most of her life, Gabby struggled to retain her composure.

"I prefer that you not call me anything at all, your grace," she said in a wintry voice, grasping the tail end of her self-respect with both hands before it could quite slink away. The child in her longed to run and hide; the woman the child had become disdained to so much as blink lest she appear weak in the face of this predator. "You will forgive me if I tell you flatly that I am surprised that you have the audacity to present yourself here."

He chuckled, coming closer. He was, she saw with the dispassionate gaze of one now safe beyond his sphere, a relatively small man, not many inches taller than she was her-self, and slim of build. His hair was gray and thinning now, where it had once been shining blond, and many lines creased a face that looked as if had too rarely seen the light of day. His nose was a hawklike beak; his eyes were heavy lidded and still keen. In one hand he held the same—she was sure it was the same—silver-knobbed walking stick.

She wondered if he carried it deliberately.

"You wound me, Gabby, truly you do. Are we not the oldest of friends? I made sure of my welcome. When I saw you and Claire at the opera last night, I was quite imbued with the ambition to renew what has truly been among the most delightful of my relationships."

Try though she might to maintain a confident exterior, Gabby felt her knees begin to shake. She shifted her weight to her stronger leg, fearing that the damaged one would be-tray her precisely when she could not bear that it should. It was difficult to breathe, suddenly, and her palms, she dis-covered as she clenched her fists, had turned clammy and cold. But circumstances were different now, she reminded herself firmly. Her father was dead. Trent had no hold over any of them.

"I have no wish to acknowledge you in any way. Please leave, and do not call again."

He smiled. She remembered that smile. It was a humor-less stretching of thin lips, giving his face more than ever the appearance of some ghastly death mask. He looked her over as openly, and rapaciously, as a hawk might prey.

"I make you my compliments, by the way. You've be-come quite a taking little thing, not just in the common way. And Claire—she is a rare jewel. One any collector would be proud to claim."

Gabby couldn't help herself. At the memories that conjured up, icy fear snaked down her spine. She took a tiny step backward. His eyes gleamed.

So riveted was she on the man in front of her that the sound of footsteps crossing the hall behind him barely penetrated her consciousness. More difficult to overlook was the tall, broad-shouldered form that appeared without warning in the drawing room doorway, then checked on the threshold to survey the scene before him with a suddenly sharpened gaze.

"Wickham." She registered his presence with blind gratitude, and held out her hand. His gaze moved swiftly from her face to that of her guest, who had turned to survey him through a languidly lifted quizzing glass, and his posture of easy negligence vanished as he came toward her.

"Introduce me," he commanded in a clipped tone, walking past Trent as if he didn't exist to take her hand and tuck it into the crook of his elbow. The warmth of his fingers was very welcome as they enfolded her cold ones. The firm muscles of his arm provided their own reassurance. For a moment he looked down at her, frowning. Meeting that dark blue gaze, Gabby felt relief wash over her like a tidal wave. She took a deep, steadying breath. Wickham's mere presence gave her strength. Scoundrel, criminal, and vile seducer though he might be, he would keep her—keep all of them—safe from Trent. This she knew with absolute certainty.

She squared her shoulders, and glanced at Trent.

"There is no need," Trent said, stepping forward and extending his hand to Wickham. The rapacious smile was gone now, and so, too, was the predatory gaze. Trent was simply a gaunt old man, elegantly dressed and bearing himself in a way that spoke of rank and wealth, but giving no indication that he was in any way a threat. Compared to Wickham, whose tall, powerful form exuded vigor, he looked weak indeed, and almost shrunken. "I am Trent, an old—very old—friend of your father's."

Wickham shook hands, but kept Gabby's hand tucked in his elbow as he regarded the visitor unsmilingly. "I had very little acquaintance with my father, I'm afraid."

Trent gave a small smile. "I am aware. You should know that for most of our lives your father and I were practically—bosom friends."

Gabby's hand tightened involuntarily on Wickham's arm. Wickham glanced down at her, and his brows knit.

"His grace was just leaving," she said in a high, clear voice that did not sound much like her own. Nevertheless, her gaze was steady as it met the Duke's. He could do her no harm now, and so she meant him to know she realized.

"I am indeed," he said, and smiled again. "Au revoir, Gabby. Your servant, Wickham."

Then he made them an elegant leg, and left.

As the sound of his footsteps died away, Gabby let go of Wickham's arm, crossed to the sofa, and sat down. She had no choice. Her legs threatened to buckle under her at any moment.

Try though she might to reason it away, she could not rid herself of this most hideous of long-standing fears.

Wickham followed her, and stood with his arms folded over his chest, looking thoughtfully down at her. Still engaged in willing her body to function properly, Gabby nevertheless registered, as she glanced up, that he was fully dressed in gleaming tasseled Hessians, biscuit-colored breeches that clung to the powerful muscles of his thighs, and an elegant coat of blue superfine tailored to showcase his build.

"What are you doing downstairs?" she managed, pleased to discover that her voice sounded almost normal now.

"Want to tell me why that man frightens the life out of

you?" he asked, brushing aside her question as the non sequitur it was.

Gabby took another deep, calming breath. Relieved of Trent's presence, she was feeling better and slightly ashamed of herself for reacting so intensely. After all, now that her father was gone she had only to bid Trent to leave.

"What makes you think he frightens the life out of me?"

Wickham made a derisive sound. "To begin with, when I walked into this room, for the first time in our acquaintance you actually looked glad to see me."

Gabby's gaze met his. "For the first time in our acquaintance, I *was* glad to see you," she admitted.

His mouth crooked into an ironic half smile as he considered her. "Keep flattering me like that, and I might just get a swelled head."

Gabby laughed, and suddenly felt almost fully recovered. Trent was a part of the ugly past, and she meant to keep him there. He could only trouble her if she permitted him to. It was foolish to react to him as if she were a helpless child again.

"What brought you into the drawing room at such an opportune moment?" she asked on a lighter note.

"Stivers sent me to your rescue. He was standing in the middle of the hall practically wringing his hands when I came downstairs. When he saw me, he all but begged me to join you in the drawing room. Naturally I did, if only to discover why."

She smiled at him with real gratitude. "Thank you."

"Now are you going to tell me why an old friend of your father's frightens you so?"

Before Gabby could vouchsafe any answer, Stivers appeared in the doorway, announcing his arrival with a discreet cough.

"Your curricle is at the door, my lord."

"Thank you, Stivers." Wickham glanced down at Gabby, then spoke to Stivers again before he could withdraw. "Have Lady Gabriella's outdoor things brought as well."

"Yes, my lord." Stivers bowed himself out as Gabby looked up at Wickham in surprise.

"From the looks of you, you need fresh air even more than I do, my girl," he said, before she could speak. "I'll take you driving in Hyde Park, where you may preen yourself and wave condescendingly at all your acquaintances, while I demonstrate to all and sundry that I am still among the living."

Gabby smiled, and allowed herself to be pulled to her feet, but shook her head at him.

"Wait a minute. You're not even supposed to be downstairs yet, much less driving a curricle. You're recovering from a bullet wound, remember?"

"Which is why I'm driving, not riding. I'm not fully recovered yet, but I'm getting there. Believe me, getting out of this house will help. If I don't, I may just run mad."

"Your things, my lord, Miss Gabby." Stivers appeared again then. A few minutes later, having tied her bonnet under her chin, permitted Francis the footman to help her on with her pelisse, and drawn on her gloves, she stepped out into a sunny spring afternoon with nary a cloud in the sky. The air was crisp and fresh; the scent of growing things perfumed it. Taking a deep breath, she was suddenly very glad to be outdoors. Smiling at some nonsense of Wickham's, she walked with automatic care down the steps.

A gleaming black curricle drawn by a magnificent pair of matched grays waited at the curb. Jem was at their heads, stroking the nearside animal's muzzle, murmuring to it as its ears twitched back and forth in response. His eyes widened as he saw her, then narrowed as he looked beyond her to find Wickham.

"Hello, Jem." Despite feeling absurdly guilty under her servant's condemning look, Gabby assumed an air of nonchalance. His answering scowl was not unexpected, and was due, Gabby knew, to the presence of the man at her elbow.

"Miss Gabby." Jem's scowl deepened as, with Wickham's help, she stepped into the curricle without further ado. Wickham came up behind her, and took up the reins.

"Stand away from their heads," he directed Jem, taking his whip in hand. Still scowling, Jem did as he was told, then, as the grays plunged forward at Wickham's behest, scrambled to get up behind.

"We won't need you," Wickham called over his shoulder, and then they were away, with Jem, arms akimbo, left to stand nohow in the street, glaring after them.

"Your groom doesn't approve of me," Wickham said with a flickering smile.

He drove well, Gabby noted with approval, maneuvering the vehicle dexterously between an overloaded wagon and a lumbering barouche. The grays were proper highbred 'uns, playfully skittish and requiring a firm hand.

Gabby laughed. "Do you find that surprising? *I* don't approve of you. And tell me, if you please, just how you coaxed him into doting on your horses, when he looks at me as if I'm fraternizing with the enemy just because I am going driving in your company?"

Wickham glanced at her and shrugged. "What can I say? He likes horses more than he dislikes me. Barnet informs me that he has watched over them like a mother over twin babes ever since they arrived from Tattersall's."

"They are newly purchased, of course. And the curricle as well." She looked at him with a gathering frown as she was reminded afresh of what a rogue he was. "You are shockingly free with other people's money, it seems."

His good humor remained unfazed. "No more than you, my girl. Oh, yes, I'm quite aware of the size of your expenditures, believe me. Challow is very good about keeping me informed. And the money you're spending does not rightfully belong to you anymore than it does to me."

This was so true that Gabby could do nothing but bite her lip, and look away. So Challow kept him abreast of her expenditures, did he? Annoyance stirred, until Gabby realized that of course Challow thought, as did everyone else, that he was dealing with the true earl of Wickham. If the reprobate beside her had indeed been Marcus, she would have been quite happy for him to know to the shilling how much she spent.

The curricle was rattling briskly through Mayfair, and the gates to Hyde Park were in sight. A pleasant breeze stirred the peacock-blue feather that adorned her bonnet, causing it to tickle her cheek. Absentmindedly she pushed it back, brushing at her cheek with her gloved hand.

"The result, however, is certainly worth the expense," he added, watching her efforts with a half smile. "That bonnet becomes you charmingly."

The glance she gave him was both startled and a little shy. Whatever she had expected from him, it was not easy—too easy?—compliments.

"You are trying to turn me up sweet," she said, rallying. "With some fell purpose in mind, I have no doubt."

His smile faded at that. "I'll make a bargain with you," he began, but Gabby, eyes widening, turned on him a look of such dismay that he stopped short.

"Oh, no, never that," she said involuntarily, shaking her head. Then, realizing to what extent she had allowed her bone-deep embarrassment to show and trying, too late she feared, to make light of the matter, she attempted a smile even as she dropped her gaze to her clasped hands.

But with the best will in the world she could not stop herself from blushing to her hairline as his words—inadvertent ones, she felt sure—brought the excruciating details of the previous night's rendezvous in his bedroom crowding into the forefront of her mind. She had not forgotten it, precisely. Indeed, until Trent appeared on the scene she had not thought it was possible that anything could drive it from her thoughts. But Trent's arrival had done just that, and the subsequent upset of her emotions had allowed her to regard Wickham primarily in the light of a friend and protector. Now she was reminded of how she had sat on his lap, and kissed him; of how it had come about that she knew that his crookedly smiling mouth tasted of brandy and cigars, and was scalding hot on the inside; of how she had learned that he could render her as shameless as any harlot, shameless enough to permit him to bare and suckle at her breast. . . .

"If you turn any redder, your hair will catch fire." This drawled observation brought her gaze flying up to his.

"I—you . . ." For once her poise deserted her, and her tongue became hopelessly tangled as she sought for something innocuous to say. As his gaze held hers, she felt mortification so intense that it curled her toes.

⚘ 27 ⚘

"**D**on't be a fool, Gabriella." His voice was crisp. "And you are a fool if you're blushing for shame. There was nothing in what we did to cause you embarrassment. It was only a kiss, when all is said and done."

But she couldn't seem to help herself. Although she steeled herself against it, the image of his black head as it had looked nuzzling at her breast was suddenly all she could see. Remembering, Gabby felt a wave of heat so intense that it really did feel as though she would catch fire. She pressed her gloved hands to her cheeks, and closed her eyes.

"Could we please not talk about this?" she asked in a strangled voice.

He chuckled, and at the sound she opened her eyes to glare at him.

"Far be it from me to embarrass a lady. But kissing is perfectly normal, you know. And it's also a lot of fun."

"Fun!" The exclamation came out before Gabby could stop it.

His gaze quizzed her wickedly. "If you didn't think so,

I'll have to work on my technique. Come, Gabriella, confess: you liked kissing me. You liked me kissing your . . ."

"If you say another word I'll jump out of this curricle, I swear I will." Gabby gripped the side of the vehicle with one hand and looked daggers at him.

"All right, I won't," he said, unexpectedly obliging. Gabby wondered at it, until she saw that they were at the entrance to the park. She guessed that he wanted to give her a chance to compose herself before they could encounter anyone they knew. Glancing away from him out over the expanse of green as they turned in through the gates, she hoped that the sweet-scented breeze would be sufficient to cool her cheeks in time.

"You're no more than charmingly rosy now," he observed encouragingly.

Gabby cast him a darkling glance. "Don't tease."

He laughed.

There were a number of other vehicles in the park, including several phaetons and a scattering of gigs. Riders on horseback were abroad as well, cantering along the paths at the side of the road. Wickham touched his hat from time to time to acquaintances, and Gabby waved. But he did not stop, although several people signaled and called out to them. Finally, having sprung his horses and pulled away from the heaviest crush of traffic, he turned his attention to her again.

"You never did tell me why you are afraid of Trent."

Gabby had thought that topic had been forgotten. She should have known better. She was beginning to suspect that he never forgot anything. For a moment she debated what, if anything, to tell him. The entire story was too sordid, and too disturbing a memory, to relate.

"He is a most unpleasant man," she said finally in a constricted voice. "He visited my father often when we were young, then less often but still regularly until his death. The last time I saw him was at my father's funeral. After that, I forbade him the house. With the servants to back me up, he has stayed away from us. Until today."

"But that doesn't explain what he did to make you afraid of him." He looped his rein easily to pass a slow-moving gig. The capes on his tan driving coat fluttered as the curricle picked up speed.

"He is one of the few human beings on earth that I am prepared to say is truly evil." Already she was feeling the creeping chill that afflicted her whenever she thought of Trent. She shook her head, indicating with a gesture that she didn't want to talk about it anymore. In an effort to change the subject, she looked pointedly at Wickham. "If we're telling life stories, it's now your turn. You may start with your true name."

"Ah, but if I told you that, then you might slip and let it out," he said with a tantalizing grin. "For now, Wickham will have to do. Personally, I'm growing quite attached to it. There's much to be said for living the life of a belted earl."

"Especially when you're a rogue on the make," Gabby muttered dryly.

His grin widened as he glanced at her. "Talk about the pot calling the kettle black. Oh, don't poker up. Not many females of my acquaintance would have the courage to spit in the eye of fate as you are doing. It is something I particularly admire in you."

Before Gabby could reply, she caught the eye of a redoubtable lady in a old-fashioned carriage who was waving frantically at them as they approached.

"Oh, no," she said. "There is Aunt Augusta, and she is waving at us. You will have to stop."

Wickham did, pulling up beside the carriage and responding with considerable charm as Gabby made him known to Lady Salcombe and her friend, a Mrs. Dalrymple. After receiving a sound scolding for not having called upon his aunt during his first days in town, Wickham was let off with a slightly mollified *Well! You possess address enough, at all events!* The talk then turned to plans for the upcoming ball, where it stayed until Wickham, pleading a crush of carriages trying to pass, drove on.

After that, they had to stop several times. Lady Jersey, with her companion Mrs. Brooke, hailed them next, looking Wickham over with interest as she demanded the story of his accident from his own lips. When that tale was told, quite mendaciously but in a wry manner that provoked much laughter from his listeners, he was treated to an account of a similar predicament that had once felled Silence's mother's uncle. When they parted, it was with Lady Jersey's promise of vouchers for Almack's ringing in Gabby's ears.

"For they are a most charming pair, don't you know," Gabby overhead Lady Jersey telling her companion as they drove off. "And the little sister—well, she is a diamond of the first water. Augusta Salcombe's nieces and nephew, so there's nothing to object to there."

"Claire will be in alt," Gabby said, settling back against the leather seat and smiling as the carriage joined the line of traffic heading for the park gates.

"What about you? Are you excited about the prospect of participating in the Marriage Mart?" Wickham asked curiously.

Gabby laughed. He had been right, she thought, the drive was just the tonic she had needed. Already Trent's visit was being relegated to the distant recesses of her mind specifically reserved for unpleasant memories. And Wickham—though she was not forgetting for a moment all the less savory things she knew of him—was seeming more like an ally than an adversary with every passing moment.

"Aunt Augusta informs me that my best hope for wedded bliss is a widower with children," she related with a comic grimace that made him grin. "And I rather gathered from what she didn't say that she meant a very *old* widower with a great many children. That being the case, you'll understand why I am not quite dazzled by the thought of my introduction into the Marriage Mart. Indeed, I'm well aware that I'm past my prime. I only go to chaperone Claire."

"So old as you are," he said mockingly. "I can give you eight years, you know."

She glanced at him with raised brows. "What, are you thirty-three? That is one more fact to add to my store of information about you. A thirty-three year old captain of some kind who knew my brother. If you let any more information slip, I may just be able to ape the queen in Rumpelstiltskin and guess your name."

Whatever response he might have made to that was lost as two riders on horseback emerged from a path near the gates, spied them, and signaled them to pull over. The smile died on Gabby's face as she recognized the equestrienne in the modishly cut green habit as Lady Ware. Eyes quite unconsciously narrowed, she exchanged rather strained small talk with the lady's companion, Lord Henderson, and at the same time watched from the corner of her eye as Wickham carried his inamorata's hand to his mouth, kissing her fingers for rather longer than was proper and then retaining his hold on her hand as they engaged in a low-voiced conversation that Gabby, with the best will in the world, could not quite overhear. She didn't need to know what was being said, however, to recognize the intimacy that existed between them. If he had kissed Lady Ware full on the lips in the middle of the public thoroughfare, Gabby thought, disgusted, he could not have made it more plain that she was his mistress.

She remembered his assertion that kissing was fun, and felt sick to her stomach.

It was as well that she had been reminded that the man was a practiced rake, Gabby thought, as the parties said their farewells and the curricle at last sped through the gates. If she had been well on her way to having her head turned by a charming manner and a handsome face, then here was an end to it. He would not catch her succumbing to his wiles again.

"You're very quiet," he observed after several minutes in which he weaved in and out of traffic and she stared fixedly at the passing scene.

"Am I? I seem to have developed a headache," she said with a mechanical smile.

He looked at her keenly. "It came on very quickly."

She shrugged. "Headaches are like that."

"If I were conceited, I would observe that it developed immediately after we left Lady Ware and her friend."

Embarrassed by his perception, Gabby made a quick recover and looked at him haughtily. "You *are* conceited, to even allow such a thought to enter your head."

He grinned at her as though her answer removed all doubt. "Admit it, Gabriella: You're jealous."

"You're mad."

"Belinda is a friend."

Gabby snorted derisively, quite unable to contain herself

in the face of that blatant falsehood. "Strumpet is more like it."

"Now, now, Gabriella, you really shouldn't say such things to me. You shock me, my dear." The glance he sent her way was teasing.

"You might at least have the decency not to carry on with your inamorata while in my company. I realize that you probably aren't familiar with the finer points of well-bred behavior, but a gentleman would never ogle his mistress while in the presence of his sister, which is what I am supposed to be."

"I did not ogle Belinda." His protest was mild.

Gabby gave a tinkling little laugh. They had reached Grosvenor Square by that time, and he reined in the horses to a more sober pace.

"You may call it what you will, but I pray you won't do it in public again. It is an object with me to keep our family name clear of scandal until Claire is safely wed."

"Do you know, Gabriella, that you make an extremely pretty shrew?" There was laughter in his gaze as he glanced at her.

At the realization that he was finding in her entirely jus-tifiable annoyance at his behavior a source of suppressed amusement, she lost her temper. Her eyes flamed at him as he pulled the curricle up in front of the house.

"And you, sir, make the very model of an insolent, vul-gar goat that I would be rid of with a snap of my fingers if I could!"

With every fiber of her being, she longed to leap down and whisk away from him without further ado. Because of her weak leg, however, she was forced to wait until he came around to help her out. In seething silence, as he secured his horses and jumped down to assist her, she stood and came to the curricle door, ready to take his hand. Instead of offering it, as the most untutored clod knew to do, and in full view of Francis the footman, who stood at the open door, and any other servant or neighbor or passerby who chanced to be watching, he set his hands on either side of her waist and lifted her down.

By the time she had both feet on the ground, she was quivering with temper.

"No, you wouldn't," he said softly, grinning down at her. "You like me too much."

Then he let her go. Eyes flashing, Gabby purposefully clamped her lips together, too conscious of their audience to let fly at him as he deserved. With regal dignity, she turned her back on him and stalked—there was really no other word for it—up the steps and into the house.

To add insult to injury, Jem was waiting for her inside. No sooner had Francis closed the door behind her than he appeared from the nether regions of the house, eyes anxious, words of reproof trembling on his lips.

Gabby glared at him before he could open his mouth.

"Don't you dare say one word," she snapped. That the warning was delivered under her breath in no way detracted from its ferocity. Taking one look at her face, Jem remained prudently silent. Gabby cast him one last fulminating glance, then, drawing off her gloves with savage jerks, began to ascend the stairs to prepare for the evening's entertainment.

❧ ❧

Late that night, when the knock came on the connecting door, she was not entirely unprepared for it. Indeed, she had just retired to bed, and could only suppose that he had been listening for her to dismiss her maid. Scowling, she glared in the direction of the door, crossing her arms over her chest as she lay in bed and vowing that it would be a cold day in his putative birth place before she would open the door to *him*.

In the event, she didn't have to. With widening eyes she heard the unmistakable sound of a key turning in the lock, then the creak of an opening door followed by soft footsteps. With as little ceremony as that he was inside her bedroom, his gaze fastening on her as she lay in bed, fortunately covered to her armpits by a pile of quilts and coverings, glaring at him.

❧ 28 ❧

"How dare you just walk into my bedroom without so much as a by-your-leave?" Gabby snapped, sitting up in bed while taking care to keep the covers clamped to her chest. Her hair, on orders from the hairdresser, who felt that sleeping in hairpins weakened delicate tresses, was confined in a thick braid down her back. Her nightgown was of thin white lawn with long sleeves and a frill around the base of her neck. Her eyes, she knew, must be bright with temper. Her jaw was tight with it.

He grinned at her teasingly. Lit only by firelight, clad in his maroon dressing gown over a nightshirt that left his lower legs and feet bare, he looked tall and broad and disturbingly handsome. Just a few days ago, she thought, she would have felt menaced by the very fact of his presence. She no longer felt the least bit menaced by him, she discovered. Instead she felt cross as a crab, edgy as a cat in a room full of rocking chairs, and ready, willing, and able to box his ears.

"I thought you might be missing your book." He held up *Marmion* as he padded toward the bed.

Gabby's cheeks reddened as she recalled the exact circumstances in which she had left the book behind.

"Give it to me, and give me the key, and don't ever, ever come into my room without permission again."

"You wound me, Gabriella. I made sure you would be most thankful to have your book restored to you."

He was laughing at her, the beast. Gabby scowled at him as he reached the side of her bed, and snatched the book he held out to her with little grace.

"There. You've discharged your errand, so you may give me the key and leave."

"With your hair like that, you look like you're about fifteen, Beth's age." His eyes twinkled teasingly.

"Get out of my room."

"Or you'll scream?"

Infuriating man. He knew perfectly well she would not.

"Or I will make sure Mary shares my chamber in future," she said with dignity.

His brows rose. "Don't I at least get a thank-you for returning your book?"

"No!"

"Then I see I'll have to take one."

Before she realized what he meant to do, he bent and, cupping the back of her neck with his hand, pressed a quick, hot kiss to her mouth.

Gabby gasped. Given such easy access, his tongue slid inside. She was mesmerized for a moment, but the image of Lady Ware was too fresh. He would not use her so. Her temper exploded, and she jerked her mouth free, letting loose with a roundhouse right at the same time that connected solidly with his jaw.

"Ow!" He jumped back out of reach, clapping a hand to his jaw, but didn't seem otherwise dismayed. Indeed, he was grinning.

"Such a violent creature you are, Gabriella," he said reprovingly.

"Get out of my room." The covers forgotten, she surged to her knees, swinging at him. He retreated, laughing.

"Temper, temper."

She growled, remembered the book in her hand, and hurled it at him. His eyes widened as he saw it coming, and he dodged barely in time. It smacked into the wall just beyond his shoulder.

He tsked. "And to think that I was always taught that the mark of a lady born was that she was gentle, soft spoken, and kind."

Maddened, she glanced at the bedside table and grabbed the nearest object to hand: a brass wick trimmer. She hurled that at him too, and then snatched up a hairbrush and flung that. He retreated before the onslaught, one hand upflung to protect his head, laughing.

Gabby leaped out of bed, hefted a small crystal clock, and prepared to give chase. There was no need. He ducked into the dressing room.

"Sweet dreams, my vicious little bedbug," he called. As she ground her teeth, moving with swift purpose to brain the graceless lout, she heard the door between their apartments close. Then, just as she gained the dressing room, the key turned in the lock.

The cowardly blackguard had locked her out.

By the time she finally returned, fuming, to bed, she had wedged a straight-backed chair firmly beneath the knob.

❧ ❧

The next two weeks passed in a whirlwind of activity. The season was in full swing, and they were soon caught up in the feverish pace of it. There were parties and dances and dinners and breakfasts, visits to the theatre and drives in the park, calls paid and returned. Claire and Beth both soon developed their own circle of friends, which was composed of unmarried young ladies of compatible temperament and similar ages. Gabby made many agreeable acquaintances of her own, but found that she was often the odd person out in any gathering of ladies. She was too old to be numbered among the unmarried girls, but the young matrons who were her contemporaries inevitably talked of husbands and babies, which left her with very little to say. Not that she bemoaned her status. She had acquired a very respectable beau of her own—a widower with children, to her secret amusement, who was quite devoted—and, more important, Claire was a raving success. Every afternoon their drawing room was packed with eligible gentlemen jockeying for a favored place on the sofa beside the Beauty; and Claire received so many bouquets and other small tokens of esteem that Gabby, not without some pride, was forced to contemplate the necessity of throwing a great many of them out. Preparations for their own ball, to be held on the fifteenth of May, proceeded apace. In addition, the vouchers for Almack's having arrived as promised, they were involved in making ready for Claire's first appearance there. These preparations included repairing a shocking lapse in Claire's education: although she could perform her part in country dances creditably enough, thanks to Twindle's tutoring and those assemblies in York, she had never been taught to waltz. Having left fashionable London behind when she had moved with Claire's mother to Hawthorne Hall, Twindle had never learned the steps, and so was unable to instruct her charges in them.

"Of course, you may not waltz until the patronesses have given you permission to do so," Aunt Augusta cautioned when she learned of this shocking omission. "But when one of them—Lady Jersey, say, or Mrs. Drummond-Burrell—presents a gentleman to you as an agreeable partner, to be unable to accept because you did not know the steps would be to risk being labeled a rustic. Nothing could be more fatal, I assure you. Well. A dancing master must be engaged at once."

Accordingly, early in the afternoon of the day before Claire's much anticipated debut at the august supper club, Gabby, Claire, Beth, Twindle, and Mr. Griffin, the impecunious young dancing master who was already, after a quartet of visits, showing alarming signs of growing infatuated with Claire, were gathered in the long ballroom at the rear of the house, practicing the waltz.

Twindle was at the piano, playing a tinkling melody from sheet music provided by Mr. Griffin. Claire, under Mr. Griffin's eagle eye, was dancing with Beth, who was, to her disgust, assigned the part of the gentleman. Gabby stood near the door, applauding her sisters' sweeping twirls about the room, which were marred only when Claire forgot that Beth was to lead, or Beth trod on Claire's slippered foot. Mr. Griffin, watching their peregrinations with the eye of an expert and ignoring, with commendable tact, the muttered threats that flew back and forth between the sisters like bullets in a war, moved with them, doling out criticism and encouragement as he deemed necessary.

The music was lovely, a magical, intoxicating tune, and Gabby found herself swaying with it without even really being aware that she was doing so. She only noticed when, to her surprised consternation, Wickham's voice said in her ear, "What, Gabriella, no partner?"

Startled, she glanced over her shoulder. He stood behind her, having apparently entered through the open door without her noticing. She had seen him only in passing since she had driven him from her chamber; she was rarely home, and neither, apparently, was he. She, at least, came home in the small hours to sleep, but whether he did or not she couldn't say. In any case, she had heard no sounds from his room at night, although, much as she hated to admit it even to herself, occasionally she would find herself lying in bed and listening hard to see if she could. She had even given up wedging the chair beneath the knob; clearly he no longer had any thought of invading her chamber. Perhaps, she thought waspishly, instead of passing his nights in his own bed he was spending them with Lady Ware.

He smiled at her then, quite as if he could read her thoughts, and the teasing quality in that smile set up her back even more thoroughly than her speculations about him and his mistress.

Knave, she thought, and skewered him with a disdainful glance.

His black hair had been trimmed, and was brushed back from his forehead in the most fashionable of styles. He was clean shaven; the hard lines of his jaw contrasted with the crooked curve of his mouth. His broad shoulders were showcased by a bottle green coat that fit him to perfection. His linen was snowy, his breeches biscuit-colored and snug, his boots tasselled and gleaming. If he was not a belted earl—and he was not—he looked the part, far more than did most of the nobles of her acquaintance.

All this she noticed with a glance, and wished she had not. Turning a cold shoulder on him, she lifted her chin a notch and pretended to ignore him. To actually do so was, of course, impossible, she discovered to her chagrin.

"I'd be happy to offer myself up in the name of contributing to a worthy cause." His blue eyes laughed at her.

"Thank you," she answered shortly, casting him a cold glance before looking away again. "But I do not dance."

❧ 29 ❧

"Nonsense," he said, and pulled her into his arms. Gabby stumbled forward willy-nilly, and for a moment found herself held close against his chest. She glared up at him, to which look he responded with a wicked grin.

"I am lame," she hissed, resisting. Furious at him for forcing her to make such an admission, humiliated because her defect was thus glaringly exposed, she put both hands against his chest and shoved. To no avail: his hold was unbreakable.

"I won't let you fall," he promised. And then he wrapped one hard arm around her slender waist, clasped her reluctant hand in a strong grip, and began to move in time with the music, slowly, counting the steps off under his breath for her edification. If she was not to make a scene—and with her sisters and the rest present she certainly did not wish to—she had no choice but to follow his lead. She did so with her head held high and twin spots of angry color dotting her cheekbones. Her eyes burned with temper at finding herself so coerced, and her lips were pressed firmly together with the effort involved in keeping her limp from becoming too dreadfully apparent.

If there was any way on earth to prevent it, she would not appear clumsy before him—before them all.

"You look like you'd give a monkey to box my ears again," he murmured teasingly. "Remember that we have an audience, and smile."

Indeed, a quick glance around told her that the others were looking their way with some interest now even as they continued with their own activities. Reminding herself that Wickham was supposed to be her brother, of whom she was quite naturally fond, she pinned a smile on her lips, and murdered him with her eyes.

"That's my girl," he approved with a lurking grin, ignoring her killing glare, and whirled her into a turn. Clinging to his shoulder for support, leaning back against the hard strength of his arm, Gabby felt her skirt bell out around her as she matched his steps. As long as she came down only on the ball of her foot on her weak side, she discovered, she could manage. She was never going to be as graceful as, say, Claire, but at least she would not fall on her face.

"Do you always ride roughshod over everyone?" she said through her teeth, the coerced smile still plastered on her face.

His eyes twinkled at her. "Only when I find that it's necessary to do so to get my own way."

She drew in her breath. "Bully."

"Shrew." He smiled at her.

"I'm surprised someone hasn't murdered you before now. I'm tempted to give it another try."

"Ah-ah, you're forgetting to smile."

He made another of those sweeping turns in response to a flourish in the music, and Gabby caught a glimpse of the pair of them in the long mirrors that lined the walls. She blinked, surprised by how well they looked together. He might be a rake and a mannerless churl, but he was also tall, dark, and powerfully built. As far as physical beauty was concerned, she was a mere candle to the blazing light of his sun, but she looked becomingly slim and pale and delicate in his arms, and in her slim, fern-green muslin, with her hair styled in its becoming topknot, she felt almost beautiful.

For the first time in her life, she realized with a sense of wonderment.

And that was not all. She was dancing—with a great deal of effort, it was true—but *dancing,* when she had thought she never would. There was the slightest hesitation in her gait—she was keenly aware of it—but, knowing now that, as he had promised, he would not let her fall, her confidence grew with each gliding step.

"See, you *do* dance," he said as the music ended, and they twirled to a stop. "And very prettily, too."

Claire and Beth came toward them then, laughing and applauding, and Twindle, clapping too, beamed at Gabby from the piano bench. Poor Mr. Griffin, with no idea that he was witnessing a noteworthy family moment, smiled gamely with the rest. Her sisters and Twindle knew, of course, that Gabby never danced, and why. They had never seen any reason to question it, or to wonder if she could, or even if she would like to. It was simply a fact of life. But now that they had witnessed her twirling in Wickham's arms, and beheld her smiling and flushed, they were glad for her, and full of praise for her achievement.

"That was lovely," she said to Wickham, for the benefit of the others, as he let her go.

"That's what brothers are for," he replied, perfectly straight-faced save for the wicked gleam in his eye.

Gabby matched that gleam with a darkling one of her own, then was distracted by her sisters.

"Now that you're here, perhaps *you* can partner Claire," Beth suggested to Wickham hopefully. "I am tired of having my toes trod on with every other step."

"I do *not* tread on your toes." Claire's response was indignant, as was the look she gave Beth. Then she placed a hand on Wickham's arm and smiled up at him beguilingly. Watching, Gabby was surprised to feel a pang of envy. Claire was so ravishingly beautiful—what man wouldn't fall instantly in love with her? Together, she and Wickham were a couple to steal one's breath.

Gabby realized, with some dismay, that never before in her life had she felt envious of Claire.

"I wish you *would* dance with me," Claire said in a charmingly plaintive way to Wickham. "Mr. Griffin cannot partner me because he must watch my steps, and the truth is that Beth treads on *my* toes. Besides, it is very lowering to be forced to dance with one's sister."

"Dancing with a brother cannot be much of an improvement," Wickham replied without any visible evidence of sympathy. "In any case, you'll have to excuse me, I'm afraid. I have an appointment for which I cannot be late."

Gabby did not realize that she had been waiting with baited breath for Wickham's answer until she slowly exhaled after he had gone.

That evening's entertainment was a soiree at the home of Lord and Lady Ashley, followed by a dance from which the Banning ladies did not return until nearly two a.m. Gabby, her experience with Wickham notwithstanding, sat with the chaperones or strolled the rooms on the arm of Mr. Jamison, her worthy suitor. As always, she did not dance, but Claire sat down only for the waltzes. Even then, Claire had a court of admirers around her, vying to bring her ices or lemonade, which caused some of the less favored girls—and their mothers—to eye her with dislike. When Aunt Augusta's coachman set them down at their door, Claire was yawning hugely behind her hand and went immediately upstairs. Gabby, realizing that Wickham, whom she had not seen since he had left the house after their waltz, was still out as she picked up her candle from the hall and noticed that a third one remained, followed more slowly. After Mary put her to bed, Gabby lay awake in the darkness for a long time, tired but unable to sleep.

Finally she realized that she was listening for Wickham to come in. He never did, at least not that she heard, but at last sheer exhaustion did its work, and she slept.

Only to find, when she awoke bleary-eyed the next morning, that the blasted man had haunted her dreams.

She next saw him in the flesh late that afternoon. Coming in from a pleasant visit to the Pantheon Bazaar where she, Beth, and Twindle had purchased all manner of improbable things, Gabby was greeted in the hall by Stivers with the news that my lord wished to speak with her in his study at her earliest convenience. Gabby was alone, Beth and Twindle having gone on to Green Park to try again to take a turn about the basin, their last attempt at doing so having been aborted by Twindle's sprained ankle, now healed. Brows lifting, Gabby paused only to hand her packages to Stivers, and draw off her gloves and pelisse, before responding to *my lord's* summons. Wickham had never asked to speak with her in this manner before, and that circumstance alone was enough to fill her with a lively curiosity, and some dread.

The door to his study was closed. She knocked, and was bidden to come in. Wickham was seated behind the big desk before the windows, smoking a cigar. He had obviously been going over some papers that were spread out before him. As he looked up and saw her, he came to his feet, but he was frowning and that was so unlike him, Gabby realized, that she was alarmed.

"What's amiss?" she asked sharply. He made a gesture indicating that she should close the door. She did, feeling her heart start to pound.

"Sit down," he said, as she turned to stare at him. He had discarded his coat, and in shirtsleeves and a gold-colored waistcoat he was, in the ordinary way of things, a sight to gladden any female's heart. Gabby was too apprehensive at his expression to notice.

"You have been found out," she gasped, remaining where she was and giving voice to her worst fear.

He grimaced. "You mean, *we* have been found out, don't you?" He shook his head. "Not that I know of. *Would* you sit down? I can hardly do so while you are standing, after all."

"What is it, then?" Relieved of one fear, Gabby immediately began to cast about for another to latch onto. At his gesture, she sat down before the desk, but instead of seating himself behind it Wickham walked around and perched on one corner, swinging one booted foot and drawing on his cigar as he looked at her meditatively.

"You don't mind if I smoke, I hope?" This was said very politely.

"No, I don't mind if . . . Oh, would you just tell me what this is about?"

He drew on his cigar again. The smoke curled around his head, and the aroma made Gabby, quite unconsciously, wrinkle her nose.

"I received an offer for your hand today."

"*What?*"

"From Mr. Jamison. A very eligible gentleman, I believe. Expressed himself just as he ought, and promised to take good care of you."

"You are funning me."

"Not at all." He puffed at his cigar. "He and I even reviewed his finances in a preliminary sort of way. They're sound enough, I believe. I congratulate you on such quick work."

"But I don't want to marry him. He is fifty years old if he is a day, and he has *seven* children. You didn't *accept,* did you?"

For a moment he looked at her without saying anything. "I didn't," he said.

"Thank goodness."

All of a sudden it occurred to Gabby that she should have been delighted at Mr. Jamison's offer. An amiable man, he was certainly preferable to no husband at all even with the twin drawbacks of his age and children, as anyone would tell her. Aunt Augusta would be sure to pronounce it a very suitable match. Before they had come to London, even without the impetus of Marcus's demise to force her hand, Gabby realized that she would almost certainly have said yes, just for the chance to have a normal life and children of her own. *What* had changed?

Wickham took another drag on his cigar, causing the tip to glow red and smoke to form a wispy wreath around his black head. Gabby's eyes widened as she stared at him.

How could she look at a portly, balding, amiable widower when *he* was all she could see?

The devil in the flesh.

"Why are you looking at me like that?" He sounded vaguely irritable, and he frowned at her.

"I should—I *should* accept Mr. Jamison," Gabby said, feeling numb. "It would solve all our problems. Mine, and Claire's, and Beth's. Instead of depending on *Claire* to marry, I should do so myself, now that I have the opportunity. We would be safe, no matter what happened."

For a moment they simply stared at each other.

"I didn't refuse on your behalf. I said that you would have to make the decision for yourself." The words were abrupt.

Gabby felt as if her heart had suddenly turned to lead. She had really no choice at all. The world she was living in was built on a foundation of sand, and she knew it. Sooner or later, someone would discover that the real earl of Wickham was dead, and then her lovely new life would collapse. The man frowning at her so pensively would disappear back into whatever nether region he had crawled out of, and she—and her sisters—would be left with nothing.

For their sakes, as much as her own, she had to do what was necessary to make sure that didn't happen.

"I have to accept him." Her throat felt scratchy. Her voice sounded strained. She looked at the man on whom she had so unaccountably come to depend, and realized that her relationship with him was as deceptive as that foundation of sand. He simply wasn't real.

"You could do better."

"No," she said baldly, facing the truth. "I can't. And even if I thought there was a possibility that I might get another offer, I daren't take the chance."

"You could trust me to make sure that you—all of you—are taken care of."

Gabby laughed. The sound was high-pitched, with just a touch of hysteria. "You! I don't even know who you really are! You aren't Wickham. One day you'll be found out, and thrown into gaol, or hanged, or—or just disappear in a puff of smoke, and there we'll be."

"The papers on my desk are meant to right the injustice of your father's will, and grant you and your sisters portions when you marry, or provide you with an income for life if you don't. I had Challow draw them up. All I have to do is sign them."

For a moment Gabby felt hope flutter like a wild bird in her breast. An income for life, whether they married or not—they would be secure. All her worries would evaporate. She wouldn't have to marry Mr. Jamison. . . .

"They are no more real than the rest." The truth struck her with the force of a blow. "Do you forget that you *are not Wickham?* Your signature would be a forgery. If—when—it was found out, the money would be taken away from us. We would be in no better case than we are now, with Marcus dead!"

"Keep your voice down."

Footsteps hurried down the hall, and were followed almost immediately by a vigorous tattoo on the door. Gabby jumped, and looked over her shoulder like a deer catching wind of a hunter. Wickham frowned, then stood and moved behind the desk before bidding whoever it was to enter.

Beth burst into the room, rushed across the floor and caught Gabby by the hand. "Oh, Gabby, the most famous thing! We've just arrived home, and there are clarinet players in the street, and a man with the most cunning little dancing monkey. Come see! You, too, Marcus."

Gabby took a deep breath, and allowed herself to be pulled to her feet. There was no more to be said here, after all. Her sister looked so carefree that she made Gabby's heart ache. Beth's future, and Claire's too, depended on her. They would be secure if she married Mr. Jamison. Anything else would be pure folly. Anything else was as insubstantial as moonbeams and hot air.

"Gabriella." Wickham's voice stopped her on her way out the door. She glanced back at him, and felt the ache in her heart intensify. He took the cigar from his mouth as their gazes met. He looked so tall and powerful standing there that it was hard to believe that he was no more solid than a shadow. "Trust me."

He'd said that to her before. Gabby racked her brain, and remembered: on the occasion when he had talked her into making her second bargain with the devil, in exchange for a kiss.

Recalling what had happened next made her pulse race and her lips quiver. For a moment she looked at him almost longingly. He had, in the end, kept his word, and acted the gentleman with Claire . . .

But this time there was, for her and Claire and Beth, simply too much at stake.

"I can't," she said, and, turning her back on him, followed Beth out the door.

30

Almack's was sadly flat. That was Gabby's verdict as, sipping lemonade at the side of Aunt Augusta, who was busy talking to a purple-turbaned matron who had been presented to Gabby as Mrs. Chalmondley, she had a moment to herself to take stock of her surroundings. The rooms themselves were of a comfortably large size, though being crowded seemed smaller, but were surprisingly shabby. The available refreshments consisted of tea, lemonade or orgeat, with bread and butter or slightly stale cakes. Dancing was the entertainment of choice, although gossip played almost as big a role. In addition, there were several card rooms that were given over largely to whist, played by certain of the dowagers, and such gentlemen as were content to settle for paltry stakes. Laughter and chatter filled the air, along with music, making it difficult to hear what any but the person closest to one said. The long windows were firmly closed, and the rooms were over warm and stuffy. The scent of perfume and too many bodies filled the air.

What made it bearable for Gabby was Claire's enjoyment. In a simple white muslin dress caught up under the bosom by silver ribbons, with more silver ribbons twined in her upswept hair, she radiated happiness and was without a doubt the most beautiful girl in the room. Several mothers of other, less popular, young ladies watched her with jaundiced eyes as she moved from one partner to another with scarcely a pause; notable among these was Lady Maud, who was present with her younger daughter. Desdemona was clad in white like Claire and, indeed, most of the young ladies present, but on her it was an unfortunate choice. With her pale coloring, it made her look decidedly washed out. Her mother had her work cut out for her to find partners for her, but, to her credit, she seemed to manage it most of the time. When she failed, Desdemona sat on the sidelines, glaring balefully at Claire until Lady Maud, catching her in the act, prodded her into a smile with a sharp elbow to the ribs.

Because she was no longer considered a girl, Gabby, fortunately in her opinion, was spared the prevailing preference for white; she wore a simple gown of lilac crepe, which, she thought, suited both her coloring and her mature status quite nicely.

Claire had already earned the approval of the patronesses, and Lady Jersey, who had hurried forward to greet them on arrival and seemed to consider them somewhat in the light of protegees, beamed on her with a benevolence that would have surprised those who had encountered the sharp side of Silence's tongue. The still more formidable Lady Sefton had even gone so far as to pronounce Claire a very pretty-behaved miss as she presented her with no less a personage than the Marquis of Tyndale, a slender, smiling young man, as a desirable partner for her first waltz.

"He practically begged me for the introduction," Lady Sefton said in a comfortable aside to Aunt Augusta as Claire twirled around the room on the arm of the Marquis. "He would be a good match for her, Gussie, if you can bring him up to scratch. A Marquis, after all, with twenty thousand pounds a year."

"Can I get you a plate of bread and butter, Lady Gabriella?" Mr. Jamison came up beside her, his question drowning out her aunt's reply. Gabby, who hadn't realized that he was present, forced herself to smile warmly at him. If she was planning to marry the man, she told herself, the least she could do was be polite.

She declined the offer, but patted the seat beside her. When he sat down with a suspicious creak that made her suspect that he might, like Prinny, be attempting to conceal his tendency toward corpulence by wearing a corset, she ignored the sound and set herself to draw him out. Soon they were chatting comfortably of his home in Devonshire—a handsome property, she could be sure of that!—and his interest in innovative methods of obtaining maximum yields from his fields. It was only when the conversation turned to his children that he gave any indication that he had it in mind to make her his wife.

"They are all of them very *good* children," he said earnestly, having mentioned each by name and described several anecdotes in which one or another had behaved in an exemplary fashion. "Poor little tykes, all they are wanting to make their happiness complete is a mother. The three youngest are girls, you know. A mere father does not always know how to go on."

Ignoring the sinking feeling that these confidences had provoked, Gabby said with great resolution that they sounded adorable.

"Indeed, I hope you will think so," he said, his gaze warming as it moved over her face. "Because—well, no doubt your brother will have told you of my visit today."

Now that the matter was fast approaching the sticking

point, Gabby discovered that she possessed the coldest of cold feet. Glancing away from him rather blindly, she chanced to find Claire's slender figure flashing in and out among the other dancers. The sight of her sister performing her part in the boisterous country dance with laughing grace was exactly the tonic she needed to bolster her flagging courage.

She could do this, for Claire, and Beth, and, in the end, when the moonbeams had faded away and the harsh sun once again glared brightly down, for herself.

"He did," she agreed, smiling at Mr. Jamison again, and hoping that he would take her momentary hesitation for modesty, or shyness, rather than the reluctance it was.

"It is my fondest hope that you will consent to be my wife," Mr. Jamison said in a lowered voice, possessing himself of her hand and looking at her very intently. Gabby glanced down at the plump, sun-spotted fingers clutching hers and had to force herself not to pull her hand away. Instead, she lifted her chin with steely determination, and smiled as she met his gaze. He continued, "You may wonder that I have come to such a decision when the acquaintance between us is of such short duration, but I am one who knows my own mind. You are exactly the lady I would choose to oversee my children's upbringing. You are young enough to deal with them energetically, yet mature enough not to be forever wishing to go gallivanting about to parties and dances; you are good-humored, and from what I have observed you appear to possess an uncommon degree of sense. In addition, I myself—well, I don't find you unattractive."

He said this with so much the air of one bestowing an extravagant amount of praise that Gabby's lower lip quivered, and her smile turned, momentarily, genuine with real amusement.

Then it faded altogether as she pictured herself on her wedding night, in his bed.

But now was not the time to be thinking of that.

"Thank you," she said, determinedly smiling again.

"Oh, look, there's Wickham. I asked him most specifically to come tonight, but as it's almost eleven I had nearly given him up. Well. What a splendid figure he cuts, to be sure."

Aunt Augusta's voice in her ear prompted Gabby to glance up. There, indeed, was Wickham. He stood just inside the doorway, resplendent in elegant black evening attire, glancing about him as he talked in a desultory fashion to another gentleman who had apparently entered with him.

"He is quite the best looking of the Bannings, I think," Lady Sefton observed judiciously from Aunt Augusta's other side. "Except for Lady Claire, of course. They are quite a dazzling pair of siblings." She lowered her voice and spoke only to Aunt Augusta, no doubt expecting that in the hubbub no one else would be able to hear her words. "I understand that the youngest one is no beauty either?"

Gabby, thanks to a sudden hush, overheard and understood the implied insult to herself, but wasn't troubled by it in the least. Wickham *was* the masculine equivalent of Claire, she thought. She observed that a great many feminine heads had turned to remark his entrance. The ladies whispered to each other behind their hands, and then let their gazes linger on him for rather too long for mere casual interest in a new arrival. Realizing that she, too, was guilty of staring, she took herself in hand, and turned her attention firmly back to Mr. Jamison.

"Your brother is coming this way," Jamison said, defeating the purpose. He had released her hand and was looking past her, and something in his expression told Gabby that he found Wickham intimidating. Of course, for all Mr.

Jamison's maturity, Wickham's consequence was by far the greater, and as for his person—well, there was no comparison. Mr. Jamison continued hurriedly: "I will come for your answer tomorrow, if I may, when we may be private together. I should never have said so much as I did, in such a public place, but you may flatter yourself that my eagerness is such that I simply got carried away."

On pins and needles at the prospect of Wickham's imminent arrival while simultaneously striving to appear unconscious of it, Gabby managed a dutiful smile and a nod for her suitor. Inwardly, she was most thankful for the reprieve.

Having resolutely refused to look his way again, Gabby felt his presence before she saw him. As acutely as she might sense heat from a stove, she felt the force of his presence as he stopped at her side. Then he said something and she could no longer avoid looking up. When she did, it was to find him looming above her, greeting Aunt Augusta and Lady Sefton with a smile, and shaking hands with Mr. Jamison, who was on his feet now, before glancing down at her.

"Enjoying yourself, Gabriella?" he asked with a lazy smile.

"Immensely," she replied with cool self-possession.

He laughed, and turned his attention to Mr. Jamison. The two men stood chatting for a few minutes, quite ignoring her, while Gabby responded at random to some remark of Aunt Augusta's that she never even heard and struggled to keep a pleasant expression on her face. He had come tonight purely to torment her, she knew—and torment was exactly the right word for what he was doing. She was hideously conscious that he stood no more than an arm's length away, though she never once glanced his way.

Suddenly he was at her elbow again, looking down at her. She had, perforce, to glance up. Something in his eyes—a wicked gleam, a teasing smile—warned her, but she was powerless to prevent what happened next.

"My dance, I think, Gabriella," he said. She looked up at him with eyes grown suddenly wide. The musicians, she realized, had struck up a waltz.

"Lady Gabriella does not dance," Mr. Jamison interjected in an urgent undertone, as though to remind Wickham of Gabby's affliction, before Gabby could reply.

"Oh, she does with the right partner," he replied carelessly. "Our steps are well matched."

"My dear, if you can dance, by all means do so," Lady Augusta muttered in her ear. "I had thought—but seeing that you *can* do so might make all the difference."

Gabby pursed her lips, but had no chance to reply to this. Lady Sefton was smiling encouragingly at her.

"You'd best hurry along, Lady Gabriella, or you'll miss your chance. Wickham is a partner most ladies would kill for! Of course, he is your brother, which I am sure quite takes the thrill out of it, but still. You may go along."

"Gabriella, you observe me still waiting," Wickham said with a smile, holding out his hand to her.

Not wishing, in so public a venue, to plead her lameness as an excuse, especially when Wickham, the rat, was perfectly capable of overriding such a concern anyway, Gabby smiled, too, and placed her hand in his, allowing him to draw her to her feet. Under Aunt Augusta's and Lady Sefton's benevolent gazes, and Mr. Jamison's slightly frowning one, Gabby tucked her hand in Wickham's arm and was thus borne away.

"You beast. I don't wish to dance. Especially not in public. How dare you force my hand in such a way?" she hissed as they walked away.

"You deserve to dance, Gabriella. Take my word for it, you don't wish to be wed to a man who doesn't realize it."

They had gained the dance floor, and he was taking her into his arms.

"What would you know about it?" As his arm slid around her waist and he took her hand in his, she suddenly looked at him with horror in her eyes. "You aren't by any chance *married,* are you?"

He grinned. "There's that unfortunate jealousy of yours again. No, I'm not married. Come, Gabriella, stop scowling at me. People will think we're quarreling."

"We *are* quarreling," Gabby said through gritted teeth, as he swung her into the dance. But she smiled at him, nonetheless, and danced, and took joy in the dancing. His arm around her was firm, his hand holding hers was warm, and the shoulder she rested her hand on was wide and strong. She knew that she was safe in his arms, knew he wouldn't let her fall, and so she was able to follow his lead with confidence, and even relax. The music was intoxicating, and, she discovered with some surprise, she was actually having fun.

"You were born to dance, Gabriella." He swung her expertly around. "You're enjoying yourself, aren't you? Your eyes are sparkling and your cheeks are pink and you're smiling at me quite nicely now."

"You are utterly loathsome, you know." But she said it without heat, and her eyes as they met his gave her words the lie.

"And you are beautiful. Here, don't color up. You blush far too easily." He was laughing at her.

Aware that her cheeks were indeed flaming—blushing easily was the curse of the fair-skinned—Gabby glanced self-consciously at the dancing pairs around them. To her relief, she saw that no one seemed to be paying them the least attention, for which she was thankful. In truth, being held so close to him was wreaking havoc with her senses. She was noticing things about him that it would be better, perhaps, if she did not. The shoulder beneath her hand was solid with muscle. The cloth of his evening coat felt silky smooth. His hand holding hers was decidedly masculine in feel, and far bigger than her own. His throat was a strong brown column, and the faintest shadow of stubble could be seen on his strong jaw. His mouth, that beautifully shaped mouth, was smiling. . . .

"There's no need to offer me Spanish coin," she said with dignity, taking care with her steps as he whirled her around with the rest of the circling couples. Balancing on the ball of her foot worked well, she thought; unless someone looked very closely, she doubted that they would be able to tell that she was lame. She found it marvelous, suddenly, that she had never before realized that she could dance. But then, until now, she had never had a reason to want to.

Her reason smiled at her, a slow, charming smile that stole her breath.

"What, don't you think I meant it? I did, I promise you. Shall I go into detail? Fairest Gabriella, your eyes are the color of small flat stones at the bottom of a sparkling clear pond. Your hair makes me think of the richest of autumn leaves. Your mouth—but there you go blushing again. I'll have to leave off, or we'll have everyone in the room wondering what we're talking about."

Gabby indeed felt another rush of heat to her face, and narrowed her eyes threateningly at him.

"I wouldn't blush if you wouldn't tease."

"What makes you think I'm teasing?"

He wasn't smiling now. Their gazes locked, and Gabby felt suddenly very, very warm. Something of what she was feeling must have shown in her expression, because, as his gaze moved over her face, his eyes darkened until they were the color of a stormy midnight sea.

❧ 31 ❧

The music ended then with a flourish. He twirled her around and they both came to a stop. Then, while Gabby was still dizzy—from either the dance or him, she wasn't quite sure—he lifted the hand he still held to his mouth, and pressed his lips to it.

"To me, you are the most beautiful woman in the room," he said softly.

She looked up at him, speechless, lips parting as she drew in a long, shaky breath. Their gazes met and held. The heat of his mouth seemed to sear her skin like a brand.

"You deserve better than Jamison, Gabriella." His voice was softer still.

All around them couples were leaving the floor. Another dancer's skirt brushed against hers, and, glancing instinctively at its wearer, Gabby intercepted a curious look. Brought back to reality just that suddenly, Gabby was alarmed by the realization that they were making a spectacle of themselves. Pulling her hand from his, aware too late that wondering glances were being cast their way, she stiffened her spine and lifted her chin with the effort of mentally pushing him away.

"I think you should take me back to my aunt." Her voice was steady, and amazingly cool.

Apparently realizing, as she had, that they were attracting undue attention, he made no dissent, but did as she suggested. They were both of them uncharacteristically silent as he escorted her from the floor. He even, she saw with a sideways glance that she absolutely could not prevent, looked a little grim. Mr. Jamison was waiting, faithful as a dog, beside her aunt. Gabby could not help but compare the two men, to Mr. Jamison's decided detriment. But, she reminded herself firmly as she released Wickham's arm to move to Mr. Jamison's side, there was style and there was substance, and Mr. Jamison was substance.

Wickham said no more than the few words civility dictated, then took himself off with a bow. Lady Maud came up just as Wickham was leaving, and settled into Lady Sefton's vacated seat.

Gabby sat down again, discreetly fanning herself, and tried not to feel disgruntled as she watched Wickham leading first Claire, and then one of her blushing friends, onto the floor. What he did or whom he danced with was no concern of hers, she told herself sternly, and prepared to listen to Mr. Jamison prosing on about his children for the rest of the night. But that gentleman was unusually quiet, and Gabby began to frown as she caught him once or twice out of the corner of her eye, looking at her a little askance. Her worst fears were realized when Lady Maud, with a malicious glint, said brightly during the next intermission, "You are to be congratulated on having acquired such a—*very* fond brother in Wickham, Gabby."

Gabby was proud of herself. Although the remark was a shock, in the face of such an emergency she didn't even change color. Instead she managed a careless little laugh.

"Indeed, Beth and Claire and I consider ourselves supremely fortunate. Wickham is the dearest creature. Having been raised in Ceylon, he has no notion of how cold-blooded we English generally are. He is most kind and affectionate to us all."

Lady Maud looked disappointed, Gabby saw with satisfaction, and to her relief said no more on that head. Even Mr. Jamison, clearly having had a question he had not asked acceptably answered, seemed to warm up after that. Gabby watched Wickham go down the room with Lady Ware, and set her teeth. It was going to be a long night.

Mr. Jamison finally excused himself and headed for the card room; Lady Maud was drawn away by one of her friends. No sooner had they gone, leaving her temporarily alone with her aunt, than Aunt Augusta leaned over and hissed in her ear: "What was Wickham *thinking*, to kiss your hand like that? It looked most odd, let me tell you, such a gesture from your brother. I declare, I could shake the boy for so forgetting himself, foreign raised or not. Everyone was staring. Well. It is certainly no wonder. I was myself."

Gabby, meeting her aunt's condemnatory look, thought fast.

"He was apologizing," she said with as much unconcern as she could muster. "We quarreled. He does not think I should marry Mr. Jamison, you see."

Aunt Augusta looked full at her then, her eyes rounding with excitement, her mouth forming a little *o*. "Never say that Mr. Jamison has made you an offer?"

Gabby nodded, feeling suddenly rather wretched. Now, more than ever, she did not want to accept. Once Aunt Augusta knew, however, the die was all but cast. "He called on Wickham earlier today."

"Oh, my dear, that's just what I hoped would happen

when I introduced you. Wickham does not favor the match? Why not, pray?" Aunt Augusta visibly bristled.

"I think he feels Mr. Jamison is rather old for me. But whatever he thinks, I mean to accept."

Aunt Augusta's face was suddenly wreathed in smiles, and she reached over to squeeze Gabby's hand with approbation. "You are a smart, good girl. Wickham knows nothing of the matter, and so I mean to tell him before he is very much older. It's all of a piece: clearly he has much to learn of our English ways. Well. It is not official yet, so I will say nothing more until it is! But you have done well for yourself, Gabriella. I am most pleased."

Gabby knew her aunt was right: in attaching Mr. Jamison, she had done better for herself than she had had any right to expect. But the prospect of being wed to him was making her feel less happy by the moment, and her unhappiness had nothing to do with his prosaic appearance or his advanced age or even his seven children.

The cause of her unhappiness with her chosen lot stood well over six feet tall, smoked smelly cigars, and had truly gorgeous blue eyes. His touch set her on fire; his kisses made her head spin; twirling around the room in his arms—and she had done that, she reflected with pride, quite remarkably well—had made her realize that his arms were the only place on earth where she wanted to be.

Moonbeams and hot air or not.

But reality was a harsh, cold thing, and reality was what she had to face. Mr. Jamison was her future; Wickham—or whatever his true name was; it said much about the idiocy of her infatuation that she didn't even know that much— was no more than a besotted maiden's foolish dream.

A dream that threatened all she had worked so hard to achieve, she reminded herself sternly. There could be no more dances, no more kisses, with him. Tonight the polite world had had occasion to look at them askance. Rumors, once started, could be ruinous, she knew. She meant to give the gossips no more opportunity to dine out on tales of her behavior, on pain of endangering everything for herself and Claire and Beth. On the morrow she would accept Mr. Jamison, then wed him with the smallest possible delay, and thus assure her own and her sisters' future.

Then she would sever all contact with Wickham.

When the inevitable happened, and he was found out, she, Claire, and Beth would be safe.

Wickham must have caught wind of the gossip as well, because he did not come near her again. He danced twice more after standing up with Lady Ware, once, crafty creature, with Desdemona and once with a female Gabby didn't know. Then, scan the crowd though her wayward eyes might, she did not see him again. After a while she assumed, with a bewildering mix of emotions, that he must have left. Mr. Jamison reappeared, and asked her, with a touch of self-consciousness, whether she would care to attempt a dance with him. When she assured him, with perfect truth, that she would not, he accepted her refusal with transparent relief and sat talking with her a while longer, until at last, at long last, it was time to go home.

Mr. Jamison had already taken his leave and she and Claire and Aunt Augusta were in the vestibule waiting for their carriage to be brought round, when Gabby suffered her second upset of the night. Stifling a yawn with difficulty, reflecting with increasing glumness on the prospect of becoming betrothed on the morrow, she stood in the shadow of one of the tall, slightly dusty potted palms that decorated the entry hall, a little way apart from the others, who were talking to various of their friends who likewise waited for their conveyances.

A gloved hand touched her bare arm just below the spangled scarf she had draped over her elbows. Gabby glanced around with a questioning smile that froze in place as she encountered, without warning, the Duke of Trent's obsidian gaze. He was standing in the shadows, in full evening dress with a greatcoat thrown over all, his hat and the ubiquitous silver-knobbed walking stick in one hand. Obviously he was preparing to depart the premises. Had he been at Almack's all the evening? If so, she hadn't seen him. Perhaps he had been hidden away in a card room, or even in some quiet corner, watching the dancing. The thought of him spending all the evening so near, and her unaware, made her shiver.

"Ill met by moonlight, eh, Gabby?" he said in a low voice, and smiled at her. "Or should I say, from my point of view at least, well met?"

Gabby, glancing around, saw that their conversation was unobserved. Claire had her back turned and was laughing at something one of her friends had said, while Aunt Augusta, her head close together with that of Mrs. Dalrymple, had walked a little way apart with that lady, arm in arm.

"Temporarily bereft of champions?" He had observed her frantic glance, and his smile grew broader. "None of them will avail you anything in the end, you know, not even that most attentive brother of yours. I mean to have what is mine."

"I have nothing to say to you," Gabby said in the iciest voice she could muster. Under the circumstances, she was proud that she could speak at all. Every instinct she possessed urged her to turn her back and walk away, but when she tried she discovered to her horror that she could not move: sheer mindless terror kept her rooted to the spot.

"You haven't forgotten the voucher, have you, Gabby? No, of course you have not. I still have it in my possession, and I *will* see it redeemed, of that you may be sure. Very soon now, in fact."

"You have no hold over me." It was an effort to keep her voice from shaking. Her pulse raced. Her heart pounded. She could scarcely breathe, and all because he was near.

He took a step that brought him nearer yet. . . .

And at that instant Aunt Augusta's carriage rattled up to the door.

"Soon, Gabby."

The chilling whisper hung in the air as Aunt Augusta glanced around, beckoning, at last. Trent brushed past Gabby and went down the steps, the skirt of his coat swirling behind him, to vanish like the vampire he resembled into the night.

But try though she might to banish it from her thoughts, Gabby could not get the encounter out of her head. Trent had exuded menace, and she was, no matter how she tried to arm herself against him, terrified.

She told neither her aunt nor her sister of the encounter. She was too shaken, the memories it revived were too painful, and she did not want to upset Claire, who clearly had not seen Trent.

For her part, Claire practically bubbled over with happiness during the seemingly interminable ride home. In answer to Aunt Augusta's prodding, she admitted that the Marquis had, indeed, been very nice, and, yes, he had said that he would call on the morrow, and they had indeed danced twice.

Glad of Claire's chatter to mask her own silence, Gabby said little during the ride home, and still less while Mary helped her undress and put her to bed. But later, when she was alone in the dark—really alone, because Wickham's apartment was, as usual, empty, which meant that she was the only living being in that whole vast wing of the house—she finally succumbed to a terrible mixture of emotions that arose from some combination of gloom over her forthcoming engagement, an aching, illicit longing for Wickham, and the horror that had haunted her for years.

To her shame, she cried herself to sleep.

❧ 32 ❧

He was, he reflected wryly as he set the candle down on the table beside his bed and proceeded to shrug himself out of his coat, just a trifle well to live. Not drunk, precisely, but definitely feeling the effects of too much cheap wine. However necessary it might be for him to put himself out where he could see and be seen, he was getting way too old to be spending his nights in dives. When he'd first come to London, its seamier side had at least had the advantage of novelty. Now he'd visited practically every gaming hall, brothel, cockpit, and hole in the wall in London, and he had nothing to show for his efforts except a newly-won wad of the ready in his pocket and a headache, neither of which had been his object. The game was growing increasingly risky, too. The longer he pretended to be Marcus, the more likely it became that he would encounter someone who knew he was not.

If his quarry was out there, he was being damned cautious. What the hell was he waiting for?

Barnet, whom he had last seen scrounging around the docks and who was still not back, although it was gone four in the morning, had put the same degree of effort into attempting to glean information from the rougher types who skulked in the alleys by dead of night. Barnet's targets were the lowest of the low, the kinds of thugs who would melt away at the first sight or sound of a swell. But Barnet had had the same degree of luck in finding what they were looking for as had he himself: that is to say, none at all.

They couldn't keep this up indefinitely, he thought wearily, sitting down on the side of the bed to pull off his boots. The situation, risky to begin with, was deteriorating rapidly. Already things were far more complicated than he'd ever anticipated. Gabriella and her sisters had added an element to the quest that made it dangerous in a way he could not possibly have foreseen.

Whatever happened, he did not want them getting hurt. Not physically, not financially, and not emotionally. Without at all meaning to, he had grown to care about what became of them. For better or worse, he felt responsible for them now.

Boots off, he walked on stocking feet to the table by the hearth, where by his orders a bottle of brandy and a box of cigars waited. Since he was already about three sheets to the wind, he figured he might as well do the job thoroughly and at least assure himself a sound night's sleep. Pouring brandy into a snifter, he absentmindedly admired the way the flickering fire turned the liquid a mercurial orange. The cigar he snipped, and lit. Then, carrying the bottle with him as well as the snifter, he settled in before the fire, alternating puffs on the cigar with swallows of brandy.

Damn fine brandy, too. Being the earl of Wickham had some compensations, he had to admit.

Physically he was bone tired, but his mind was restless. His thoughts returned to the dilemma he'd been wrestling with for some days. He could not stay in his present guise indefinitely, that much was clear. It was always possible that one of these days he would encounter someone who knew him, or had known Marcus, and the jig would be up. If that didn't happen, his quarry was bound to make his move sooner or later, and then events would progress with the speed of a winning horse at Ascot. Before that happened, there were things he had to see settled.

Three things, to be precise: His "sisters."

Beth was a charming child, as uncritically affectionate as a puppy. She had accepted him as her brother from the first, and he had, by infinitesimal degrees, with the thing done before he'd ever really become aware that it was beginning, played the role so well that he felt like a brother toward her now in truth. He could not let harm come to Beth.

Claire, beauteous Claire, was, as he'd recognized from his first glimpse of her, as ravishing a female as any he'd ever seen in his life. She was a young Venus, a dazzler, with the kind of looks that could bring strong men to their knees. Any man, setting eyes on her, would think instantly of candlelit bedrooms and smooth cool sheets. But then he'd discovered that she was sweet natured, slightly shy, fiercely loyal to her sisters, and as young and naive as any other miss of eighteen. He'd also discovered to his considerable surprise that his taste did not run to innocent buds, however beautiful. He still admired Claire's looks—no man could help it—but his admiration was purely objective now. In fact, by the time he had made admittedly rather dishonorable use of Gabriella's fear that he might attempt to seduce her sister to tease her into kissing him, he'd had absolutely no intention of stepping over the line with Claire. He had grown fond of her, and wanted the best for her. In short, he felt like a protective big brother to her, too.

And finally there was Gabriella. Gabriella was the surprise, the wild card in the deck, the punch line at the end of the joke—and the joke, he feared, was on him. A hoity-toity, sharp-tongued old maid who had never, even in the first bloom of youth, been a beauty, she had intrigued him from the first. But who would ever have believed that he would get to the point where just looking at her could make his loins ache?

Not he. It was ridiculous, and he knew it, and could even laugh at himself because of it. But the dismal truth was that he, who had had more high flyers in keeping than almost any man in Wellington's army, wanted her so badly that he would have gladly walked over a river of hot coals to get to her bed. Knowing that she was asleep, right now, on the other side of that door was enough to make him have to grit his teeth and look away to avoid getting to his feet and heading temptation's way. The cream of the jest was that she wanted him, too. He had no doubt about that. Her physical response, when he touched her, was unmistakably fiery and intense. And the way she looked at him sometimes—well, he wasn't a fool, and he wasn't a green boy with no experience of women. He knew what the look in her eyes meant.

He could bed her any time he chose. He knew that as well as he knew his own name.

But she was a lady, and, he had no doubt at all, a virgin. Even though he was no earl, he was gentleman enough to respect that. He could not simply seduce her, and then leave.

But he could not stay.

That was the crux of his dilemma. He wanted her fiercely, hungrily, to the point where he was deliberately making himself drunk with brandy because he could not otherwise sleep, knowing that she lay abed just beyond one closed door, to which he had a key. But he could not take her, because he could offer nothing of himself beyond the taking.

And she deserved more, far more, than that.

Jamison. The picture of Gabriella's plump, balding suitor rose in his mind's eye, making him frown. The sharp pang of dislike he felt for the fellow surprised him. Then he realized the dislike for what it was, and had to laugh at himself.

He, who had had women fawning over him from the time he was a stripling, was jealous of a fat fifty-year-old widower with seven children.

It was ludicrous. It was hilarious. But the thought of Gabriella wedding—*bedding*—the man drove him insane.

As he had told her tonight, she deserved better than Jamison. But that, then, begged the question: what—or rather, who—*did* she deserve?

A man with no name he could admit to, no identity he could claim, who would leave her as soon as the job he'd come to do was done?

Even he was forced to admit that Jamison's stolid security didn't look half bad compared to that.

He poured himself more brandy, and sank lower in his chair, stretching his long legs out before him, drinking and smoking his cigar as he numbed himself, he hoped, into oblivion. Still, thoughts of Gabriella would not leave him in peace. Quite irrationally—and he was still sober enough to realize that he was being irrational—he found himself blaming the whole thing on her. She had been a thorn in his side from the first moment he had laid eyes on her. And she was a thorn in his side still.

As he had told her tonight—and he shouldn't have, he knew better, knew that people who played with fire quite often ended up getting burned—she had somehow, in his eyes, grown more lovely than any woman of his acquaintance. Her slim shape, her pale skin and cool gray eyes appealed to him in a way the lusher charms of the women he usually bedded no longer did. Belinda was a case in point:

he hadn't visited her bed in weeks. He doubted that he ever would again, although she was clearly eager that he should. He hadn't set up another mistress either, although he could not remember ever before in his adult life having gone so long without a woman.

But the only woman he wanted he couldn't, in honor, have.

What was it about Gabriella? he wondered moodily, swallowing the remaining brandy in his glass at a gulp. Was it the way she had of looking at him sometimes like he was a street sweeper and she was the bloody queen? Or was it the quickness of her tongue, or the telltale way she blushed, or the sparkle in her eyes when she laughed?

Or was it her courage? She had more than any man he had ever met. Fate had handed her a raw deal, and she had stood up and spit in its eye and dared it to try to defeat her. She had stood up to him, too, from the beginning, when he'd done his best to frighten her out of her wits. She was brave enough to come to London when any other woman would have gone into mourning for her poor dead brother in Yorkshire and waited for someone else to decide her future. She was brave enough to contemplate marriage with a man she knew damned well would make her miserable, because she saw it as the best way to obtain security for herself and her sisters. She was brave enough to hold her head high and dance in defiance of the infirmity of her leg.

He'd seen heroes in Wellington's army who weren't half as brave as that.

When he had realized that his taste didn't run to sweet young things like Claire, he had discovered, too, what it did run to: the intelligence and gallantry and passion that was Gabriella.

He wanted her with an urgency that, lately, seemed ever

present. And yet, he wanted to protect her, too. Earlier tonight, when he had realized that he had provoked a miniscandal by kissing her hand at the end of their dance—and it was getting harder and harder to remember that he was supposed to be her brother—he had subsequently partnered half a dozen females he had no desire to stand up with just to keep from adding fuel to the fire by allowing the gossips to say, too, that she was the only woman he danced with.

Whatever happened, he didn't want her to be hurt. Not by him, or anyone else.

And he wasn't about to let her marry Jamison. He couldn't stay with her, but he could save her from that. And he meant to do what he could to make her, and Claire and Beth, safe before he had to go.

His cigar had burned down to a nub, he noticed at a glance. And the brandy bottle was very close to empty as well. Getting rather unsteadily to his feet, he stubbed out what was left of the cigar, took one last swallow of brandy, and began to unbutton his waistcoat.

He would go to bed. If sleep did not come to him now, when he was so drunk the bed looked like he was seeing it through the small end of a telescope, it never would.

His waistcoat was off, and he was working his way down the buttons of his shirt, his movements slow and careful because drink had rendered his fingers clumsy, when he heard something from the apartment next door.

His head came up, and his hands stilled. Frowning, he glanced toward the adjoining door.

At that moment Gabriella screamed.

❧ 33 ❧

Trent was there, in the darkness with her, striking her with his cane, meaning to . . . to . . .

Gabby screamed, and screamed again. Shatteringly. Heartbreakingly.

"Gabriella! Gabriella, wake up, for God's sake!"

Strong hands closed over her upper arms, shaking her, rousing her from the nightmare that held her in thrall. Her eyes blinked open, and for a moment, still fighting free of the terror, she cringed as she stared groggily up at an indistinct dark shape looming above her. Her heart pounded. Her skin crawled. It was a man's shape, rendered black and featureless by the faint orange glow of the dying fire. A man's hands, wrapped around her arms. A man's breath, brandy-soaked, warm on her face.

In that next split second she recognized him, would have recognized him, she thought, in the darkest fissure in the deepest corner of hell. Her own personal devil, come to steal her soul.

"Oh, it's you," she breathed on a shuddering sigh of relief, and her tense muscles went limp. Perversely, now that the dream was gone, she began, in a bone-deep reaction that she couldn't control, to shake.

"Yes, it's me," he said. "Don't worry, Gabriella, I have you safe."

His voice was warm, and deep, and soothing. It, and his presence, and even the smell of brandy, which she quite liked, and cigars, which she didn't, made her realize that there was truly nothing to fear. She took a deep breath, and then another, trying to stop the tremors that racked her limbs. But they sprang from some place deep in her subconscious, apparently, because with the best will in the world she couldn't get them to stop.

"You're shivering."

"I know. I can't seem to help it." She took another deep breath. She was lying on her back now with her head on her pillow, the covers neatly tucked around her waist, shaking so badly that her teeth chattered. Clenching her fists, she willed the tremors to stop. They did not.

"You're not cold?" His voice was gentle.

Gabby shook her head. Trent's face loomed in her mind. . . .

"Bad dream?"

She shuddered. "Hold me," she whispered, shamed at her own need.

"Gabriella." His response was swift. The covers shifted, and then he was sliding into bed with her, stretching his length beside her, pulling her into strong arms. By the time they were settled her head rested on his chest and his arms were wrapped around her waist. She shifted slightly so that she could look up at him, one hand twining in the soft linen of his shirt. His eyes gleamed at her through the darkness. She could make out his features now, just barely. He was frowning, so that his brows nearly met over his nose and his mouth—that beautiful mouth—was grave.

"You screamed," he said.

"Did I?"

"Like a banshee."

She shuddered again, remembering, and his arms tightened even more.

"I'm so glad you heard me." All of her usual defenses were down. The dream had unsettled her so that all she could do was cling to him as the only safe port in a terrifyingly rough sea. Closing her eyes, she snuggled closer yet. His solid warmth attracted her like a magnet. In the aftermath of the dream she felt cold, so cold, and hideously vulnerable. It was as if she were a little girl again, alone and afraid, with no one to protect her. . . .

The hand that had been gripping his shirt loosened, smoothed the cloth she had wrinkled, and discovered that his shirt was unbuttoned almost to the waist. Her fingers just brushed the mat of hair thus exposed. Drawn by the heat of his bare skin, intrigued by the tensile strength of his wide chest, she let her hand rest in the fur. Her fingers moved idly among the crisp whorls.

He said nothing, but lay very still. Something brushed the top of her head, and she wondered vaguely if it could be his lips. Opening her eyes, she saw that her hand looked very white and slender lying atop the thicket of black hair. She could feel the long, hard length of him through the thin lawn of her nightdress, and registered that he was still fully dressed, in breeches and a shirt, and stockings. Her own feet were bare, and she rubbed her toes along his silk-clad calves, loving the hard warmth of him, greedy to make contact with him in any way she could.

"I should perhaps warn you that I am a trifle drunk."

The words were said carefully, and his hand came up to still her fingers, which were playing almost of their own volition with his chest hair.

Gabby glanced up at him. "Umm. You smell like a brewery."

"And you smell like—vanilla." A slight smile curved his lips. His eyes were mere slits now, gleaming in the firelight as he looked down at her. His hand lay atop hers, not permitting it to move but not lifting it away from his chest.

"It's the soap I use. I had a bath before I came to bed."

He said nothing in response to that. Beneath her palm, she could feel, very faintly, the steady beat of his heart. Wrapped so closely in his arms, besides the scent of brandy and cigars, she could smell the barest hint of leather and the faint, musky aroma that she had learned was man. Her shivers were lessening, eased by some combination of the heat of his body and the comfort of his presence. Her breasts were pressed flat against his side; one of his hipbones nudged her stomach. Her cold toes wedged between his silk-clad calf and the mattress, seeking heat.

Everywhere they touched, her skin tingled.

"Tell me about your nightmare." His voice was low, slightly husky, and commanding for all that.

She took a deep breath, distracted from her growing awareness of her body's response to his, and instinctively curled her fingers around the hair she touched; her nails lightly scored the surface of his chest. He winced, and, realizing that she was hurting him, she eased her grip with an apologetic caress.

"Gabriella."

She shook her head, wanting the nightmare simply to slip away as it had so many times before, unwilling to extend its horror by putting it into words.

"Was it by any chance about Trent?"

She quivered, and glanced up at him, wide-eyed. His arms tightened around her, pulling her so close against him that she could feel the hard outline of his hip bone pressing into her skin.

"How did you—what makes you think that?"

His hand stroked the back of her head, found her braid, and slid down its length before toying with the end, which was bound with a scrap of blue ribbon.

"Servants are an unending source of information. When I saw how Trent terrified you, I had Barnet ask around. Trent was in some way responsible for your damaged leg, wasn't he?"

Gabby's breath caught on a little gasp. Her fingers clutched his chest hair again, but this time he didn't seem to notice. His hand was at the base of her spine now, spread flat against the first gentle flare of her bottom, pressing her close.

"Tell me." There was no doubt, this time, that it was a command.

For a moment Gabby hesitated. She couldn't speak of what had happened, had never been able to speak of it. Not to anyone, not her sisters or Twindle or Jem. All these years she had kept the events of that night bottled up inside—and they had visited her in the form of nightmares. Over the years, though, the nightmares had become less frequent, and finally had nearly ceased altogether. The one tonight was the first she had had since her father's death. It had been brought on, no doubt, by her hair-raising encounter with Trent.

Then she realized: here was the one person she could tell who wouldn't be frightened by the knowledge or somehow put in harm's way by it. Who was neither a servant nor a woman, and who was, moreover, only a visitor to their insular little world where wealth and nobility conveyed on one all the powers of a medieval king.

She could share her burden with him with really no more consequence than talking to herself.

"He—I—my father—I was twelve years old," she began haltingly, loosing her grip on his chest hair and smoothing her fingertips over the abused patch. She did not glance up at him, but kept her gaze on her hand. The short black hairs curled around her fingers. . . . "My father had—house parties. He was confined to a Bath chair in his later years, you know, so rarely left Hawthorne Hall. His friends came to him. They were a raffish group: mostly noblemen and their mistresses. They drank, and gambled, and—and, well, I'm sure I don't need to tell you what else went on."

"I can guess." His voice was dry.

"Yes, well, one night my father apparently ran low on funds. He invariably gambled away every pound of income the estate brought in; I am sure, if the property hadn't been entailed, he would have lost that, too. It was past four in the morning when a servant came to summon me from my bed. My father desired to see me most urgently, he said. I was not even to take time to dress. Accordingly, I rushed to his side in my nightgown and wrapper, expecting to find him at, perhaps, death's door. He was in his rooms on the second floor: by that time he rarely went downstairs anymore. There I discovered nothing more dire than my father and Trent playing cards. It was a few minutes before I realized that *I* was the wager on the table."

He made an inarticulate sound, and his arms tightened around her. She took a deep breath and went on.

"My father had lost a great deal, it seemed. The pile of cash and vouchers in front of Trent was high. After a few minutes in which they both ignored me, my father beckoned me over and pulled me around to face Trent. Will she do, he asked. I was too young to really understand what was going on, but I knew enough to be embarrassed by the way Trent was looking at me. I was frightened of him, a little, but at that point my father frightened me more. So I just stood there as Trent nodded. My father wrote something on a piece of paper, said *twenty thousand pounds against one virgin girl child* in a gloating kind of way, and pushed the note across the table to Trent. They played, and my father lost. Then he went away. The wheels of his Bath chair squeaked as he left." Gabby's eyes closed. It was all she could do to keep her voice from shaking. "I can still hear the click as he turned the key from the outside. I was locked in, alone, with Trent."

He made a sound under his breath. Gabby paused, her fingers closing over his chest hair again, suddenly unable to go on. She could hear his heart beating strongly beneath her ear. It was all she could do just to breathe.

❧ 34 ❧

"The bastard tried to rape you." It wasn't a question. His voice was harsh. Gabby could feel his hands ball into fists against her back, scrunching the thin lawn of her nightdress within them.

"He told me to take off my clothes." Gabby's voice was ragged. "He seemed to think that I would obey. When I wouldn't, he grabbed me. I got away, but he hit me with his cane—the same cane he carries now—as I was trying to get out the door, and knocked me down. Then he hit me—again, and again. I managed to get away a second time, and get on my feet. When he came after me again, I—jumped out the window. It was a long way to the ground. I fell—I remember it was a beautiful, starry night, and warm for September, and for a moment I almost felt like I was flying—and landed on the terrace, which is made of stone. The fall knocked me out, and broke my leg. I—when I came to I was in terrible pain, and still so frightened. Almost too frightened to call for help, but finally I did. Nobody came until it was light. Then Claire saw me lying on the ground from the nursery window, and came running down."

Gabby trembled uncontrollably at the memory.

"What the hell kind of father did you have?" His voice was harsh.

"A monster. He hated all of us, hated everyone. He—he blamed me, afterward, because the debt had not been paid, and he still owed Trent the money. I think he offered me to Trent again, when I was better, but Trent was not interested any longer because I was—crippled." Her voice caught on the last word.

He swore under his breath with a fluency that should have shocked her, and cradled her against him, rocking her in his arms, stroking her hair, her back. His lips brushed her forehead, her temple, her cheekbone. . . .

But before she could allow herself to accept the comfort he offered, there was one more thing she had to tell him.

She took a deep breath in an attempt to steady her voice. "He—for some reason, now that we're in London, he seems—interested—in me again. He—was at Almack's tonight. He said—he said he still has the voucher. He said— he was coming for me, to collect on it. Soon." With the best will in the world for it not to do so, her voice shook.

His arms around her were suddenly as taut as steel bands. The warm, resilient body she lay against stiffened and stilled. His breathing deepened in a way that spoke of anger being put under careful control. Gabby suddenly remembered her first impression of him: that he was a very dangerous man.

"Trent threatened you tonight?" His voice was surprisingly devoid of emotion.

Gabby nodded, swallowing. Her throat was too dry to permit her to speak.

"Don't worry about it: I'll kill him for you." The words were said with as little force as if he were commenting on the weather.

Gabby's eyes widened. He could not be serious—but she

knew instinctively that he was. She went cold with fear as she imagined him making an attempt to do just that, and instead being killed himself.

Her hand closed quite unconsciously on his chest hair again as she glanced up at him in a panic.

"No! No, please don't. Trent is very powerful. He is immensely rich, and besides that, he has—unsavory connections. I don't want you to get hurt. Please."

There was the tiniest pause.

"Gabriella."

She could feel a lessening of rigidity in the arms that held her. His body seemed to relax a trifle, too. Even his breathing gentled.

"Yes?"

"Did you know that that's quite the nicest thing you've ever said to me?"

In the midst of her panic, she was stunned at the note of amusement that had crept into his voice. His eyes glinted down at her in the familiar teasing expression. The smallest curve touched his mouth. She knew him well enough to know that despite his sudden levity he had not just abandoned his stated intention to kill Trent for her; clearly the problem was that he didn't appreciate the threat the duke represented. Her fingers tightened on his chest hair. Her hands were suddenly very cold. In any straightforward confrontation with Trent, Wickham must inevitably prevail. But Trent was not straightforward. He was underhanded and evil, and with his power and resources he need do no more than express the wish to have Wickham killed for it to be done.

"Ow! You're hurting me," he complained. One hand came up to close over hers, gently causing it to flatten on his chest and thereby release his chest hair.

"I shouldn't have told you," she said desperately, ignoring his non sequitur as she lifted her head to look directly into his eyes. "You must stay away from him, do you hear? He'll have you killed. He can order . . ."

"Gabriella," he interrupted, still smoothing her hand. "You need have no fear for me: I can take care of myself quite well, thank you. Trent won't harm me, and I will undertake to make sure that, *if* I let him live, he will never come anywhere near you again. You may safely leave the matter in my hands."

"You don't understand," she protested with a catch in her voice, making an abortive movement to clutch his chest hair again, which his stroking hand immediately quelled. "He won't do it himself. He'll order someone to kill you, and pay them well. And they will. Please, please promise me you'll stay away from him."

"You must just trust me." He sounded maddeningly placid as his fingers toyed with hers.

She made a despairing sound. "You are not invincible, you know, you big looby. Why, even I managed to shoot you."

His smile widened. "True, but in my own defense I must point out that I was not expecting such a proper young woman as you seemed to be at the time to harbor such a nasty, violent streak."

Gabby practically ground her teeth at his refusal to take her warnings seriously.

"Trent will stop at nothing," she insisted, scanning his face anxiously for some sign that she was getting through to him. "Having you killed wouldn't give him any more trouble than ordering the swatting of a fly."

"Gabriella," he said, and the glint in his eyes was pronounced now. "If I were conceited, I might interpret all this concern for my safety to mean that you have a care for me."

Blindsided by the notion, Gabby could only stare at him

for a moment, unblinking as an owl. That she had a care for him . . .

The suggestion shook her to the core. Because, she realized with a sinking sensation in the pit of her stomach, it was too horribly true. She did have a care for him, and more than just a care. Over the course of their acquaintance, she had come, by the smallest of baby steps, to depend on him to a remarkable degree, to consider him a dear friend, and more. Although, in the cool light of day, she knew—*knew*—that he could disappear as suddenly as he had arrived, tonight, wrapped tight in his arms, she discovered that hot air and moonbeams were possessed of an irresistible magic all their own.

I've fallen in love with him, she thought. Her eyes, wide with her new knowledge, locked with his.

"I don't even know your name," she whispered, appalled, as the rational part of her mind screamed in protest over what her rash heart had done.

"Nick," he said, his eyes never leaving hers. "My name is Nick."

His hand cupped the back of her head, and slowly, oh, so slowly, he pulled her mouth down to his. Then he kissed her.

❧ 35 ❧

*H*is lips were firm, and warm, and gentle. He kissed her softly, tenderly, with exquisite care, while her bones liquified and her blood turned to scalding hot lava in her veins.

Gabby closed her eyes and opened her mouth to his and let him steal her soul with nary a protest. *Nick.* It wasn't much, and for all she knew it might not even be his real name. A good many unsuspecting persons knew him as Marcus, after all. But, she discovered, it didn't matter. She was his, whoever he was, for however long he wanted her. Her body knew it instinctively. Her heart was a recent convert. Caught up in the heat of the moment, her mind accepted it, too. She had no thought of right or wrong, no thought of threat to the neat future she had struggled so hard to secure, no awareness of anything except him, and the way he made her feel.

Nick, she thought again, wonderingly, then said it aloud, and wrapped her arms around his neck, kissing him back. The kiss changed; suddenly it was no longer gentle at all. He rolled with her, so that she was on her back and he was looming above her, propped on his elbows. One hard, heavy thigh slid across hers, rucking up her nightgown as it went, and she quivered at the excitement of it. He kissed her as if he were starving for the taste of her mouth, and her heart began to pound. His tongue plundered and invaded, caressing hers, warring with it. She responded shyly at first, and then with increasing boldness as her breathing grew ever more erratic.

He tasted of brandy and cigars, and she couldn't get enough of the taste. His jaw was prickly with bristles, and she loved the masculine feel of it brushing over her skin. His hands cradled her face, caressing her cheeks, her temple, positioning her mouth to deepen the kiss. She surged up against him in response, pressing her breasts to his chest shamelessly, wanting only to get closer to him yet. Against her hip, she could feel, hard and insistent, the turgid evidence of his desire.

"Gabriella." He lifted his head then, and his voice was faintly unsteady. Her eyes fluttered open in response, and her gaze flickered over his face. *Nick.* Her impossibly handsome Nick. "Gabriella, I . . ."

"Shhh," she whispered, one hand sliding behind his head to draw his mouth down to hers again. She no longer wanted to talk, or to listen to him talk. She wanted only to kiss him, to go on kissing him until she expired from the pleasure of it. She was on fire from his kisses, dizzy with them. . . .

"Gabriella, listen." He resisted the pressure of her hand, keeping his mouth from touching hers even as she pulled his head down and lifted her lips to seek his. His eyes, glittering with the restless fire of black diamonds in the dim light, moved over her face. "I told you, I've had too much to drink. I can't just play, not like we've done before, not tonight. I want you so badly I'm hurting with it, and I'm afraid, if I don't get out of your bed, right now, that when the time comes I'm not going to be able to get out of it at all."

But even as he warned her, his gaze flickered to her mouth, and his hand slid sideways to trace the soft curve of her lips. As if it, too, had a mind of its own quite independent of his words, the hard bulge that was silent testimony to his desire rocked against her hip.

Lips parting instinctively as his thumb brushed over the line between them, Gabby looked up at him. Her breasts throbbed against the solid warmth of his chest. Her thighs quivered beneath the weight of his. She was mad for him, aching for him, starving for him.

Whatever happened, whatever the consequences, she could not just walk away from this. She might never again, the whole rest of her life, feel the way she felt with him.

"I don't want you to get out of my bed," she said, her voice surprisingly steady.

His eyes narrowed. "You don't know what you're saying. Tomorrow . . ." His voice was hoarse.

She caressed the warm skin at the nape of his neck, and wound her fingers in the thick cool silk of his hair. With the best will in the world to resist, she thought, he was still allowing his head to dip toward her mouth.

"I don't care about tomorrow," she whispered, and lifted her head from the mattress to find his lips.

"Gabriella." It was a guttural groan as her lips touched his. Then he surrendered. Suddenly his hands were all over her, caressing her breasts, sliding over her belly, stroking her thighs. Gabby was gasping, crying out, writhing, helping him as he pulled her nightgown up and off, quivering as she lay naked on the bed while he pulled his shirt over his head, then with quick, savage movements, freed himself from his

breeches and stockings. Even before his knees slid between
hers, her legs were parting to admit him. The man part of
him touched her woman part, prodded, and she gasped at
the burning, stretching sensation as it began to invade her
most intimate flesh. At the sound he stopped. The muscles
of his back seemed to bunch beneath her hands, and he
pulled his mouth from hers to take a couple of deep, gulp-
ing breaths. His shaft was ever so slightly withdrawn.

"We'll take this slow," he said in her ear. His breath was a
warm soft whisper that caused her to turn her mouth
blindly toward his again.

His shaft rested against her inner thigh, hot and throbbing
and swollen with need, but he made no further move to claim
her. He kissed her mouth again instead. Her arms wrapped
around his neck and she kissed him back with feverish abandon, and quite forgot about the thing between her legs.

"You're beautiful." He lifted his mouth, and smoothed
wayward tendrils of hair back from her face with a hand
that was not quite steady.

"So are you."

He smiled at her then, a heartbreakingly sweet smile,
and kissed the tip of her chin. His mouth slid down her
neck, and he turned his attention to her breasts, caressing
them, suckling them, gently nibbling on her nipples, until
Gabby was on fire with the pure pleasure of it. Her heart
pounded. Her pulse raced. Her breathing deteriorated to
fast little gasps that sounded as if she had been running for
miles. Finally, when her hands were buried in his hair and
she was offering her breasts up to him quite shamelessly,
his hand slid down her body to the secret place between her
thighs. She was burning hot there, and damp, melting and
so far gone with passion that she no longer cared if she
melted. When his hand found the nest of curls and stroked

it, she moaned. When it went lower still, she lay helpless and quivering as he touched her where she had been dying to be touched without even knowing what it was that she wanted. He stroked her, found a tiny little nub that she had never even dreamed existed, and rubbed it. Tongues of flame raced over her body, and she cried out.

Then his fingers slid inside her.

Gabby's breath caught, and her nails dug into his shoulders. The slow penetration of her body by first one finger, then two together, made her loins clench and burn and ache. She gasped, then arched against his invading hand, begging it for—something. Her hips moved in a circular fashion, and his body suddenly went stiff as a board. For a moment he lay perfectly still.

"God in heaven," he muttered thickly. "This is going to be the death of me."

Her lids fluttered up, and her eyes met his. His were black with passion, blazing down at her, intent.

His fingers were still inside her. He pulled them slowly out, then pushed them in again, watching her all the while.

"Do you like that?" His voice was guttural now. His lips parted as his breath whistled between them.

"Yes," she gasped, clinging to his shoulders, lost to all sense of shame. Her body tightened, wept, quaked. "Oh, yes."

"I want you more than I have ever wanted anything in my life." The words were a groan. His gaze flicked over her face. "All right, then."

His hand left her body and he moved on top of her, supporting his weight on his elbows. Her legs parted instinctively to receive him. His thighs slid between hers and suddenly his shaft was once again probing at the hot, wet place his fingers had readied for it.

As she felt him there, entering her that first little bit, the aching within her intensified until she was shuddering with it. Her thighs trembled. Her body burned. She wanted . . . She wanted . . .

He pulled out, then pushed back in again.

Gabby cried out, and his mouth claimed hers with a sudden fierce ardor. Her hands slid up his back. His skin, she discovered, was damp with sweat. His muscles flexed, and he pushed himself farther inside, until it seemed that he was wedged up against a barrier within her.

Her virginity. She was giving him her virginity. She recognized that with the last tiny flicker of sanity that remained to her, and realized too that, even if she could, she would not stop him now. She would die if he stopped now.

Then his muscles flexed again, and he seemed to gather himself. Suddenly he gave a mighty thrust and broke through the barrier.

The pain was sudden, and scalding. Gabby whimpered, stiffening, digging her nails into his back in surprised protest.

"I'm sorry." His eyes were narrow coal-black slits that gleamed down at her. He whispered the apology against her lips even as he pushed himself farther inside, stretching her, filling her to the point where she was sure she must burst.

"That—hurt," she managed unevenly as the worst of the pain began to recede.

"I know." He pressed a soft kiss against the corner of her mouth. "It won't hurt anymore. I—oh, God, Gabriella."

She did not resist, but could not help the involuntary tensing of her muscles as he began, slowly, as if he couldn't help himself, to move. He was sweating like he had put in a long day's labor under a hot sun. He held his weight from her with arms that trembled, and eased himself slowly in and out.

As he had promised, there was no more pain, although some of the magic was definitely gone.

But when he bent his head to kiss her breasts, and at the same time pushed deep inside, to her own surprise she moaned. That one small sound seemed to make him lose all sense of restraint. He groaned in answer, and she felt a tremor rack the long back she clutched. Suddenly his movements changed. They were no longer gentle at all. He drove savagely within her, his thrusts growing ever more fierce and fast and deep. His breathing came in quick harsh pants; his body pounded hers mercilessly into the mattress.

He had become a greedy predator, while she was semi-re-luctant prey. The intensity of his passion made her feel taken, overwhelmed. If it had been anyone but him she would have struggled, fought to get free. But instead she lay quiescent beneath him, her hands clutching a back made slippery by sweat, as he made her most thoroughly a woman.

The one thought that swirled through her brain was, if it was like this with a man she loved, what would it be like with one she didn't? At the thought of Mr. Jamison per-forming such an act upon her person, she shuddered.

Apparently her shudder was all it took to send him over the edge. He muttered her name, buried his face against the side of her neck, and thrust inside her so hard that she feared he might split her in two. Then he held himself there for a moment, impaling her with his flesh, gripping her hipbones with fingers that dug into her tender skin. He groaned, and his body seemed to convulse. Finally, at long last, he went limp.

Gabby lay there, staring up at the ceiling, her hands rest-ing nervelessly atop wide shoulders that, along with the rest of him, pinned her to the mattress. The man weighed a ton. He was hot and heavy and sweaty and certainly not the Prince Charming of every maiden's dream. She had wanted him, and she had certainly gotten what she wanted.

In future, she cautioned herself, she might be well advised to be careful what she wished for.

He lifted his head then, and met her gaze. She tried to smile at him, but it was a weak effort. Grimacing, he rolled off her, then gathered her up so that she was lying against his side. A muscular arm wrapped around her waist held her in place; otherwise, she would have scrambled off the bed and out of his reach, as he somehow seemed to guess.

He picked up her hand as it rested rather limply on his chest, carried it to his mouth, and pressed his lips to her palm. Then, still holding her hand, he glanced at her.

"I'm perfectly agreeable," he said with the tiniest suggestion of a twinkle, rubbing her hand over the prickly roughness of his cheek, "if you wish to box my ears."

This had the surprising effect of making her smile. Just a small smile, it was true, but genuine nonetheless, and welcome after the emotional and physical trauma of the last several minutes. She remembered suddenly that she was in love with him, quite madly really, and why. Among other reasons, she thought, had to be counted that teasing glint in his eyes.

"I don't wish to," she responded primly. "Now."

He eyed her. "And so what did you think of your first sexual experience?"

She hesitated, and her cheeks pinkened. To talk about it—did people really talk about such things? She had no idea. But he was asking, so apparently they did. Besides, worrying about maintaining a decent decorum seemed rather foolish under the circumstances. He was naked, she was naked, and they were in bed together and she was draped all over him and damp with his sweat and juices and he had just done things to her that she had never imagined anyone would do. Certainly her every pretension to modesty must have flown out the window some time since.

"It was fine." The word was a small pale thing to describe the fiery awakening of her body and then the sobering aftermath, she reflected, but it was the best she could do.

He laughed, then groaned, and kissed her palm again. Then he rolled out of bed, scooped her up in his arms before she had any idea what he meant to do, and headed toward his room with her.

❧ 36 ❧

"**W**hat are you doing?" Gabby demanded, scandalized, even as she automatically curled an arm around his neck. To be naked in bed with him was bad enough; but to be naked right out in the open air, and carried about in his arms, was far worse. She could glance down and see every inch of her skin from her neck to her toes: her breasts, no bigger than oranges, their creamy skin capped by small erect nipples, still rosy from his recent attention to them; the mahogany triangle of curls that he had just thoroughly explored and claimed; the slender curves of her thighs, draped over the hard brown muscles of his arm, complete with, on the left one only, faint scars, pearly white now and no wider than her smallest finger, that marked where her bone had broken through her flesh in two places that awful night so long ago. If it had not been for the scars, she reflected, no one would know, just from looking, that there was anything wrong with her leg.

"I need a smoke, and a swallow or two of brandy to clear my head, and then you and I, my girl, are going to have a talk."

That sounded like a promising enough agenda, especially

when he set her carefully down on the edge of his bed, dropped a quick kiss on her mouth, and provided her with a pitcher of water, a basin, and a cloth, before proceeding to turn his back. As she gave herself a quick sponge bath, she eyed his back with a great deal of interest. He was as naked as the day he was born, and, seemingly, not a whit bothered by it. Not that, aside from modesty, which he didn't seem to possess in any appreciable amount, he had anything to be bothered about. From his wide shoulders to his sleekly muscled back to his long, powerful-looking legs, he was more masculinely gorgeous than even the Greek statues at the museum. She observed his buttocks with particular fascination. She already knew they were smooth and firm to the touch. Now she saw that they were nice to look at, too. Very nice.

"Nick," she said experimentally, having finished her sponge bath, run her fingers through her now loose hair, and pulled on his dressing gown, which had been lying very conveniently across the foot of his bed. Holding a snifter of brandy in one hand and a lit cigar in the other, he actually responded to the name, turning with an inquiring look to face her. She was sitting up against the headboard by this time, her legs curled beneath her, feeling appreciably better now that she was both clean and minimally decent.

What she had been going to say next died on her lips as she got her first good, full frontal look at a naked man.

The sight practically stopped her breath.

She had known that his shoulders were broad and that his arms bulged with muscle. She had known about the wedge of black hair on his chest and how it tapered to a trail leading straight down over his hard-as-a-washboard belly. She had known about his male appendage, and how, when sated, it hung in a semi-somnolent state from its bed of black hair. She had known about the red, puckered scar

just above his left hip—she had given it to him, after all—
and even about the other scar, jagged as a lightning bolt
and paler than his skin, that snaked down his right thigh.

What she hadn't known was how looking at him like
that would affect her. She felt her eyes widen, and her
mouth go dry.

"What?" he asked when she didn't say anything. Gabby's
gaze rose to meet his, and she realized, to her embarrassment, that he had turned around in response to something
she had said. The problem was, she couldn't remember exactly what that was. Oh, yes; his name: Nick.

"I just wanted to see if you answered," she said, a shade
tartly. "I would imagine it's hard to keep your identity
straight, when you seem to have a name *du jour.*"

He chuckled, swallowed the small amount of brandy in
his glass, and set the glass down. Then he put his cigar in
his mouth and came toward her, gloriously naked.

"Back to being a shrew again, are we? You must be feeling better." He removed the cigar from his mouth as he
reached the bed, and stubbed it out in a receptacle on the
bedside table. "Nick is my real name, I promise."

"Nick who?" She met his gaze with a touch of wariness
in her own. The state of his body, which had changed considerably just over the course of their conversation,
alarmed her. He looked ready, willing and able to . . . Could
men do that more than once a night? Apparently they
could. But *she* could not. Or at least, she didn't want to, and
so she meant to make perfectly clear to him.

He gave her a charmingly crooked smile, and sat down
on the edge of the bed. "Why is it that women are never satisfied, I wonder? I tell you my name's Nick, and you say,
Nick who? I make love to you, and you say it was fine.
Gabriella, *fine* is not a word that a man likes to hear in that

context. I think, if we try again, we can certainly improve on *fine*."

"Wait." When he leaned forward, clearly meaning to kiss her, she placed a detaining hand on his chest. "I . . ."

His hand came up to grip her wrist, holding her hand in place. Beneath the crisp mat of hair and the warm, resilient layers of skin and muscle, she could feel the steady beating of his heart against her palm.

Her gaze met his. The fire in his room was only minimally bigger than the one in her own, but it provided enough light for her to plainly see the hard planes and angles of his chiseled features, and the intent look in his eyes.

"No matter how carefully it's done, the first time is never good for a woman," he said quietly. "And to make matters worse, I'd had too much to drink. I lost control at the end. I should have been gentler, but I wanted you so damned much that I just couldn't slow it down. Forgive me."

"Nick." But her resolve was melting in the face of those blue eyes. "It isn't your fault. You warned me. I told you to go ahead."

"Are you sorry?" He brought her hand up to his mouth again, and pressed his lips to her knuckles. The warmth of his lips sent a little shiver coursing down her spine.

"No." She swallowed, knowing as she said it that she spoke nothing but the truth. "No. I'm not sorry."

"You are the most beautiful thing I have ever set eyes on in my life," he said then, in a deeper tone, lowering her hand but not releasing it. "And I'd cut off my right hand sooner than hurt you again." A tiny muscle jumped at the corner of his mouth. Then he seemed to shiver, and when he spoke again his voice was lighter and brisker. "I'm freezing, and you, in case you haven't noticed, are wearing my dressing gown. How about if we just get into bed together and talk? I won't do anything you don't want me to, I give you my word. And you can ask me all the questions you want."

Gabby looked at him rather suspiciously. That last sounded too good to be true. It made her think of balky horses and metal pans filled with corn.

Which, indeed, proved to be the case. Having been cajoled into bed with him—although she had categorically refused to give up his dressing gown—she lay wrapped in his arms with the covers piled high atop them both. She was cozy and comfortable and warm as toast, and perfectly content to watch him wind a thick skein of her all-too-abundant hair around his fist in an absentminded kind of way, then unwind it before repeating the operation all over again.

"Nick who?" was her first question.

He slanted a half-exasperated, half-amused look down at her. "If I told you, would it make any difference?"

"It might," she said. "Try me."

He laughed, and pressed a quick kiss to the end of her nose.

"All in good time," he said.

"You said I could ask you anything I liked," she reminded him. Her hand rested on his chest. Her fingers spread out of their own accord, burrowing through the thick mat of hair. While the covers were tucked cozily around her shoulders, they only covered him to the waist. When she had, in the spirit of helpfulness, tried to tuck them closer around him, he had pushed them down to their current level. Which was quite all right with her. She found the sight of his wide, black-furred chest, broad bare shoulders, and heavily muscled arms impossibly appealing.

"I did, didn't I?" He glanced at her with a lurking smile. "But I didn't say I was going to answer."

"Oh, you." She was not surprised by the evasion, but she gave his chest hair an admonitory little tug anyway.

"Ow!" His fingers unwound from her hair and captured the hand on his chest, flattening it. "There's that nasty, violent streak I was talking about showing itself again."

"The only times I've been nasty and violent toward you, it's been well deserved," she said severely, then glanced back at their joined hands. The feel of his chest was intoxicating despite her recent disenchantment with some other parts of his anatomy, she reflected. His skin was so warm, and the muscles beneath were so solid. . . . She moved her fingers experimentally.

He took a deep breath, and freed her hand to push the covers even farther down, so that he was just minimally decent. His navel, his hipbones, the puckered scar where she had shot him, all were revealed.

"I thought you were cold," she said, frowning up at him.

The faintest of smiles curled his mouth. "Not anymore."

"Oh," she said, as she got his meaning.

"Yes, *oh*."

"You can't possibly—I mean, you don't want to do that again, do you?" Faint consternation colored her voice.

"The thought had crossed my mind, I must admit."

"Well, I don't." The words were very firm.

He laughed.

"Gabriella," he said, in a slightly altered tone. "You like touching me, don't you?"

She slanted a look up at him. As she was at the moment lightly stroking his chest, there wasn't much point in denying it. "I—yes. I guess."

"Why don't you then?"

Her eyes widened. "What do you mean?"

"I like it when you rub my chest that way. I like your

hands on me. I could show you some other things I like, if you'd let me."

The look she gave him must have been suspicious, because he grinned at her.

"You're looking at me like I'm the spider and you're the fly. Sweetheart, I'm not going to make you do anything you don't want to do. If you don't like something, just say so, and we'll stop right there."

It was the caressingly uttered *sweetheart* that did it. That, and the twinkle in his eyes.

"What do you want me to do?" Not that she minded, not really. As long as all he wanted her to do was touch him, that is.

"This." With his hand atop hers, he guided her fingers over his chest, over each flat male nipple, which to her surprise hardened under her touch, then down, over his belly, over his abdomen. Gabby's fingers tingled at the feel of him. His skin was smooth and warm and rough with hair, and felt nothing at all like her own soft silky flesh. Touching him was a pleasure, she discovered; she could gladly have gone on touching him for the rest of the night.

He let go of her hand when, of its own accord, one of her fingers decided to explore his navel. She remembered how she had wanted to do that before, without a towel to come between his skin and hers. . . . She delved in and out, then stroked the surrounding abdomen. His firm, muscular belly was such a contrast to her own. . . .

"Don't stop there," he said when she paused to consider the contrast of her slim white fingers with his shades darker, hair-roughened flesh. His tone was teasing, but there was a husky note underlying the words. Gazing at him, arrested, she realized that he wanted her to go lower yet. When his hand covered hers again, and started to guide hers down, she didn't resist. He kicked the covers down around his feet, and the object of the quest was suddenly obvious.

A tingle raced down her spine as she looked at it. Dear Lord, no wonder that thing had hurt going inside her. It should be clear to anyone of the meanest intelligence that it simply could not fit. It must have been intended for a larger female than she.

When she said as much, he laughed uproariously.

"That almost makes up for the *fine*, I guess."

She frowned at him, uncomprehending. "What?"

"Nothing. Gabriella, I'm dying here. Touch me. Please."

She was not proof against that *please*. When, allowing his hand to guide her, her fingers closed around him, it was all she could do not to pull back. It felt so—foreign in her hand. Before, when he'd been ill and had put her hand on him, it had been much smaller, although the contact had been so brief details had hardly registered. Now it was huge and thick and hot, with slightly damp, velvety smooth skin. She squeezed it, just to see what would happen.

He sucked in his breath, drawing her attention to his face. With fascination she saw that his jaw was set, and sweat beaded his brow. His lips were slightly parted as he breathed through clenched teeth, and his eyes were narrow glittering slits as he met her gaze.

"Am I hurting you?" she asked, preparing to let go.

"No." The words were forced through his teeth. "Oh, no. That feels—good."

"It does?" Interested now, she sat up, and squeezed again. He made a low guttural sound that was a cross between a groan and a growl.

"You can also—do it like this."

His hand closed over hers again, demonstrating silently how to please him. Kneeling at his side, she repeated what he taught her until he stopped her, suddenly, by grabbing her wrist and pulling her hand away from him.

She looked at him inquiringly.

"That's enough." His breathing was labored. For a few minutes he simply lay there with his eyes closed and his hand wrapped around her wrist. Finally his lids lifted, and he looked at her, smiling a little wryly as their gazes met. Then he sat up.

"Gabriella." He was very close. She was sitting back on her haunches by this time, and still the top of her head didn't quite reach his chin.

"Hmm?"

"Will you trust me to show you something else?"

By now she was more interested than nervous. "What?"

He still held her wrist. His other hand came up to cup the nape of her neck. For a moment he simply stroked the tender flesh there without replying. Then he bent his head, and touched his mouth to hers.

❧ 37 ❧

$\mathcal{B}$y the time Gabby realized that they were once again lying down, and he had somehow managed to divest her of his dressing gown and was at that moment positioning himself between her thighs for another assault on her person, she was so lost in the throes of passion that she could do nothing but cling to him and wait, martyrlike, for the pain she only just now remembered. He'd beguiled her with kisses, first on her mouth and later on her breasts and belly and even her soft inner thighs. Then, to her shocked surprise, he had even kissed the very core of her, loving her with his mouth until she was trembling and gasping and writhing with passion.

Only then, when she was mindless with pleasure, had he moved between her thighs. And still her foolish, forgetful body was hot and wet and ready, burning with the fire he had ignited, wanting, needing, craving—him.

He was far too big, she remembered frantically as he probed the opening. Her eyes opened wide, but his mouth was on hers and before she could pull it free and order him to stop he was pushing inside, stretching her, filling her— but there was no pain.

Instead it felt—almost wonderful.

"All right?" he asked then, his voice thick, as he lifted his mouth from hers at last and looked down at her.

"Yes." She must have sounded a little doubtful, or perhaps her eyes were still wide, because, despite the hard passion that suffused his face, he gave her a wry little smile.

"Trust me," he said, and she discovered, somewhat to her own surprise, that she did. His shaft was huge and solid and hard as a rock inside her, but he wasn't using it, just holding it deep in there, and the result was—amazing. She moved her hips experimentally, just to see what would happen, and the resultant fiery clenching of her loins around him made her gasp. He smiled again, quite differently than before, then bent his head to press his lips to the tender spot just below her ear. Still he didn't move the lower part of his body. She rocked her hips against him again just because she couldn't help it, and hot tendrils of pleasure shot through her belly and down her thighs. When she moaned and shivered in delicious response, he answered by sliding his hands beneath her thighs and lifting them until her knees were bent on either side of him.

"Wrap your legs around my waist," he said in her ear.

Gabby drew in her breath, but did as he told her, and found, as she twined her limbs around him, that she was trembling with anticipation. Then, finally, he began to move. With each slow, sure thrust she cried out, arching her back, clinging to him.

"God, you feel good." His words were guttural. Gabby scarcely heard them. Her heart pounded in her ears. She gasped, cried out, got lost in a sea of sensations that she had never even imagined existed. The melting she had experienced before had turned to pure liquid fire, and it was shooting through her veins, undulating along her nerve endings, making her feel as though at any minute her body might burst into flames. As he felt her response he began to thrust harder, faster, driving himself into her, and this time she welcomed the fierceness of his taking and responded with a hungry urgency of her own. Finally his hand slid between their bodies, found the very heart of her desire, and stroked her there, and her passion spiraled out of control.

"Nick, Nick, Nick, *Nick!*" she sobbed against his shoulder as suddenly her world seemed to explode into searing pinwheels of fire. Long, exquisite tremors racked her body. She clung to him, shaking, gasping as shooting stars of pleasure sizzled through her veins.

His arms tightened around her in response, and, shuddering, he plunged deep inside her as he found his own release.

When Gabby finally floated back to earth and opened her eyes, it was to discover that she was lying flat on her back with him propped up on an elbow beside her, watching her with a lazy, annoyingly self-satisfied smile playing around the edges of his mouth.

"What do you think? Did we manage to improve on *fine?*"

From the look of him, he knew the answer very well.

"I'm not going to answer that. You're too conceited already."

He laughed, bent his head, and kissed her. "You'll tell me one of these days," he said, quite cheerful. Then he yawned hugely, gathered her close against his side, and fell almost instantly asleep.

Before Gabby had time to feel affronted, she too was asleep, wrapped close in his arms.

When she awoke, she was in her own bed, and Mary was creeping around her bedroom building up the fire and generally readying the chamber for the day. The cold light of early morning was peeping around the edges of the curtains. She was, Gabby discovered as she stretched, quite naked, and immediately the events of the night replayed themselves in her mind. She had slept with Wickham—no, Nick. Nick now. *Her* Nick. She had thrown her cap over the windmill with a vengeance, given a nefarious rogue whose true name she could not even be sure of the most precious gift she had to give, and whistled Mr. Jamison and security down the wind, all in one mind-bogglingly glorious night.

And the wonderful thing about it was, she didn't regret it one bit.

She stretched again, and suddenly became aware of the slight soreness between her thighs and the unusual tenderness of her breasts. Recollecting the cause with utmost vividness, she smiled dreamily up at the ceiling.

Nick. She had given herself to Nick.

"I'm sorry, mum. I didn't mean to wake ye up," Mary said contritely, looking up from where she was sweeping ashes from the hearth.

"That's all right, Mary." Smiling at the maid, Gabby felt a sudden spurt of alarm. Had Wickham—no, Nick now, and that had better be his real name if the rogue knew what was good for him—left any evidence of his presence behind, like his breeches, or a stocking? She had a horrible vision of his clothes being strewn about the carpet.

She couldn't sit up to check, of course. She had to stay in bed with the covers up to her neck in case Mary should discover that she was naked. Sleeping naked was quite shocking in and of itself, even without having a gentleman's discarded clothing discovered in one's bedchamber. The only thing more scandalous would be for the gentleman himself to be discovered sleeping in her bedchamber—or for her to be discovered sleeping in his.

Where she had been until, she guessed, roughly an hour before.

She had the vaguest recollection of Nick carrying her to her own bed. Thank goodness he had woken out of the deep sleep he had fallen into for at least long enough to do that. It was quite likely that he had also removed his clothing from her room at that time, she thought. Whatever else he was, he was far from being a flat.

As she thought of all the things that he was, and acknowledged that she was wildly in love with him despite them, she felt a most unfamiliar bubble of happiness start to grow inside her.

"You can go ahead and prepare my bath, Mary. And bring my breakfast up."

"It's early to be gettin' up, mum," Mary said doubtfully. "Just gone half past seven, it is. 'Course, you're not the only one up with the chickens this morning. My lord's been out of the house for this hour past."

Gabby's eyes widened a little at this. "My lord—you mean Lord Wickham?" It was going to be quite a trick, she realized, to keep his names straight—Wickham in public and Nick in private; she had almost stumbled then. Oh, dear, the situation was growing increasingly complicated. "He is gone from the house?"

"Yes, mum. He left an hour since, and his man, that Mr. Barnet, with him. Barnet saddled the horses himself. Your Jem was real put out about that, when he came into the kitchen this morning. Said Mr. Barnet had no business in the stables."

Gabby stared at Mary. Nick—and Barnet—had gone somewhere on horseback. If he had simply gone out for a morning ride—a very early morning ride, and this after a night most energetically spent—he wouldn't have taken Barnet. Would he?

A hideous thought assailed her. Was he—please God he was not!—going to confront Trent?

The very idea made her feel faint.

"Run downstairs and get my breakfast, Mary. I am getting up."

❧ ❧

He did not come home that day, or that night. Pleading a severe headache, she spent almost the entire day in her room, on tenterhooks, waiting for him to return home. But he did not.

Mr. Jamison called, and was sent away, not too unhappily, with the intelligence that Lady Gabriella was too unwell to see him. He was not the only visitor, according to Claire, who, along with Beth, stopped in at intervals to check on her. Nearly a dozen gentlemen had called, and almost as many ladies: a sure sign of social success.

"Tomorrow you must get yourself downstairs and accept Mr. Jamison," Aunt Augusta informed her severely, after having ascended to her chamber with the express purpose of providing her with a recipe for a *tisane* that she knew from her own experience cured headaches without fail. "There is still some talk about Wickham's extraordinary behavior toward you, I'm sorry to say, although I've managed to squelch most of it. Well. Maud Banning has a vicious tongue on her, and always has, and she doesn't like you and most particularly Claire. I've no doubt she's at the root of it, and very few people—certainly none of sense—pay her any heed. But still, it will be as well for you to get Mr. Jamison locked up. There's many a slip 'twixt cup and lip, you know, and suitable marriage prospects for a girl of your age aren't exactly thick on the trees."

Gabby agreed to that, and if her agreement was somewhat listless Aunt Augusta put it down to the effects of the headache, and went away.

By the next morning, when Nick still had not come home, Gabby was beside herself with fear. She had scarcely slept all night, so hard had she listened for him. And she had actually looked in his chamber twice, just to make certain that she had not missed him when he came in. But he didn't come, and thoughts of him being injured or killed by Trent began to take horrible possession of her mind.

What else would keep him from home at such a juncture? After the night they had spent, surely, surely, he would not just leave? Without a word?

Too worried to care about anything but Nick, she sent for Jem.

"You want me to go see if that swine of a duke is still in town?" Jem asked with disbelief. Like Stivers, he knew Trent of old, and held him in extreme dislike, although Gabby had never revealed Trent's part in the fall that had broken her leg. "If you don't mind my askin', why exactly?"

"Because—because Trent said something insulting to me. I told Wickham and he said he would kill Trent for me. And he left very early yesterday morning, and has not come home since."

"It seems to me, Miss Gabby, that you're tellin' that *imposter* entirely too much about yer personal affairs," Jem said severely.

"Jem, please, just do as I ask." Some of Gabby's wretchedness must have been apparent in her voice, because Jem's expression changed to one of concern.

"He's properly cozened you with his smooth talk, has he? You keep the line with him, Miss Gabby. He's trouble, pure and simple."

"Jem . . ."

"I'll go, if you're wantin' me to. But I'm telling you straight out, it's not likely that anything's happened to him.

What's more likely is that he's simply come across a better scam, and taken himself off."

When Jem returned to report that Trent was still in London, still going about his business normally, and he had not, from inquiring judiciously in the stables and among the servants, picked up any scent of Wickham or Barnet coming anywhere near the duke, Gabby felt ill.

The possibilities associated with Wickham's disappearance were endless, and none of them, from her perspective, were good.

Pleading residual exhaustion from the previous day's headache, Gabby excused herself from expeditions proposed by both Claire and Beth, and went upstairs immediately after luncheon. It was ignoble of her to stoop so low, she knew, but perhaps, if she looked through Wickham's—Nick's—oh, whoever's—room, she would find some clue as to why he had left so precipitously.

Without a word.

That was the part, she thought, that truly bothered her. After the night they had spent, after what they had been to each other, surely, surely, he would not purposely have left her for this length of time *without a word*.

She entered his chamber through the connecting door, feeling like a thief in the night. At this time of day, the servants were likely to be busy with chores elsewhere in the house, but still she would not like to be discovered going through Wickham's things. It would look most odd. . . .

His apartment was, in a strange kind of way, comforting. In his dressing room, a few shining black hairs still clung to his brush. His highly polished Hessian boots, with their dangling tassles, had been placed side by side in a corner. Several fresh neckcloths hung over the back of a chair. She opened drawers, feeling increasingly guilty as she rummaged through their contents, but found nothing beyond cufflinks and the usual jewelry and gewgaws that a gentleman of fashion might reasonably be expected to possess. In his bedroom, there was even less that was personal: a collapsible spyglass placed on the mantle, a box of cigars and a bottle of brandy on the table near the fire, a book on military history on the table by the bed.

Nothing to tell who or what he really was; nothing to tell where he was.

Feeling guiltier than ever, she pulled open the single drawer in the table beside the bed.

The first thing she noticed was the smell. A heady smell, sweet and cloying, like roses past their prime. Wrinkling her nose at it, she almost smiled. Such a scent was unlikely to appeal to Nick, although, she thought with a gathering frown, it did seem faintly familiar. Then her eyes fell on the collection of unsealed, neatly folded notes that graced the drawer, and she knew.

The scent came from Lady Ware's *billet doux.*

❧ 38 ❧

eading another person's mail was reprehensible. Gabby knew it, knew she should close the drawer and walk out of the room. To do so was utterly beyond her. She picked up one of those perfumed notes, and began to read.

Besides fulsome words of love, they contained erotic descriptions of the things *mon cher Wickham* had done to Lady Ware, or things she wanted him to do.

By the time Gabby had finished—there were perhaps six notes in all—Gabby felt as if she had sustained a mortal blow. She could feel the blood leaching from her face; her stomach churned, and she feared she would be sick.

Some of the acts described in the notes she had experienced first hand. *Mon cher Wickham* had introduced them to her, too.

"My lady!"

Mary's voice from the other room brought her head up. Putting down the note she had just finished, she closed the drawer, and walked with deliberate steps toward her own apartment. She no longer worried about being caught in Wickham's chambers. She no longer worried about anything to do with Wickham at all. She could almost hear the cautionary tone in which he had uttered, on that never-to-be-forgotten night when she had allowed herself to be seduced by one who was, in Jem's words, a right blackguard, the word *tomorrow*. She couldn't say that he hadn't warned her, in his fashion, that tomorrow would come.

And it had.

Her fear for him now seemed foolish. Worse, it seemed pathetic, like the unwanted clinging of a love-smitten old maid. Of course he had not thought to leave word for her when he had taken off with Barnet for whatever reason. What they had done together might have meant the sun, the moon, and the stars to her. To him, it was no more than a little pleasant exercise undertaken in female company, the type of thing he clearly indulged in with different and various women almost every night. Nothing special at all: the knowledge tore at her heart.

"Oh, mum, there you are!"

Gabby had walked right through to her bedchamber without even realizing it. Mary was there, first smiling at her, then frowning.

"Is your headache back, my lady?" she asked sympathetically. "You're that pale."

"Did you want me for something, Mary?" Gabby asked, surprised at how cool and composed her voice sounded. Inside, she felt wounded, no, shattered. But the best thing about having lived with the kind of father she had endured for most of her life was, she had learned how never to let an injury show.

"Mr. Jamison is here, my lady, and Lady Salcombe—she's here too—bade me come up and tell you so. Shall I tell them you're unwell, my lady?"

Gabby took a deep breath. If Mr. Jamison was here, it

could only mean one thing: he wished to make her a formal offer.

She would be a fool to turn him down. She could only thank God that she had come to her senses in time.

"No, Mary, I'll come. Just let me wash my hands, and tidy my hair."

Gabby washed her hands, and Mary repinned her hair. Then Gabby went downstairs. With every step she took, she could not escape the sickening scent of past-their-prime roses. No matter how she scrubbed, Lady Ware's perfume would not come off her skin.

ॐ　ॐ

The following night was Claire's come-out ball. Despite the frenzied preparations that had, under Aunt Augusta's direction, taken place around her, Gabby had almost forgotten about it. If it had not been for Claire to bully her into her dressing room and Mary to bundle her mistress into the bath and dress her and fix her hair, she might have pleaded illness and stayed abovestairs. In this case, claiming that she was unwell would not have been far from the truth. She had not been able to eat more than a bite or two for the last three days, and she could not sleep at all.

Wickham had still not come home. He had been gone without a word for nearly three full days.

"I am going to *kill* that boy," Aunt Augusta hissed in Gabby's ear as she took the latecomer by the arm and hustled her into place in the receiving line. The older woman was resplendent in purple satin, with a magnificent diamond necklace and a trio of ostrich plumes adorning her silver hair. Clad in a ballgown of dull gold lace over an underdress of gold satin, Gabby knew that, between her magnificent aunt and her beautiful sister, she was overshadowed, and was content to have it so. "He is the *host*. What will everyone think if he is not here?"

Her eyes swept over Gabby and Claire, who stood beside her sister looking like a fairy princess in purest white, with spangles, and a simple strand of pearls. "You both look just as you ought. Gabriella, pinch your cheeks. You are by far too pale."

Then the first guests began to come up the stairs.

The ball was a smashing success. As the evening progressed, a palpable sense of excitement hung in the air. All of fashionable London was in attendance, the ladies in their most extravagant ballgowns and their finest jewelry, the gentlemen elegant in their best evening attire. Aunt Augusta overheard several guests describe it as a *dreadful crush* and, knowing that for the highest of accolades, was almost giddy with triumph. Wickham's absence, while still galling, as she confided to Gabby in an occasional muttered aside, was not being overly remarked on, as she had had the good sense to ascribe it to a death in a distant branch of his mother's family. And Gabby's own less-than-decorous behavior with her brother seemed to have been forgotten.

"Though how Wickham can have gone off without a *word*," Aunt Augusta said with disgust as Mr. Jamison went off at her instigation to fetch her a glass of punch, "you must some time explain to me. Well. It would be wonderful if we could announce your engagement at our own ball, but without Wickham here we cannot do it, I suppose. It will have to wait until he returns."

If he returns, Gabby thought, feeling the hard cold knot of pain that had not left her since she had read Lady Ware's missives tighten in her stomach. Though she had always known him for a womanizing cad—among many other, probably worse, things—she had idiotically allowed herself to imagine that their relationship had evolved ino something unique. Having been so foolish as to permit herself to fall in love with him, she could not just pluck the feelings she had for him from her heart like a troublesome splinter. They were lodged in place for, she feared, quite a while. The difference was that she was no longer blind to what he was: a charming rogue, no more, no less.

And she had a life to live, and sisters to provide for.

Mr. Jamison would make her a good, steady husband. Better than she deserved.

She had accepted him yesterday, knowing full well that she was coming to him defiled. But she meant to do her best to make herself into just the wife he wanted.

It was the least she could do, when, in accepting him without revealing her altered state, she had made herself into a liar, and a cheat.

"I suppose that's the last of them. After we've greeted these, we may as well join our guests," Aunt Augusta said, observing that the line on the stairs had slowed to a trickle. In the hall below, the servants in their livery were scurrying away with the last of the cloaks and topcoats. The closing front door blocked the sound of departing carriage wheels.

Gabby greeted the latest arrivals, and then, taking Mr. Jamison's proffered arm, turned to enter the ballroom. Claire, who had been dismissed from duty earlier, skipped down the room with other couples to the strains of a merry quadrille. Her partner, Gabby saw, was the Marquis of Tyndale, who was looking quite smitten as he gazed at Claire. More guests milled around the edges of the floor. A few unfortunate debutantes who had not yet been asked to dance sat in chairs along one wall, their white dresses easy to spot among the more colorfully clad chaperones. Desdemona was among them, and beside her Lady Maud sat with a smile on her face that could have been carved from granite as she exchanged conversation with the lady on her other side. Taking pity on her cousin, Gabby vowed to dispatch an eligible gentleman her way as soon as she could, then turned her attention elsewhere.

The room was long, and narrow, and already growing over warm, though it was still fairly early in the evening. The long windows that looked out on to the garden were flung open, and filmy curtains fluttered in the breeze. Dozens of candles burned in gilded sconces. More candles shed their light from sparkling crystal chandeliers overhead. Flowers and greenery were banked in the corners, and the mirrors set into the wall reflected it all. The orchestra, hired for the evening, played beautifully, and the air was filled with infectious music and the sound of laughing, chattering voices.

Gabby circulated on Mr. Jamison's arm, and was introduced to his sister, and several of his particular friends. She chatted with her own friends, and, without seeming to be so, was aware of a rising stream of comments linking her to Mr. Jamison that was just one of many tributaries to the river of gossip that was the *ton*'s lifeblood. The only bad moment in what was otherwise a tolerably enjoyable evening came when the orchestra struck up the first waltz.

She had a sudden vivid memory of waltzing with Nick.

"Would you care to . . . ?" Mr. Jamison offered gallantly, indicating the floor.

Gabby smiled at him. He was a kind, good man, and it was not his fault that she had fallen top over tails in love with a handsome scoundrel instead of appreciating her good fortune in attaching a man like him.

"I really don't dance," she said with a smile. He looked relieved, and led her down to the supper room instead.

❧ 39 ❧

*A*fter three days spent mainly in the saddle, Nick was dead tired. Trotting beside him, Barnet looked as weary as he felt. Approaching the mews through the narrow alley that ran behind the row of fashionable houses, they both heard the music at the same time and looked at each other.

"Hell, I forgot about Claire's thrice-damned ball."

"I'd say you're in for a rare trimming, then, Cap'n." Barnet sounded annoyingly merry at the prospect. "Miss Gabby'll 'ave your 'ead on a plate. And Lady Salcombe. That old lady's been plannin' this thing with more care than Napoleon plots 'is campaigns. She's gonna chew you up and spit you out."

"Just whose side are you on, Barnet?" Nick asked sourly. His mood was not improved by the wide grin he got in return. To cap his enjoyment, the groom who emerged from the stables a few moments later to take their horses was Jem. He scowled when he recognized them.

"So yer back, are ye?" he said with a marked lack of respect as Nick swung down, and handed him his reins. Barnet did likewise and was rewarded with a growl.

"How are the ladies?" Nick asked, both because he truly wanted to know and because he had come to the reluctant conclusion that this old fool was going to have to be tolerated for Gabriella's sake.

"Jest dandy," Jem said in a grim tone that in no way matched his words. He started to lead the horses away, then turned around to glare at Barnet. "You can put your own bloody horse up." He thrust Barnet's reins back at him. "I ain't your bloody groom." His jaw tightened, and he slanted a glance at Nick. "I ain't yours, either, when you comes right down to it. 'Cause you ain't he."

"Crabby old coot," Barnet said as Jem stalked off, leading Nick's horse. "One of these days I'm goin' to plant 'im a rare wisty castor, Cap'n, not bein' able to 'elp meself an' all."

"Well, you can't." Nick's reply was short. "Miss Gabby wouldn't like it."

Barnet made a disgruntled sound, and headed into the stables with his horse.

Left alone in the dark, Nick walked quickly through the back garden. He stuck to the shadows near the shrubberies, walking across the grass rather than following one of the meandering brick paths, trying to stay out of the patches of light that spilled from the windows of the ballroom along with music and laughter and chattering voices. If he could do it, he would prefer to reach his chambers without being spotted. He hadn't had a bath since he'd left, and to his own nostrils he smelled about as ripe as three-day-old garbage. He hadn't had a shave either, or a change of clothes. In his opinion, anyone who looked less like an earl than he did at the moment would have been hard to find.

But—he thought, he was almost sure—he'd found what he'd been looking for. He'd only meant to be gone for perhaps half a day, but one thing had led to another and suddenly, the answer to the whole riddle had dropped into his lap, and half a day had stretched to three.

Now all he wanted to do was see Gabriella.

However the whole convoluted mess unraveled, one thing was crystal clear: she was now his. In taking her virginity, he had committed himself, although under the circumstances honoring that committment was going to be tricky. They'd just have to work out the details as they went along.

He was smiling faintly as he let himself in the back door and took the servants' stairs two at a time. The question was, just how much had she missed him?

If he was lucky, and he always had been, the answer, which he hoped to give her a chance to demonstrate in the very near future, would be *a lot.*

"Marcus! Marcus!"

He looked up in surprise. Beth, clad in a demure white dress, was sitting on the landing just above him, her black-slippered feet resting side by side on the step beneath her. For a moment he couldn't think what she was doing perched there. Then he saw the plate in her lap, and smiled in sudden understanding: she'd obviously been raiding the supper room.

"Where have you *been?*" She got to her feet, beaming at him, and came down to give him a quick, one-armed hug. He hugged her back, realizing that he was as glad to see her as if she were in truth his little sister, and, as he released her, tweaked her chin. "You're missing Claire's ball. Aunt Augusta is *livid,* and Gabby's upset, too—at least, *I* think she's upset. *She* claims she's been sick." Beth abruptly wrinkled her nose, and stared at him suspiciously. "What is that smell?"

He had to grin, even though his interest had been

caught—more than caught, really—by her previous statement. "Me, I think. Never mind that. Did you say Gabriella's been ill?"

"That's what she says." Beth looked at him earnestly. "*I* think she's upset because she's agreed to marry Mr. Jamison. She doesn't like him above half, you know."

"*What?*" He stared at Beth, thunderstruck.

She nodded vigorously. "Didn't you know? Well, Gabby said she didn't need your permission when I asked her, but I thought you *knew.*"

"I knew Jamison was going to make Gabriella an offer," he said carefully, trying to keep clear in his mind that, as far as Beth was concerned, it was their mutual sister they were discussing. He was so tired it was difficult to think straight, let alone keep all the threads of the web of deceit he'd woven from getting tangled in his mind. "It was my understanding that she was going to refuse."

Beth shook her head. "She said *yes.*"

"Are you certain?"

Beth nodded.

"When?"

"He came and asked her yesterday. She accepted. Aunt Augusta wanted to announce it at the ball tonight, but she said she couldn't if you didn't get home." Her voice trailed off, and she looked at him with a growing frown. "But you're home now, aren't you? If you get changed and go downstairs, you could still make the announcement."

"Like hell," he said, before he thought.

Beth seemed to see nothing out of the way in that. "That's what I think. Gabby doesn't really want to marry him, I can tell. Maybe *you* can stop her. She won't listen to me."

"I'll do my best." He started up the stairs again, giving a

quick tug to one of Beth's red curls as he passed. "Thanks for warning me."

"I'm glad you're home," she called after him as he reached the landing and headed down the hall toward his rooms.

When Barnet showed up some fifteen minutes later, he was already out of the bath he'd had one of the footmen prepare, dressed in black evening breeches and white silk stockings, and half shaved.

"Some valet you are," he commented acidly, scraping away.

"There's no need to get snippy with *me,* Cap'n. I can't 'elp it if Miss Gabby found 'erself another feller while we were away." Barnet searched the wardrobe for his master's coat, shook it out, and hung it over the back of a chair.

"So you heard that, did you?" There had never been any keeping secrets from Barnet, and most of the time he didn't bother to try.

"Talk of the mews. And the kitchen. They say she's anxious to wed as soon as can be."

The razor slipped, and Nick swore as a bright dot of blood appeared on his cheek. Barnet made a choked sound that could have been either a cough or a laugh. Nick shot him a sideways glare.

"Makes a nice turnaround for you, though, don't it? Usually females is climbing all over each other to get to you."

Nick wiped the last of the soap from his face and tossed the towel aside. "Mind your own damned business, why don't you? And hand me my shirt."

When he was dressed at last, he headed down the front stairs, quickly but with at least a little of the decorum befitting an earl. He was almost at the bottom, waving off

Stivers who had stepped out to greet him, when something, a sound, a movement, made him glance to the side.

There, in the drawing room, was Gabriella. She was with Jamison. From what he could see the two of them were alone, and the fat fool was clasping her tightly in his arms.

Kissing her.

For a moment Nick stopped dead. Anger, possessiveness, and a thick hot tide of primitive feeling that he recognized with some distaste as jealousy warred for supremacy in his breast. Finally they joined forces. His jaw clenched. His eyes glinted.

And he walked with carefully controlled aggression toward the entwined pair.

❦ 40 ❦

"What the hell is this?"

That was the first Gabby knew that he was home. Her head turned so swiftly that her neck hurt. For a moment it was enough to simply know that he was safe. Her eyes drank him in: he was clad in impeccable black evening clothes that fit his broad shoulders and long, powerful legs to perfection. His black hair was brushed back from a hard, handsome face that looked stern now, and even angry. His eyes—yes, certainly he was angry—were a stormy dark blue. They glinted dangerously at her.

Her first, idiotic thought was, nobody, but nobody, looks like Nick.

Her second was, I'd like to break his neck.

Mr. Jamison, clearly cowed by the intimidating presence of the man glaring so fiercely at them, removed his arms from around her with a swiftness that made her stagger. She had to catch hold of a nearby chair to keep from losing her balance. Perversely, she blamed that on Nick, too, and gave him back glare for glare.

"Sir—um, my lord—my affianced wife—ah . . ." Mr.

Jamison, red-faced, was stammering more like a schoolboy than the fifty-year-old, prosperous landowner he was.

"Gabriella," Nick said, ignoring Mr. Jamison and addressing her in tones of stark outrage, "were you *kissing* him?"

Gabby smiled at that. Her chin lifted, and her voice, when she spoke, was very clear and cold.

"Yes," she said, "I certainly was."

For a moment they stared at each other in charged silence.

"Nothing havey-cavey here, you know. Your sister's accepted my suit. Um, she's going to marry me. No need for you to be upset, my lord, although I certainly honor your sentiments in desiring to protect your sister. . . ."

"Mr. Jamison," Gabby said sweetly. "Perhaps we should return to the ballroom."

"Uh, yes, certainly. If you like." He proffered his arm to her, and Gabby tucked her hand in it. With no more than a final scathing look for Nick, she prepared to sweep past him.

"Gabriella." He stopped her as she tried to do just that by the simple expedient of catching her arm. She looked down at where his long brown fingers gripped her slender white arm just above the elbow, then glanced up to meet his gaze. Her eyes flashed. "A word with you, if you please."

"No," she said baldly, and jerked her arm free. Her other hand was still tucked in Mr. Jamison's arm, and she practically propelled him from the room. She could almost feel Nick's hot breath on the back of her neck as he stalked behind them.

"Lady Gabriella," Mr. Jamison remonstrated, looking as unhappy as he sounded. "Your brother—perhaps you should—no wish to have bad relations in the family—he is your guardian, after all."

"He is *not* my guardian," Gabby said through her teeth. Recollecting herself, she added, "I am of age."

"But still . . ."

They reached the ballroom then, and Gabby pinned a smile on her face. Behind her, Nick was stopped the instant he stepped over the threshold, and engulfed. Glancing back as she hurried Mr. Jamison across the room, she saw that he was shaking hands with Lord Denby, while Mr. Pool and Sir Barty Crane waited for his notice. Lady Alicia Monteigne was closing on him from the left, with Mrs. Armitage in tow, and Aunt Augusta, having clearly spotted him from where she stood talking with an acquaintance, was headed straight toward him like a ship in full sail.

"Hah!" Gabby said with satisfaction, steering Mr. Jamison toward where Desdemona once again sat with the chaperones. Nick would come after her as soon as he could, she knew, and she meant to have a weapon to hand.

"I do think you were rather hard on Lord Wickham, I must say. I thought you were quite fond of him, to tell you the truth. It has certainly seemed . . ." Mr. Jamison's voice trailed off. "But no doubt something has occurred to put the two of you at outs. It is most unfortunate, if so. Do you think you might see your way clear to making it up with him? I was hoping he might be persuaded to announce our engagement tonight. The quicker it is known, the quicker we can get the wedding over with, you know." This attempt at humor on his part fell on deaf ears. In the act of sitting down, Gabby had been waylaid by Claire.

"Marcus is back," Claire said excitedly, having just run from the floor between dances. Her partner, young Mr. Newbury, followed her, looking besotted, as men always did around Claire. "Have you spoken to him? Did he tell you where he's been?"

Before Gabby could answer, she was waving at their "brother." Watching him wave back, then excuse himself from the crowd around him and head purposefully their way, Gabby found herself, for one of the few times in her life, feeling cross with Claire.

"We're so glad to see you," Claire trilled as Nick reached them. Smiling, she stood on tiptoe to peck his brown cheek, and he took her hands in his, twirling her around to admire her dress.

"Ravishing as always," he said with a smile.

"Thank you." Claire laughed up at him as he released her hands. Gabby caught herself looking baleful, and once again pinned a smile on her face. "We've been worried about you, Gabby especially. You really should not go off without letting us know."

He slanted a glance down at Gabby. "Obviously not."

The band struck up again.

Claire said, "Oh, dear, where is Mr. Newbury? It is his dance. Oh, there you are, Mr. Newbury. I'll talk to you later, Marcus, Gabby, Mr. Jamison."

With that she headed back out on the floor.

"Dance, Gabriella?" Nick stood directly in front of her, frowning down at her.

"I don't dance," she said with bite. She had to look up the whole long length of him to meet his gaze, and she didn't like it. To be so tall gave him, she felt, an unfair advantage.

He looked impatient. "Of course you do."

Beside her, Mr. Jamison, who was looking rather wide-eyed as he glanced from one to the other, shook his head. "No, she really doesn't. I ask her all the time, and she says the same thing: 'I don't dance.'"

Nick's eyes narrowed.

"Do you really wish to dance?" Gabby asked him before he could annihilate Mr. Jamison with a few well-chosen words.

"Yes, I do."

She smiled and turned to Desdemona, who was sitting on her left. There was an empty chair between them, so she had to touch the girl's arm to get her attention.

"Wickham was just saying how much he wanted to dance," Gabby said in a voice that was raised to be heard over the music. "I cannot, of course, but perhaps you . . . ?"

"I'd love to," Desdemona said quickly, standing up. Trapped, Nick had no choice. With no more than a single killing glare for Gabby, he smiled and offered Desdemona his arm. Gabby smiled sweetly at him as they walked away.

"Shall we get some refreshments?" she asked Mr. Jamison. The refreshments were set out in the dining room, and that was where she meant to be before Wickham came off the floor.

"If you'd like a glass of punch, I'd be glad to fetch it." Mr. Jamison stood up, looking more than a little put out.

"I'll come with you."

Unfortunately, Aunt Augusta caught them before they were more than halfway to the door.

"Isn't it the most fortunate thing that Wickham has returned?" she said to Gabby, her purple plumes nodding enthusiastically. "Well! I daresay he never intended to miss Claire's ball at all. I talked to him about announcing your engagement to Mr. Jamison tonight. He says he will be glad to, just as soon as he has a chance to talk with you to make sure it's what you want. I must say, you are very fortunate in having acquired such a *thoughtful* brother, Gabriella. Most brothers are not that way at all."

"So that is why he wanted a word with you," Mr. Jamison said, nodding and looking relieved. "You should speak with him the first chance you get." He glanced at Aunt Augusta. "I was thinking we might have a June wedding, Lady Salcombe, but I wanted to get your opinion on . . ."

The two of them were soon nattering away about the good and bad points of summer weddings, a subject which seemed to interest them both mightily while it interested Gabby not at all. Standing a little apart from them, Gabby felt the weight of a heavy gaze on her back. Glancing around, she saw Nick bearing down on her. He was scowling, his blue eyes glinting unpleasantly as they met hers. Gabby resigned herself, lifted her chin, and stood her ground.

"Stop glowering, you're making a spectacle of yourself," she said under her breath as he reached her.

The smile he gave her was a mere baring of his teeth.

"If you try to fob me off one more time, I'm going to make a spectacle of myself the likes of which you have never seen, I promise you."

Mr. Jamison glanced around just then, and saw him. "Oh, my lord, Lady Salcombe and I have just been wondering whether you would be good enough to make an announcement of Lady Gabriella's and my engagement. . . ."

The orchestra struck up a waltz.

Nick looked at her. Gabby knew what was coming even before he did it.

"My dance, I think, Gabriella," he said through his teeth, and clamped a hand around her wrist so that, in order to break away from him, she would be forced to engage in a most undignified struggle—if it could even be done at all. He glanced past her at Mr. Jamison, and nodded rather curtly. "I will let you know what I decide."

Then he practically dragged Gabby onto the floor.

≈ 41 ≈

"Suppose you explain yourself," he began unpleasantly as he swung her into the dance.

For a moment Gabby merely glared at him, so taken aback by his audacity that she was bereft of speech.

"I do not owe you, of all people, any explanation at all," she said when she found her tongue, her voice dripping icicles. "You seem to keep forgetting that you are *not* my brother."

"No," he said with an ugly glint, "I certainly don't forget that."

Unable to help herself, Gabby flushed scarlet at the obvious implication. That he could embarrass her so easily maddened her.

"You are a swine," she said through her teeth.

"What were you doing kissing Jamison?"

"Is there any reason why I shouldn't kiss him? We *are* engaged."

His hand tightened on hers, his arm hardened around her back, and he swung her around in a movement of the dance. Gabby had, perforce, to cling to his broad shoulder. Out of the corner of her eye, she caught just a glimpse of her gold lace skirt swaying against his legs. She had been so angry that she had scarcely been aware of what she was doing; now she realized that she had been waltzing almost without effort, her weak leg instinctively compensating for its disability without any thought required on her part at all.

"The hell you are." He said it almost pleasantly, but when Gabby looked up at him his eyes were hard as agates.

"You're jealous," she said on an incredulous note. "Of Mr. Jamison."

Then she laughed.

Those hard eyes flashed blue fire at her.

"So what if I am?" he said harshly after a moment. "It seems to me that you gave me every right to be. Or did I just imagine that you were naked in my bed only a few nights ago? If so, I apologize."

Gabby's jaw slackened. Then her teeth shut with a snap. She was so angry she could feel fury building inside with tangible heat.

"After which you disappeared for three days without a word," she said, and smiled at him with the false sweetness of a crocodile.

"So you got yourself engaged to Jamison to teach me a lesson. Is that it?"

"You flatter yourself."

"Were you worried about me while I was gone, Gabriella?" His expression was mocking. "Claire said you were."

Gabby's back stiffened. His hold on her was unbreakable. She could feel his legs brushing against her skirts. If there had been any hope of escaping, she thought, she would have jerked herself from his arms there and then and walked away.

But of course she could not do that. They were in the middle of a dance floor, for goodness' sake, surrounded by dozens of other waltzing couples and very likely hundreds of watching eyes.

"Is that what you think?" she asked, dredging up a mocking glint of her own. "I'm not surprised. I think we're both agreed that you tend to be a trifle conceited."

"What I think, sweetheart, is that you're throwing this little tantrum because you've discovered that you're madly in love with me."

At the jeering note in his voice, Gabby felt as if she'd been stripped naked right there in front of everyone. She wanted to wilt, to melt away like butter in the sun, to escape from him in any way she could. The charge was so true that it cut like a knife. And to think that he could make it, and call her *sweetheart* in that derisive tone, after he'd taken her virginity and left her without a word and . . .

She remembered Lady Ware's perfumed notes. Doubtless Lady Ware was madly in love with him, too.

And probably many others as well.

The knowledge was soul shriveling.

"You make me sick," she said, the words icily clear, and before she thought she drew back her hand and slapped him hard across the face.

The sound pierced the music and talk and laughter like a pin puncturing a balloon. He stopped dead, releasing her as he lifted a hand to probe his cheek. She could see the mark her hand had made quite clearly; it was white at first, and then began to fill with dark blood.

The first she remembered of their audience was the hissing sound she heard. Glancing around, she discovered that they were increasingly the cynosure of all eyes. The couples nearest them had stopped to stare. Others were stopping as well, as though wondering what the commotion was about, and even those who were crowded around the edges of the room were beginning to crane their necks and look. Gabby glimpsed Claire, craning with the others, a puzzled expression on her face as if she was not sure what had happened. On the other side of the room, Aunt Augusta stared with obvious horror. Beside her, Mr. Jamison gaped.

The hissing sound she had heard had been dozens of people gasping at the same time.

She had just ruined everything, including herself and probably Claire.

Without so much as another look at the man who had brought her to this, Gabby turned on her heel and, as quickly and gracefully as she could, fled the room.

"Gabriella." Her name, uttered in a hoarse voice, followed her.

Nick. He would be coming after her, of course.

She didn't want to see him. Not now, not ever again.

As she reached the hall, she turned and went down the servants' stairs.

Quite how she ended up in the back garden, she couldn't have said. She was numb with despair; in, she thought, a state of shock that thankfully protected her, for the moment, from feeling more than she could bear.

Ruined, ruined, ruined.

She had lost everything, including Nick, purely because of her own foolishness. But then, she reminded herself, none of it had ever really been hers in the first place. They had all existed on borrowed time since they'd come to London. And tonight time had run out.

Like Nick himself, everything—the parties, the clothes, the beaux, all the trappings of life in the *ton*—had been woven of hot air and moonbeams.

The end had been implicit in the beginning. The only wonder was that it had lasted as long as it had.

She was walking in the shadows now, skirting the patches of light that spilled from the ballroom's second-story windows, rubbing her bare arms against a night that was too cool for her low-cut gown. A slight breeze blew, making her skirt rustle. The music still played; she could still hear laughter and people talking.

With Aunt Augusta to oversee it, she had no doubt that a frantic attempt to cover her *faux pas* was being made.

But everything would be very different with the dawning of a new day.

She was looking back at the house again when, without warning, a hand came out of the shadows and closed over her arm. She jumped, glancing around, expecting that Nick had caught up with her at last.

What she saw instead made her go weak at the knees. Her mouth went dry. Her pulse began to race.

A pistol was pointing straight at her heart; she was staring at a hideously familiar face.

"Ill met by moonlight once again, it seems, Gabby dear."

❦ 42 ❧

$\mathcal{G}$abby had no sooner recognized Trent than she heard Nick calling her.

"Gabriella!"

Trent's hand tightened on her arm with enough force to hurt her. The sudden pain made her gasp.

"Be quiet." Trent sounded suddenly ruthless as he jerked her against him, holding her so that her back was to him, wrapping his arm around her throat and squeezing just enough so that her breath was temporarily cut off. Gabby grabbed his arm, her nails digging into the fine wool sleeve of his coat. The mouth of the pistol was shoved against her temple. She didn't have enough breath even to squeak. Cold terror snaked down her spine. Her pulse drummed in her ears.

"Gabriella!"

Nick was coming toward her, whether drawn by some slight sound or by instinct, she couldn't have said. Trent had drawn her into the deep shadow cast by the shrubbery. The pale sliver of a moon overhead illuminated only the center of the garden. Nick was walking down the path. His tall form was no more than a black shape in the moonlight.

She was fighting for every breath, but her fear, suddenly was all for him.

"Gabriella!"

He saw her then. Or at least, he saw something, though perhaps nothing more than a stray moonbeam glinting off a gold thread in her dress. Clearly he didn't see Trent, or realize that he was walking into danger. He changed course, coming toward her swiftly. Gabby tried to cry out, couldn't, and felt her palms grow damp.

"Gabriella, for God's sake . . ." His voice was husky.

"Ah," Trent said with satisfaction, and pushed her forward until they both stood revealed in a patch of moonlight. His arm was still around her neck; his pistol was held to her head.

Nick stopped dead. His eyes flicked over Gabby once, then moved past her to Trent. They were suddenly black and shiny as pieces of jet.

"Let her go."

Trent laughed. "My dear boy, you can't be serious."

"You can't get away."

"Well, now, you know, with Gabby here for a hostage, I almost think I can." He pushed the mouth of the pistol so hard against her temple that it felt as if he might be going to shove it through her skull. Gabby whimpered. The small sound was immediately choked off by the tightening of his arm around her neck. She remembered then that Trent was cruel. That he enjoyed being cruel.

She shivered. Her body was suddenly icy cold. Blind panic threatened to overwhelm her. She had to deliberately force it back.

"If you hurt her I'll kill you." Nick's voice held a deadly certainty.

"Are you threatening me, Captain? Oh, I beg your pardon, it's Major now, isn't it?" The arm around Gabby's throat eased its grip just the smallest bit, and she took a deep, shaken breath. Then it tightened again. It was torture, being able to breathe and then not, and she was certain he intended it as such. "Congratulations on your promotion, by the way. You *do* know he's not your brother, don't you, Gabby? Yes, of course you do. But do you know who he *is?* Major Nicholas Devane, Wellington's premier spy catcher."

There was a sneer in the last words. Gabby's eyes widened on Nick. He was working for the government? She had wronged him from the start.

"And you're the latest spy I've been trying to catch." Nick's voice was silky with menace.

"You're very thorough. I make you my compliments. I thought I had covered my tracks quite well. Actually, I've been watching you since you arrived in London. Pretending to be Wickham was quite a good trick, I must admit. It took me several weeks to ascertain that the real Wickham was truly, as he was supposed to be, dead."

"You had him killed."

Gabby could feel Trent's shrug against her back. She could breathe again now, a little, as he was focused on Nick. "It went against the grain—the son of a friend, you know—but that idiot Challow sent a sealed letter Matthew had given him for safekeeping to the new earl, along with a box of other papers. That letter identified me as a spy for the French. Really, the knowledge that he had it was all that kept Matthew alive for so long. Matthew had many flaws, but he didn't like betraying his country. Only the fact that he was in the direst financial straits enabled me to persuade him to allow Hawthorne Hall to be used as our meeting place. It was so remote, you know. And Matthew had lost all that money to me, and had no other means of paying. But he wrote that letter, and told me so. Of course, once it fell into the hands of Matthew's son I had to retrieve it. I don't believe it had been in his possession a week when I, er, got it back."

"You mean when you had the letter stolen from the house and Marcus killed on the off chance that he had read it."

Trent smiled. "That's right. I couldn't be sure, of course. But obviously he did read it, or you and I wouldn't be here. He sent for you, didn't he? But what puzzles me is how the devil he knew of your existence. Most don't, you know. Even in the military. I pride myself on being one of the few."

"Marcus was my cousin. His mother and my mother were sisters. We grew up together in Ceylon. My father was a military man, his was an earl. Our paths diverged at a young age, but we remained close. I don't mean to let you get away with killing him, you know."

"Ah," Trent said, with something that sounded very much like satisfaction. "The weak link in the chain. There always seems to be one. You were hoping I'd think you really were Wickham, having survived the attack and come to London, weren't you? Did you actually expect me to go after you without checking?"

"One can always hope."

"One final question: What put you on to me?"

"You did." Nick smiled, but it wasn't a pleasant smile. "You should never have threatened Gabriella. That was your fatal mistake."

Trent laughed, and glanced around. "Well, I must say I've enjoyed making your acquaintance at last, but it's time for me to go. I didn't actually come here for Gabby, you know. I came to kill you. But she is a nice bonus. Matthew promised her to me years ago, actually, and I've always meant to collect."

He began to move backward, dragging Gabby with him. She clawed at his arm to no avail, choking as her breath was almost totally cut off again. The pistol ground into her skull, hurting her. Despite the cold, she was sweating with terror, both for herself and for Nick. The time for conversation was over, she feared. Trent was the only one with a weapon, and he was unlikely to let either of them live. She guessed he was only drawing Nick as far away from the house as possible before he shot him. Gasping for breath, heart racing, she stumbled as much as possible to slow Trent down, but he was surprisingly strong.

If Nick realized what Trent was up to, he gave no sign. He kept pace with them, step by step, drawing, Gabby thought, steadily closer to her by the smallest of degrees, his focus all on her captor now. His face, as a shaft of moonlight struck it, was utterly expressionless. His eyes were black shards of ice, and they never left Trent's face.

"You can't get away, you know. By now the courtyard will be surrounded." Nick's voice was almost conversational.

Trent chuckled. "You'll find I don't bluff that easily."

"No bluff. I've had someone following you since early yesterday. By now, there are a dozen of my men on the other side of that hedge."

"I seriously doubt it, Major."

"Let Gabriella go, and maybe you and I can do a deal." To Gabby's ears, Nick's voice was harder than before, with a fine sharp edge to it that reminded her of a knife. He didn't sound like the charming, mocking Nick she knew. He sounded like—a man as cold and ruthless as Trent. The thought made her shiver. It also gave her hope.

If anyone could stop Trent, it was Nick.

She realized that Trent had dragged her almost all the way to the east corner of the garden, where there was a gap in the hedge.

At the thought that she might soon be alone with Trent, and at his mercy, panic once again threatened to overwhelm her. Her chest tightened. Her stomach churned. She could feel cold sweat breaking out all over her body. . . .

But no, she told herself, no. She must just trust Nick.

Gabby's heart pounded like a kettledrum as she realized that, very soon now, Nick was going to have to make his move, or one or both of them would be lost.

"I may be mistaken, but I believe I hold all the cards in this hand. No deal, Major."

"*Now*, Barnet!" Nick barked the command. Gabby's heart leaped into her throat with a combination of hope and terror before she remembered that it was the same toothless ruse he had once used on her. . . .

❧ 43 ❧

*N*ick dived for Gabriella just as the pistol went off. At such close range the explosion was deafening. The bullet whizzed harmlessly past his ear as he fell with her to the ground, twisting to take the force of the landing on himself. Just as he'd expected, Trent had fired at him instead of Gabriella. Thank God he hadn't miscalculated. At the thought of what could have happened had Trent not reacted as predicted, Nick began to shake.

From all corners, his men rushed to surround Trent. They were quiet, efficient, well trained. Trent fought, tried to break free, but was quickly overpowered and bound. A few guests began to emerge from the house, drawn no doubt by the shot. They were peering in the direction of the disturbance. Nick, lying on the cold hard ground with Gabriella's warm, soft shape in his arms, left the whole group of them to do what they needed to do. He'd been searching for Trent for months, ever since it had become clear that a spy with access to top secret government papers was passing details of Wellington's army's movements to the enemy. Ironically enough, he'd gone after Trent for Gabby. He wouldn't have looked at him else. But in digging into Trent's background, he'd discovered enough information to convince him that the duke was the man he sought.

His focus now was all on Gabriella.

Her silky bare arms were locked around his neck as if she would never let him go, her delectable breasts were snuggled close against his chest, her face was buried in his shoulder, and, like him, she was shaking.

"Oh, Nick." Her voice trembled, too.

His name on her lips was the sweetest sound he had ever heard. He hugged her tight, kissed her ear, which was all of her his mouth could reach, and inhaled the sweet scent of vanilla.

"Are you all right?"

Her shivering seemed to be lessening by degrees, he thought. His had almost stopped. It had been entirely on her account, anyway. He had been more afraid for her tonight than he had ever been for anyone else in his life. Now what did that tell him?

"Yes. Are you?"

"Besides losing about ten years off my life when I thought he was going to shoot you before I could get to him? Fine."

"I was afraid he was going to shoot *you*."

Now that was promising. He smoothed a hand down her back. The lacey dress she was wearing left her shoulders and most of her shoulderblades bare.

"Gabriella."

"Hmm?"

"Look at me."

She was still trembling, long fine tremors that chased each other through her limbs, but she did as he told her. Her eyes were mysterious dark pools in the moonlight. Her lips were parted as she looked up at him. He had to distract himself from those lips. He focused on her eyes instead.

"Remember what I said before you slapped me in the ballroom?"

Her brow darkened, and she frowned at him. "Yes, of course I remember."

"Something about thinking you were madly in love with me?"

Her frown grew more pronounced. "You don't need to repeat it," she said with faint hauteur.

He smiled. He couldn't help it. That innate high-and-mightiness of hers was just about the first thing that he'd noticed about her. He had discovered, to his own surprise, that he liked pride as well as courage in a woman. Especially when they came all wrapped up in delicate bones and porcelain skin and eyes the color of rain. . . .

"Are you smiling?" Her tone was ominous.

"The reason I said that," he continued hastily, before she could get mad at him again, "is because I've discovered, to my own everlasting surprise, that I'm quite madly in love with you." As he said it, he knew that he meant it more than he had ever meant anything in his life.

Her eyes widened. Her breath seemed to catch. The hands that were still linked behind his neck tightened. She tilted her face up toward his.

"Oh, Nick." She smiled at him rather tremulously. All of a sudden her heart was in her eyes. "I do love you, Nick."

His back, thankfully, was to the growing crowd. They lay on the short prickly grass, deep in the shadow of an over-hanging bush, wrapped in each other's arms. Her frothy gold skirt was all tangled around his legs, her half-naked bosom was pressed firmly against his chest, and he felt not the small-est inclination to change a thing. Neither, apparently, did she. Thinking about it, Nick supposed with a dawning grin that the presence of the crowd that was even now spilling out from the ballroom was reason enough to get to his feet and pull her up with him: if he and Gabriella were spotted, their guests would be even more scandalized than they were already. As far as they knew, what they were seeing was the earl of Wickham lying in the grass kissing his sister; who had, moreover, not thirty minutes earlier in the middle of a crowded ballroom, already very publicly slapped his face.

He didn't give a damn. He kissed her anyway.

"Cap'n! Cap'n!" Barnet was calling him, his voice urgent. Nick registered that, glanced around, and came rolling to his feet quick as a cat as he saw the stranger rushing toward him in a low murderous streak across the grass. Clad all in black with a mask over his face, the man could only be an assassin. Nick's senses went on high alert. Barnet was pounding behind the attacker, running like a horse for the finish line, but it was all happening too fast. Crouching, cursing under his breath, Nick faced the assailant unarmed. Thank God Gabriella was behind him. . . .

It was the last logical thought he had. A pistol exploded, and something hit him hard in the chest. Looking down, he saw a bright blossom of crimson staining his waistcoat right in the middle of his chest.

He groaned.

Behind him, Gabriella shrieked.

He was still staring stupidly at the spreading stain on his waistcoat when at least four of his men tackled the assassin and brought him down. Barnet reached him half a heartbeat later.

"Cap'n! Cap'n!"

Nick looked up at his longtime henchman in stunned disbelief. "Not now," he said unsteadily, his voice already beginning to slur. "I'm not ready. There's Gabriella. . . ."

"Ah, Cap'n." Barnet wrapped his arms around him

tightly as Nick's knees began to collapse. With blurring vision, he registered that his unit, bearing Trent and the assassin with them, had already melted away. Like shadows in the night . . .

"No," he managed one last protest.

"Nick!" Gabriella's horrified scream broke through the buzz that was beginning to fill his ears. "Nick! Nick!"

"Get her out of here," he breathed. Then, as blackness rose up to claim him, he took a final shuddering breath and collapsed.

Fifteen minutes later, with Barnet forcibly holding a hysterical Gabriella at a decent distance, Nick's men long gone and the entire population of the ballroom now gathered around, a hastily summoned surgeon pronounced Marcus Banning, seventh earl of Wickham, dead.

✤ 44 ✤

Fittingly enough, that year it was cold in June. It didn't matter: Gabby spent as much time outdoors as she could, wrapped up against the chill, walking, endlessly walking, over the moors. She walked so much her leg ached continuously, and then she walked some more. She walked until she was exhausted, until she had to knead her thigh before she could move properly in the mornings, until her limp became pronounced. She walked because it was the only way she knew to extract a few hours peace from the long stretch from midnight to dawn when she was haunted by nightmares, and aching, poignant dreams.

She was thankful, in a way, to be back at Hawthorne Hall. Out of the whole rest of her life she had just this little time left to spend at her childhood home. Cousin Thomas—the eighth earl of Wickham now—had allowed them to travel back to their former home to pack up their personal belongings before he took permanent possession of the estate. They had to be out for good in three more days.

Despite the scandal that she had brought down on them all, Aunt Augusta had offered her and Claire and Beth a permanent home with her in town. And the scandal was huge.

Mr. Jamison had withdrawn his offer; Gabby had suffered several cuts direct from people she had considered friends; and everywhere she went there were those who would look at her with contempt, then whisper behind their hands. She couldn't really blame anyone: all of fashionable London believed that they had watched her falling in love with her brother, and then witnessed his subsequent murder by an unknown gunman in the courtyard of Wickham House. Gabby had told no one, not even her sisters, anything different, but at least her sisters, in the matter of her supposed love affair with their brother, seemed willing to give her the benefit of the doubt. Barnet had come to see her on the day after Wickham's death, along with a high-ranking official from the war department. They had asked her, in the interests of national security, not to reveal the true identity of the man who had died that night. She had agreed never to do so.

Sometimes she wondered, in passing, if she would have been killed if she had not agreed.

Nick was dead, only no one knew it. Everyone, her sisters, her aunt, the servants, everyone except Jem, thought she mourned so for her brother Marcus, with whom, in the court of popular opinion, she had been convicted of conducting an illicit love affair. It would have been almost funny, if in the aftermath of Nick's death she had not felt so terribly forlorn.

She could not share the depth of her loss, or the degree of her pain, with those she loved best. So she walked the moors alone, and grieved.

"Miss Gabby, it'll be gettin' dark soon. You need to come back to the house now."

Gabby looked over her shoulder, and smiled at Jem. He was worried about her, she knew. His voice was gentle whenever he spoke to her now, and his eyes when he looked at her had an almost grim expression that she had seen in them only once before, right after she had broken her leg and it had become apparent that it was not going to heal properly. He had taken to following her about, too; not that he let her see him, much, but whenever she was out close to dark, or near a bog or some other potentially treacherous place, he always seemed to turn up. She knew what he was doing, and appreciated his care of her.

Claire and Beth were worried about her, too. Gabby knew it, and tried her best to act as if she were in reasonable spirits while in their company. They mourned the man they had known as Marcus, too, but not like she did.

She didn't grieve for a charming but only recently met brother. She grieved for the man she loved.

At the time, she had thought the funeral was a nightmare. Nearly a thousand people had turned up in Westminster Abbey to pay their last respects, or to gawk and gossip, she hadn't been able to decide which. And she hadn't cared.

Now she knew that the real nightmare was living on after the funeral. Her world had turned to ashes and was peopled by shadows; she felt as though something inside her had broken—her heart, perhaps?—and would never again be whole.

And no one knew.

"I don't know about you, but I'm gettin' cold."

Gabby turned, summoned a smile for Jem, and, walking at the old man's side, headed back toward the house. A brisk wind carried the scent of gorse on it. The setting sun was reflected in the lake near the house. Hawthorne Hall itself brooded against the skyline, looking as dark and gloomy on the outside as she felt inside.

She walked up the shallow front steps and let herself into the house. Jem was behind her, but he headed off for the kitchen as soon as they were inside. Claire and Beth heard her enter and came out into the hall as she was taking off her cloak and gloves. They had been together in the front salon, watching for her, she guessed. A fire blazed in the hearth.

"You look frozen," Beth said in a falsely cheerful tone as Gabby hung her cloak on the clothes tree near the door and laid her gloves on the big round table in the center of the hall. Beth took Gabby's hand and drew her in toward the fire. When they reached it, Gabby gave her sister's fingers a squeeze and stretched her cold hands out to the blaze. The truth was, no matter how many fires were built or how large they were, Gabby never seemed to get truly warm anymore. "You shouldn't stay out so long."

"You're getting way too thin, Gabby." Claire, who had followed them into the salon, looked Gabby up and down with concern. They were all wearing black again, for their purported brother. Gabby knew she looked like a wraith in her slim, long-sleeved gown, but she didn't care.

She didn't care about anything anymore. No, that was wrong. She did care about her sisters. For them, she managed to summon up a smile.

"Did you finish bundling all your old clothes up for charity?" Gabby asked with an assumption of briskness. She would not, if she could help it, wear down Claire and Beth's spirits by letting them see how low were her own.

"What makes you think charity wants them?" Beth asked starkly. "They're the veriest rags."

They all laughed a little at that. Claire moved over to the window.

"You know," she said, picking up a handful of silk curtain and holding it up to the meager light that still filtered through the glass. "These are dry-rotted. Perhaps we should take them down, and contribute them, too."

"Lady Maud specifically instructed us to remove only our personal belongings from the house, remember?" Gabby said dryly. "I think we'd better leave the curtains right where they are. Next thing you know, she'll be accusing us of theft."

"Someone's coming." Claire had dropped the curtain and was looking out the window with interest. Gabby and Beth went to join her. Visitors at Hawthorne Hall were sufficiently rare as to render them all wide-eyed with curiosity.

The dying light made it impossible to see anything but the barest outline of a closed carriage drawn by a pair of horses with a lone driver on the box.

"You don't suppose Cousin Thomas has come early, do you?" Beth asked, putting into words the truly appalling thought that had occurred to them all. The carriage slowed in front of the house, and they all watched the driver pull up his horses. Then the carriage door opened.

"It's a single gentleman," Claire said, frowning, as they watched the silhouetted figure step down. She glanced around at her sisters. "Who could it be, do you suppose?"

"Let's go find out."

By mutual consent, they went into the hall. Gabby and Claire were not as quick as Beth. They had barely reached the entryway when Beth pulled opened the door.

The man walked up the outside steps in a leisurely way, quite as if he owned the place. He was wearing a many-caped greatcoat with a curly-brimmed beaver pulled down well over his eyes, and the setting sun was behind him, so it was impossible to make sure of anything except that he was tall.

But something about the way he moved . . .

Gabby stared. Then as he stepped up into the hall, into the light, her heart started to pound.

"Nick." At first she merely whispered it as her shaking hands rose to press against her breast. Then, on a glad cry, "*Nick!*"

Even before he took off his hat she started to run.

Gasping, crying, laughing, all at the same time, she threw herself into his arms. They closed around her, sweeping her off her feet, crushing the breath from her lungs, swinging her around in a wide circle before setting her back on her feet again.

She looked up into the twinkling blue eyes she'd thought she would never in this life see again, and felt suddenly faint.

"Nick," she croaked, locking her arms around his neck. Then he bent his head and kissed her.

It was a long kiss, a fervent kiss, a kiss between lovers, and when he lifted his head at last Gabby was not surprised to discover Claire and Beth staring at them agog. Still wrapped in his arms, she looked around at them, but before she could say anything, or indeed, think of anything to say, Nick spoke.

"Claire, Beth, as you will have no doubt guessed by now, I am *not* your brother, so you can stop looking at your sister and me like that. My name is Nick Devane."

"Thank goodness," Claire said devoutly, closing her mouth. Beth nodded fervent agreement. Then they both rushed toward him. Keeping one arm around Gabby all the while, he hugged each of them in turn. Then he looked down at Gabby again. She was leaning against him, with both arms wrapped tightly around his waist. She couldn't seem to look away from him, and knew she was smiling idiotically as her gaze drank in his face. Happiness bubbled up inside her, a wonderful radiant happiness that warmed her down to her previously icy little toes. Miracle of miracles, Nick *wasn't* dead. He had come back to her.

Nick kissed her again, not as thoroughly as before but still quite thoroughly enough. She wrapped her arms around his neck and clung, and kissed him back.

When he lifted his head at last, he was smiling. She smiled back at him dreamily, still clinging to his neck, not one whit bothered by the interested audience of her sisters. She felt like she had just awakened from a long and terrible nightmare. . . .

"I take it you've missed me," he said in a husky tone, and at last got around, with a backward kick of his boot, to closing the door, which had been permitting chilly bursts of air to swirl around them all.

Gabby blinked at him. Now that she was sure he was real, not a ghost or a figment of her grief-disordered imagination or even hot air and moonbeams, she was beginning to get her bearings again.

"*Missed* you?" she asked incredulously as his question sank in. Anger began to simmer inside her. "You low-down dirty rotten *scoundrel,* I thought you were dead."

She shoved furiously at his shoulders, and whisked herself out of his arms.

He smiled at her. "Gabriella . . ."

"Do you have any idea what I've been going through?" She was raging now. Her heart pounded, and she could feel hot blood staining her face. "I thought you were *dead.*"

"I'm sorry, I . . ."

"You're sorry." She yelled the words at him, so angry now she was practically vibrating with it. A red tide of rage floated before her eyes. Her breathing quickened. Her chest heaved. Claire and Beth, still fascinated spectators, instinctively backed up out of the way as Gabby glanced around. A small, leather-bound book lay on the table near her gloves, and Gabby snatched it up and hurled it at him. He dodged behind a chair, grinning, and the book slammed harmlessly into a wall behind him. "You're *sorry.* Oh, is that supposed to make it all right? I went to your *funeral.*"

A leather card case was next. Nick dodged again, grinning, then started to work his way toward her, avoiding missiles and keeping various pieces of furniture between them as he came.

❧ 45 ❧

"I couldn't help it," Nick protested, ducking a well-aimed candle snuffer. "Gabriella, listen a moment."

Gabby's roving gaze spied Barnet, newly come on the scene with Jem and Mrs. Bucknell and Stivers and Twindle and a host of other servants drawn by the noise.

"And you." She pointed a shaking finger at Barnet. "You let me think he was dead. No, you flat out told me he was dead. You brought a government official to see me. You came to his funeral and you *cried*."

Barnet shrank back inside the doorway from which he had just emerged. "Orders, miss," he said feebly, looking scared.

"Orders!" Gabby screeched, looking around for something else to hurl.

"Now, don't start throwing things at Barnet," Nick chided, having almost reached her by this time. "He's Sergeant George Barnet, by the way, who used to be my batman, and he *was* following orders. For that matter, so was I."

He reached her then, in a quick lunge, and grabbed her arms. Gabby glared up at him.

"How could you do that to me? Do you know what it's been like? I thought you were dead."

At that she burst into noisy tears that hurt her throat and stung her eyes. Nick's grin vanished. He looked down at her with sudden compunction, then without another word scooped her up in his arms as if she weighed nothing at all.

She had almost forgotten how strong he was.

She wrapped her arms around his neck and buried her face in his shoulder and wept as if her heart would break.

"Gabriella, shh. I'm sorry," he said in her ear. This time he sounded as if he meant it. Then, as she continued to sob and gasp uncontrollably, he added to the room at large, "I think we need some privacy here. A study or something where we can sit and talk. A room where there's a fire."

She was shivering uncontrollably in his arms.

"Bring her this way, Captain." The speaker was Jem, and the tone was only faintly grudging. As Nick carried her along the hall, Gabby glanced up to find Jem holding the door to the office open for them. Then another fit of sobbing racked her—she didn't seem to be able to control them at all—and she buried her face in his neck again, wetting his coat with her tears.

"Thank you, Jem," Nick said.

Jem's reply was heartfelt. "I never thought I'd live to say this, Captain, but I sure am glad to see you. I've never seen Miss Gabby in a state like she's been."

Gabby felt Nick's answering nod. Then he carried her into the office. Gabby heard the door shut behind them. A moment later he sat down in front of the fire with her in his lap.

"Gabriella." He kissed the side of her jaw. His lips were warm; his whiskers were scratchy. Perversely, the familiar sensations made her sob harder. "Sweetheart, don't cry.

Please. I'm sorry. They had to make it look like I was dead. I knew they were going to do it sooner or later, I just didn't expect it to be right then. The assassin was fake; he was one of my men. He hit me with a bladder full of pig's blood. Barnet pressed a pressure point on my neck and put me out like a light. The rest was acting."

"You let me think you were dead!"

"I may catch spies, but I'm still a soldier. My orders were not to tell anyone, not even you. I had no choice. I came as quickly as I could." He slid his mouth along her jawline to her ear, and added persuasively, "I really couldn't keep pretending I was the earl of Wickham for the rest of my life, you know. If I did that, how could I ever ask you to marry me?"

That, not unnaturally, made Gabby quit crying and sit up. She sniffled a few times and scrubbed at her wet cheeks with her hands. Then she looked at him with a suspicious expression that made him smile.

"*Are* you asking me to marry you?"

"Yes, I am."

She frowned at him. "I don't want to marry a soldier."

His smile widened. "You're in luck. I just sold out. Barnet, too, actually."

Her frown turned into a scowl. "Then how, pray, do you propose to support a family?"

His eyes twinkled at her. "This would probably be a good time to tell you that I'm a very rich man. I propose to buy a property—you can pick it out if you like—and move you and your sisters and any of the servants who care to come with us into it. I haven't had a home in a long while; I think it's time I had one again."

"Aunt Augusta's already offered us a home," Gabby said with a haughty lift of her chin.

"Your choice is clear, then: Aunt Augusta or me."

Gabby glanced down, hesitated, then looked up at him again. "What about Lady Ware?"

His brows knit. "Belinda? What about her?"

"You should know that I happened to see some of her—letters." Her voice was faintly truculent. Inside she was afraid, so afraid, that he was going to say the wrong thing. She would never, ever be able to share him with a mistress. She loved him far too much for that. Though, she supposed, she would rather share him with a mistress than have him go away again. She didn't think she could bear that.

"Gabriella, did you go through my drawer and read my mail?" His tone was severe.

Gabby nodded guiltily. "I was afraid something had happened to you. I was trying to find anything that would help me think where you could be."

He eyed her, then suddenly chuckled. "I wish I could have seen your face! Belinda's notes are pretty blue."

"I'm well aware, believe me." Her response was dry.

His brow knit. "*That's* why you accepted Jamison. You were jealous of Belinda." He started chuckling again.

She scowled at him. "Well, *you* were jealous of Mr. Jamison."

"I was, wasn't I? Pray don't remind me." He smiled at her. Her hands rested in her lap; he picked one up and carried it to his mouth, and kissed it. His eyes were suddenly serious as he lowered her hand and looked at her. "All right, Gabriella, I admit it: there are lots of women in my past. But I give you my word that, if you marry me, you'll be the only woman in my future."

She looked at him consideringly for a moment, while her heartbeat quickened and her pulse began to race. Then she started to smile. "I love you, you know."

"Is that a *yes?*"

"Yes. Oh, yes."

He gathered her close against him. She wrapped her arms around his neck and kissed him with all the pent-up love and longing she'd been holding at bay for weeks. When he lifted his head at last she looked up into those beautiful blue eyes and knew she had finally found her heart's home.

"I love you." His voice was low and husky as he touched his mouth to hers again. "I'll spend the rest of my life showing you how much."

"Nick . . ." Shaken to the core, her heart swelling with love for him, Gabby found she couldn't say another word. So she kissed him again instead.

∂ ∂

Later, much later, they were lying together on the carpet in front of the fire. The door was locked, the household was long since abed, and their only cover was his greatcoat, which he had spread over them both. Beneath it they were naked, their bodies entwined. He was flat on his back with one arm bent behind his head. His eyes were closed, and he gave every appearance of being asleep. Gabby was using his chest for a pillow when a sharp popping from the hearth brought her lids fluttering up.

For a moment she merely blinked sleepily at the fire as she tried to determine exactly what it was that woke her. Suddenly another ember crackled and popped even louder than the first, and her eyes widened. Then she smiled.

It was in front of this very hearth that she had made her bargain with the devil, after all. And now here he lay beside her, in the hard, handsome flesh.

She ran a hand over his black-furred chest, and slanted a look up at him to see if he stirred. He didn't.

The fire popped insistently again. Her smile widened and her hand slid down.

Speaking of the devil, he was hers now, and she wasn't giving him back. She meant to marry him, too.

But in the meantime, she thought with a naughty twinkle as her hand found what it sought, it wouldn't hurt to bedevil him just a little bit.

Pocket Books proudly presents

Shameless

Karen Robards

Coming in hardcover from Pocket Books
on April 13, 2010

**Please turn the page for a preview of
Beth Banning's story, *Shameless***

April 1817

It was, Lady Elizabeth Banning thought ruefully as she looked up into the reddening face of her latest fiancé, all the fault of her damnable temper. Again.

"Are you telling me that you're *jilting* me?" William demanded incredulously. The Earl of Rosen was of average height, with a slightly stocky build that Beth suspected would, in middle age, run sadly to fat. But just now, at age twenty-six, his square jaw, regular features, speaking blue eyes, and thick fair hair worn à la Brutus were enough to ensure that he was held to be a very handsome man by those of the fairer sex. Of course, that assessment was undoubtedly helped along by the fact that he was also possessed of an income of something in the nature of twenty thousand pounds a year.

Which she was, regrettably, in the process of whistling down the wind.

"I am not jilting you. I am telling you that I feel we should not suit."

Standing in front of one of the pair of tall windows, thickly curtained in claret velvet, that adorned the far wall of the small, book-lined library of Richmond House, her brother-in-law the Duke of Richmond's palatial London home, with

William less than an arm's length away, Beth was conscious of a draft curling around her shoulders. They were left bare by the fashionable décolletage of her slim, high-waisted frock of gleaming gold silk, its color chosen with care to set off her fiery curls. Really, the room seemed surprisingly cold despite the fact that a fire crackled in the hearth in deference to the crisp temperatures of the early April night. Instead of shivering, though, she folded her arms over her chest, lifted her chin, squared her shoulders, and held William's increasingly incensed gaze without flinching. Conversations of this sort were never easy, as she had learned from far too much experience. Still, it had to be done, and she had already put it off too long.

"You cannot be serious. My *mother* is here." William was practically quivering with outrage. His mother, Lady Rosen, was one of the *ton's* highest sticklers, and over the course of the last two Seasons had made no secret of her opinion that Beth was *fast*. Beth had little doubt that William's announcement that he meant to marry her had brought floods of tears and recriminations down upon his head.

"I am really very sorry." Beth looked up at him remorsefully. The idea that he had stood up to his formidable mother for her made her feel even more guilt. She *was* sorry. Their engagement, which at the moment was known only to their immediate families, was of a little more than a week's duration, and she had regretted it within hours of accepting his offer. She should have told him so immediately, of course. But he was such an eligible *parti*, while she, at twenty-one and embarked on her third Season, was no longer in the first blush of youth and well past the age at which most of her contemporaries married. Having brought William up to scratch mostly, she admitted to herself, to spite his acid-tongued sister, she had thought, hoped, wished, that if she tried very hard, this time things might be different.

They were not. She had tried her best, and still her stubborn heart refused to cooperate. She liked William well enough. She did not, however, love him, and she knew now she never would.

She could not marry him.

Had she not, three weeks ago, overheard Lady Dreyer, William's high-in-the-instep older sister, insisting to Princess Lieven, the most toplofty of the Almack's patronesses, that no matter how much he dangled after her William would never be so foolish as to make Lady Elizabeth Banning, with her shocking reputation and scandal-plagued bloodline, an offer, she would never have accepted him in the first place.

But she had overheard, and the dye was cast. The remark had both hurt and infuriated her, and when William, with, admittedly, some considerable encouragement on her part, did indeed come up to scratch, she had accepted him on the spot. Suspecting even then that she would live to regret it, she had added the proviso that they tell no one outside their immediate families until her brother-in-law the duke, who stood in place of her guardian since both her parents were dead, should come up from the country, from whence he had arrived, most unexpectedly, earlier that evening. Still, whispers of an engagement had run like wildfire around the *ton*, so much so that Beth had actually found herself in the absurd position of seriously considering marrying the man simply to keep the gossips from saying she was playing fast and loose with yet another gentleman's affections.

Fortunately she was not yet as foolish as that.

"I spoke to your brother-in-law not an hour since." William was breathing hard and his hands had closed into fists at his sides. "I told him then that I hoped to be able to announce the engagement at midnight tonight, and he made no objection."

"Which is why I am telling you now," Beth said. Her older sister Claire, Duchess of Richmond, had told her of William's conversation with her husband, which was why Beth was giving William his congé in the middle of Claire's ball. The timing was less than ideal, Beth knew, and she blamed herself for delaying until circumstances forced her hand. William was angry, as he had every right to be. She, on the other hand, would remain cool and composed. With that laudable objective in mind, her tone was eminently reasonable, and she laid a placating hand on his forearm as she spoke. The sleeve of his bottle green satin coat, which he wore with a pale yellow waistcoat and white inexpressibles, felt smooth beneath her fingers, but the tension of the limb beneath spoke to how very far from being placated he actually was. "*Before* the announcement is made. That way, neither of us need suffer the slightest degree of embarrassment."

"*Embarrassment.* . . . " William's eyes bulged and his face went from puce to purple. "My God, they are already betting on it in the clubs. At White's, the odds are five to one against me getting you to the altar and ten to one against you actually going through with the ceremony and becoming my wife."

"How dreadful." Beth was genuinely shocked. Her lips pursed, and she shook her head in disbelief as her hand dropped away from his arm. "Gentlemen will truly bet on anything."

William sucked in air. "Is that all you can say?"

"I'm sorry," she offered again. Muffled by distance, the lilting strains of the first notes of the quadrille reached her ears. They had exited in the midst of a country dance which had clearly run its course. She had pounced on William as soon as she had spotted him in the ballroom, but as he was more than passing fond of his own voice, it had taken her some time to detach him from the group he'd been edifying with a detailed account of his role in some long-past hunt. Now, with the quadrille striking up, Mr. Hayden, to whom she rather thought she'd promised the next dance, would be searching for her. Time to end this. "But when you have had time to reflect a little, I'm sure you will agree with me that it's for the best. Truly, we should not suit."

"But . . ."

Prolonging this served no purpose. She started to turn away, adding with finality, "Pray excuse me. I must return to the ballroom now."

"Wait." He caught her arm above the elbow, his fingers gripping just a little too hard for comfort. She turned back to him with raised brows. "It's too late to draw back. I've sent the announcement to the papers. It is to run in tomorrow's edition."

"Oh, no." Beth thought of the torrent of gossip that would sweep over her—over her family, over William and his family—in the wake of her publicly crying off from yet another engagement, and winced inwardly. There was so much notoriety attached to the Banning family name already that this would be in the nature of heaping coals upon an already smoldering fire. The resulting blaze would be intense. Her eyes went to the clock on the mantel. It was a few minutes past eleven p.m. Almost certainly, the presses would already be printing. There was little chance of withdrawing the announcement now. "You should not have done so."

"You mean, I should have remembered that you have jilted two previous fiancés and expected you would do the same to me?"

She didn't like the tone of that, but she had to admit that, from William's point of view, she probably deserved it.

In any case, there was no undoing what was done. She gave him a small, wry smile. "Well, at least you may take comfort in the fact that no one will attach the least blame to *you*."

"You are right about that." From his expression, the fact did not please him. "But the scandal will besmirch us all."

Catching her other arm, William jerked her toward him. Taken by surprise, Beth found herself coming up tight against his chest. The top of her head reached the bridge of his nose, which meant that they were almost eye-to-eye for a pregnant moment as their gazes collided. Supremely conscious that she was in the wrong—and also that a good portion of the *ton* was present at her sister's party and would thus be able to hear any loud altercation that occurred inside the library—she confined her reaction to firming her lips and narrowing her eyes at him warningly.

"William . . ." she began.

He rushed on, cutting her off, his fingers tightening around her arms until they dug painfully into her soft flesh, clearly undeterred by the fact that she was now rigid against him and her eyes were starting to shoot off sparks.

"But, of course, this is nothing new to you, is it? I am but one in a long line, after all! You left Amperman practically on the steps of the church, and you threw Kirkby over less than a week before the wedding. I should have been warned. Indeed, I *was* warned! Everyone I hold dear advised me against making you an offer. 'She's shameless, a hardened flirt,' they said. 'There's bad blood in that family. Look at the father, wed four times, a drunkard and a dreadful loose screw. Look at the sisters, both the subjects of sordid scandals. Shocking reputations, the pair of them, and the third girl's no better,' I was told more times than I can count. But more fool I, I chose to disregard those who I now perceive to have had my best interests at heart, even my own mother. And this, *this* is my reward!"

By the time he finished, he was breathing hard. The aspersions he had cast on her sisters' characters caused Beth's slim, black brows to snap together in an ominous line over her delicate nose. Her delft blue eyes took on a decidedly militant sparkle, and a flush—that curse of all redheads—heated her porcelain skin. Still, mindful of the gathered company that would dearly love to add yet another page to her family's already overflowing book of sins, she kept her composure, albeit with an effort.

"If this is how you see fit to behave, I am very glad I decided we should not suit." Her tone was icy, and she disdained to struggle, although she had little doubt that she would have bruises on the morrow from where his fingers were digging into her arms. "Unhand me, if you please. I repeat, our engagement is at an end, and I wish to return to the company."

"Unhand you?" William's mouth took on an ugly twist, and a hard gleam appeared in his eyes. He shook his head at her. "Oh, no. You'll not play fast and loose with *me*. I've not the smallest desire to become the laughingstock of White's, or the subject of my friends' pity, or the world's jests. You gave your word, and now you *will* marry me."

"Now there you're out: I won't." There was a decided snap to her voice as her patience frayed. Beth attempted to pull her arms free without success, her determination to be cool and collected almost lost in a hot rush of temper that she just managed to keep from getting the better of her by remembering the proximity of a potential audience. "Let me go at once."

"No." With a quick move that caught her by surprise, William snagged a hand in the neckline of her gown and yanked. The delicate silk tore like paper. Gasping, looking down at herself in disbelief, Beth realized that the top of her dress had been all but ripped away. Only the fluttering gold ribbons tied beneath her breasts kept the ruined garment from dropping to her feet. Except for the flimsy barrier of her near-transparent chemise, she was now naked almost to the waist.

The firm white curves of her generous bosom swelled indecently above the filmy muslin undergarment that revealed almost as much as it concealed.

"What the *blazes* do you think you're doing?" Her eyes flew to his even as her hand clapped over her décolletage in an attempt to shield as much of her flesh as possible from his view. For the moment, at least, the shock of it was enough to practically immobilize her. "You must be mad."

"Aren't you going to scream? Half the *ton* will no doubt come barreling to your rescue if you do." He gave her a sneering smile. As Beth attempted to jerk her arm free, his fingers tightened until they were digging into her in a grip that no amount of tugging could break. If she hadn't been so angry—and so increasingly alarmed—she would have winced at the pain of it. "I, of course, will explain that I was simply overcome with lust for my affianced wife, and you—you will have a choice of marrying me at once, or being utterly, completely ruined."

Beth instantly envisioned the scenario he described and was appalled. Smirking, he grabbed the shoulder of her chemise and yanked. The flimsy cloth ripped with a sharp tearing sound. Only her hand pressed to her breasts kept the garment from disintegrating completely, and prevented her from being utterly exposed.

"You *pig*. Let me go!" Maddened, Beth kicked him, but from his reaction, or, rather, the lack of it, the contact clearly hurt her toes in their soft slippers more than his rock-solid shin. Hampered by her inability to use either hand, she nevertheless fought furiously to tear herself free. "I'll never marry you. Never, do you hear? No matter what."

Despite her rising fury, Beth was careful to keep her voice down lest someone in the milling company that filled the house to overflowing should overhear. To her horror, she realized that he was right in his estimation: if anyone found them like this, the scandal would be insupportable. If they didn't wed immediately, the doors of polite society would be closed to her forever. She would be well and truly ruined. The prospect was terrifying. Though she might flirt with being outrageous, and enjoy fulfilling the expectations of those who called her scandalous just to prove that their gossip meant nothing to her, she had no stomach for finding herself a true pariah. And the resulting firestorm of scandal would scorch her family, too.

"Oh, I think you will." William smiled that sneering smile at her again even as her eyes shot pure poison at him. Then, grabbing her other arm in such a way that she lost her protective grip on her tattered chemise, which immediately fell so that her breasts were now completely bared, he took a good, long look—and shoved her roughly away from him.

"Oh!" Taken by surprise, Beth staggered backward. The small, sharp cry escaped her lips before she could clamp them together, but she managed to swallow the rest of it even as the edge of the Egyptian-style settee caught the back of her knees. She lost her balance, sitting down hard upon the slippery silk seat.

"You'll pay for this, you . . . " There were no words bad enough to do her feelings justice. She started to bounce back up, quivering with fury, both fists at the ready and never mind that she was now in truth indecent, when he threw himself on top of her, forcing her down into the settee.

He lay on top of her, his weight pinning her down, his hands imprisoning her wrists, licking and kissing the delicate cord at the side of her neck.

Beth shuddered with revulsion. She heaved beneath him, jerking her head to one side, craning her neck to escape his disgusting onslaught, all to no avail.

"Get off me! You disgust me, you *cretin*." The fact that she hissed rather than screamed the words at him in no way detracted from their venom. "How dare you attack me like this? How dare you?"

"You'll wed me, one way or another."

"Pray disabuse yourself of that notion! I never will!"

His lips, open and wet, found her averted mouth then, and to her disgust he thrust his thick, wet tongue inside, so far that it felt like it was going all the way down her throat. Gagging, cringing with distaste, suppressing a scream only with the greatest of effort, Beth tore her mouth free, bucking and writhing like a mad thing in a frenzied effort to extricate herself. Her efforts paid off: dislodged, he fell heavily to the floor. Unfortunately, he took her with him, then flipped her onto her back and flung himself atop her again even as she tried to scramble away. The impact knocked the air from her lungs. He trapped her with his weight, grabbing her fists and forcing them above her head, where he pinned them to the thick Turkish carpet. The hard round buttons on his coat and waistcoat dug into her tender breasts as he ground his lower body suggestively against hers.

Dear God, I hate this, she thought, revolted. And she knew that this, this imposition of his flesh on hers, was at least part of the reason why she could not stomach the idea of marriage. To give a man the right to use her so at will. . . .

She could not do it.

"Get off me! Get off, do you hear?"

Panting, struggling for all she was worth, she merely succeeded in shifting them both sideways. Breathing hard, still firmly atop her, he forced his knee between hers. He was, Beth was sickened to realize, glancing down between them to ogle her breasts.

"You'll sing quite another tune when you are my wife." His

voice was thick. He licked his lips. His eyes still fixed to her bosom, he lowered his head . . .

"*Get off.*"

He meant to put his mouth on her breasts.

"*No.*"

Galvanized by revulsion, heart thumping wildly, fighting to get away with every ounce of strength she possessed, Beth managed to jerk an arm free at last. Attention thankfully diverted, he grabbed for it, but she was too fast: fist clenched, she punched him in the temple so hard her knuckles stung.

"*Ahh.*" He reared up with a curse, face contorting viciously, and grabbed for her hands—both were free now—as she pounded him about the head and shoulders.

"Think you there will be no reckoning for this, you wantwit? I'll see you dead over it."

"Wed, rather," he panted.

"*Never.*"

Shaking with fury and fear, heaving in a futile attempt to throw him off, she went for his eyes with her nails. There was now no doubt in her mind that, if she didn't stop him by screaming for assistance or some other means, he meant rape.

Even as her nails gouged his skin he slapped her, the blow heavy and shocking. The force of it caused her head to snap to one side and briefly disordered her senses.

"*Strumpet. Jezebel. Jade.* I'll school you to mind your manners with me. When you are my wife . . ."

Stunned, Beth lost the sense of his words as she found herself staring blindly into the fire. It twinkled merrily at her, oblivious to her distress, and she realized that she was now lying within arm's reach of the fireplace. Then he caught her chin, wrenched her face around, and ground his mouth into hers again.

No. No.

At the renewed assault of that sluglike tongue, Beth went cold with horror. She felt a wave of nausea.

The fireplace tools.

The image of them as she had just seen them standing beside the hearth snapped into sudden sharp focus in her mind.

They were close. Within reach.

No sooner did she realize that than she reached out for them, her groping fingers finding and identifying the ornate silver stand, the small broom, the poker. His mouth left hers—*I'm going to be sick*—only to find her throat again; he caught her tangled skirt and dragged it up, over her knees, despite her struggles.

Her fingers closed desperately around the poker's smooth iron shaft. An instant later the heavy metal bar arced through the air as she slammed it down smartly against the back of his head.

To her alarm, William merely stiffened, shaking his head a little, his eyes widening as his head came up just enough so that he could stare down at her in disbelief. Terrified that she had not done the thing properly, she hit him again with all her might. The resultant *thunk* made her think of a melon splitting.

He made a little sound like a kitten mewling.

Heart pounding like a runaway horse, she watched with a kind of dreadful fascination as his eyes rolled back in his head and his mouth went horribly slack. Then he collapsed on top of her without another sound, pure dead weight.

Thank God, was her first thought. Her second was, *Oh, no, have I killed him?*

Shaking, heart thudding, breath rasping in her throat as she struggled to suck air into her lungs, Beth lay beneath his motionless body for a moment in near shock as visions of her own lifeless body swinging from the gallows at Tyburn flooded her mind. Then she realized that she could feel his chest moving, hear the faint wheeze of his breathing, and felt a quick upsurge of relief.

Not dead, then.

With that reassuring thought, she recovered some of her wits. Gritting her teeth, willing her poor trembling body to move, she tried to wriggle out from beneath him without success. Unfortunately, there was no budging him. He was simply too heavy.

I'm trapped. What now?

From the distant ballroom, she heard the last flourishing notes of the quadrille, and panic seized her. At any moment someone could open the library door and find them like this.

Beth never knew from whence she summoned the strength to shove him off, but she found it. Wedging both hands beneath his shoulder, she heaved, then heaved again—and it was enough. William rolled limply onto his back, his outflung hand catching and parting the sumptuous velvet curtains that they had been standing in front of earlier, when she had first told him that the engagement was off.

She had just rolled onto her hands and knees in preparation for jumping to her feet when something caught her eye. Impossibly, a boot was planted there between the curtains. A man's large black riding boot, scarred and creased from wear, and liberally flecked with mud.

For the space of a couple of heartbeats, her gaze stuck there, riveted.

The boot was attached to a leg, Beth saw as her gaze rose along it inexorably. A long, muscular leg encased in snug black trousers. The leg was attached to lean masculine hips. . . .

It was then, with a jolt of pure shock, that the truth registered: There was a man standing in the window embrasure. Until that moment he had been concealed behind the curtains. A tall, broad-shouldered, darkly handsome stranger clad all in black save for the merest hint of white that was his shirt, silhouetted against the grayer black of the moonlit night beyond. His lean face was absolutely expressionless. His crow-black hair was tied back in a queue. Without the muffling effect of the heavy curtains, cold air rushed in across the small balcony that overlooked the garden. Remembering the earlier draft on her shoulders, Beth felt certain that the tall French window had been open all along.

He had climbed in through the window . . . *why?*

Having shot to his face, her eyes now locked with his. They were as black and hard as pieces of jet. Cold, pitiless eyes that stared narrowly back at her, their expression so menacing that her breath caught.

In that frozen instant she realized, too, that he held a pistol in one hand.

Beth's eyes widened. Her heart skipped a beat. Her mouth went dry.

Said pistol was now aimed directly at her.